"One of the best erotic romance writers writing today!"
—Ecataromance

Praise for the novels of Sarah McCarty

"[A] pulse-pounding paranormal."
—The Road to Romance

"Masterfully written."
—The Romance Readers Connection

"Powerfully erotic, emotional, and thought provoking."
—Ecataromance

"Has the WOW factor . . . characters that jump off the pages!"
—Just Erotic Romance Reviews

"Toe curling."
—Fallen Angel Reviews (recommended read)

Running Wild

Sarah McCarty

HEAT
New York

THE BERKLEY PUBLISHING GROUP
Published by the Penguin Group
Penguin Group (USA) Inc.
375 Hudson Street, New York, New York 10014, USA
Penguin Group (Canada), 90 Eglinton Avenue East, Suite 700, Toronto, Ontario M4P 2Y3, Canada
(a division of Pearson Penguin Canada Inc.)
Penguin Books Ltd., 80 Strand, London WC2R 0RL, England
Penguin Group Ireland, 25 St. Stephen's Green, Dublin 2, Ireland (a division of Penguin Books Ltd.)
Penguin Group (Australia), 250 Camberwell Road, Camberwell, Victoria 3124, Australia
(a division of Pearson Australia Group Pty. Ltd.)
Penguin Books India Pvt. Ltd., 11 Community Centre, Panchsheel Park, New Delhi—110 017, India
Penguin Group (NZ), 67 Apollo Drive, Rosedale, North Shore 0632, New Zealand
(a division of Pearson New Zealand Ltd.)
Penguin Books (South Africa) (Pty.) Ltd., 24 Sturdee Avenue, Rosebank, Johannesburg 2196,
South Africa

Penguin Books Ltd., Registered Offices: 80 Strand, London WC2R 0RL, England

This is an original publication of The Berkley Publishing Group.

Cover art by Phil Heffernan.
Cover design by George Long.

First edition: June 2008

Library of Congress Cataloging-in-Publication Data

McCarty, Sarah.
Running wild / Sarah McCarty.—1st ed.
p. cm.
ISBN 978-0-425-22150-1
1. Werewolves—Fiction. 2. Erotic stories, American. 3. Occult fiction, American. I. Title.
PS3613.C3568R86 2008
813'.6—dc22 2008008110

PRINTED IN THE UNITED STATES OF AMERICA

10 9 8 7 6 5 4

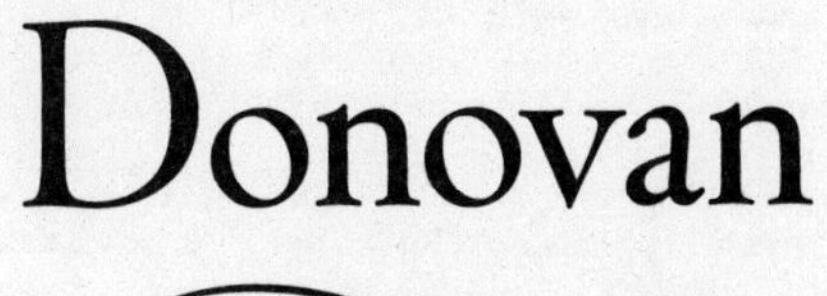
Donovan

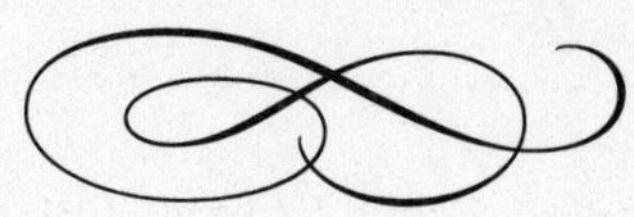

One

It was going to be one of those nights.

Donovan took a pull on his beer and sighed. Just one thing after the other, none of them good, with the exception of the woman approaching the glass doors of the dilapidated town's only point of entertainment, a combination bowling alley, bar, and pool hall. She had promise. She was about five feet three and packing more attitude than a were during a full moon. With her figure obscured by a too-big parka and most of her face hidden by a knit hat pulled low, it was hard to make out much in the way of detail, but he had an impression of vibrant femininity, delicate features, and a wide mouth pressed to a flat line of determination.

The woman hit the door hard, arms outstretched, body rigid. Her light brown hair blew back from her face in an aggressive surge. The neon light from the signs crammed into every inch of window space flared across her expression, revealing a collage of emotion—fury, desperation, resolve—that flickered in synch with the uncertain light. Fury.

She was clearly on a mission. Donovan took a steadying sip of his beer as the door opened and the cold night air wrapped around him, for a split second clearing the stench of smoke and human sweat and replacing it with the snap of the building storm.

"Shit." Wyatt leaned forward. His gaze cut from the woman to the group of hell-raisers in the back room playing pool. The front legs of his chair hit the concrete floor with hollow thumps.

"Trouble?" Donovan took a deep breath, instinctively reaching for the woman's scent. It came to him, light and airy, spiced with the feminine essence his inner wolf had spent its whole life searching for.

"I'm hoping not."

From the tone of Wyatt's voice, he didn't have much hope. Donovan watched as the woman skirted the bar, ignoring the bartender's greeting, and headed toward him, her destination clearly the back room. He might not be able to tell her shape in the too-large winter coat, but her jeans-encased legs were slim and long for her height, and her scent—Goddamn, her scent. As she passed his table, it wrapped around him in a long-awaited hug, sinking deep beneath his skin, deep enough to embrace his wolf. Deep enough to make it howl in primal recognition. Donovan sat up straighter in his chair. She was definitely trouble.

Donovan motioned to the woman's back. "That's one pissed-off woman."

"That's Lisa Delaney." Wyatt pushed his chair back. "And she's got a right."

"Boyfriend step out on her?" A boyfriend would be a complication, but nothing he couldn't handle. A husband would be a more difficult obstacle.

"Worse." Wyatt got to this feet. His badge caught a fragment of the florescent light, a dim reflection of the power the man actually wielded. Donovan wondered if anyone in this tight-knit community knew a werewolf enforced their laws.

"Much worse," Wyatt muttered as the woman snatched up a discarded pool cue and headed for the back corner where four men, who looked to be in their twenties, were playing a competitive match that was fast degenerating to the level of aggression.

It wouldn't be a party Donovan would choose to join if he were female. The men were too bored, too drunk, and too impressed with themselves. A bad combination in any species. The woman didn't hesitate or veer from her course, however, just clutched that pool cue and took one deliberate step after another. If she were wolf, he'd say she'd just marked her prey.

The hairs at his nape prickled a warning. "What's worse?"

"A woman with her back against the wall and her dander up." Wyatt didn't take his eyes off Lisa as she cleared the doorway. "Shit, I was afraid of this. C'mon."

Lisa Delaney reached the group of hell-raisers before Donovan took three steps. The mouthiest of the group—the one who'd been posturing the most all evening, the one everyone referred to as Buddy—glanced up.

"Well, look who's here. Come to pick up where your sister left off?"

The woman's "Yes" reached Donovan across the distance—soft, husky, loaded with tension. Without breaking stride, she drove the pool cue forward into the man's groin. Buddy screamed and clutched his balls. Like every other man there, Donovan flinched. And, like every other man there, he moved forward. The woman swung again, a vicious uppercut that snapped Buddy upright and back into the wall. He grabbed his nose and shouted for help. One of his friends stepped forward. A man from a neighboring table grabbed the younger man's arms and locked them behind him. A quick glance showed his other two friends similarly restrained by hard-faced, impassive townsmen. Wyatt took up a protective stance near Lisa but made no move to interfere.

Understanding sank in. Whatever this was, it was personal. And deserved.

Lisa flipped the cue around and swung for the man's midsection. "It was her first date, you bastard."

The base connected solidly. Air whooshed out of Buddy's lungs. He doubled over. The next blow landed across his back. Donovan thought he heard a rib crack. Before Buddy hit the floor on all fours, he was sniveling like a baby.

"Her first everything," Lisa snarled.

She swung again. Buddy hollered for help, throwing up his arm, blocking the blow, screaming again as his forearm took the brunt. The hard-edged men forming the boundaries for the tableau didn't twitch, just stood impassively, observing from under their baseball caps. The woman raised the cue again, her breath dragging into her lungs with the force of the emotion tearing at her.

"And you hurt her."

It was almost a sob.

Buddy drew his knees up and huddled into a ball, covering his face with his arms, leaving Lisa with a clear shot at the back of his head. She didn't take it.

"Damn you, you hurt her."

Donovan glanced at Buddy. It didn't take a genius to piece together the motivation behind the attack. The piece of shit curled on the ground had taken advantage of an innocent young woman. Someone related to this woman.

Light caught on the tears pouring down Lisa's face, the hatred in her eyes, the helplessness in her soul as she wrestled with the right and wrong of what she was doing.

"You had no right to hurt her."

The next swing didn't have the strength of the others. It bounced off Buddy's thigh. "She didn't deserve it."

Another blow, another lessening of force. A barely visible trembling began in her arms as the reality set in.

Lisa didn't have it in her to kill the sniveling son of a bitch. Donovan moved to her side and caught the cue as it raised again. Surprise jerked her face up. Her eyes were a brilliant blue, full of tears and a pain that just about ripped out his heart.

Adrenaline spiced her scent anew as she took in his size and the easy strength with which he held the cue. A primitive, instinctive feminine call of distress, one to which any male wolf was obligated to respond. It hit him harder than it should, more personally than it should. Donovan lifted the cue higher, increasing the tension between them. "You've either got to make the call to kill him, or leave him for the law."

She yanked at the cue, glaring at Buddy, who rolled to his back moaning.

"I don't have to do a damn thing."

Her muscles were no match for his. The cue stayed put. "Yes, you do."

"The law won't do anything to a piece of dirt like him."

Donovan glanced over to Wyatt. "That true?"

Wyatt's mouth settled in a grim line. "The county prosecutor refused to press charges."

"Because Buddy's mother bought him off," Lisa growled, drawing her foot back. Buddy cringed. Lisa didn't kick him, just watched him grovel, a strange tension in her shoulders.

Wyatt sighed. "True. But it doesn't mean the law's going to be that lenient with you if you take this any further."

"I don't care." Lisa yanked at the cue. Donovan relaxed his grip on the next tug, letting her reclaim it, shaking his head at human law. No plea from a momma would have saved a man who'd touched a were female. Her menfolk would have been judge, jury, and executioner, and if she didn't have a man, that job would have fallen to the pack's Protectors. In his pack, that meant either he or his brother would have stood for the woman. Pack law was absolute in matters like this.

The set of Wyatt's mouth expressed his own dissatisfaction with human law as he delivered the truth. "You've done about all you can here, Lisa."

She glared down at Buddy, her expression hidden by the hat and the fall of her hair. Stale smoke swirled around her head in an acrid veil as she blew out another harsh breath. "No."

"Yes."

Wyatt reached for the cue. Donovan's lips curled over a snarl so low only another wolf could hear it. Wyatt cut him a glance. Donovan shook his head and folded his arms across his chest. The woman would have her say, however she wanted to say it. Wyatt stepped back, a flick of his eyebrow indicating his surprise.

Buddy took advantage of the distraction to get his feet under him. Using the wall as a brace, he pushed upright, holding his nose and his side. Blood seeped between his fingers as red and as hot as the anger pouring off him. "You fucking bitch."

"Absolutely." Lisa drove the pool cue between the window of his hand and his arm, finding the soft spot beneath his Adam's apple, holding it there as Buddy's eyes flew wide. As she was about eight inches shorter than her opponent, it made for an optimally painful angle. "And if you ever come around my family again, you'll find out just how big of one I can be."

Buddy's response was a harsh gurgle that had the men around them shifting uncomfortably. Donovan adjusted his position to better cover her back and waited. There was only one way this could end, and it wasn't going to be in violence. Lisa Delaney did not have the heart of a killer, even if she wanted to at that moment.

That hunger poured off her. The need to see the man suffer, the desire to have the wherewithal to kill him, followed slowly, sadly, by the eventual acceptance that she didn't have it in her to finish the job. Buddy took advantage of the hesitation and shoved the cue. Lisa took a step back, first one and then another, driven by Buddy's strength and the smirk on his face now that he had the upper hand.

Another step back and she was almost up against Donovan. The heat of her body caressed him from chest to toe in a subtle enticement. He closed the distance between them, reached around, and added his strength to hers. She cast him a shocked look over her shoulder as his chest came up against her back before whipping back around, grabbing the pool stick, and throwing her weight against it. He adjusted the angle slightly, pushing and lifting until Buddy was once again back against the wall, this time dangling on the end of the cue, his smirk gone, his face taking on a blue cast that didn't bode well for his survival.

"If you want to say something, you might want to get on with it," Donovan prompted as Lisa hesitated.

"I can handle this."

"Wasn't arguing that you couldn't, just thought you might want to get whatever it is said before he passes out."

She risked another glance at him. For a brief moment her body rested against his, taking his support. The rightness of it sank to his soul. Inside his wolf howled "Mine" so loudly it seemed impossible she didn't hear.

Wyatt did. He gave Donovan a strange look before stepping forward. "You need to let him go, Lisa."

"So he can do it again? To someone else?" She shook her head and gripped the cue harder. "No."

"If he does, he'll be caught."

"And his mother will just buy him out of it again."

"No. She won't."

Donovan recognized the promise behind the statement. Wyatt hadn't gone completely native on him after all. Good. That would make his job easier. Buddy jerked to the side. Lisa stumbled. Donovan slid a hand around her waist, bracing her back against him. The soft, feminine muscles of her abdomen shuddered beneath his touch. She was scared and unsure, caught in a situation she wasn't equipped to handle, but she was determined to see it through. The woman had guts.

"You can't promise that," she told Wyatt.

"I can promise you that if you kill him, your sister will be without a guardian. Without protection."

Buddy made a strange gurgling sound in his throat, sort of like he was swallowing his tonsils dry. Donovan felt another shudder go through Lisa as she looked at Buddy's purpling face, the cue, her hands above his own on the base. With a small exclamation, she dropped the cue and stepped out of his embrace. The impact of wood hitting the floor set everyone in motion. Bystanders stepped back; Buddy stumbled forward. Donovan caught Lisa's hand and tugged her aside.

Buddy grabbed his throat. His friends rushed in, kicking the cue. It rolled across the cement floor with a disjointed rattle.

Lisa stared at it, at Buddy, at the group of men supporting him. Her hands balled into fists. Everything she wanted to say was there in her eyes, along with the knowledge that it wouldn't make a difference. Nothing she did was going to change what had happened, and short of killing Buddy, nothing was going to remove the threat he presented.

Her lip lifted in a fair imitation of a snarl. "Don't come near me or mine again."

With the same determination with which she'd entered the bowling alley, she turned on her heel and left, as strong walking out as when she'd walked in. Damn, she was something.

Donovan followed her, his pace slower, his strides shorter. He had no desire to catch up to Lisa while she was still inside. He grabbed his coat off his seat. Halfway across the room he heard it, the rustle of clothing as Buddy moved, the murmur of outraged voices feeding a sense of injustice. He turned. Buddy glared after Lisa, his bruised and bloody face warped with hatred. Shaking off the friends holding him up, he pushed away from the wall, swaying on his feet.

"This is not over, Delaney," Buddy yelled to Lisa's retreating back. He included all the bar patrons in the next glance as he wiped the blood from his face and muttered, "Not by a long shot."

The threat snapped Donovan back. Five strides and he was in front of the bastard. He grabbed him by his bruised throat, lifting him easily with one hand, suspending him above his head, letting him flail, letting him feel the full force of his wolf, the razor edge of his claws over his jugular and spinal cord before snarling, "She doesn't have it in her to gut your sorry ass, but I do."

The bite of ammonia stung his nostrils. Donovan dropped Buddy, snorting in disgust. The coward had pissed his pants. He spun around and pulled up just short of running into Wyatt. With a jerk of his thumb he indicated the man standing in a puddle of his own urine. "They call us animals? Hell, they're not even housebroken."

Two

START damn it!"

Lisa turned the key again. The starter whined, but the engine didn't catch. She needed to get out of here. Buddy and his friends weren't going to take his humiliation sitting down. She glanced back at the bar. A man's silhouette filled the door, blocking the light, before stretching into the night. The stranger in the bar. She and her sisters hadn't lived here long, but in a town as small as Haven, one only needed a day to know everyone, and strangers stood out.

Especially one like that one. Tall, dark, and virile. If she hadn't been in a rage, she might have just stopped and drooled on first sight. She'd originally thought Wyatt the most handsome man she'd ever seen, but the stranger had another element to him that froze a woman in her tracks. Maybe it was the thick mane of hair he wore to just past his shoulders that gave him that bad-boy look. Maybe it was the way his cheekbones slashed so aggressively above the square set of his jaw. Maybe it was the barely civilized aura he wore like other men wore jeans, casually and naturally, but whatever it was, it had slipped beneath the "I have no time for this" grip desperation had had on her love life the last few years and renewed her interest in the opposite sex. In the middle of her rage and revenge, no less. That had to be some load of testosterone he was carrying around.

The pool-hall door opened, spreading the yellow flare of light into the hazy pattern of color cast by the neon signs. The man stepped forward into the haphazard joining of shadow and light outside the door and then just . . . disappeared. She blinked and squinted through the escalating fall of snow, her hand on the ignition key. She searched the area, following the trajectory of his path. He didn't turn up. She remembered the way he'd come up behind her, held the cue when she'd faltered. She'd never been so scared or so terrified as when her anger had ebbed and she'd stood there realizing what she'd done, but then he'd reached around her, surrounding her in power, and her fear had evaporated.

She scouted the darkness, noting the isolation of the parking lot, the black of the night. Her fear came back full force. Men just didn't disappear, and men who did, while she sat isolated in a dark parking lot, were men to be avoided. She turned the key again. The starter wheezed a command. The engine ignored the order.

"C'mon, Bessie, don't do this to me now."

The engine grunted and sputtered but didn't catch. "I've got a nice, fresh bottle of oil at home for you if you start." She thought she detected a perking in the engine. "Not the cheap stuff either," she crooned. Another sputter. Another false hope. She paused and glanced around, every sense on red alert. There was nothing she could see. Just white drifts of freshly fallen snow touched by moonlight, painting an illusion of life over a town too stubborn to admit it was dead. The old leather seat crackled a protest against the cold and her movement as she leaned forward and caressed the dash. "You'd like that wouldn't you? Fresh oil, with maybe just a touch of additive to spice it up?"

It was crazy to think sweet-talking a vehicle was going to fix what a repairman had warned her was going to take hundreds of dollars to correct, but she didn't have a spare penny. She and her sisters had sunk every cent of their small inheritance into the old farm at the edge of the national park that they hoped to build into a thriving retreat for photographers and naturalists. Haven might be thirty miles from the bustling tourist town of Bender, Montana, but it bordered the same park and therefore should cater to the same tourists. Its highest allure, though, was definitely that the property carried half the price of properties in more popular areas; but even at half the price, the inn had cost them every penny they'd had. Without her older sister Heather's job, they wouldn't have been able to swing the renovations. That being the case, sweet talk was all she had to offer the truck. The howl of the wind swept the heavy flakes into an impenetrable wall of white, encouraging the desperation she was keeping at bay. And she was fast running out of strength to push back.

She flexed her fingers inside her gloves to relieve the stiffness from the cold. The temperature was dropping rapidly. She hoped her sister remembered to bring in more wood. If this turned into a blizzard, they were going to need it. The old furnace wasn't that reliable and their supply of oil was getting low, but thankfully, the house had come with a woodstove and a mountain of firewood.

The wind gusted, buffeting the truck. She wiped at the fog condensing on the window. A rap to her left ripped a scream from her throat. She spun around. It was him—the stranger from the bar. And no matter how safe he'd made her feel in the middle of that foolish confrontation, out here in the elements he scared the bejeezus out of her. Probably because he looked so at home in the wild storm.

She didn't open the window, just hollered through. Not that safety glass offered that much protection, but it was better than nothing. "What do you want?"

"To get you out of here." He motioned to the front of the truck. "Pop the hood."

If she popped the hood he could do all kinds of nastiness to Bessie. Then again, since Bessie was in a funk and not cooperating, how much worse could he make things?

She reached under the dash and pulled the lever. The metal gave with a loud thunk. He walked around and lifted the hood, obscuring her view of everything but the multipainted surface. She heard the support scrape into place, then silence. The man could be doing anything to her precious truck, from ripping out wires to fixing them. A flare of light to the left caught her eye. Another silhouette stood in the doorway. Besides the stranger, there was only one other man in town with that wide-shouldered, lean-hipped build. Only one other man who walked into the night like he owned it. The sheriff.

For a second the snow swirled and Wyatt disappeared like the stranger had, but she blinked and he was back, striding toward her through the storm with the same commanding presence. She wondered if the two were related. It would at least explain the stranger's appearance in town. And the odd way both seemed to master the space around them.

She opened the door and slid to the ground. The wind ripped through her coat with ruthless efficiency. The severity of the weather was just one more thing she and her sister had underestimated in their decision to move from the city. Lisa huddled into her coat and walked to the front of the truck where the stranger was bent over, fiddling with what looked like an octopus of wires.

"Do you know anything about engines?"

He didn't look at her, just worked at one particular connection. "Nope. I just like to play with the wires."

She couldn't blame him for the sarcasm. It had been a stupid question. "Can you fix it?"

"I'll let you know in a bit."

In a bit she'd be a popsicle, but no way was she going back in the bar. She shoved her hands into her pockets and shivered. "Thanks."

"You're welcome." He glanced over. His deep brown eyes seemed to hold all the warmth she was missing. "Why don't you wait in the truck?"

"I'm fine."

The immediate shiver that shook her belied her claim.

"So I see." He straightened. It struck her again how tall he was, well over six feet. And she just cleared five. They'd look ridiculous as a couple. Her hormones didn't care. They watched in breathless anticipation as he unfastened the elk horn buttons on his heavy shearling coat. As if hearing the call, the wind blew again, pressing his shirt against the powerful expanse of his chest. The fabric buckled into the flat planes of his stomach, revealing the long lines of muscle that flowed into his lean hips and strong thighs.

Her hormones started a chant more suited to a strip joint than a parking lot. *Take it off. Take it all off.*

She licked her lips. "Thank you for the help in the bar."

"You're welcome."

He shrugged out of his coat. She took a breath and held it. He didn't reach for his shirt buttons, which was just as well. Below zero or not, she had an awful feeling that one glimpse of his chest would have her going up in flames. At the very least, reaching out and exploring the delineation of muscle she could just make out through the black cotton of his shirt. Just the thought of doing that had her knees so wobbly, all it would take would be the touch of his finger and she'd fall back in the snow in a wanton sprawl. "You are aware it's below zero out here?"

He swung the coat around her shoulders, tucking the collar under her chin before fastening the button. "Judging from the way you're shivering, I'd say yes."

The coat was warm from his body, saturated in his scent, an

addictive, pleasing aroma that had her taking a deep breath. And then another, before she caught herself. Good grief, what was it about him? "I can't take your coat."

"I won't need it for a bit."

Everything was *a bit* with him. "In a bit you'll be frozen stiff."

She reached for the button. His hands caught hers. "No."

A simple word, a low, drawled command, delivered with the expectation of being obeyed.

"I don't take orders from you."

"I don't imagine you take orders from anyone," Wyatt said, coming up beside her, "but in this case you might as well consider it a reasonable suggestion."

A sound erupted from the stranger's chest. It sounded distinctly like a growl. Wyatt stepped to the side, the smile in his voice showing in the crease at the corner of his mouth. "Donovan can be temperamental about hi— a woman suffering."

She ignored the hesitation. "Donovan will just have to adjust."

She wiggled her hands. Donovan's finger under her chin tipped her face up. His thumb smoothed along her jaw in a caress that lingered in sensitive nerve endings. Was he as affected by her as she was by him?

"No," he told her quietly. "He won't."

As if to prove his point he buttoned the rest of the buttons so fast that his fingers were a blur of movement, effectively trapping her within the heavy folds. She stood there in the dark between the two men, Donovan's coat sheltering her from the cold the same way he'd sheltered her from the repercussions of her violence earlier.

She folded her arms across her chest beneath the coat. She wasn't used to being taken care of—didn't know what she was supposed to do now. Protest his high-handedness or stay secure against the cold? His coat was warm, very warm, and his scent spread to her skin—totally masculine, totally pleasant. She couldn't remember a man's scent affecting her like this, but she could inhale his forever.

The backs of his fingers brushed her cheek. "Wyatt's going to take you to his car while I take care of yours."

She raised her brows. "He is?"

Wyatt put his hand on her shoulder. "Apparently so."

She planted her feet, wincing as the soles tingled a protest. "I don't think so."

Donovan frowned. "There's no need for you to be cold."

"There's no need for you to freeze, either."

His expression softened. "I'm not cold."

Amazingly, he didn't appear to be. He stood there in the bitter storm as relaxed as if it were eighty degrees, while her feet were turning to blocks of ice. She stomped the feeling back into them. He glanced down, then back at Wyatt. "Take her to the car."

The surety of the command made her decision for her. "You don't give me orders"—she ducked out from under Wyatt's hand—"and I'm not going anywhere."

She worked her hand through the front placket and set to work on the buttons. "And I refuse to be warm at someone else's expense."

"The only one suffering is you," Donovan countered.

"You have to be cold."

He shrugged. "I won't be for awhile, but your feet are cold now."

"My car is right over there." Wyatt pointed across the lot.

As if she didn't know that. The fancy lights sitting on top were a dead giveaway. She set her chin. "I'm fine."

She wasn't leaving anyone alone with her truck. It was the only thing standing between her family and destitution.

"I can vouch for Donovan."

She rolled her eyes. "The innocent act doesn't look good on you, Sheriff."

"I was shooting for trustworthy."

"I'm fresh out of trust." Good-looking men who thought their looks would get them special consideration were way down on her list these days. And men who looked like Wyatt and Donovan, well, a woman would be a fool to trust them. "I'm staying with my truck."

Wyatt glanced at Donovan and shrugged. "I tried."

Donovan made that rumbling noise again. Lisa lifted her foot off the ground, just a bit, more a shift of weight than anything, but as if she were a magnet, both men reacted immediately, their gazes dropping to her poorly shod foot. In a move too fast to see, Donovan had her in his arms. Even through two layers of coat, she could feel the hardness of his muscles as they shifted. And this close, there was no avoiding his scent. If she'd thought it addictive before, it was positively heady now. He shifted her higher and opened the truck door. The leather seat creaked as he set her on it. He didn't step away. She could see the amber flecks in his brown eyes. The way they caught the light was both beautiful and mesmerizing. She placed her palms against his chest. He wasn't cold at all.

"You're so warm," she marveled as an endless amount of energy poured off him to her, making her palms tingle with an awareness that defied description. Her breath caught in her lungs as his hands skimmed down the sides of the coat in a rustle of intent. Everything in her focused on the path of those hands, the nerve endings under her skin coming alive at the subtle pressure, straining for the ghost of sensation as his fingers passed over her hips, down her thighs . . .

"You're not," he drawled in a voice as low and easy as his touch. The heat from his palms settled over the point of her knees, igniting a fire in her belly. His fingers rested on the outside while his thumbs pressed on the inside. "But I can do something about that."

She waggled her elbows in the coat, going for humor to fight the embarrassing onslaught of need. "I thought you already had."

He pushed her knees aside and stepped in. Desire shot through her in a white-hot bolt of need as his groin nestled into hers. He was hard and ready. His low, totally masculine chuckle as she gasped only fed the invisible fire licking over her flesh.

"What are you doing?"

He leaned in, his eyes seeming to glow, that strange energy wrapping around her, drawing her in as his fingers slid under her hair to cradle her skull. "Staking my claim."

Three

He didn't claim her mouth immediately. Donovan had waited too long for this moment, this first kiss with his mate, to charge in. He savored the puff of astonishment that brought the moistness of her breath to his skin, the essence of her scent to his nostrils. He leaned in a bit farther, teasing himself with the heat of her mouth, the whispered gasp of his name.

"Donovan . . ."

He tipped her head back and growled, "Yes, *Donovan*."

Her eyes flared open at the primitive sound. He didn't give her time to assimilate the strangeness, just fitted his mouth to hers, holding her still for the sweep of his tongue, savoring the addition of her taste to her scent. He cataloged it all, imprinting it on his soul. This was his mate. The woman created just for him.

She held still beneath him, not moving, not immediately returning his kiss. He took full advantage of her hesitation, learning the textures of her mouth, the sensitive areas, how the stroke of his tongue along the inner lining of her lower lip caused her to shiver and press closer. How the brush of his tongue along hers brought another type of stillness. A breathless anticipation.

Her fingers curled into his chest. Eight pressure points of heat. He flicked his tongue along the flat edge of her teeth before tempting her with another glide along her inner lip. Her mouth moved under his, the aphrodisiac in his saliva working into her system the way it would with any human, but doubly potent with his mate.

She moaned. He took the feminine husk of sound into his lungs on a slow breath, tilting her head back farther, drawing her against him, resenting the thick barrier of the coats that kept the softness of her breasts from him. He wanted her naked in his arms, flesh to flesh, heartbeat to heartbeat, their bodies joined and desire burning brightly. He wanted privacy to explore all the ways he could bring pleasure to her eyes and soft, throaty moans to her lips.

Donovan dragged his mouth from Lisa's, struggling for control, his body aching with the need to possess her. She was here. Finally here. Snow crunched beneath a booted foot. Wyatt. His wolf reared within and bared its fangs, aggressively possessive of this miracle, not willing to tolerate any male near her. Not even his cousin and leader.

Donovan kissed Lisa's cheek, struggling against the violence of his instincts, rooting himself in the reality of his senses. Her skin was like cool satin, smooth like cream, sensitive at the corner of her mouth. He lingered there, relishing the tiny unveiling betrayed by her gasp, needing to know more. He had to know every curve, every secret sensitive spot, every private longing, every treasured dream. He had to know everything about her.

"Yes," he whispered as he kissed the hollow under her cheekbone, following the shallow path back toward her ear, stopping to nibble at the lobe, satisfaction blending with the pound of his pulse as she gave a little shiver and tilted her head back, offering him more. "Give yourself to me."

Her answer was an airy sigh and the stroke of her fingertips against his chest. The bones of her jaw were fragile, the cord of her neck providing an erotic lure to more sensitive places. He followed it down, nibbling along the soft flesh until he ran into the edge of her collar. Unbuttoning his coat, unzipping hers, he growled with frustration, even as she frowned a protest at the loss of sensation. There were too many barriers between them. He jerked the zipper down to her chest before continuing his journey to the seductive hollow where the taut line angled into her shoulder.

A touch of his tongue to the vulnerable spot. Another jerk in her respiration. She liked that. He tightened his grip, holding her in place for another kiss, another taste. He'd starved for her for so long, waited so long, he'd almost given up hope.

"Sweet," he whispered. "You taste very sweet." He slid his hand up her thigh, luxuriating in the soft, enticing curve that led to the pleasing fullness of her hips. His fingers sank into the firm flesh. "Do you taste this sweet everywhere?"

He had to know. His canines stretched and ached with the same demand that pounded in his cock—to claim her, to mark her undeniably as his. He slid his arm around the small of her back, arching her chest into his, pressing his teeth into her skin, laving the sensitive flesh, sucking it into his mouth, connecting them in this small prelude. Every shiver she made as he prepared her to take his bite shook loose another growled "Yes" from his chest. This was the woman he'd waited for. His woman. His mate. He wanted to throw back his head and howl. He wanted to scoop her up in his arms and hide her away. He wanted . . . her.

The hand on his shoulder brought his head up. "Donovan."

He shook off Wyatt's touch, his gaze locked on Lisa's parted lips, her dazed expression, the slumberous passion in her eyes.

"Get the hell out of here, Wyatt."

"So you can claim her?"

Donovan focused on the pulse racing in Lisa's throat and the red mark a few inches to the right. If Wyatt hadn't stopped him when he had, that transitional bruise would have been replaced with the permanence of a mating mark. He touched the spot. She was receptive, prepared. "Yes."

Wyatt folded his arms across his chest. "I can't let you do that."

The snarl started in Donovan's toes. He turned slowly, letting Lisa's hands drop from his chest. His claws extended. His muscles contracted and expanded in preparation for the change. "Are you challenging me?"

"Hell, no, but neither am I going to allow you to commit suicide through mating lust."

Donovan blinked, bringing Wyatt's face into focus. His cousin waved his hand toward Lisa.

"Think man. She's human, damn it! You're a Protector. Think of what marking her will cost you both."

Behind him, Lisa groaned. Donovan turned back. Her hat was askew, dipping over one brow. Awareness was replacing the dreamy expression in her blue eyes, and embarrassment was sweeping a tide of red color into her cheeks. Hell. Hopefully she was still too far gone to process what Wyatt had said.

He pulled her face into the hollow of his throat, tucking her hips to his, her chest to his, listening to the rapid beat of her heart, breathing in the spice of her arousal, every cell in his body demanding he mark her, his conscience warning him of the unfairness of it if he did.

Her hands worked from between the lapel of his coat, slid up his hips to his waist, leaving a trail of fire in their wake and an anticipation almost impossible to manage as her nails dug into his side through his shirt. There was no shyness in the tug that notched his groin to hers, no regret in the moan of satisfaction as the hardness of his cock found the softness of her pussy, just pure feminine bliss. A bliss he had to ignore if he planned on living with himself. There were times when being a Protector was damn inconvenient. "Lisa."

She stiffened. He repeated her name, drawing her out of the haze into the present. Her grip lightened, slid around, pressed. Donovan let her put a few inches between them. His wolf snarled a protest at even that small separation.

She stared at him, shock and fear in her eyes. For a second he wondered if she'd heard the mental protest, but then her fingers came up to her lips, and he understood. It was her response to him that shocked her. He stared back, keeping his expression bland. She was going to have to get used to it. True matings were passionate affairs.

Another blink, a deep breath, and Lisa glanced over at Wyatt, her fingers moving to the mark on her shoulder. She cleared her throat and shifted forward on the seat.

"I think I'll take you up on your offer of a lift."

The image of her in a car with another male—cousin or not—snaked another low growl past Donovan's control.

The low rumble of noise vibrated against Lisa's hands, chasing the last of the cobwebs from her brain and the lethargy from her muscles. The hairs on the back of her neck stood on end. The swell of desire racing through her system broke against the wild energy spilling off Donovan. Danger screamed through her mind, but rather than running in fear, everything in her demanded she move forward, back into his arms, back into the flames. She'd always had a soft spot for bad boys.

She placed her finger in the middle of his chest and pushed. "You, Donovan, should come with a warning label."

She was rather proud of how that came off. Sophisticated. Worldly. Unimpressed. And they'd said those years of grammar school plays were a waste of time.

Donovan stepped back, but his gaze never left her face. She had the impression he was cataloging every flicker of expression, every betrayal of emotion. "I could say the same about you."

She slid off the seat into the small space she'd created. The flakes were coming down harder now, catching on her hat brim, blowing into her eyes. She blinked one of them off her lashes. "It was just a kiss."

"It was more than that."

She shook her head and licked her lips, tasting the coolness of the storm and the heat of his desire.

What are you doing?

Staking my claim.

The man certainly was intense. She took a step to the left, away from the door. He obligingly made room, those dark eyes searching hers. She shook her hair over her shoulder, grabbing the coat when it threatened to slip off. "No, it wasn't."

"I could tell you why."

The way Donovan was looking at her was different than the way any man had ever looked at her. Like, for him, she was the one who'd put the *X* in sex. Like he just needed two minutes and a bit of privacy to show her heaven in his arms. How in heck was she supposed to resist a man who looked at her like that? In the next instant she knew. She bluffed. "Are you trying to creep me out?"

He didn't even blink, just kept watching her with that lazy manner that was seduction itself. "No."

She was suddenly glad the sheriff was standing only five feet away. It kept her from doing something stupid like asking him where he was staying. "Then I'd prefer you tell me you can fix my truck."

"I can, but it's not going to do you any good tonight."

"Why not?"

He brushed the accumulation of snow off her hat. "In this storm, all those bald tires will do is land you in a ditch."

She stepped back and started walking. He closed the door behind her.

"Bessie would never betray me that way."

He came up beside her, seemingly impervious to the cold. Out of the corner of her eye, she studied him, taking in the flatness of his stomach, the power in his thighs, and finally the shadowed image of the erection stretching across his groin. The man was definitely blessed. Her gaze lingered. His cock jerked beneath the denim. She licked her lips as her womb clenched with the same want.

"Bessie?" he asked.

She cleared her throat and patted the hood of the truck. "Bessie."

She didn't have to look at his face to see his smile. It was clear as day in his voice. "You named your truck?"

He didn't have to make it sound so illogical. "I'm sure you've named a thing or two yourself."

Donovan looked at her as if he had no idea what she was talking about when everyone knew the first thing a man did name was his penis.

"No, I haven't."

She stepped around him. "Just my luck. A great kisser with no imagination."

"I've got imagination," Wyatt offered.

Behind her, Donovan made that noise again. She ignored him. Her heart wasn't in the smile she flashed Wyatt. She was tired, depressed and she still had a lot of work ahead of her before she could go to sleep. Delaney's Bed-and-Breakfast's grand opening was only a month away. "Do us both a favor, and for the rest of the night, keep it to yourself."

"About done in?" Wyatt asked.

She nodded, glancing at the door to the bar. "I shouldn't have lost my temper."

"You had reason."

"Maybe." She hunched down inside the coats as they approached Wyatt's SUV. "But Buddy isn't going to forget tonight anytime soon."

Wyatt's lips flattened to a straight line. "He will if he knows what's good for him."

Buddy wasn't the type to see reason.

Wyatt changed the subject. "How's Robin doing, by the way?"

"Honestly?"

He nodded.

"I don't know. She seems to think that because she was beat up and not actually raped, it's okay to pretend nothing happened."

"Pretending won't do her any good."

She didn't need to turn around to know who was talking. She'd recognize that smooth drawl anywhere. "Aren't you supposed to be fixing my truck?" she asked Donovan.

"We've already covered that."

"You covered it. I didn't agree. It's my truck." She looked pointedly over her shoulder at him. "I win."

Her sense of victory didn't even get off the ground before she stepped on a patch of ice. Her right foot slipped out from under her. Inside the coat, her arms flailed as she tumbled backward. Donovan caught her as naturally as breathing, as if he'd expected her to slip. He didn't let go when she got her balance back, just kept her tucked into his side and guided her across the ground, as if she were something delicate and fragile. As if he hadn't just seen her march into a bar and deck a man with a pool stick.

As if she'd conjured her fear with the thought, the door to the bar opened and two men exited. Lisa snapped her head around. The men passed out of sight before she could see where they were going. They'd better not be planning on messing with Bessie.

She twisted, trying to keep them in sight. Donovan's arm was in her way. She planted her feet. He kept walking. She stuck her foot between his. By rights they should have landed in a heap, but Donovan had the reflexes of a cat. He kept them both upright through a miracle of coordination that released a curl of heat inside her. Good grief, the man was a walking pheromone.

He held her by the arms with an easy strength. "What in hell are you doing?"

She resisted the urge to step forward and press her lips to the hollow of his throat, to touch the tan of his skin with her tongue, to taste his heat. "Getting your attention."

His hands dropped from her arms and folded across his chest. He didn't seem to notice how those broad shoulders of his blocked her view. "You've got it."

She motioned with her fingers. "You're in my way."

He glanced behind him, one eyebrow cocking as he noticed Buddy's friends crossing the lot. "You didn't have enough fun inside?"

She shoved her hands back in her pockets, remembering the violence that had overtaken her, its inevitable death that would have left her helpless except for the intervention of this man. She stepped to the side, tracking the two men's progress. "More than enough."

"Then why the interest in those men?"

"I don't want them to hurt Bessie."

"I think Bessie is past the hurting stage," Wyatt interjected.

Buddy's friends didn't appear to be interested in her truck. That was a relief. Without Bessie, she and her sisters would never have everything done in time for the grand opening. "I'll have you know Bink Riddle swore to me she's got at least another fifty thousand in her."

Wyatt rolled his eyes. "Bink would throw his soul on the line if he thought it'd sell a car."

She shrugged. "Maybe, but not this time."

"What makes you so sure?" Donovan asked.

Try as she might, she couldn't detect any skepticism in his voice or expression, just an easy confidence she'd love to bottle. "Instinct."

His eyebrows lifted. "And what do your instincts say about me?"

She didn't even have to think on the answer. It just came popping out, riding the frost of her breath and the heat in his gaze. "You're trouble. Pure, unadulterated trouble."

His slow smile spread across her feminine side with the smoothness of butter, coating it with a rich layer of desire. "I don't see you running away."

She blew a snowflake off the end of her nose. "That's because when it comes to trouble, I've got the brains of a goose."

"So what's the problem?"
"Your timing."
"What about it?"
She spun on her heel, frustration driving her past Wyatt and his knowing smile. "It sucks."

Four

SHE thought his timing sucked? Donovan smiled grimly as he followed Wyatt's big SUV through the blinding snowstorm. She ought to look at it from his perspective. Here he was, on a critical mission for his pack—retrieving their leader—and he found his mate. His human mate, forbidden to any wolf, but most especially to a Protector.

He ran his tongue over his lips, gathering up her unique taste, shuddering as it rippled along his senses, igniting them anew, feeding his frustration. He'd waited a hundred years for this moment, this destiny, and now tradition declared he had to walk away.

But he couldn't. Even if he could ignore the pull on his senses, which he wasn't sure was possible, he couldn't. She was in trouble. She needed help. He was here. It was his duty to provide her security, as a Protector and as her potential mate. She'd bound him to her with that one desperate glance that asked for everything and expected nothing.

The big SUV slipped on the slick road. His reflexes easily handled the small skid. Ahead, he could make out Wyatt's SUV sliding into the next curve. The roads were getting treacherous. He clenched the steering wheel as the SUV ahead straightened.

He hadn't wanted Lisa in the car with another man, her safety in another's hands. He'd wanted her with him, under his protection. And she would have been, if Wyatt hadn't backed her small defiance with an escort into his SUV. Damn Wyatt, he'd known how much putting her in his vehicle would drive Donovan crazy, knew how it would prick his wolf to have Lisa in such close proximity to another male. Knew it and reveled in it. It was payback for the pressure Donovan was going to put on him to return to his rightful place. Donovan couldn't do much about his leader's defiance, but Lisa's could and would be handled.

He remembered the angry glare she'd cut him, as if her refusal to respond to the attraction between them was his fault. She couldn't tease his wolf and expect to walk away scot-free. Then again, maybe she could. She was human, with no concept of what he would require from her if he chose her as his mate. If . . .

Damn it! When had it gone from *impossible* to *if*?

The SUV pulled into a dark driveway that wound through the trees. As a wolf, Donovan approved the seclusion. As a man with an unclaimed woman with a threat against her, he found definite downsides to being so far off the beaten path. He turned down the driveway, noting the thickness of the forest and brush, the denseness of the canopy that slowed the fall of snow and blocked the moonlight. The perfect hunting ground for predators.

The driveway ended in a circle at the base of a large Victorian-style home. Immediately, the front door opened. Light flooded the yard and two silhouettes, one small and slight, the other taller and stockier, ran down the steps. Donovan was out of his truck and at the passenger door of Wyatt's vehicle before the women reached it. Both women pulled up short. The younger woman bore a strong similarity to Lisa in features and scent. Her sister.

The older woman had a much more lived-in face. Both women blinked at him with identical expressions of confusion on their faces at his sudden appearance. This close there was no missing the bruises on the younger woman's pale face. They were hard to look at on one who radiated such delicacy and gentleness of spirit. No wonder Lisa had gone crazy.

Donovan bit back a snarl as the younger woman took an anxious step forward and peered around him, her scent enveloping him in shades of his mate and something else. Something not right. Something that brought forth every protective instinct he had. He grazed his fingertips over the discolored flesh on her cheekbone. His family now.

She flinched away and eyed him warily.

He smiled reassuringly at her as he closed his fist over his anger and brought it under control. Behind him, he could hear Lisa cursing.

"Who are you?" The older woman asked, pulling the young woman back.

The door latch clicked. The panel struck his back.

"A pain in my butt," Lisa grumbled from inside the SUV. Donovan didn't immediately move. The door rapped him in the spine again. He held firm, keeping Lisa in the vehicle as he ascertained the safety of the area. No strange energy or scent came to him on the wind. He nodded to the waiting women as he stepped away from the door, blocking the opening with his body as he held out his hand for Lisa to take. She glared at him. He waited patiently. With a huff, she put her hand in his. The contact sent sparks dancing up his arm. He breathed in her scent as she brushed past him. Her elbow in his gut took him by surprise.

"Back off."

He raised an eyebrow at her. She scowled right back. The woman didn't have a lick of caution. He liked it.

"Lisa?" The older woman questioned, breaking the moment.

Lisa pushed around him. "Carol, thank you so much for staying with Robin."

Carol didn't take her eyes off him, the wariness in her gaze hinting at the predator she sensed lurking beneath the surface. Donovan smiled his most sympathetic, friendly smile at her. Not an ounce of caution left her expression. In fact it got worse. So much for his brother Kelon's suggestion that they could blend. Humans might not have the sharpest senses in the world, but they had survival instincts just like every other living creature, and he apparently set them off.

He turned his attention to Robin. The younger woman gasped and took a step back. Lisa scooted around him and positioned herself protectively in front of her sister. As if her small body could stop him from doing anything he wanted. He didn't waste his smile on her. He was a threat to her and she knew it. Just not in the way she suspected.

"This is my cousin, Donovan McGowan," Wyatt said, coming around the front of the car and easing the tension with the normalcy of introductions.

"Your cousin?" Lisa asked, looking between the two men. "Why didn't you mention he was a relative before?"

Wyatt shrugged. "You didn't ask and the circumstances of your meeting didn't leave much time for introductions."

Color flared in Lisa's cheeks. Her glare deepened to accusation as she flashed those blue eyes at Donovan, as if everything was his fault. "There was plenty of time if you'd wanted to mention it."

Donovan didn't take his gaze off her lips. He loved the way they plumped around vowels, caressing the syllables a little longer than most. Or maybe he was just so tuned to her that it merely seemed that way. "I was distracted." He waited a crucial second, which had her sucking in her breath and shaped her mouth into a perfect O, before he continued smoothly, "Trying to fix Bessie."

"Oh no." Robin rubbed her hands up and down her arms, shivered, and glanced at Lisa. "Bessie broke down again?"

"Yes." Lisa frowned as she really looked at her sister. "Why don't you have a coat on?"

"Why are you wearing two?" Robin shot back.

For all her fragile appearance, the younger sister apparently had the family spirit.

"She was cold," Donovan filled in.

"And you're not?" Robin asked, apparently just noticing that he wore only a shirt.

"I'm getting there."

Wyatt shrugged out of his coat and wrapped it around the younger woman, steering her to the wide steps that led up to the wraparound porch. "If Donovan hadn't stepped in when he did, you just might have had a reason to be concerned about your sister."

Robin looked over her shoulder. "Oh Lisa, what did you do?"

Lisa's mouth firmed. "What needed to be done."

Robin planted her feet on the third step and twisted inside the coat, relying on Wyatt's support to keep her from falling. Accepting his aid came easily to her, as if she was used to being helped. Donovan earmarked the information for future investigation.

"Buddy's family is really big around here."

Lisa's mouth took on that stubborn set. "Not big enough that he can hurt you and get away with it."

Robin closed her eyes and asked, "How bad is it?"

Donovan's "As bad as it gets" easily overrode Lisa's "Not bad at all."

Robin opened her eyes. "Don't take this wrong, Lisa, but I'm going with Mr. McGowan's assessment on this."

"You don't even know him."

"But I know you, and you have a habit of lying to protect me."

"Not always."

A gust of wind kicked the temperature down a degree or two. Donovan put his arm around Lisa's shoulders. "You two can discuss this inside."

Lisa stiffened even more. "Who the heck are you to tell me what to do?"

Your mate.

It popped into his head, rumbled in his throat. He bit it back because he didn't think she'd appreciate the claim even if she understood it. His dry "A concerned citizen" twitched the corners of Wyatt's mouth. The other wolf understood exactly the conflict going on inside him. And was enjoying it, the son of a bitch.

Donovan flipped him off behind Lisa's back. That just made Wyatt's smile broaden and Robin's eyes narrow. Wyatt tried to urge her up the steps. She shook her head, her gaze dropping to where Donovan's fingers curled possessively on Lisa's shoulder. Understanding softened her expression.

"You're here to protect her."

He was now. "Yes."

"I don't need protection," Lisa protested.

Robin nodded, ignoring Lisa. She licked her lips and leaned more heavily against Wyatt. "Good. She overreacts sometimes."

"I do not!"

Donovan paid no more attention to her denial than Robin had. "I noticed the tendency to take on too much."

"It's just been the three of us for so long."

"Three?"

"We have another sister."

"She's here?" He didn't scent another woman.

Robin shook her head. Behind them Carol's car started.

"Not yet," Lisa muttered as she shrugged out from under his arm. He let her put some space between them, inhaling the spice of her arousal as it stretched between them.

Robin sighed. "You told her?"

"Of course! You were hurt—she had a right to know."

Robin pushed Wyatt away. "Did it ever occur to you that I might not want anyone to know?"

"Why?"

"Because I was stupid." Her grip on the coat was white-knuckled. "So green I couldn't tell a lech from a good date."

"You weren't stupid," Wyatt countered. "Just trusting."

"Call it whatever you want, but what happened the other night isn't anything anyone wants broadcast far and wide."

"He hurt you!" Lisa interjected.

Robin shook her head. "And you just had to respond personally rather than letting the law handle it."

"The law wasn't going to do anything!"

"And now, by alienating the town, we could be forced out of here, lose our money, our future, and our dreams." Robin pushed her hair out of her face. "Because of me. Again. What do you think would be easier for me to take? A few bruises or that?"

Lisa paled, her eyes wide as the wind blew tendrils of hair around her face. Instinct demanded Donovan take her in his arms, hold her while he made her world right. Except he didn't know the details, or what that would take. He could only make one promise.

"No one will force you out of your home."

Neither woman spared him a glance.

"It's not that clear-cut, Robin," Lisa protested. "There are limits to what we can allow."

Robin snorted. "And we've reached ours. Everything we have is sunk into this place. This *is* rock bottom for us."

"It's a new start."

"Yes, and one I value enough not to risk losing it over my poor judgment."

"You're not going to lose anything."

The women didn't give Wyatt any more credence than they had

given him, which wasn't much consolation to Donovan's wolf, who wanted Lisa to look to him for everything.

Lisa stood beside him, her teeth sunk into her lip, her expression a struggle between defiance, apology, and anguish as Robin moved up a step. She reached out and steadied herself on the porch railing. "This was my last chance for a normal life, Lisa."

What in hell did that mean?

Lisa's breath broke on an "I know."

"I don't want to spend it worrying about you."

"You could think of it as the change you've always wanted."

"Not one I want to live with." Robin looked over at Donovan, the steel in her nature shining past her fragile appearance. "If you've got a bag in that SUV, you might as well get it out."

"He's not staying here," Lisa countered.

"I say he is."

Lisa yanked at the coat from within. "You're not the only person who lives here, Robin."

"No, but I'm one-third owner of the house." She motioned Donovan toward his truck. "Consider whatever part of the house he's in as my third."

"Damn it, Robin! I don't want him here."

"I do."

"Why?"

Robin cocked her head to the side as if considering the question. "Because he's got that big, mean, don't-mess-with-me look of a rottweiler on steroids that could be a deterrent to any repercussions from your trip into town today, and because"—she shrugged and a smile touched her lips—"he bothers you in a way I've never seen you bothered. It's interesting."

"I don't want to be bothered."

Robin's smile was sugar sweet. "Then maybe you should consider him a trial guest."

There was no doubt Donovan would be a trial.

Donovan headed back to his SUV. Snow crunched under his

feet. Lisa's teeth snapped audibly together before she muttered, "Don't bother getting anything. You're not staying."

He opened the door and pulled his duffel bag out. The door shut with a decisive click as he looked up. "Why not? I've been invited in."

Five

HE'D been invited in.

Donovan had put particular emphasis on *invited*, as well as a lot of satisfaction. The realization lingered in Lisa's mind, taking on a darker meaning as she slapped hamburger into patties. She couldn't help remembering the lore that said a vampire couldn't enter a person's home without being invited. Vampires didn't exist, but the two men sitting at the inn's restored farmer's table certainly could pass for the mythical beings. They had the blatant sensuality and magnetism that fed the mystique.

"A penny for your thoughts," Wyatt said, taking a sip of coffee.

"I was just thinking all I needed to do was to slap some fangs on you both, call the tabloids, and we'd be booked for the next year with guests wanting to gawk at the sexy vampires frequenting our little bed-and-breakfast."

Donovan choked on his coffee. Wyatt slapped him on the back, his cup suspended over the table, the contents sloshing over the rim with the violence of his movements.

"You think we're vampires?" he asked.

"Of course not." She rolled her eyes. "I'm just saying, if you all wanted to put in some fake fangs this coming Halloween, we could all make some good money."

Donovan carefully put his cup on the table. His head canted to the side. His eyebrow rose. "What if I don't want to be a vampire? What if I'd prefer to be a werewolf?"

She studied him. "I think you look more like a vampire."

For some reason that sent Wyatt into a fit of laughter.

"I'm not a damn vampire," Donovan growled.

Patting another burger into shape, she restrained herself from rolling her eyes again.

"Fine, then don't be a vampire." The burger landed on the tray with a thunk. "Be a werewolf. What difference does it make?"

She washed the grease off her hands at the sink.

"A heck of a lot if you don't like vampires."

She opened the broiler door and looked at Donovan over her shoulder. His deep brown eyes glittered back at her through his lashes. The tug on her senses was immense. "Did you have a bad experience with a vampire in your youth?"

"You might say that." He pushed his coffee away.

She jumped as the broiler door snapped closed. They were really going to have to adjust the tension in that thing before somebody lost a hand. Reaching out, she pulled it back ajar. Hot air blew her hair back from her face. She turned around, struck anew by Donovan's magnetism.

"I still think you'd make a heck of a vampire."

The look he shot her was hotter than the heat coming out of the oven. "Tough."

He really was touchy on that subject.

Robin popped her head around the door. "I fixed up the back bedroom for our guest."

The back bedroom was across the hall from hers and in the family wing. Teasing images of sneaking across the hall popped into Lisa's head. "What was wrong with the guest wing?"

Donovan's gaze grazed her cheek with the softness of the touch. "I don't want to be a problem."

Like heck he didn't. The man had already said he wanted to be everything to her with that kiss that had practically pulled her soul from her body. And she wasn't as adverse to the idea as she should be, Exhibit A being how aware of him she still was, to the point she knew from her body's responses every place his gaze touched. When her lips tingled, she knew he was looking at her mouth. When her breasts swelled and filled with a foreign ache that drew her nipples taut, she knew his gaze had lowered. When her knees weakened and her stomach sucked in, she also knew it was time to take back control. She liked to be the one calling the shots in a relationship.

"I get the feeling you love trouble and all the problems that come with it."

His lips twitched. His gaze came back to hers. "It has its attractions."

Meaning her.

Robin pushed her bangs off her forehead and interrupted the moment. "I would have put him in the presidential suite, except the heating system is out there."

"We just paid to have that fixed!"

"I guess we didn't read the fine print that said it would be a temporary fix."

"I can take a look at it if you want."

Lisa eyed Donovan. "Do you fix heaters as well as you fix cars?"

The chair back squeaked as he leaned against it. Totally in control. Totally, mouthwateringly sexy. "Pretty much."

"In that case, we'll take fifty dollars off your room rate for as many days as it takes you to fix it."

"I'm paying rent?" he asked, taking a sip of his coffee.

She eyed the way the breadth of his shoulders stretched his shirt across his chest, the cotton tucking around his arms hinting at the power beneath. Her mouth went dry. She followed the flex of the muscles of his throat as he swallowed, noticed a hint of moisture on his lip. She licked hers, imagining how he would taste flavored with coffee and desire.

She indulged her interest, visually tracing the swell and dip of muscles as they flowed down his arm to the large bones of his wrists. He had well-shaped hands, strong with long fingers and clean nails. They looked capable and big. Big enough to encompass her ample breasts. The mental image knocked the starch from her knees.

Oh God, if he ever put those hands on her she'd sizzle and pop just like dinner. She closed her eyes at the thought of being his dinner. For sure, Donovan knew how to make a meal of a woman. Sensual knowledge was written in the fullness of his lips, in the way he carried his body, the way he looked at her . . .

She clenched her hands on the stove door handle as her womb throbbed with raw hunger. She'd always thought nature had neglected her in the sensuality department. It just went to prove that nature had a sense of humor. Finding out she could pop and sizzle with the best of them at a time when she couldn't indulge was a cruel joke. "Absolutely."

She named an amount double what they'd been planning on charging. He didn't even bat an eye. The corner of his lips did twitch, though.

"That seems fair."

It wasn't and they both knew it. So did Wyatt, if his expression was anything to go by.

"If that's settled," Wyatt cut in, "do you think you could manage to pull those burgers out of the fire?"

Oh shoot! They were burning. She yanked the door open, waving at the smoke, and grabbed for the broiler pan. She moved too fast, catching her arm on the edge. The skin seared instantly. "Ow!"

Wood scraped across wood, and between one blink and the next, Donovan was at her side, pulling her arm up. She thought it was to look at the wound, but he kept pulling until his breath was on her skin and then his lips scalded deeper than the burn. Her breath froze in her lungs as she stared at his mouth on her arm. His eyes locked on hers as his tongue flicked over the sensitive area. They were black, so black, there wasn't any softness of brown left.

"What are you doing?" she managed to get out.

"Making it better."

"By kissing it?"

"It's the human way."

She frowned at the odd turn of phrase. "That's an old wives' tale."

He lowered her arm and cocked a brow at her. There was no reason for it to take her breath away. It still did.

"Are you telling me it doesn't feel better?" he asked.

The muscles in her forearm quivered under his touch. The room went airless and everything fell out of focus. Except for his eyes. His eyes called to something deep in her. Beckoned. Enticed. She remembered the passion in his kiss, the power in his thighs, the thrust of his cock as it pressed against her cleft. A hungry whimper slipped past her lips.

"Should I take that as a yes?"

"I think you can take that as anything you want," Robin interjected from the doorway.

Dear God, she'd been gawking at the man like a schoolgirl!

"Do you men think you can handle finishing up supper?" Robin continued. "I need Lisa to help me with something."

"Yes," Donovan answered. Still she couldn't move. He tucked her hair behind her ear, his fingers lingering on the sensitive skin beneath. "Go with your sister, seelie. I'll take care of dinner."

Seelie? "What's a seelie?"

He turned her. "Care for your sister." With a dip of his head, he whispered into her ear before giving her a push, "She's not feeling well."

That snapped Lisa out of her haze. Her hand dropped to her side, pressing on the scar. Her gaze locked on her sister, a familiar panic riding her nerves. Robin was pale, her bruises standing out in a grotesque array against her white skin. Oh God! He was right! "Robin?"

Robin shook her head. "Not here."

Lisa passed Wyatt as he sat at the table. "She'll be fine, Lisa," he said. "She's just upset."

Lisa shook her head. He didn't know, couldn't know. Robin was living on borrowed time, and only a miracle would change that. Unfortunately, they seemed to have used up their store of miracles, and now there were just their wits and prayers to get them by.

It wasn't going to be enough.

Six

"YOU got a miracle tucked in your back pocket?" Donovan asked Wyatt as he glared at the rusted, grimy valves of the old furnace.

"Nope, but I've got a wrench."

"That's not going to cut it."

"The old girl's that far gone?"

"The old girl's dead. Someone just forgot to bury her." He slapped the side of the fifty-plus-year-old contraption.

"Shit, the Delaneys don't need to hear that."

Donovan leaned out from behind the behemoth of a furnace. "And they're not going to."

"They're going to notice when the room doesn't heat up."

"They don't need the worry."

"By *they*, you mean Lisa?"

"I mean they." He held his hand out for the wrench. "The family of my mate is my family."

Wyatt handed him the wrench. "Does that mean we get to go calling on Buddy tonight?"

Anticipation spiced Wyatt's tone. Wyatt was always up for a fight. "Aren't you worried about violating the human law you represent?"

"I'm here to learn, not convert."

"Which means?"

"I want Buddy's blood as much as you do."

No one could want it more than he did. The man had hurt the sister of his mate, threatened his mate. He ratcheted down a loose bolt. "Careful Lisa doesn't hear you saying that or you'll find yourself sporting fangs come Halloween."

"Might be worth it. She does seem to find vampires sexy."

He yanked too hard. The bolt stripped. Shit. "She'll change her mind."

"When you show her your canines?"

He imagined that, flashing his canines an instant before he sank them into her shoulder, imagined her cry as the bliss stole through her, as he plunged into her . . . His cock hardened. He swore again before saying, "Yes."

Wyatt shook his head. "It won't work, Donovan. You're a Protector. The pack will never allow you to mate with a human."

He slid out from behind the furnace. "It's not the pack's call."

"They'll make it their call. There are too few Protectors left. The pack needs you."

"The pack needs its leader."

"My father's the leader."

"Your father's dying."

The tension in Wyatt's shoulders was the only indication the news effected him. "Tough old weres like him don't die."

"They do when their mates pass."

Wyatt flinched. "Helen died?"

"You know how she liked to run in wolf form. She was shot by hunters. Apparently, she was too wounded to change back, and without her mate there to help, she was unable to heal."

"Damn." Wyatt ran his hand through his hair. "Did he bond himself to her after all?"

"No. You know how worried he is about the pack's future."

"But?"

"Without her, he's wasting away." And in a hurry to impress upon Wyatt the necessity of the old ways before he passed. A battle Donovan wasn't sure he should win, but it wasn't his place to say. He guarded the laws, not created them.

Wyatt studied Donovan from under the bridge of his hand. "You're here to return me to the pack."

"It's my job."

"It's also your job to mate with a female were and provide the pack with future protection."

Donovan felt the claw of guilt, the pull of duty. "I know my destiny."

"But you're considering throwing it away, turning your back on your pack?"

"A mate only comes to a wolf once." In recent years the longing for one had begun to interfere with everything he did, frustration growing in proportion to the conviction that a mate would not come for him. But one had. His grip on the wrench tightened.

"Then you understand why I'm not going back."

"It's not the same. If I leave, Kelon can carry on the line. You're Alpha. There is no one else."

"I won't lead the way it's always been."

"As Alpha, you can do what you want."

"The pack is too steeped in tradition to hear what I want. They'll follow the old ways right into discovery or extinction."

"Then you'll have to change their minds."

"The way you will, convincing them that taking a human mate won't weaken the line?"

Donovan forced his grip to relax. He tossed the wrench into the toolbox. "Yes."

"They'll challenge her until she's dead, and you know it."

Donovan's spine snapped taut. Adrenaline rushed through his system. "They will not harm her."

Wyatt stepped back, letting him out of the small space. "Because you say so?"

Donovan inclined his head. "That, and because they'll know that were she to die, I would follow."

"And what about those that believe mating physics don't hold with human mates? That a wolf cannot form a life bond with a human? What will you do when they attack? Kill the people you've spent your life protecting?"

"If they attack my mate, yes." He wouldn't have a choice. He would have to fight to defend her because she would be unable to help herself. Weres were born, not made, and while mating with him would change Lisa's physiology, allowing her to live his life span, it would not make her wolf. The belief that a werewolf's bite converted a human was human embellishment on the mating process.

"The ones attacking her will be your friends and loved ones," Wyatt retorted, driving his point home. "Do you really think you'll find it easy to kill them?"

An image rose in his mind, Lisa with her soft white skin ripped by wolf claws, her throat torn open by wolf canines. With her human frailty she'd be easy prey. Rage bled red into his vision. His muscles drew tight. A snarl rumbled up in his chest.

"I guess that answers my question."

Donovan blinked and looked down. He didn't remember the thought to change, but he was half-morphed. He met Wyatt's gaze, the agony of the realization shooting through him.

"I've seen you face certain death at the hands of a flock of vamps without losing control, but you're standing here half-morphed just thinking about harm coming to Lisa." Wyatt shook his head. "From your own people."

Donovan closed his eyes and absorbed the truth as he reversed the change. The answer was a guttural expulsion of pain. "Yes."

Wyatt didn't flinch, just tilted his head to the side and asked, "A man can't live torn between such choices, cousin, which begs the question. Are you prepared to walk away from Lisa?"

Give up his reason for being, the other half of his soul? How did a man make such a choice? How did he decide the right of one over the other?

"Maybe."

Wyatt sighed. "I think you're kidding yourself."

"About what?"

"About whether you should." Wyatt bent and closed the toolbox. "Our beliefs teach us a mate is a blessing chosen for a wolf by the Creator before his birth." The latch snapped closed with metallic finality. "It's always struck me as the height of arrogance that our culture decided that we get to pick and choose which blessings a male gets to accept."

He straightened and met Donovan's gaze, the ache of loneliness inside common to all unmated wolves reminding Donovan that Wyatt had lived a lot longer than him, and all that time alone. "For what it's worth, I think you should welcome the gift and see where it takes you."

"Even if it takes me out of the pack?" Being packless was worse than death. Abandoning duty was punishable by death.

"Even then." Wyatt shrugged. "You and your brother have served the pack well, risked your lives countless times, borne wounds that would have felled lesser wolves in defense of were law. There should be a reward for that."

Donovan grimaced. "By becoming one of the lost?"

Wyatt's gaze held steady, making him wonder if the other man had sensed the growing darkness within him.

"By finding your soul."

It was a poetic way of putting the rightness Donovan felt at breathing Lisa's scent. "I'll think on it."

"While you're 'thinking' on it, remember, as Alpha I'll be doing my best to change views on mixed matings within the pack."

He didn't sound optimistic—just sad. It didn't take much thought to figure out why. Not only was that going to be a virtually impossible task, but for it to even have a chance, his father had to die, because Big Al was not a proponent of diluting were blood.

"I'm sorry about your father."

"I never thought the old coot would die."

"Helen was his weakness." As Lisa would be his.

Wyatt shook his head. "No, she was his joy." The toolbox rattled as he shifted his grip. "His mating to my mother was not a true mating, but sealed through pregnancy. I remember, as the years passed, seeing the same haunted look in his eyes that I see growing in yours. Our kind are not made to live alone."

"Pack can be a substitute." It was a knee-jerk response, a teaching instilled in him from his earliest memories.

"Can it?" Wyatt asked, the too-old look in his eyes moving to his expression.

Donovan couldn't be less than honest. He had thought so before he met Lisa but now . . . ? "I don't know."

Wyatt motioned to the door of the small utility room.

"After seeing the shell of the man I thought was my father grow into the man I admire, seemingly overnight, with the advent of Helen into his life, I'm not sure any man should walk away from his destiny."

Donovan was a Protector, sworn to give his life for any member of the pack. A wolf sworn to put pack first over any personal need. Sworn to place pack before a mate. "I have my duty."

"One from which I'm giving you permission to walk away."

Guilt, desire, hope—they all clawed for dominance, each one a betrayal of the purpose to which he'd pledged his life. He inclined his head. "The consideration is appreciated."

Wyatt shook his head. "You are one stubborn bastard, I'll give you that." Donovan stepped back, protocol demanding the Alpha go first. Wyatt paused as he came abreast. "You should take my offer and run."

"You're not my Alpha."

"I will be."

"And when you are, we'll discuss it."

"Do you think Lisa will wait that long?"

Donovan didn't need to answer. Wyatt read the answer in his eyes. "Dad's that bad?"

He didn't blink. "Yes."

For all that Wyatt's expression remained calm, there was a wealth of anguish in his scent. He passed through the door, waiting on the other side.

"So what can we do about that furnace?" Wyatt asked, motioning to the nonfunctioning behemoth.

"We're going to order a new one and pretend we fixed this one."

"Do you think the Delaneys will fall for that?"

"We only need to keep them distracted away from the house until such time as the new furnace is installed. After that, it'll be too late."

"True. But they're an independent sort. Not like our women."

Donovan knew that already. Lisa's defiance, unheard of in a were female, aroused his dominant instincts. His cock twitched at the challenge, and his wolf prowled with the thought of accepting that dare, of proving to her that he was the stronger, the one whose orders she would follow, in and out of bed. The strength of the urge, the violence of the need shook him. He was dangerously close to the edge of his control and that couldn't be. The violent matings that wolves were prone to could leave a human badly injured. He would need to teach Lisa submission before they mated for her own safety. "Then I guess we'll just have to coax them around to the idea."

"Those women could be hard to convince."

But at least one of them could also be very soft and melt against him like butter with the right incentive. "Then I guess we'll have to rely on my stubbornness to carry the day."

"Well, if you're going to apply your stubborn side . . ." Wyatt's smile faded. He grew serious. "Human or not, Donovan, I'm glad you found your mate. And I'm doubly glad she looks to be a match for that obstinate side you harbor."

Donovan smiled. "You just remember how much you like my stubbornness when I'm hauling your ass back to the pack."

The other man just laughed. "I'll keep it in mind if I decide to ascend to Alpha."

Donovan took the toolbox from Wyatt. "Ascending to Alpha isn't a choice."

"Neither is claiming your mate."

He nodded, acknowledging the point, heading up the basement stairs, the anticipation racing through his blood at the thought of seeing Lisa again. It easily compared to the thrill of battle. "So I'm beginning to believe."

CLAIMING a mate wasn't a choice.

The knowledge came back to haunt Donovan later that night. Fresh snow puffed over the landscape, blanketing everything in a gleam of white. More snow was falling. It was colder than a well digger's ass, yet he could see Lisa standing on the porch, wrapped in a comforter, staring out into the night, frowning as if all the answers in the world were just past the darkness that cloaked her human vision.

Gliding soundlessly through falling flakes of snow, he stopped at the tree where he'd left his clothes. The wind blew in his face, ruffling his fur, bringing with it her scent. He inhaled deeply, holding it as his anchor while he shifted back into human form and grabbed his clothes from where he'd left them draped over a tree branch. The run had settled his nerves, relaxed him into his purpose. Coming home to her scent merely cemented the rightness of his decision. Pack or not, he wasn't walking away from Lisa.

As soon as he was dressed he headed toward her, the feeling of coming home getting stronger with each step. A hint of moisture at the corner of her eye shimmered under the porch light. She was crying. He took the knowledge like a punch in the gut. She shouldn't be crying. Nothing that could bring sadness should ever touch her.

She should be sheltered, pampered, protected from everything in the world that might take a smile from her face. He was her mate, destined to be her strength, her voice, her haven.

Another tear formed. Nothing moved in her expression while that drop of moisture slowly slid down her cheek. He deliberately stepped hard on the top step, knowing the board would creak as well as he knew she wouldn't appreciate him seeing her cry. She would see it as a weakness rather than a gift of trust given by a female to her mate.

The board creaked. Her head snapped around, lips parted in a startled gasp. His cock, hungry from the previous waft of her scent, twitched and stretched in a pointless longing to feel the softness of those lips against its hardness.

Through the next two steps he imagined she was wolf, envisioned her greeting him in the proper way a female wolf did when confronted with a male as aggressively turned on as he was—dropping her gaze, hands at her side, offering no resistance. He carried the image a step further, imagined himself closing the distance between them, pulling that soft mouth to his chest and holding her against him as he bathed in her scent and her touch, letting her draw the dangerous edge off his arousal with the brush of her lips.

"What are you doing out here?"

The illusion vanished under the snap of her question. The aggressive need to claim and mark did not subside, however.

"Enjoying the night." He came up beside her. "A better question might be what are you doing out here just wrapped in that." He motioned to the quilt.

The only indication of her shrug beneath the bulk of material was the slight rustle of cotton. "I'm warm enough."

A glance down revealed the tips of big, pink fuzzy slippers peeking from beneath the pastel quilt.

He didn't know any woman who would be caught dead in them. Lisa wore them without apology. "I like your slippers."

To his surprise, her face crumpled into a heartbreaking precursor to a sob. The "Thank you" she forced past her compressed lips was hoarse. "They were a gift from Robin."

"Compliments aren't supposed to make you sad, seelie."

A tear leaked down her cheek, followed quickly by a second. Her body jerked as she took a breath. The anguish in her scent pulled him to her. He wrapped his arms around her shoulders, tucking her into his chest. Even in the bulky quilt she felt small to him, dwarfed by both the material and him. "I don't know what that word means."

He brushed a kiss on the top of her head. "It means you're not alone."

She didn't look at him, just stared straight ahead. "Can I ask you something personal?"

"Yes."

The immediacy of his answer seemed to give her pause. She tightened her grip on the quilt before asking, "Just how much trouble *are* you?"

Was she worried about Buddy and his friends? He turned her around and tipped her face up with a hand under her chin. The way she followed his direction eased some of the aggressive hunger in him. "Trouble enough that I can see to whatever you need done."

She blinked. "No questions asked?"

"No questions asked."

"Why?"

The natural bow of her mouth shaped the syllable in a sexy pout. He touched his thumb to the center of her bottom lip as the question trailed off. "Because you asked me to."

She leaned back, depriving him of the sensation of her lips moving against the sensitive pad. "Wow, you must have a rap sheet a mile long."

She didn't seem entirely put off by the idea.

"You think everyone asks me to do something illegal?"

"Technically, I haven't asked you to do anything."

"True. And I haven't named my price."

Instead of pulling away, she leaned against him. Something was very wrong. Lisa was not a dependent woman.

"Are you bad enough to make me forget everything for an hour?"

"What's the problem?"

She shook her head. "Just answer the question."

She was his mate. Legend said he could burn sanity from her mind. "Yes."

She let go of the quilt. It slid downward. Instead of making a grab for it, her arms glided up his chest with the same smooth rush, seemingly oblivious to the cold that had to be biting through the silky sheer nightgown that skimmed over her back and hugged the full curves of her buttocks. "Prove it."

There wasn't enough honor in his soul to keep his hands away from that lush flesh. He cupped her rear in his hands, pulling her up against him. "You want me to make love to you."

He didn't make it a question. She didn't pretend that he should have.

"Nothing so permanent." The tips of her fingers slid under the collar of his shirt, instinctively seeking his flesh as her gaze met his. "But I want you to make me forget."

"What?"

She shook her head. "That doesn't matter."

It mattered a hell of a lot, but he wasn't a stupid man. His mate was standing in his arms, giving him license to claim her. He'd deal with the other later.

He lowered his head, breathing in more of her intoxicating scent, honor bound to inform her of her choice before proceeding. "If you do this you'll be making love with a wolf."

"God, I hope so. A lack of experience would not be endearing right now."

His laugh choked to a groan as her thigh rode up his. He helped her, curling his fingers into the softness of her buttocks, lifting her as he breathed against her parted lips. "There'll be no going back."

She closed the distance between them, her full lips cuddling into the firmness of his the same way her belly cuddled his cock. "I'm only interested in going forward."

"Good, so am I. Wrap your legs around my waist."

Seven

DONOVAN tasted as good as she remembered—spicy hot and male—felt as good against her as she remembered, the hard slabs of muscle welcoming her with hollows in all the right places. And his smell . . . she all but whimpered when he crushed her against the unyielding planes of his chest. He smelled like the promise of every earthly delight she'd ever imagined. Raw and masculine, the perfect indulgence. She'd love to bathe in his scent, breathe it every minute of the day. She settled for inhaling it now, gasping as it fed the ravenous hunger rising within her. The flesh between her legs moistened and unfurled in welcome.

"Make me forget," she moaned as she locked her ankles tightly. He was the only one who could make her forget the looming loss.

His lips nipped at the edges of hers, sending tiny sparks shooting inward where they gathered in an ever-growing pile of embers just waiting for the right moment to burst into flame.

"Forget what?" he asked as he ignored the invitation of her parted lips to trace the curve of her lower lip with his tongue, the rougher texture of the caress bringing a few of the embers flickering to life. He moved to the sensitive corner of her mouth, lingering and probing. A bolt of lust hit her so hard she whimpered and leaned away in self-defense.

"No." The world spun as he whipped them around. His forearm pressed into her back as he pinned her against the house. She shuddered as the icy chill blended with the burning heat. His tongue touched that spot again. The effect was no less electric. She jerked and twisted her face away. He rumbled a growl and then captured her chin between his fingers. His eyes burned like black fire into hers. His chest expanded with another hard breath as he ground out, "No, you accept what I give you."

Oh God, that was hot. Totally and completely hot. She'd never had a man give her an order in bed before. "I like that."

"What?"

"You're letting your bossy side out."

For a second he stared, as if not quite believing what he'd heard, then his eyes crinkled at the corners and he caught her lower lip between his teeth, nipping gently before saying, "That's good, because I'll probably get a lot bossier before the night's over."

"You will?"

The smile in his eyes spread to his mouth as he studied her expression. There was no doubt he liked what he saw. Which was in itself unique. She'd never seen herself as particularly sexy.

"Definitely."

She turned her head, teasing herself with the tickle of his five o'clock shadow against her cheek. Her lips burned where the moisture of his caress lingered. She stole a taste. Scent blended with flavor, creating a demand for more. "I love the way you smell."

It was his turn to hesitate, then she felt his smile push against her lips. "You smell pretty damn good yourself." The dip of his head brought his mouth to the hollow of her throat. "Hot, spicy, needy woman."

Needy. She wasn't needy all the time. It was important he understood that. His mouth opened, his teeth tested the cord of her neck, stealing her voice, drawing her arousal to a fine point of breathless anticipation.

"Just for tonight," she managed to groan.

"For more than tonight."

She shook her head.

Donovan kissed his way up her neck—moist, nipping kisses that sent shivers down her spine and shards of delight edging between anticipation and desire. He reached the too-sensitive corner of her mouth, tickling the wild hunger to flare.

"No going back, remember?" he growled before his mouth fitted to hers, sealing her gasp between them, trapping them both in a burst of carnal desire that left no room for argument. Each breath was a raw intake of need. Each movement a drive for completion. His lips parted from hers. His grip flexed, pulled, separating the globes of her rear, opening her more. "Come here."

Lisa wrapped her arms around his neck and tightened her ankles behind his back, rubbing her mouth against his. "I am here."

"No, you're there." He supported her with one hand under her hip, before he stepped back in, pinning her between the heat of his body and the hardness of the wall. There was no give in either. Especially not in his cock, which he notched firmly in the vee of her thighs. "I want you here."

"Oh God." Here was good. Very good. Very hot. Perfect.

She pressed back against him so hard it hurt. The tiny bite of erotic pain only made her want more, need more. He shifted his grip again, holding her on that precipice while the storm raged around them in silent devastation. Trees snapped as the wind blew, and inside Lisa, the last bit of resistance snapped, too.

Donovan thrust up. Lisa's head dropped back under the whip of sensation as he drew her hips down in quick counterpoint, dragging her soft folds along his thick length. The thin nylon of her panties was no protection from the divine rasp of female over denim-covered male. Her forehead hit his shoulder as the throb of passion splintered through her. "How do you do this to me?"

"The same way you do it to me."

She liked that, liked knowing she wasn't the only one burning here. She opened her eyes. He turned his head at the same time she did. Her mouth found his, parted, invited.

He was slow to pick up the cue, continuing with the teasing she couldn't stand, tormenting her with the promise of the passion to come while his hips pulsed his length along her wet crease. Her panties bunched to the side, and then there was only his jeans keeping her from his hard cock. She reached between them and found the first button. It was a struggle, but she got it undone. She fumbled for his zipper and almost sobbed when she found another button. "Why do you wear button fly jeans?"

It took forever to get the darn things undone. The fly finally gave with a jerk. The thin line of hair on his stomach pricked the back of her hand. The ridges of muscles quivered and jerked.

"I wish I could see."

He made that rumbling noise in his chest again. The reverberations wended their way deep into her core. His stomach sucked in, giving her more room to work. She wedged her hand deeper.

Her nipples peaked. She twisted against him. Oh, that was good. She did it again. Harder. He rumbled again. Louder.

"That is so sexy."

The sound came again, deeper, harsher, the inherent command rippling along her arousal, tugging it past her reserve as his fingers clenched in her hair, tilting her head to the angle he wanted, which was perfect for his kiss. His head lowered. His eyes seemed to glow.

"I just knew you were going to be like this," she whispered. By working her fingers down she was able to cradle his cock against her fingertips.

"Like what?"

His mouth was just a scant dip of his head from hers. Her lips tingled. "Wild."

She was counting on that wild side of him coming out. Especially tonight when she wanted to be driven out of her mind, out of her worries, by the sheer physical chemistry that pulsed between them.

"I'll keep it in mind."

She tilted her head back, shaking her hair out of her face, knowing the exact moment his gaze dropped to the front of her nightgown, knowing he could see the tight beads of her nipples against the semisheer fabric—maybe even make out the outlines of the areolae. "You're going to have to do better than that. You're going to have to drive every other man out of my mind."

He went stiff against her. That rumbling sound came harder, shorter. He didn't like hearing about other men. "Any particular man you want gone?"

"Dr. Steven Holcomb."

"Why?"

"He's always disappointing me."

That low rumble kicked up to a sound that couldn't be called anything less than a snarl. "You won't be disappointed in my bed."

"Prove it."

"It's a mistake to challenge a wolf."

"Why?"

She arched her spine, contorting a bit in the small space to offer him her breasts. He took a step back; she arched further. His hand in the small of her back arched her still more, until her spine was strung as taut as the tension within her.

"It brings out our dominant side." His lips closed over the tip of her breast, hot and firm, possessing it completely with the barest of grips.

"Oh." She struggled for balance before just giving up and letting him support her. It felt so good to let someone else handle the basic stuff. "I've always wanted to be dominated."

He went very still, then his lips drew back and the sharp edge of his teeth bit ever so slightly into the base of her nipple, sending hot little spikes of pleasure shooting inward.

His expression took on a feral cast and there was something strange about his eyes. "You just have to bait the beast, eh?"

She should have been terrified. She wasn't. What she was was incredibly turned on, to the point that, if he just gave her a little more pressure on her clit and paid a little more attention to her breasts, she'd come.

"If you're talking about this"—she rubbed her fingertips along the part of his cock she could reach—"absolutely."

"Hell!" A twist of his wrist and her head was in the position he wanted. That she wanted. His mouth came down hard on hers. Her lips parted under the pressure of his, accepted the thrust of his tongue, the dominance of his personality. That addictive essence of his kiss spread through her, sank to her bones. So good. So familiar . . .

Oh heck, she'd just known he was going to be the kind of man that didn't leave a woman her defenses, but built the fire so hot that she didn't have an option but to burn with him. She'd never had a lover like him. Lisa shuddered, wrapping her fingers around his cock, pulling with her thighs, bringing him to her. She'd been completely deprived and never known it.

"More."

He lifted her up. "All you can take, seelie."

His weight settled against her. Mouth to mouth, chest to breast, cock to pussy, hope to dream.

"Oh God," she gasped as her back came against the cold wall again. "When?" Her shiver took the heat from the question.

Donovan's hands clenched on her rear, each finger as hot as a brand.

"You're cold."

"It doesn't matter."

His hand came between her back and the wall. He bent with easy strength, taking them both down far enough that he could grab the quilt. "We can make love where it's warm."

"We can make noise out here." If she waited until she got inside the house, she'd lose the momentum, be forced to remember all she was trying to forget. Something he obviously didn't get.

"You can scream for me inside."

He let her feet slide down his sides . She felt adrift without his support. She tried again. "I'll scream louder out here."

He cupped her cheek in his hand, the brush of his thumb against her lips was as gentle as his knowing smile. "Want to bet?"

THE old house creaked under the force of the storm. The sheets rustled as Lisa lifted her hips. The filmy gown slid down her smooth thighs, pooling at her groin, tempting him with a hint of the softer flesh below. Bold as brass, sweetly shy, soft and hot, his little mate was a picture of contrasts, lying in the dark on the big four-poster bed. She'd changed positions three times before settling on her current one. Donovan definitely approved of her choice. Propped on her side, gravity provided him with a mouth-watering view of her plump breasts as they tempted the edges of the silky triangles of material that struggled to contain them. If it weren't for the ruffled trim on the ultrafeminine garment, he'd know the color of her nipples. He licked his lips. All it would take was a nudge from his chin and the satiny peak would be revealed for his attention.

He paused, his boot halfway off, lust surging through his body in an ever-growing wave as her fingers played with the pale peach hem, lifting it a bit more, unwittingly taunting his wolf to the fore. And along with his wolf came the aggressive hunger. Releasing his boot, he eyed the spot on her inner thigh where lean muscle gave way to womanly softness. His canines ached. He ran his tongue over them, not taking his gaze from the creamy spot. When this was over, when they were both sated, he'd mark her there.

The boot hit the floor with a dull thud. Lisa jumped, fingers clenching, eyes big. While she clearly couldn't see him, there was enough ambient light that he could appreciate every rich curve.

Every sultry invite, like the small shimmy that quivered through her breasts at her start.

If he was closer, he could have absorbed that start against his chest, stilled the vibration with his lips, soothed her nervousness with his kiss. He needed to be closer. He tugged off his other boot.

"Nervous?" he asked.

"Impatient might be a better description."

She couldn't be as impatient as he was. "Turn on the bedside light."

"I like the dark better."

"Hmm." He bet she did, but she couldn't hide from him, from this. The bed dipped as he braced his hand on the edge. Awareness flared in her eyes as he got close enough for her human senses to detect. He reached up and turned on the light. "But I want to see you."

Her inhale was a near soundless gasp as light flared. Alarm darkened her irises to indigo before her gaze dropped and locked on his chest. The flash of pink as her tongue slid over her lips drew a growl of appreciation from his throat. Her gaze didn't leave his chest.

He flexed his left pectoral. She blinked. Something foreign and soft moved in his chest. She blinked again as he flexed the right. Like hell she wasn't nervous. He flexed both pectorals together. That got two blinks and the hint of a smile.

Placing his knee on the bed, he eased over her, using his greater size to leverage her back. "You have the prettiest smile."

Her palm flattened on his chest as the pillows cradled her in a puff of down. "And you have a great chest."

He stopped when he covered her, nudging her thighs apart with his knees before coming down over her, thigh to thigh, hard to soft, chest to breast. He worked his hand between the pillow and her skull. The fine strands of her hair slid across his skin like cool silk.

"You could always introduce your pretty smile to my chest."

Her brows arched up and that smile widened. "Would you be hinting that you'd like my mouth on you?"

Oh yeah. He closed his eyes, concentrating on where her flesh touched his—the points of her nipples, the pads of her fingers, the plumpness of her mound. "It would only be fair as I intend to have mine all over you."

The bite of her nails into the hard muscle of his chest spoke of her appreciation.

Lust charged through him as, outside, the barometer dropped. His skin registered the change, his ears the increased power of the wind as it buffeted the house, and inside, he felt the desperation feeding Lisa's desire. Donovan touched her temple where purple veins created a fine tracery beneath the surface, another reminder that she was human. Fragile. He frowned and tamped down the aggressive hunger.

"What?"

He slid his fingers deeper into the silk of her hair. "I'm just reminded that I'm going to have to be careful with you."

It was her turn to frown. "What if I don't want you to be careful?"

The brush of his lips over hers, a quiver in her breath, and he had his control back. This was their first time together. It would set the tone for the rest of their relationship, and as wolves mated for life, the care he showed her now would resonate with them for the rest of their lives.

"I'll be careful anyway."

"You really have no idea of who I am," she groaned.

He couldn't resist the smooth cream of her skin. His lips found her temple, lingered on the pulse there before skimming the bridge of her nose, the arch of her cheek. Perfect. She was so perfectly soft, so perfectly rounded. Perfectly created to rouse his wolf. But she wasn't wolf. She would never survive the rake of his claws, the wildness of his bite.

"For sure you're a sweet, tempting mystery." A nudge with his chin under her jaw exposed her neck. Her scent, a combination of soap and woman, was stronger here. Infinitely rich, powerfully seductive. His cock jerked in his pants. The bite of pain centered the lust flowing through him. He was born for her, and she for him. Tonight would seal that bond. After their joining her cares would be his to soothe. Her worries his to quiet. Her enemies his to eliminate. Her pleasure his to grant. His claws extended, digging into the covers.

"Mine." He growled the word against the side of her neck.

She arched into the pressure of his kiss. "For tonight."

A scrape of his teeth along the taut cord of her neck corrected the statement. Her fragile nails dug into his skin. The shudder that rippled through him echoed the one that had her twisting on the blankets. Feminine arousal, sweet and addictive, flowed into the space between them, wrapping him in a blanket of certainty. "Incredible."

"What?"

"You." He touched his tongue to her skin, his eyes closing as her taste flowed under her scent, different yet the same. "You really do bring out my wild side."

Her thighs clung for a heartbeat before falling open as her nails scraped down his torso, too light to stimulate him to mating fever, but enough to send need tearing at his control and lust diving for the invitation.

"Good."

"No. Not good." He couldn't scare her, hurt her. "Not this time."

Maybe not ever.

He took a breath, and she took advantage. Shifting into the cradle of his thighs, nestling the thick wedge of his cock into the moist vee between her legs, she worked her hand between them, its destination clear. His balls drew up tight, anticipation snapping to a fine inner hum. He was losing control. Grabbing her hand, he pressed it into her stomach.

"Spoilsport."

"Yup."

Goose bumps sprang up along her flesh. He followed them like bread crumbs down the trail of her torso. Her head canted to the side, facilitating his exploration. The overt sign of submission blunted the razor edge of need slicing at his purpose. His gaze fell to the spot where he'd marked her earlier. The spot was as untouched as the day she was born. No remnant of his claim lingered. He tightened his grip in her hair just as her hand slipped down the open fly of his pants and closed around him. Hotter than fire, the open caress seared deep. His woman, taking him in her hand. Damn, he wasn't going to last long if he reacted so strongly to everything she did.

He tugged her face into his chest, breathed the order across her ear, focusing on the point where his mark should be. "Come here, seelie."

"Are we going to go through that again?"

Lust flavored with laughter. Another difference between human and were mating. One he actually liked. He nipped her earlobe, holding her close, as the subsequent whip of sensation shot through her, gentling her in the wake of his wildness. "Yes."

"Why?"

He shook his head, unable to convey to her what a wolf female would have understood instinctively about the give-and-take of first matings. She watched him, lips faintly parted, the gown twisted across her torso, the material only a few shades darker than her exotically pale skin. Her breasts quivered with her rapid breathing. "Because I want it."

"And we're always going to do what you want?"

The plump little lobe of her ear beckoned. He took it between his canines, biting down gently, soothing as she gasped and flinched, laving the mark with his tongue, steadying her as the aphrodisiac spread through her system, gritting his teeth as her small fingers gripped, tightened, milked.

She turned her head, meshed her mouth with his, parted her

lips, and ran her sweet little tongue along the seam of his mouth, tempting him again. "Donovan . . ."

The whisper of his name flowed over his control, settling on it, destroying it. "Do you want me, Lisa?"

"Yes."

"Do you accept me?"

"God, yes."

He could feel his wolf struggling for dominance at her answer. Feel it fight for supremacy as it always did in moments of high adrenaline. Want coarsened his voice. He flicked the sensitized lobe with his tongue. "Then offer yourself to me."

He expected her to be shocked, to pull back. If she had done that he could have controlled the wildness inside. But she didn't. Instead, she smiled at him. A totally witchy smile that reached deep and tapped that part of him he was trying to keep hidden. Her fingers closed around his cock again, caressing him with little pulses of pleasure. Her other hand dropped to her shoulder and slowly, ever so slowly, pulled the strap down her arm, revealing milky white flesh that swelled and lifted.

She held his gaze, a woman challenging her man, daring him. "What would you like me to offer?"

The material hovered on the tip of her nipple. All it would take was a puff of air, a pulse of his breath and it would slip free. Her fingers started a slow trek across her chest, the back of her nails cruising the rise and fall of the full curves, almost careless in the caress they bestowed as they brushed across the lush flesh he hungered to taste, drifting toward the other strap.

He let her play, enjoying the show. His cock swelled, challenging the restriction of her grasp. The slightest of hesitations when she reached the strap indicated her surprise. Weres were very similar to humans, but there were some differences, size being one of them. In a blink, she had the falter in her smile covered with more of that bravado that fooled so many. He shook his head. "You don't have to hide from me, Lisa."

"Who's hiding?"

He tucked his thumb into the corner of her mouth. "You're worried."

"Just adjusting my expectations."

Downward, if that little frown had been anything to go by. "I'm going to be very careful of your pleasure, seelie."

"Why do you keep calling me that?"

He pressed. Her lips parted and he could see the white of her teeth, the pink of her tongue beyond. "It's a very old endearment."

"That's not telling me anything."

Lowering his head, he captured the last syllable with his lips, absorbing her gasp and another of her shudders as his tongue slipped along the inner lining of her lip.

"Oh!"

"What?"

Her tongue met his. Her palm pressed flat to his shoulder pressing hard, before her fingers curved in, the nails nicking him in tiny crescents of demand. "You taste so good."

The aphrodisiac. A necessity amongst his kind. It prepared the women for the violence of wolf mating. On some level he'd always resented it, but now, gliding his hand down her rib cage, feeling how small Lisa's bones were compared to his, how delicate the muscles covering them, how finely she was made compared to a were female, he was glad. He wanted her screaming, but not one note did he want to be caused by pain. It took conscious effort to retract his claws before he slipped his hand over her stomach and covered her mound. His fingers nestled between the plump folds, welcomed in by sweet moisture. The engorged nub of her clit strained against the inside of his knuckle. He curled his fingers, drawing the tips up the moist crease, holding her gaze as he did, watching it darken as he neared that sensitive peak, watching her pupils flare as he crested the tip, paused, stroked, flicked.

He continued holding her gaze as he drew his fingers through her juices and then brought those same fingers slowly, deliberately to his lips. Shock and embarrassment, along with a hot flick of arousal, chased across her expression as he placed his fingers in his mouth. Her essence flowed across his taste buds in a shocking claiming as powerful as any aphrodisiac.

"You taste pretty damn good to me, too."

"I can't believe you did that."

"I told you I was going to have my mouth all over you."

Her hand slipped between them. "But not there!"

A smile forced its way through the hard surge of lust. "How can a woman so bold be so innocent?"

"I am *not* innocent."

"If you don't know that's the place I most want to taste, then you're as innocent as a newborn baby."

Her eyebrows rose. Two tugs and she had her hand free of his pants and latched on to the back of his head. He let her. There was nothing she could do that could deter him.

The upper slope of her breast drew his mouth. He pressed an openmouthed kiss on the high slope before following it downward. The silky material of her bodice snagged on his beard-roughened chin, retreating in the wake of his advance. A sharp gasp marked the rasp of his chin over the point of her nipple. He was quick enough to catch the expression of pure pleasure that raced across her features.

"Think how good it's going to feel when I do that to your clit."

A small mewling sound was her only response. Greedy man that he was, he wanted to hear it again. He rubbed gently. She jerked violently, but she didn't make that intriguing little moan. A glance up revealed that she purposely withheld it. Her blue eyes glittered at him from beneath her lashes—defiant, challenging. He again dipped his fingers between her thighs and growled a warning. That got a reaction. Cream poured over his fingers as her pussy clenched in a hungry kiss. She liked it when he growled.

"Hold still."

She thrashed beneath him, her hips bucking up into his hand. "I don't want to."

Exasperation cozied up to desire. "Try."

Another buck of her hips and it became clear she needed incentive. With a little searching he relocated her clitoris. It was hard and distended, and he soothed its hunger with a light touch. She froze. He did it again. Using her gasps as a barometer, he modified his touch until he found the gentle circular motion that broke her breath into choppy gasps.

Gentle—damn she would have to rise just like that to a gentle touch. Gentle, when everything in him said to take, to claim, to mark.

He dropped his forehead to her stomach, rubbing it against the nightgown. "You're killing me, seelie."

Her fingers twisted in his hair. She tugged. He ignored the order. "I'm not the one dawdling."

No, but only because she didn't understand what was at risk. "My apologies."

"Never mind apologies. Just hurry."

He kissed the hollow of her stomach, smiling as the soft flesh rose and fell with her labored breathing. He increased the pressure of his stroke as he worked the hem of her gown up with his chin.

Pinning her thighs with his shoulders, he caught her wrist and pulled her hand away. He placed it on the spot on her stomach that he'd just kissed. Her fingers cupped, as if holding on to the memory.

"Keep it there."

"You're really not going to—"

"I am, and you're going to enjoy it."

Too late, she tried to snap her legs closed. "Says who?"

"Says me and every happy little nerve ending in your body."

"I haven't even had a shower tonight!"

It would take too much concentration to figure out why that

mattered. Not when he could smell the rich cream of her arousal. After his years of waiting, speculating, hoping, there was only so much a woman could ask of a mate. And waiting a second more was too much. With a slice of his claw, her panties fell aside and then there was nothing between them. Not material. Not time. Not distance. Nothing.

At the first touch of his tongue she gasped. At the second, she cried out. At the third, she pulled the pillow over her face and let her thighs go lax. Which suited him just fine. No man, wolf or human, wanted any distraction when faced with a feast like the one before him.

She was as pretty here as everywhere else. Swollen with need, damp with desire, the inner lips unfurling with an eagerness that throbbed in his own blood. Another deep breath, another flood of the absolute rightness of this woman, this moment. He settled in to enjoy, laving her softness, drinking of her beauty until the pillow could no longer muffle her screams. Tension hummed through her muscles, spiced her scent. She was close, very close. The only thing that held him back was the old wives' tale that said good fortune flowed through the union that started right. And right meant Lisa came on his cock this first time.

Donovan tucked a finger into the well of her vagina. Her muscles convulsed. He drew back, cushioning her clit on his tongue, not giving her any additional stimulation while he tested her channel. He gritted his teeth as her muscles clamped down on the press of his finger. Small. She was small and tight. He eased his finger deeper. Her back bowed off the bed. Silken muscles rippled in strong pulses, drawing him in.

"Donovan!"

Even through the pillow he heard her need, felt it. Echoed it. His balls ached and pulled up. He wasn't going to last much longer, either.

With a last regretful kiss, he left her pussy, slipping his finger free, but he couldn't leave her skin. Not totally. His need was too great, her allure too potent. It took about fifty kisses to reach the tip of her breast. Another ten to reach her mouth. Her hands pulled him higher, into her kiss. Tears on her cheeks moistened his skin. Strands of her hair caught on his jaw.

"Donovan."

"Right here."

"You promised to make me forget."

"I know." With his free hand he shoved his jeans down, freeing his cock. "Just give me a minute and I'll give you everything I promised."

"I don't want everything. Just you. Now."

He braced himself on the bed. The mattress sank. She leaned into the dip, took his thumb in her mouth, held his gaze, and sucked. It was his turn to draw a hoarse breath as warning tingles raced up his spine. "Damn, don't get me thinking along those lines or bad luck will follow us for sure."

"Bad luck?"

He shook his head, more to dispel the images than to answer her question. "Never mind. Just superstition."

Focus. He needed focus. With quick efficiency he lined up his cock, tucking the fat head into the slick opening. Her eyes flew wide as she felt the extent of his arousal. His eyes closed as he felt the searing heat awaiting him. He opened them when Lisa released his thumb.

She'd passed nervous, left desire, and was now fully centered on alarm. "No, seelie, don't be afraid."

Her smile was forced. "I think I got a little more than I bargained for."

In more ways than she understood, she had, but it was his duty to soothe such fears, ease her into his life, care for her in all ways. The anticipation went deeper than sexual. He pressed against her, maintaining the connection when she would have moved away. "I know what I'm doing."

She glanced between them to where they joined. Her return

glance was frankly skeptical. "I'm sure you do, but I don't know if the condoms I bought are going to fit."

Ah hell. He'd forgotten about that aspect of human mating rituals. Weres didn't carry disease and pregnancy—a rare occurrence amongst wolves—was longed for. "Condoms?"

He dodged her hand as she reached up and back. When he realized she was reaching for the nightstand drawer, he opened it for her, his breath hissing through his teeth as her muscles parted the barest bit, teasing him with the heat beyond. In the drawer was a small box.

Jealousy clawed at him as he recognized it. With difficulty, he kept his voice even. "You keep condoms by your bed?"

"I believe in being prepared." She met his gaze. "Do you have a problem with that?"

"Not at all."

He ripped the box open, exerting the violence inside on the paper container. The sheaf of condoms whipped against the side of the drawer.

Lisa turned at the small racket, the tight bud of her nipple skimming along his chest. "What happened?"

He'd lost his temper. Something he hadn't done since he was a kid. He grabbed the sheaf.

"My hand slipped."

"Oh."

She settled back on the bed, her fingers dipping down his abdomen, tangling in the line of hair beneath his navel, continuing to advance in a series of evocative tugs down to the base of his cock. Anticipation gathered in his blood. Even though he knew it was coming, nothing could have prepared him for the heat of her fingers, the tightness of her fist. A lightning bolt would have been less devastating.

He closed his eyes and ground his teeth, instinct guiding the thrust of his hips. Lisa didn't flinch, just followed his lead, falling into his rhythm, milking him to the pace he set.

He tossed the packets on the bed and grabbed her wrist. She looked down. Her grip tightened and her smile grew. "Feeling ambitious tonight?"

"Are those all you have?"

"Yes."

His teeth closed over her earlobe, stopping just short of biting, holding her on the edge. The bed dipped as he shifted to his side. There was the tear of a condom wrapper. "Then no, I don't think I'll be setting any records."

Her smile didn't falter, but her eyebrows rose.

"You realize you just set the bar pretty high for yourself, right?"

"Uh-huh." He opened the packet and looked at the contents. The condom was going to be too damn small. Shit!

"What's wrong?"

He bit down. She shivered and gasped, and the warm rain of her pleasure bathed his cock, eroding his determination to do this her way. To make her comfortable. "I don't think these are going to fit."

Her hand slammed into his shoulder, knocking him back. He rolled onto the pillows. She came over him, her expression as fierce as any wolf's. She yanked the condom out of his hand.

"They'll fit."

They did, barely, encasing the tip in a choke hold that supported his flagging control. Something he wasn't sure Lisa appreciated. She seemed determined to drive him wild. Or maybe it was herself she wanted wild. Either way, he was up to the job. When he had her back under him, his cock stretching her that first tiny bit, her breast in his hand, her nipple under his thumb, he kissed her again. Hard and deep, tempering her aggression with his own, taking control away from her, kissing her until she softened and went compliant, until she moaned his name in acceptance. With surprise, he notice the surgical scar on the right side of her abdomen, making a note to ask her about it later.

"That's it." He brushed the hair off her face. "Just let me handle this."

"Why do you get to set the pace?"

"Because." He pushed in, feeling the small, silken muscles strain and resist before relaxing and taking him that first inch. Even through the condom, her heat burned. Tempted. "I'm the one with his reputation on the line."

"Oh."

Her frown deepened as he worked in small pulses. Her nails bit into his shoulders, pulling him down. Contrarily, her thumbs pushed him back as the uncertainty he could feel in her body rose at his possession. His wolf snarled a protest, reacting instinctively to her resistance with the urge to dominate. Her palms opened on his shoulders, pressing as her body absorbed the intrusion of his. Another "Oh" burst past her lips. Breathy, feminine, higher in pitch, richer in inflection, blending with the sweet perfume of her desire. He inhaled both. Damn, nothing had ever been like this.

He held steady within her, struggling for control as she adjusted to his size, shuddering as she clenched around him, enticing him deeper. He pushed the hair off her face again, searching her expression for signs of discomfort, finding only the same agonized pleasure along with a sense of wonder.

The wonder held his attention, lured him. He wanted to feed it, nurture it, explore the newness of it with her. Hell. His gaze dropped to the pebbled hardness of her nipple as it shivered atop her breast with her next breath. Who was he kidding? He just wanted to explore her.

"Are you okay?"

It took a good five seconds for her lids to lift, revealing the deep blue of her eyes. "No."

It was his turn to frown. "What's wrong?"

Her palms slicked down over his shoulder blades, the hollow of his back, and then up the rise of his buttocks, where they came to a stop. The edges of her nails bit into the hard flesh. "I'm a starving woman, and you're holding out on me."

He let her pull him closer, watching carefully. "Maybe I just want to be sure you can handle what you asked for."

"I can handle it. Trust me."

"Do you accept me?"

"If I say yes, will you get on with it?"

Another smile broke through the hard edge of passion. "Yes."

"Then absolutely." The bite of her nails left no doubt what she was talking about. He gave it to her, gathering his muscles before thrusting deep. He slapped his hand over her mouth just in time to cover her scream as her orgasm tore through her.

That wasn't the only thing to tear. The thin latex condom ripped under the pressure of his thrust. He didn't care, couldn't care, because now there was nothing between him and her but the slick heat of her channel and the drive for completion. She arched up, another scream coming on the heels of the first as she took all of him. He accepted the invitation, setting his teeth to her shoulder, growling as his climax exploded through him, biting down, feeling the glands at the side of his mouth release the hormone that would leave the shadowy mark. Holding her pinned between his teeth and his spasming cock, he branded her as his.

Forever.

Eight

LISA started crying near dawn, harsh, tearing sobs that made Donovan want to go out and kill whatever had upset her. But all he could do was hold her until the worst of the storm passed, until her sobs were only hiccups. He brushed his lips across her temple, her tears spreading over his lips in a salty wash. "I promise I'm disease free."

She blinked at him. "What?"

"You can't catch anything from me because the condom failed."

"The condom broke?"

"Yes."

"Oh, great."

So the broken condom wasn't the issue. Which only left two things. He caught the next tear on the edge of his finger. "I also can't get you pregnant." Unless he wanted to, and then only if fate smiled upon them.

She sniffed and swiped at her cheek. "I guess that makes you the perfect lover then."

"Not perfect. Not if I leave you crying in the aftermath." He brought the tear to his lips.

She waved him away. "It's nothing."

He frowned. "You're crying."

She frowned back. "So?"

"What hurts you, I want to fix."

That didn't please her at all. Another swipe followed by a glare.

"Maybe I'm just crying because you brutalized me with that monster cock of yours."

His hand opened over her buttocks, nestling the curve into his palm. "Is that the truth?"

"No, but it could be."

"I was very careful with you. *Gentle*."

Lisa sniffed back another sob at the extra emphasis on the word *gentle*. Her tears had nothing to do with him, and it wasn't fair to make him think they were. She opened her mouth to tell him so. He cut her off.

"You're not hurt."

There was no way he could know that. "That is an incredibly arrogant assumption."

"But no less true. Now, why are you crying?"

How could she tell him everything? She didn't even know him. "It's none of your business."

The thumb that had been stroking her cheek tucked under her jaw and pressed. She didn't have any choice but to look up. He was as gorgeous as ever, his features softened with lambent satisfaction, his eyes dark with an emotion she was too bleary-eyed to discern. While she no doubt—thanks to her crying jag—looked like a hag. A hag with flyaway hair and puffy eyes and a red nose. She reached over and fumbled for the light switch. She couldn't reach. She flopped back on his chest, pressing her face against his shoulder. She was really making quite the postcoital impression on the guy. "I hate the lights on all the time."

He studied her face, lingering on her eyes. He caught her hand in his, bringing it to his lips before placing it over his heart. The bed shifted as he reached back and flipped the switch. The small consideration was almost enough to make her start crying again. With a sigh, she resettled her head on his shoulder. "I really wish I had met you at some other time in my life."

He took on that peculiar stillness she'd noticed a few times before. "Why?"

His chest hair was crisp under her palm. She rubbed, focusing on the slight rasping noise rather than on how awkward she was making this. "I think we could have had something special."

"We have something special." His hand covered the place on her shoulder where he'd bitten her. The mark warmed and burned. Goose bumps sprang up on her skin and between her legs. The spot pulsed with expectation. The man had a kinky side, and she definitely liked it.

"This was a one-shot thing, Donovan."

"You made love to a wolf, Lisa. There's no going back."

She rolled her eyes. There was ego and then there was ego. "Look, I get you're a Romeo, and I'm grateful for your experience, but you haven't exactly ruined me for other men."

Technically, that could be a lie, but it wasn't one she was admitting to.

The grip on her hair tightened. One minute she was cuddled into his shoulder and the next she was flat on her back on the bed, and he was looming above her. "I damn well better have."

That was too much. She slammed her hands into his chest, intending to push him off. She might as well have slammed her hands into a brick wall. The shock of impact radiated up from her wrists. She gritted her teeth against the pain and snapped, "Well, you haven't, so get over yourself."

He growled. There was no other way to describe the rumble that came from his chest. Her pussy, as always, tingled at the primitive sound and then, contrary to the anger building within her, softened in invitation. The bed lurched as his knees wedged between hers. "There won't be any other men, Lisa."

She could feel him all around her—all muscle, all male, and not completely in control.

She wiggled up, ran into the barrier of his arms, and stopped. She scooted down only to run into the broad head of his cock. The man was not only irritating, he was insatiable.

She snapped her chin up. "That's not your call."

He brushed his knuckles down her cheek. "For as long as you're with me, seelie, I will be the only one."

"Stop calling me that!" She pushed off his chest. "And get off me."

"Why?"

"Because you're being obnoxiously overbearing."

"But you like it."

"I do not."

"Your body says otherwise."

Trust a man to pick up on that! "The fact that I'm attracted to you physically has nothing to do with whether or not I want to have a relationship with you."

Another stilling pause. "It doesn't?"

The way he said that gave *her* pause. "No."

He didn't move, didn't speak. She couldn't stand the silence. "I've been sexually attracted to a lot of men with whom I decided not to have a relationship."

Though it was pitch-black in the room, she swore she could see his eyes. Not distinctly, but there seemed to be a break in the darkness, almost a glow. Goose bumps raced over her skin again. Tension entered his muscles. He didn't let her up, didn't crowd her more, just stayed propped above her . . . thinking?

Finally, he broke the silence. "You'd be more comfortable with your choice with time?"

He talked like it was a done deal. "When I get around to making a choice, time will be a necessity."

His hand slid behind her head, weaving through her hair. His lips touched hers. "You're denying what's between us?"

"No." Yes. Was she? Making love with him had changed something between them. Something she couldn't identify. Maybe that's where her problem lay. She didn't like mysteries.

"You don't sound sure."

"I haven't made up my mind yet."

His teeth closed over her lobe, stopping just short of biting, holding her on the edge. The bed dipped as he shifted. His other hand worked under her. In one of those smooth moves that showcased his strength and secretly thrilled her, he rolled to his back. He didn't remove his hands. Clever man. If he had, she could have been off the bed in a heartbeat. Between her thighs, his cock throbbed, the pulse an echo of her heartbeat. Another disturbing connection in a series of them. He was right. There was something between them. Something powerful and scary, and if she were inclined to believe in fairy tales, incredibly right.

And she simply didn't have time for it.

"I told you, your timing sucked."

"I don't agree."

Why was she not surprised? "I can't handle anything more than this with you right now."

"This being . . . ?"

"Sex when we get the urge." The last syllable came out on a high jerk as the warmth of his hand cradled her breast, offering support for the full globe.

"And if I told you I didn't have a problem with that?"

"I'd call you a liar."

His thumb passed over her nipple. "Why?"

He'd paid a lot of attention to her breasts through the night. The peaks were still tender, almost raw. She jerked under the sensation that was just short of pain.

"You're too intense for me," she managed to gasp.

"I'm just right for you." The stroking of his fingertips up and down her spine stopped. Pressure from his fingers between her shoulder blades eased her forward. "Come here."

Lust, white-hot and immediate, clenched her womb, contracted her muscles, dragged a whimper past her throat. He'd said that so many times during the night, and each time she'd obeyed, he'd made her come a different, more exciting way until she'd lost track of how many times, how many ways. She shook her head, almost helplessly. "No."

He didn't give her any choice, drawing her down toward his mouth. "Shh. You need soothing."

Soothing? Was that what he was calling it now? She yelped when the heat of his mouth enveloped her nipple, strained against the curl of his tongue, but her strength was nothing compared to his and all she could do was brace herself for the pain.

It never came. Instead, as when she'd burned her arm and he'd kissed it better, there was heat, the stroke of his moist tongue, and then, no more pain. He suckled gently until the tension left her muscles.

"Give me your other breast."

The soft command came out of the darkness. Lisa didn't think to hesitate, merely shifted position and waited a breathless second for the claiming she knew would come. It came with the same delicacy, the same care. She closed her eyes as her discomfort eased. His steadying grip on her hip added a sense of security to the sense of being cared for. He was as meticulous at soothing that breast as he had been with the other. When he settled in to suckle, she stifled a yawn. He released her nipple with a slow glide of his lips. Arousal, always humming beneath the surface when she was with him, perked despite the weariness dragging down her lids.

"Tired?"

She nodded. Once again, he reversed their positions in that smooth indescribable way he had. She parted her thighs, desire and exhaustion battling for supremacy. He slid off the bed. She had an impression of a shadow and then his mouth was on hers—hot, experienced, completely carnal in its demand for a response. A response she couldn't hold back even if she wanted to.

When it came to this, he was her master. When Donovan pulled back, she went with him, clinging to the feeling, the connection.

"Shh." His fingers encircled her wrists, drawing her arms down from around his neck, lowering her back to the pillows.

"Hold that thought."

She closed her eyes as he left the room, using the occasional squeak of the floorboard to track his progress to the bathroom. There was the sound of water running, a few more squeaks, and he was back at her side. The covers slid down. His hand on the inside of her thigh made her jump. The warm cloth he pressed between her thighs made her moan. Then sigh. As the cloth cooled she pushed at his arm. She was too raw for anything to touch her.

"Sore?"

She cracked an eyelid, for all the good it did her. She couldn't see a thing, whereas he seemed to be able to find whatever he wanted with an unerring accuracy. She'd bitch about the unfairness of it if she weren't so tired. "Yes, and don't get any ideas about soothing it."

The covers slid down. "Too late."

She pushed at his head as it neared her hip. "I'm serious, Donovan."

"I wouldn't be much of a wolf if I left you like this."

"Trust me, it wouldn't hurt your reputation a bit."

He wasn't deterred. "I'm not taking the chance."

She put her hand over her mound. He took it in one of his.

"Donovan—"

She never got to say more. His tongue smoothed over her raw flesh. Pain spiked in a flash only to disappear before she could finish her gasp.

"Shh. Let me tend to you."

The hand he placed just above her pubic bone didn't give her any choice. And then she didn't want one. The warm stroke of his tongue covered her flesh in a soothing massage that drained the tension from her muscles and made room for the weariness to take hold. Sleep beckoned. Her hand dropped to his head. His hair was cool against her fingertips.

"I'm sorry."

With a light kiss to her folds, he stopped his ministrations. There was a slight sting on her inner thigh and a spike of pleasure that shot to her core. Before she could protest, he gave a gentle tug on her shoulder and she rolled over. He straddled her thighs. His fingertips started easy circles on her shoulder blades, stealing the tension away. "Why?"

She rested her chin on the back of her hands. "I'm so tired."

"Then sleep."

She could feel his cock resting heavily against her buttocks. She forced her eyes open and pressed back, and some strength returned to her muscles. "It's not fair to you."

"You let me worry about fair." He patted her hip. "Sleep."

As if his permission was all her body had been waiting for, tiredness rolled over her in a blanketing fog. As the haze closed in on her, her memory nagged at her. There was something she needed to do. Something important. She struggled to remember. His cock jerked. It came to her then. "You'll remember to get condoms tomorrow?"

His hands paused midstroke. His "Yes" was cloaked in a hot growl of displeasure.

She frowned. He might be the sexiest thing out there, but she wasn't going to continue to risk life and limb to experience him. "You promise?"

He resumed his massage. "I promise."

"Good." She yawned and wiggled deeper into the pillows. "Because I think I'm going to want you again."

"I'm counting on it."

The promise drifted with her into sleep.

Nine

"YOU'RE back early."

Wyatt looked over his shoulder as Donovan entered the kitchen. "I wanted to talk to you."

Fragrant steam rose from the coffee he poured into a cup.

"About what?"

Wyatt turned and leaned back against the counter. His eyebrow cocked as he took in Donovan's appearance. "I take it you made a decision about Lisa."

"What makes you say that?"

"The fact that you look like a cat dragged you in through a knothole backward." He motioned with the cup. "And the fact that you have Lisa's scent all over you." With a wave, he indicated the farmer's table and chairs. "Have a seat."

Taking a seat meant the third degree. If Wyatt didn't make such damn good coffee he might have given it a pass. Donovan grabbed a cup off the mug tree as Wyatt took a seat in the chair nearest the pot. The man did have a serious caffeine addiction. And he did make good coffee.

"I take it you made your choice?" Wyatt asked as Donovan took a seat across from him.

"Yes."

"Does Lisa know she's no longer a free woman?"

Donovan stretched. His body was pleasantly tired, completely sated, and yet throbbing with expectation. He hadn't felt this alive in decades. "Not yet."

This time, displeasure gave Wyatt's eyebrows that lift. "You claimed the woman and didn't tell her? And you're a Protector?"

Donovan set his jaw and took a sip of coffee. It was as good as always. "I didn't break the law."

He didn't like the way Wyatt sat back in the chair, his fingers settling carefully around the mug. "You just gave it a hell of a bend."

Donovan refused to feel guilty. "I told her she was mating with a wolf. I told her there was no going back. I asked her if she accepted me." He met Wyatt's gaze directly. "No laws were broken."

Wyatt cocked an eyebrow at him. "Did you ask her if she believed in werewolves?"

"The subject never came up."

Wyatt shook his head and took a sip of coffee. "I bet."

Donovan expected him to say more. As his next Alpha, Wyatt could feel entitled to say a hell of a lot. Not that it would matter. Lisa was Donovan's mate. Nothing, not even death, could change that, but Wyatt had very strict views on right and wrong, and there was no telling what his association with humans had done to his perception of a male's right to his female.

"You're going to have to tell her, you know."

"No shit."

"But?"

"For now she has enough on her plate, so I've decided to humor her with an affair."

Wyatt choked on his coffee. "Human style? With all the precautionary trappings humans bring to a relationship?"

Donovan gritted his teeth and slapped the were on the back, harder than necessary. It didn't do any good. There was no distracting Wyatt from the humor of the revelation. Donovan snarled the "Yes" through his teeth.

Wyatt laughed out loud. "Shit. I wish I could have see you rolling on a condom."

Donovan covered his annoyance with a large swallow of coffee. "The damn things are useless. It broke every time on the first thrust."

"Bet Lisa was thrilled to discover that."

She'd actually been oblivious, too lost in the passion to notice at first. Dismayed when she had, and while she could trust him implicitly, she'd done so too easily when he'd assured her he was disease free. That trusting side of her nature was one he'd have to monitor. It could endanger her. "I'll be going out today."

"You think any store in this podunk town is going to carry condoms to fit werewolf cock?"

"No, but I promised to try."

More laughter. "And you always keep your promises?"

"Yes."

"Well, look at it this way, when you reveal to her what you are, you can reveal to her that they're unnecessary."

"Somehow I don't see that lessening the shock."

"No, probably not, but it will give you something to look forward to."

It couldn't come soon enough for him. He hated anything between his cock and her sweet flesh.

Wyatt sobered, and leaned back in his chair. "Did the subject of what has her and Robin so upset come up?"

"It did, but I got distracted."

Wyatt smiled. "I've got to tell you, Protector, I'm getting a whole new image of you."

"Shut up, Wyatt."

"Is that any way to talk to your leader?"

Donovan paused, his coffee cup halfway to his mouth. "You're going back?"

"Was there any doubt?"

No, actually there wasn't. Donovan had never doubted that Wyatt would do the right thing. "I sort of expected you to put up a bit more of a fight."

Wyatt sighed. With the blunt tips of his fingers he tapped out a rhythm on the side of the cup. "From what you said yesterday I don't have time to indulge in temperamental displays."

Donovan had never known Wyatt to be temperamental in his life. Stubborn, yes. Angry, yes. Deadly, yes. But never temperamental. "The old guy is in a hurry to join his mate."

Wyatt finished his coffee in a fast swallow, the muscles of his throat working too hard for a simple drink. The bitterness of grief tempered his scent, but when he brought the cup down, nothing of his distress showed in his face. "I only have one problem with leaving here."

"What's that?"

"You will be alone to deal with Buddy and company."

"No one's covering for you when you're gone?"

"My deputy."

There was more apology than faith in Wyatt's tone. "I take it he's not the type to inspire confidence. When are you leaving?"

Wyatt's chair scraped across the floor as he stood. "Now." He grabbed his hat off the back. "I called Kelon last night. He should be here in a few days."

"I'm sure he was thrilled."

"He sounded his usual enthusiastic self."

Donovan just bet. He knew exactly how Kelon had taken the news. Kelon was all hard edges and strong purpose. In the old days, Donovan had still been able to make him laugh, but in the last few decades, Kelon had grown more and more serious, until Donovan couldn't remember the last time he had heard his brother laugh. The long wait for a mate, the hardest thing for a wolf to endure, had worn down his optimism.

Donovan looked around the cheery kitchen, thought of the women upstairs, of how much hope they had invested in the place and the danger that could take it away. While Donovan didn't think it would take them too long to set Buddy straight, there was still the issue that had sent Lisa to his bed last night. It had to be something big. Now that they were mated, it was his responsibility to deal with it. He sighed and shoved his cup away, getting to his feet. And that meant he needed his brother. "Kelon will adjust." He held out his hand. "Safe journey, Wyatt."

Wyatt shook it and then settled his grey Stetson on his head. The brim shaded his eyes, leaving visible only the slightly grim set to his lips and the scent of purpose to indicate how he felt. "You take care yourself, Donovan. I'll be pissed if I have to come back to claim a body rather than my number one Protector."

"I'll keep that in mind."

Wyatt turned and opened the door. For a split second he stood framed in the entry, the cloud-filtered wash of dawn throwing his powerful silhouette into stark relief. Cold air whipped through the opening and wrapped around Donovan's feet. A chill went up his spine. Wyatt might be going home, but there were many who wouldn't welcome him or the change he stood for. And he'd be facing them alone. Above Donovan's head, floorboards creaked as Lisa moved about. Donovan stood, torn by his loyalties, bound by his oath. Committed to his mate. Obligated to his leader.

Wyatt stepped onto the porch, turned, and caught his gaze. Understanding flashed in his eyes. "Your duty is here, for now."

It was, but it didn't make it any easier to watch his Alpha rising go unprotected into what could be a potentially dangerous situation. "At least call Kelon back."

Wyatt smiled. "I can handle a few challenges."

Pack could be stubborn when clinging to tradition. And not all wolves put honor before results. Plumbing clunked a protest as the shower turned on. Unease crept through him. "Watch your back."

Wyatt nodded. "I'll do that."

The door closed behind him with a decisive click.

TWENTY minutes later, Lisa entered the kitchen. Donovan was expecting a smile. He didn't get one. As a matter of fact, she didn't look at him at all, just grabbed a cup and headed straight for the coffeepot as if it perked lifeblood. He caught her arm when she got close enough. With a hitch of his forefinger under her chin, he tilted her face up. She'd been crying.

He stroked his finger along the salty path the tears had taken. Something in his chest twisted. "You've been crying."

"I just got soap in my eye."

He might have believed that if her hands weren't clenched so tightly on the blue coffee cup that the knuckles shone white. He debated broaching the subject there and then, but the longing with which she looked at the coffeepot changed his mind. "Need coffee?"

"God, yes."

He chuckled. "Not a morning person, hmm?"

She still wouldn't meet his eyes. "Not if I can help it."

"That's gonna make it pretty tough running an inn, isn't it?"

"I'll adjust."

"I imagine you will."

She cut him the glare. "Was that a crack?"

At least she was looking at him. He pulled a chair out from the table and guided her into it. "Nope. Just stating the facts." She sat, her forehead in one hand, the empty cup held up in the other. The silent order made him smile.

"Your strength is something I admire." She didn't say a word as he poured coffee in the cup. "You take cream and sugar?"

"Yes to both. Three sugars and a quarter way full of cream."

He looked at her. "Are you having dessert or coffee?"

She pushed her damp hair out of her face. "If you have a problem making it like that, get out of the way and I'll do it myself."

He held up his hand before she could stand. "I'll do it. I just never heard of anyone taking it that way."

"Well, now you have." From the way she was sitting in the chair, shoulders set, arms crossed, bottom lip slightly pouted, she was clearly spoiling for a fight. He put cream and sugar in the coffee as instructed, turned around, and leaned back against the counter.

"So I have."

She motioned to the mug in his hand. "Are you going to give me my coffee, or what?"

"For a price."

"What would that be?"

She was a suspicious little thing. "A kiss."

It took a second, but some of that tension left her shoulders. "Do I have to come over and get it? Because now that I'm down I don't feel much like getting up."

He smiled and pushed off the counter. "Nope. I'm in an obliging mood this morning."

It only took three steps to get to her side. Her head fell naturally back into the support of his palm. A glance down showed her looking up at him, the memories of the night a seductive promise in her eyes. Her lips parted.

She wanted his kiss. The knowledge went through him with the hot burn of lust. The anticipation that had been simmering in his blood burst to a boil. He leaned closer, sliding his hand off her shoulder, down over the edge of her collarbone to the soft lapel of her pale yellow shirt with its neat row of small white buttons. Flimsy barriers to the flesh he sought. Holding her gaze, he unbuttoned the first, smiling when her pupils dilated. He moved on to the second, and then a third. She swallowed. Hard.

A tiny push was all it took to move the material aside. Satisfaction blended with passion as his mark came into view. Red now, but it would soon turn to a shadow under the skin. Permanent, along with the change to her scent, declaring her unavailable to all other males.

Her gaze followed his. Her fingers covered the mark, rubbed as if to remove it.

"No." He caught her hand in his. "I like it."

She blinked a couple of times. Before she could fully regain her senses, he closed the distance between them. His hand circled her breast. Her breath exploded into his mouth. He inhaled, taking it deep, noting the difference, the blend of him and her. The rightness of it.

He slid his tongue past the seam of her lips, groaning at the impact. Like gasoline to a fire, desire flared between them. She tipped her head back, inviting his kiss, the uninhibited welcome pushing him past good sense and caution, beckoning him until all he wanted was more. More of her, more of the feeling that was building.

He grabbed the back of the chair, keeping her from falling as he deepened the kiss. Her arms worked up between them, fingers pressing into the nape of his neck, feminine and sweet in their possession of his soul. He'd never had this with another—instant passion mixed with so much more, a feeling of past blending into present. The sensation of a future opening up . . .

Her nails cut into his skin in a seductive demand. Eight little pinpricks of pleasure. He closed his eyes, searching for the discipline that had stood him well all through his life. He could hear her sister moving around upstairs, and there was that whole issue of her coffee getting cold. A mate didn't let that happen the morning after claiming unless he wanted to hear about it for the next few hundred years.

He slipped his hand behind her skull, pulling her up for one last kiss a split second before he heard the creak of the top stair on the back staircase. He rested his thumb against the corner of her mouth, keeping her lips parted, ready as he put a half inch between them.

"Robin's coming downstairs."

She blinked, but the dazed look didn't immediately leave her eyes. Smiling, he pressed his lips to her forehead, breathing her scent again, knowing he'd never get tired of the way she smelled, of touching her. The floorboard before the threshold creaked. Pushing Lisa's cup in front of her, he sat in the chair adjacent, hiding his arousal. He lifted his cup as Robin came into the room. "Morning."

She looked between them and frowned long enough that he wondered if she was going to have issues with the relationship, and then she smiled. It should have brightened her face. Instead it highlighted the weariness there. "Morning, Donovan, Lisa."

A glance over at Lisa showed her frowning at Robin. Robin glanced at the coffeepot, then at the cupboard as if weighing a choice. As she stood there her scent drifted to Donovan. The something wrong—it was still there. He turned his attention back to Lisa. She was studying her sister, too. And tears hovered in her eyes.

It dawned on him then. Robin was why she cried at night. Robin sighed and opened the cupboard above the stove. Inside were bottles of prescription medicine. She grabbed first one and then another, and another. No one had that many prescriptions without it being a major issue.

"Aren't you feeling well?"

Robin braced her hands against the counter. He started to stand. Lisa's hand on his thigh stopped him.

"I'm just feeling a little nauseous."

"I can take you into town to see the doctor."

"The snow's too bad."

"Nah, it's just a dusting."

Robin turned to lean back against the counter. She tried to

make it look casual, but he could tell she was weak. He made it halfway to his feet before Lisa hissed, "Sit down."

He hesitated. It went against the grain to ignore a woman in need. Lisa's nails dug into his thigh. He sat. Grudgingly.

The smile Robin shared with Lisa was shaky. Shakier still when she included him. "If the meds don't take care of it, I'll let you know."

"You do that."

She gathered the pill bottles. "I'm just going to lie down for a bit longer."

Donovan waited until she cleared the landing before he turned to Lisa. "She's what you wanted to forget, isn't she?"

She licked her lips and took a sip of her coffee. Her hands shook and some coffee spilled. She grabbed a napkin off the middle of the table and wiped it up.

"She's been sick for a long time. Since before our parents died." She rested her forehead on her fist, the trembling spreading up her arm and then to her body. "It's not fair. She's worked so hard, had just started to dream." She dropped her forehead into her palm. "And now this."

"What is *this*?"

"The worse possible scenario."

He was grateful Protectors were trained in interrogation techniques. It gave him the ability to contain his impatience. "Explain."

The back stairs creaked. Lisa glanced guiltily after her sister. "It's not my place to say."

Maybe it was; maybe it wasn't. But she would tell him. Her lip slid between her teeth. But not here, where her sister could overhear. He pulled back her chair, took her hand, and helped her up. She needed to get out of the house, away from her guilt. "You can whisper it to me on the way to town.

She reached back and made a grab for her coffee. "It's a secret."

He didn't slow down, but he did give her enough room to get her cup. "I won't tell anyone."

SHE wasn't going to tell him. It didn't matter how much Donovan tortured her with understanding silence, the secret was Robin's to tell, and Lisa wasn't violating her confidence. She slammed the truck door closed, glaring at Donovan as he came around the side of the vehicle while watching her with those knowing eyes that tempted her to confide.

Snow crunched under her boots as she stomped up the steps to the glass door of the pharmacy. She reached for the doorknob. He was there before her. No matter what she wanted to do, he always seemed to be ahead of her. It irritated her to no end. He held the door open for her. Her "Thank you" was forced. As she passed through, his fingers grazed her back. The bulk of her coat protected from all but a whisper of sensation, but nothing could protect her from the intimacy of the memories. Heat burned her cheeks. She quickly stepped into the store, darted into the center aisle, paused next to the antacids, and took a deep, steadying breath.

Donovan came up behind her.

"Is there a problem?"

"I have a headache."

As with every other time she'd mentioned she had a problem his arms came around her. Comfort flowed over her, and for some strange reason her worries seemed silly. She ducked out from under his arm, checking around to see who had noticed. "Stop that."

"Stop what?"

"Comforting me." She wanted to grind her teeth. She wanted to turn into his arms. She couldn't do either. "What if someone saw?"

His eyes narrowed. "They'd see a man holding a woman."

She folded her arms across her chest and glanced down the

aisle. For sure, Honey Brandt, the pharmacy tech, was listening. She had a bird's-eye view from her spot behind the elevated counter at the back of the store. "It could cause a lot of trouble for you," she hissed.

"Why are you whispering? And why are you worried about it now?"

Because she'd just remembered Honey was related to Buddy. "Look, this was a really bad idea."

She tried to put some distance between them. She made it as far as the length of his arm before he hauled her back.

"Why?"

"Honey Brandt is Buddy's aunt, and she thinks the sun rises and sets on him."

"So?"

"From the glare she's giving me, Buddy's spun her some big lie, and I doubt she's going to sell me *anything*, let alone condoms."

Donovan glanced at the woman behind the counter. Lisa knew what he saw. A pleasant-faced older woman, with round glasses sitting atop plump rosy cheeks, giving the impression of openness and warmth. Nothing could be further from the truth. She waited for Donovan to smile at the woman the way people always did when meeting Honey. He didn't.

"Then I'll buy them."

"She won't sell them to you either if she thinks you're with me."

"That remains to be seen."

He headed off down the aisle, dragging her with him. Unless she wanted to pitch a fit for Honey's benefit, she had no choice but to follow along. The closer they got to the counter, the clearer Honey's displeasure grew. Donovan pulled up short in front of the small display of prophylactics hanging beneath the pharmacist's counter.

Honey's "Good morning, Lisa" was colder than the air outside. Her tone was completely different when she greeted Donovan. Which just went to prove Donovan's appeal was as potent on women in their forties as it was on women in their twenties. She pinched his wrist.

"Morning, ma'am."

Donovan cocked an eyebrow at Lisa, a hint of mischief hovering at the corner of his mouth, and she knew, just knew, what his retaliation for that pinch was going to be.

He waved to the array of boxes, and without a lick of embarrassment asked, "What's your preference?"

She didn't have a preference, had never bought a condom in her life. The ones she'd had had been purchased by her older sister, Heather, the woman who thought of everything, prepared for everything. The one who'd taken on the state and kept them together after their parents' deaths fifteen years ago when Heather was only eighteen. Heather could probably just walk in a store and buy the damn things without batting an eyelash. But Heather wasn't here, and she didn't have Donovan to deal with. Lisa pretended Honey wasn't listening to every word and slapped a smile on her face. "I think your preference would be the way to go."

The mischief was in full force now. He shrugged those big shoulders, drawing Honey's eyes. "You're the one who wants them; I'd prefer to have nothing between you and my skin."

The appreciation in the other woman's gaze got Lisa's goat more than his teasing. The man might be testosterone on the hoof, but he didn't have to be advertising it. She grabbed a box and set them on the counter. "These should do it." She turned her smile on Honey, dragging her into the small confrontation. "Don't you think?"

Honey blinked. Lisa had to wait two heartbeats for her to tear her gaze off Donovan's face. She looked at the box. A flicker of disappointment crossed her expression. "We sell a lot of them."

To women customers, she'd guess. Lisa was willing to bet not many men bought condoms designed to desensitize. Only women hoping to improve a man's staying power did that.

Donovan grabbed the box and turned it toward him and read

the cover. His eyebrow tipped up. "You weren't sore enough this morning?"

She set her teeth. "There's always room for improvement."

He cupped her cheek in his palm, the gesture innately intimate, implying a connection that went deeper than sexual. "You're going to have to toughen up before we start shooting for longer sessions." He put the box back on the hook and grabbed another. "We do, however, have to do something about the fit."

He pulled her in for a kiss. Out of the corner of her eye, she saw the words *extra large* printed on the box. When the kiss was over, her knees were weak, and the interest was back in Honey's expression.

"Optimist," she muttered with the breath he left her.

"Yeah. I'm guessing their definition of extra large isn't going to fit the need."

Flicking a finger at the box, she conceded the game. "We'll take those."

Shaving her hand in her pocket, she grabbed for her wallet. The glance Honey sent her was disgusted.

"I've got it," Donovan drawled, the same reprimand in his tone that was in Honey's gaze.

"Fine." She shoved both hands in her pockets. Good God, who knew there was a protocol to buying condoms?

"Do you want to pick up Robin's Tacrolimus refill while you're here?" Honey asked.

Though the wording was civil enough, there was a definite sneer around Robin's name. Lisa bristled. Donovan's hand brushed hers. Comfort or warning? She didn't care. This woman's nephew had brutalized her sister. She wasn't taking any insults off her. She opened her mouth.

"We would, ma'am," Donovan answered, his drawl as smooth as butter.

"Do you have the money yet, Lisa?"

Lisa gritted her teeth. Honey knew she didn't. Along with being a pharmacy and general store, the place was also the post office, and neither Robin's disability check, nor the monthly check from Heather had arrived yet.

"I have it." There was a difference in Donovan's drawl that snapped Lisa's head around, an inflection in his tone, a warning rumble beneath the syllables. Honey must have felt it, too, because a wariness entered her tone as she grabbed a bag from under the counter. "It's very expensive."

She named the price. Donovan didn't bat an eye. "Thank you."

"You're not paying for my medication."

"I'm not." He calmly handed over the bills. "I'm paying for Robin's."

"I can carry my own weight."

Again his hand came under her chin. She didn't need any encouragement to raise her face. Resentment did it for her. "But why should you when I'm here?"

"Because I'm a grown woman who doesn't need a man to take care of her!"

He didn't get angry. He just stroked his thumb over her cheek in that soothing, possessive way he had, and said in his deep drawl, "But you're my woman, and the pleasure of providing for you is mine."

It was such a chauvinistic thing to say, she shouldn't have been touched, but she was. Ridiculously so. "That is such an outdated idea."

"It's what my people believe."

"You're not from around here?" Honey asked as if she didn't already know he wasn't one of the once-bustling town's remaining one hundred residents.

"No."

"I didn't think so. Can't imagine a man from around here with that attitude."

"Any man worth his salt knows how to care for his woman."

The phrase "his woman" set her teeth on edge. "Could you try to sound less caveman-like?"

"I'll try, but I'm not giving any guarantees."

Cutting Donovan a glare, Lisa grabbed the bag from him. "Do you have any other archaic notions I should know about?"

"I've got a few."

"Let's hear them."

"I believe my woman's problems are mine to solve, her concerns mine to take on, and"—he looked over her shoulder at Honey—"her enemies mine to eliminate." He nodded to the older woman. "You might want to pass that on your nephew."

Honey took a step back. Lisa headed for the door. Donovan fell into step beside her.

"That's some list."

"I've got my priorities straight. That's not something you have to worry about."

Except his priorities didn't reflect hers. "Great."

He beat her to the door and held it open. Cold air rushed into the store. She sighed. He was a very stubborn man. "Can we go get my truck now?"

Ten

APPARENTLY, she could get Bessie, but she couldn't drive her. Lisa sat in Donovan's warm SUV, staring out the tinted window while Donovan fiddled under Bessie's hood, seemingly impervious to the cold. She rolled down the window and called out for the third time, "I am perfectly capable of driving my own truck home."

A sound came from under the hood. Though she couldn't make out a word, she recognized the tone of a curse when she heard it. When Donovan glanced around the hood, his expression was as calm as could be. His "I'm sure you can" was beyond patient.

She rolled her eyes.

"I know you're just humoring me."

"Then why keep asking me the same question?"

"I'm hoping the wand of enlightenment will strike you." His smile flashed, sexy and masculine, summoning every nerve ending in her body to perk up.

"Don't hold your breath."

She probably shouldn't. Donovan was definitely going to be a demanding lover. Combine that with that nurturing streak he had, and she would have to stay on her toes to keep from being totally wrapped in cotton wool.

"You know, humoring me will only get you so far."

He leaned around the hood again. "And how far would that be?"

"It might get your butt stuck here."

"Uh-huh."

Well, heck. He could at least look worried. "Are you almost done?"

"Closer than the last five times you asked me."

"How close is that?"

"About two minutes now."

Great. She sat back in the seat. At least she'd be able to get to the wallpaper in the front parlor today. "Good. Let me know when you're done."

The hood slammed down. Donovan gave it a pat. "I'm done."

She opened the door. "Thanks. I've got a ton of things to do today."

Donovan waved her back. "I think I'll take this opportunity for Bessie and I to get acquainted."

She rolled her eyes. "You just think I can't drive."

Snow crunched under his boots as he approached the truck. He braced his elbows on the window frame. "What I think is that I don't want you driving on these roads in the snow with those bald tires."

"What difference does it make if you're the one that goes over the cliff, or I'm the one that goes over the cliff?"

He touched his finger to her nose. "The difference is I couldn't live with the latter."

"And what about what I could live with?"

His fingertips slid down her cheek. "In this case, what I want matters more."

How was she supposed to argue with that? The man would rather die than see her hurt. It was like something out of a romance novel. Except this wasn't a romance, this was real life, and things like this just didn't happen to her. She watched him walk to the old truck with that broad-shouldered, lean-hipped arrogance that was so much a part of who he was.

Men like *him* didn't happen to her.

He slid inside her battered pickup truck. He closed the door without having to fight with the stubborn spot that caught halfway down. Did nothing ever go wrong for the man?

With a flash of Bessie's headlights, he indicated she should go first. She put the big SUV in gear. The engine purred with a rumble that reminded her of Donovan when he got emotional. She patted the wheel. "Just don't go getting temperamental on me, okay?"

The truth was, for all her brave talk, she wasn't used to driving on snow, let alone on roads that were only half-plowed with one or two inches of snow still covering everything.

She cautiously turned onto the highway. The tires held fast, unlike what she saw happening behind her. Even under Donovan's control, Bessie slid on the road. Maybe Donovan had a point. Maybe they really did need to fix those tires. She hated to think of Bink lying to her, though. It was a bad omen for their new life.

Then again, he hadn't really lied to her. He'd said the tires had another five thousand miles in them. He hadn't said the truck would drive worth a damn.

She took her foot off the accelerator until Donovan caught up. When he flashed his lights, she depressed the accelerator, creeping forward at a slower rate as they approached the incline, but it scared her every time the tires slipped or the back sashayed. She bit her lip, leaning forward studying the road as if she could spy the next slippery spot. As she did, she conceded another point. Maybe it was better he was driving her truck. He seemed to be quite capable at correcting skids, handling them the way he seemed to handle every upset. With calm confidence. She needed to learn to do that.

All too soon, they left the town behind and the paved road turned to dirt. Driving was worse here. She kept the big SUV in the tracks they'd made coming down the mountain, employing a little more pressure on the accelerator as they started to climb. About a mile up the road they passed Deep Hole Road. Her grip on the wheel was white-knuckled. Up ahead was one of the more treacherous parts of the road. Sharp turns with steep drop-offs on the right, and the only thing that functioned as a guardrail were the big trees growing along the side. In good weather, she'd thought them stately, natural protectors, but now, with going off the side a real threat, they looked about as substantial as toothpicks. She severely doubted they would stop her truck from tumbling all the way to the bottom of the ravine.

She pulled her eyes from the drop and locked them on the road ahead. She had no reason to be afraid. This was just a simple trip up the mountain to go home. The truck wasn't slipping, wasn't doing anything but progressing slowly and surely under her control. She had no reason to worry. Out of the corner of her right eye, she saw a souped-up SUV waiting at Deep Hole to turn onto the main road. The vehicle was familiar, but she couldn't remember who it belonged to. She lifted her pinky in greeting, hardly the customary wave, but it was all she could manage. She was that nervous.

Creeping through the intersection, with only one sashay when she hit a cross rut, she made it to the other side. A rumble from behind had her checking the rearview. She blinked. The big SUV had pulled out between her and Donovan. The conditions of the road didn't seem to bother the driver at all. He came up fast behind her—a big, mean SUV with a jacked-up chassis and jaws painted on the front. Instinct demanded she speed up to put distance between her and the reckless driver, but the next curve was a tight one and as the road was too narrow to pass, the driver was just going to have to stay behind her. She licked her lips and forced her hands to relax on the wheel. As long as they stayed behind her, she was fine.

Another glance in the mirror, and again that nagging sense of familiarity, and then recognition. The truck belonged to one of Buddy's friends. One of the less savory of his friends—the one who'd spent time in jail for assault. The speed of the SUV's approach took on a whole new meaning. Her heart started racing like a freight train. They wouldn't, would they?

Two seconds later, she had her answer. The truck gunned forward, tires spinning, engine whining. At first they didn't gain, but then those big tires gripped the road and the truck filled the rearview in a parody of teeth and danger. There was a thud and a jerk and then the landscape spun out of focus as her SUV lost traction. Behind her Bessie's horn bugled a warning as the rear end of the SUV slid to the right. The steep drop-off loomed before her. Oh, dear lord!

Turn into the skid. Turn into the skid.

The refrain echoed in her mind, riding her panic. She turned, too much or the wrong way, she wasn't sure, but instead of straightening, the truck went into a slow spin. She slammed both feet on the brake pedal. The truck didn't slow or stop, just continued to spin in slow motion toward the drop-off. Her scream lodged in her throat along with her heart and her breakfast.

Oh, God! The snowbank wasn't big enough to hold, not at this speed. She was still turning the wheel, still pumping the brake, when Buddy's friends sped by, barely missing her, honking their horn. An impression of middle fingers being held up, then she was back watching the scenery go round. One more turn and she'd be at the edge. She pressed her forehead to the wheel, helpless, terror and nausea battling for dominance. The roar of a truck engine jerked her head up. She had an impression of gray and primer orange, and then she was thrown sideways against the door as something struck the front of the truck. The gray and orange blur kept going, blowing through the snowbank in a plume of white.

Donovan!

Lisa twisted about as her vehicle crashed into the mountain wall, hung up on a rock, and came to an abrupt stop. Her cheek throbbed from where it had struck the window. Oh God, Donovan.

She fumbled with the seat belt, yanking it free, her breath coming in hard drags as she stared at the spot where Bessie had gone over the edge. "Donovan!"

The driver's side door was wedged against the mountain wall. She slid across the seat. Yanking on the handle, she kicked the passenger door open and jumped out. A look up the road showed no sign of Buddy's friends. No sign of help. A look down showed no sign of help, either. Oh, God!

She ran, slipping and sliding across the road, until she got to the point where Donovan had gone over. Peering over the edge, she couldn't see the truck—but she could see the path it had plowed through the snow. She didn't stop to think, just jumped feetfirst down the steep incline, grabbing at small trees and branches as she went to break her speed, calling Donovan's name, the lack of response feeding the blackest of fears.

Her foot caught on a branch near the bottom of the first incline, pitching her forward. She did a face plant in the snow, coming to stop against something soft. She grabbed hold. Donovan's coat. Oh God, Donovan's coat. He'd been thrown from the truck.

"Donovan!"

A low moan was his only answer. At least he was still alive. Thirty feet below, Bessie listed in a crumpled heap against a boulder. Thank God Donovan had been thrown. He never would have survived the wreck. She turned around and crawled up beside him. He was half-buried in the snow. Blood was everywhere, bright red or pink, depending on how close it was to his body. Her first instinct was to panic. Her second was to vomit. The third was to find out how badly he was hurt. She went with the third.

There was a huge gash on his forehead. Judging by the sharp, unnatural angle, his upper arm was broken. She fumbled with the buttons on his coat. Her fingers were shaking so badly she couldn't grab the smooth surface. The sob she'd been holding back ruptured from her throat. She ripped off her gloves and tried again.

"What the hell did you think you were doing, Donovan?"

The button edged in the hole. She jerked it through, repeating the process five more times, her fingers burning with the cold, her eyes burning with tears. "Is this another one of those archaic notions you hold so dear? Sacrificing yourself for others? For me?"

She ran her hands down his sides beneath his coat. It would really help if she knew what a broken rib felt like. She felt more cuts and the horrible sensation of her hand sliding inside his body. She screamed. The brittle sound carried on the air and echoed around them. She let the reverberations fade away before she steeled herself and pushed his shirt aside.

There was a hole in his side. Probably torn open by a tree limb. She could see pools of blood interspersed by greyish whitish stuff and nothing else she wanted to identify. She wanted to grab the edges of the wound and pull it closed. Her hands hovered over the horrible sight, as if it were really possible to do such a thing. She took a breath, and then another, focusing on the sheer normalcy of breathing in and out, as if that could return what she was looking at to normal. It couldn't.

He was hurt. Badly. She had to get him to the hospital, but how to do that was the next mystery. She didn't have a cell phone to call for help, couldn't get him back up the mountain, and couldn't fix him here.

"You're in quite a fix, sexy."

She brushed a length of nearly black hair off his forehead. Blood soaked the strands, smearing across her fingers. The spot on her shoulder where he'd bitten her burned with heat. The heat traveled down her arm to her fingers.

She rested her fingertips against his temple, straining to feel the pulse, the strange heat intensifying. She remembered the way he'd backed her in the bar, strong and indomitable, looking like all he'd needed to stomp Buddy and company was a word from her. She remembered his expression just before he'd kissed her that first time—wildly passionate, deeply satisfied, and incredibly sexy. But mostly, she remembered how he'd held her while she cried, strength and compassion and tenderness in his hug.

"I didn't even know men like you existed." She leaned forward and kissed the one blood-free spot on his cheek. "Damn it, don't you die before I find out what this is we have."

There was a rustle of fabric on fabric. Something touched her thigh in a whisper of sensation. "That had better be your hand."

Please let it be his hand and not some creature they'd disturbed.

His lids lifted slightly. "What are you going to do if it's not?"

The question was strained. He had to be hurting so badly. Behind his lashes, she could see the glitter of his eyes.

The sob she'd been trying to hold back broke from her throat. She shoved her knuckles against her teeth to stop the next one. He was conscious. That had to be a good sign. "Scream blue murder," she rasped.

The corner of his lip twitched. "I don't like a screaming woman."

Snow crunched under her knees as she shifted closer. "Then you'd better tell me that's your hand."

"It's my hand." His good hand came up. She caught it in hers before he could do more damage to himself.

"You've been crying."

Bringing his hand down to her lap, she rolled her eyes. "Of course I've been crying. You wrecked my truck."

He winced halfway into his smile. "I guess that means you'll have to take the cost out of my hide."

A tear dripped down her cheek and splattered on his coat. "You don't have much hide left."

"I'll be all right, seelie. I just need to lie here for awhile."

"You can't lie here. You'll bleed to death."

"Can you carry me up the hill?"

"No."

He closed his eyes. "Then let me rest a minute."

That was the craziest thing she'd ever heard. He couldn't just lie there bleeding to death. She pressed her hand harder against the gaping wound in his side. "I should go get help."

His fingers wrapped like vises around her forearm. "No. I don't want you out there unprotected."

She didn't have it in her to point out to him that he wasn't much protection the way he was. Taking off her scarf and wadding it up into a pad, she pressed it to his side. The place where he'd bit her burned like fire. "I've got to do something."

"Then talk to me."

"About what?"

He grimaced before saying, "Tell me what's wrong with Robin."

What did keeping that secret matter now? "She had a kidney transplant last year. Her second. Her last tests weren't good. She seems to be rejecting the transplant."

"Ah, that explains why her scent is wrong."

"Excuse me?"

He shook his head and frowned. "I meant, that's why you worry."

That might be what he'd meant, but that wasn't what he'd said. But what he'd said didn't make sense. "Have I ever mentioned you're a very strange man, Donovan?"

She pressed harder against his wound. The pressure bandage seemed to be working. The flow of blood was stopping. And while she knew it was her imagination, the opening of the wound felt narrower.

"I'd rather hear how sexy you find me."

Was it her imagination, or did his voice sound stronger?

"I'm sure you would, but after scaring the bejeezus out of me, you're going to have to work back up to that kind of compliment."

He didn't answer, just took a deep breath. Probably to manage the pain. He had to be in so much pain.

"You gave Robin the kidney, didn't you? That's the scar on your right side."

"Yes. Unfortunately, mine didn't work out, and she had to go through it again."

The wind blew down the mountain. Trees swayed, branches crackled, and trunks creaked a protest. She knew just how they felt. She was just as helpless against the forces shaping her life. "What are we going to do, Donovan?"

"About getting me back up the hill? Or about our relationship?"

She glanced up the mountain, and then back at him. "I don't know. Take your choice. Both are impossible."

His hand turned in hers, bringing her bloody fingers up to his lips. He pressed a kiss to the back. It was an old-world gesture. Courtly, masculine, and possessive. So very Donovan in nature. Staring at the red snow beneath him, she had to blink back the tears again. He'd lost so much blood. Too much. Oh God, she didn't want to watch him die.

"You see both as impossible because you only believe what you can see, and everything else you relegate to fairy tales."

There was something strange about his eyes. A light expanded behind his pupils. Blacker than the rest of his iris, it glowed from within with an iridescent power. She took a deep breath, inhaling his scent. He always smelled so good. Her shoulder ached as if on fire. She couldn't look away. Couldn't breathe.

"I need for you to do something for me, Lisa."

"What?"

"I need you to set my arm."

He had to be kidding. He had a gaping hole in his side, a gash in his head, and Lord knows what internal injuries, and he was worried about his arm? "That can wait until we get to the hospital."

"It must be done now."

She looked at his arm, at the break just above the elbow that gave it such a bizarre bend. She opened her mouth, and then closed it. How could she tell him her fears? That he was dying out here in the wilderness with just her at his side? And all because he'd stepped in to save her. Again. "I don't know if I can do it." Because that sounded so callous, she amended, "At least, without vomiting."

This time, she didn't stop him when he reached up to cup her cheek. She needed the comfort of the gesture, because, God help her, she was going to set the break. It was the least she could do.

"You can do it."

Her smile felt as shaky as her confidence. "If it heals all funky, you can't hold it against me."

"You just get the bones in alignment, and I'll take care of the rest."

Like he could take care of anything. Lisa gently eased his coat away from his shoulder. His indrawn hiss of breath flayed her with guilt.

"I'm sorry."

"You're doing fine," he ground out. "Just get the coat off."

She did, as cleanly as possible, discovering it didn't do any good to blink against the tears—they came anyway, driven by every staggered breath he took, every twitch of muscle that accompanied the removal of the garment.

And when she was done removing his coat, she discovered it wasn't over. There was still the shirt in her way. Tears she couldn't stop overflowed her control, seeping into the outline of his hand, slipping beneath, bonding them together in this moment of pain and pointless hope. In a voice so tight it squeaked, she said, "I've got to take off your shirt now."

His thumb stroked across her cheekbone, gliding on the evidence of her guilt. "No, you don't. Just grab hold above and below the break and pull until you feel the ends snap into place."

She had a vivid imagination. It didn't take much speculation to figure out what that was going to feel like. Her gorge rose. She gave him a smile she hoped wasn't as green as she felt. "Piece of cake."

With hands that shook, she grabbed. His biceps were so big, his forearms so developed, she had little purchase. She dug her fingers in and pulled. Her hands slipped. Her nails raked across torn muscle.

"Pull harder," Donovan gritted out through clenched teeth.

What the hell did he think she was doing? "I am pulling hard," she snapped. "We can't all be muscle-bound hulks."

"Shit."

She let go. He collapsed against the snow. Only then did she notice the sweat beading his brow. More guilt.

I can't do this.

As soon as the thought entered her head, she pushed it back. The man had risked his life for hers, and all he was asking in return was that she set his damn arm. Sitting back on her heels, she studied the situation. "I need a brace."

He reached for his upper arm with his left hand.

If only that would do it. "That won't work. The angle is off."

Two feet behind him a rock jutted out of the snow. It was high enough, yet still small enough to do the job. However, that two feet might as well be two miles. He couldn't be moved. Donovan's glance followed hers.

"Good plan."

His knees came up and his heels dug into the ground. She made a grab for him. "Don't move! Your back could be broken."

"It's not."

"You can't know that."

His gaze met hers. That strange glow was more pronounced. "I'm aware of my injuries."

"But there could be some you can't feel."

"There are some things that you're going to have to accept are different for me, Lisa."

"I've got news for you, bud: once you get past the reproductive organs, there's not that much difference in our anatomy."

He didn't answer. Instead, he pushed himself across the ground.

She jumped up after him. "You're going to kill yourself!"

He kept his attention on his goal. "I thought you thought I was dead already?"

Her foot caught on a hidden root, pulling her up short. She yanked it free. Donovan made it to the rock before she reached him.

She dropped to the snow beside him. "You are a stubborn man, McGowan."

"And you're a beautiful woman."

He turned on his left side and she reached over, supporting the length of his arm as best she could on either side of the break. "Flattery will get you nowhere."

A rivulet of sweat dripped down his temple. She couldn't even imagine the pain he was in. He should be weak, his smile shaky. Instead his smile was as arrogant and as sexy as she'd ever seen it.

"Are you sure?"

She flexed her fingers, not able to touch him because touching meant committing to going forward with setting his arm. "Positive."

They stayed like that for a good minute, him waiting, her stalling before he shifted his shoulder into a better position.

"Seelie?"

The softness of his tone demanded that she look at him. She didn't want to. She knew what he was going to say. It was time. She raised her gaze to his, knowing she was going to expose herself for the coward she was. "What?"

Understanding was in his eyes. "Set the arm."

Like it was that easy. Just grab, yank, cause untold pain and lord knows what harm, and it would be all over. On the next flex, her fingers curled into her palms. Just . . . set the arm.

Lisa took another breath. It didn't seem big enough, deep

enough to sustain her through what she had to do. "Tell me again how easy this is going to be," she finally managed.

"You just grab my arm above the elbow and pull and the bone edges snap into place, slick as snot."

"You couldn't make that description a bit more attractive?"

"I'll do better next time."

"I've got news for you, there's not going to be a next time. As soon as we get out of here, I'm killing those two."

Donovan laughed, actually laughed.

"You'd better not be laughing at me."

She grabbed his arm. His left hand dug deep into the snow, anchoring himself. His "I'm not" was tight. She braced her hands and feet and took another breath. And then, on a whispered prayer, pulled. The bones snapped into place with a horrible, grating vibration. Donovan's whole body jerked and his breath snarled out.

"I'm sorry. I'm sorry." She couldn't stop saying it, couldn't stop stroking his chest through his shirt, brushing his hair off his forehead as he wrestled with the pain. She leaned forward and kissed that one clean spot on his cheek again, savoring the warmth of his skin, the proof that he was still alive. "I'm so sorry, Donovan."

Finally, his good arm came around her, pulling her down into his left side. His voice was hoarse as he said, "You did good."

Snow melted into her jeans and cold bit through her skin. She didn't care. She tucked her hand under his coat and lay against him, letting him hold her close, letting him comfort her with the slow brush of his hand down her arm. "I never want to do anything that horrible again."

His lips brushed her hair. "I know."

"What do we do now?"

"We wait."

She carefully angled her head back to see his face. All she got was a view of the underside of his jaw. "For hell to freeze over, and us with it?"

"No." His head tilted back. Tendons in his neck became more pronounced as tension entered his muscles. His hand paused in midstroke down her arm. "For me to heal."

"That will take weeks. I don't think we'll make that."

"Actually"—he eased her to the side—"I only need a few more minutes."

"That's not possible."

"For a wolf, it is."

A moment of dizziness assaulted her. She braced herself on her hand. Snow gave beneath her weight, and she lost her balance. There was an awkward moment during which Donovan steadied her. She wiped the snow out of her face. The chill went deeper than her skin.

"You're not a wolf."

His dark gaze didn't avoid hers.

"Yes, I am. A werewolf, to be exact."

He said that with such certainty that she would have called him a nut, except he stood with a grace that should have been impossible. As if he hadn't just tumbled down a mountain, as if he didn't have a huge gaping hole in his side.

The softness left his expression as he looked up the hill. "Buddy's friends are coming back."

He glanced down at her, the wildness she'd sensed on that first meeting settling into his features, changing him to something she didn't quite recognize. Something wild, primitive, and deadly. He cupped her chin in his fingers, his big body between her and the threat from the top of the hill. As if all that muscle and bone was any good against bullets.

"I want you to head over to those rocks and crouch down. Don't say a word and don't draw any attention to yourself. No matter what."

No matter what? That did not sound good. She shook her head, the move hampered by the grip he had on her chin. "I'm not leaving you."

He didn't let go of her chin, just forced her to keep her gaze on his, to see what she didn't want to accept. "You don't face the danger, Lisa. That's not how it works."

She stepped back. The wind blew his coat and shirt open, revealing the flat washboard of his abs. She couldn't look away. His abdominal muscles rippled with strength beneath his tanned skin. His *intact* tanned skin.

She blinked but nothing changed. The wound was gone. The only legacy was a dark line amidst the tanned flesh and the wash of drying blood fading into the denim of his jeans.

She took another step back, horror overriding fear. "What are you?"

With one stride, he closed the distance she'd put between them. "I'm wolf."

The claim took on impossible significance. "What does that mean?"

The demand came out a harsh croak.

"I'm a werewolf. And you need to get to safety."

"No." She didn't know if she were denying the impossibility of his claim or the impossibility of leaving him to fight alone.

He kissed her hard, his tongue sliding over hers, stealing her protest, leaving only a soft exhale of his name in its place. He pulled back. This close she couldn't miss the power emanating from him, or the glow in his eyes. The glow that marked him as something other than human.

"Later I'll explain everything to you, but you will obey me now."

"No." Of the hundred fractured thoughts and words scattered through her mind, that was the only one she could get out.

He pulled her into his chest, against the body she'd made love to the night before. The inhuman body.

"I can handle this, seelie." The stroke of his hand down her back was hauntingly familiar in the surreal landscape of her thoughts. So was the confidence in his voice.

"I'm a Protector. It's what I do."

Car doors slammed, snapping her out of her paralysis. Her hands balled into fists against Donovan's shoulder. Men were coming to kill them. She didn't need to deal with anything more devastating than that right now. She pushed away from Donovan's embrace. Feeling strangely calm, oddly detached, she asked, "Can you handle them?"

"Yes."

She bit her lip as shadows crested the hill, slithering over the snow, growing with every heartbeat. They only had seconds to come up with a plan. "What are you going to do?"

His eyes glowed. He touched the bruise on her cheekbone in a featherlight caress. "I'm going to kill them."

Eleven

LISA was in shock.

Donovan pulled his battered SUV into the driveway of the inn. Beside him, wrapped in his coat, Lisa huddled against the door, unmindful of the wind that whipped through the broken windshield, exhaustion emanating off her in waves. He supposed he should be grateful that he hadn't had to kill the men while she watched, that they had looked over the edge and panicked, tearing off in a roar. He couldn't imagine how much deeper Lisa's shock would have been had she seen him kill with his bare hands. His being wolf was going to be hard enough for her to accept without her witnessing that side of him unleashed.

"We're almost home."

Her only response was a faint nod of her head. The bruise on her cheek had darkened since the accident. He wanted to lean over and kiss it. Heal it. Heal her. The tires slipped in a rut. Yanking the wheel, he righted the vehicle. He wished he could right things between them as easily. "Are you going to talk to me?"

She made him wait until the car pulled up in front of the inn before giving him an answer as she reached for the door handle.

"No. I don't think so."

As fast as he was, she was faster. He rounded the side of the SUV just in time to catch her as she fell.

"You need to rest."

She looked at him vaguely. "Why?"

"Healing me took a lot out of you."

The door to the inn opened with a familiar squeak.

"I can't heal people."

"You can heal me."

He scooped her up in his arms. Her hands automatically crept around his neck.

"Why?"

"Sharing energy is part of the bonding between mates."

It was a measure of her shock that she didn't automatically deny the bond between them. He glanced down. The lack of response could also be attributed to the fact that she'd fallen asleep.

Footsteps sounded on the stairs. Snow crunched under light, feminine footsteps. Donovan didn't need to turn around to know who approached. The wind carried Robin's scent before her.

"My God, what happened?"

"We're fine, but a couple of Buddy's friends ran us off the road."

He headed for the house. Robin skipped to keep up. "Why?"

"I guess they take exception to him being humiliated by a woman."

"And they tried to kill her?"

"They were trying to kill me." He hitched his shoulder, keeping Lisa's head from lolling backward. "She was driving my truck."

"Like that makes it any better." Running ahead, Robin opened the door, looking at his bloodstained clothes. "Was she hurt?"

He stepped into the warmth of the house. The scents of cleaning products and freshly baked bread surrounded him. "Only when she tried to help me."

"There's no way you'd hurt her. You love her."

He stopped dead. "Lisa would say I haven't known her long enough to love her."

"Lisa would say a lot of things to avoid being vulnerable."

"You believe in love at first sight?"

She preceded him up the stairs. Keeping her hand on the rail for balance, she said over her shoulder, "I believe things work out the way they're supposed to, no matter how hard we try to change them."

There was an acceptance in her tone that raised the hairs on the back of his neck. He took in her pallor, the weariness with which she carried herself. The ugly bruise that had spread its yellow and green pattern over half her face. "And you believe you're fated to die?"

She grimaced. "Lisa told you, huh?"

"She worries about you."

"I know." They reached the landing. "I just wish—"

"What?"

She shook her head and sighed. "I just wish the date with Buddy had gone differently."

His head snapped up. "You couldn't possibly want to have slept with that bastard."

"No, it's just"—she stopped in front of Lisa's door, her hand on the knob—"I was so sick growing up, about all I could do was read." Her smile was shy, feminine, endearing. It hurt, hearing of her dreams while looking at the evidence of how the night had turned out. "I knew Buddy wasn't a prince. I was just hoping he could be princely for a night. Just long enough . . ."

She didn't finish.

"Long enough for what?"

She sighed. "For me to touch the edges of the magic you and Lisa have."

Before she died.

The unspoken words lay heavy between them. Hell. Robin deserved magic. She deserved life. It was not in his power to grant her the latter.

A light blush colored her cheek. Her gaze flashed to his. "Stupid, huh?

"No, just very human." He stepped through the door and headed for the bed. She followed.

"Lisa will be okay. She's just going to sleep for a few hours."

Her eyebrows rose. "And you know this, how?"

He laid Lisa on the bed. Human mates did not have the resiliency of were mates. Healing was often an instinctive thing for them. A sharing of which they had no control and which frequently ended with them giving too much, too fast. "I just know."

When he straightened, Robin was watching him with those too-old eyes. "You're more than you appear to be, aren't you?"

"No."

The brusqueness of his reply just made her grin. "That's okay. You don't have to tell me. I'm really good at figuring out puzzles."

"Leave this one alone."

"When it involves my sister?" She folded her arms across her chest. "I don't think so."

It was a complication he hadn't anticipated, hiding what he was from Lisa's family. The original plan had involved taking her away, maybe eventually into his pack. But that was no longer possible. He knew Lisa well enough to know that she would never leave her sister. He had a wolf's sense of family, which meant he would also never ask it of her. "You'd be happier letting it ride."

"Nah, mysteries drive me nuts."

Despite the gravity of the moment, he smiled. "Trust me, you don't want to unravel this one."

"You can have my trust when you have hers."

"Fair enough."

Pulling off Lisa's boots, he slid her lengthwise on the bed and pulled the covers over her. Convincing Lisa to trust him again was going to take some doing. He glanced at Robin. "I'm going to secure the house. Would you stay with her?"

She looked out the window. "You think they'll come here?"

He wouldn't put anything past the two. The house had too many entry points for one wolf to guard. He'd rest easier about security once Kelon arrived. To Robin, he merely said, "Nah, I'm just cautious."

Twelve

LISA was awake. Donovan stood outside the bedroom door and listened to the change in her breathing that signaled a return to consciousness. He reached for the doorknob, then hesitated. Uncertainty was a strange feeling for him. One he hadn't felt for a long time. Since he was a kid actually. It just went to show how a mate could change a man.

He opened the door. Lisa rolled to her side, her arm tucked under her cheek, a smile on her lips. Caught between sleep and aware, she obviously didn't remember what had happened that day. Donovan smiled back at her, wanting this moment of peace, knowing what was coming.

"You're awake?"

"What time is it?"

He braced his hand on the chair by the door and tugged off his right boot. "Three o'clock."

She yawned and stretched luxuriously. Midstretch, she frowned. "I napped?"

He made short work of his other boot, dropping it before

heading across the room. He stripped off his shirt with the same speed, dropping it by the bed. "You napped."

Her eyes went to his chest. He'd noticed she did that a lot. He ran his fingers through the light dusting of hair there. Her gaze followed every move. Her tongue came out to touch the bottom of her lip. His fingers stilled as his imagination took over.

He could easily imagine that moist little tongue flicking over his flesh like darts of fire, teasing his nipples, licking a path down his abs, before testing the strength of his muscle with the edge of her teeth. He reached for the fly of his jeans. Lisa stopped him with a smile and come-hither motion of her fingers. "Why don't you let me do that."

The jerk of his cock pulled him forward into the reach of her grasp and her hand surrounded him with heat. Even through the denim, his body reacted—searching, stretching, straining for the connection he needed. "It works for me."

Her smile was witchy, a lure unto itself.

"So I can see."

It was unfair to take advantage of her half-awake state, but then again, it was unfair of her to take advantage of his need for her. Seducing him with the touch of her hand, the press of her kiss through denim, the soft pop of the button, the quiet rasp of the zipper, the anticipation of her mouth . . .

"You're playing in dangerous territory, seelie."

Her eyebrows rose, accentuating the mischief in her eyes.

"What makes it so dangerous?" The thin blade of her nails trailed from his navel to the open fly of his pants. A burning whip of sensation sucked in his stomach. The back of her fingers touched the too-sensitive skin of his lower abdomen.

"Is it how much you like the touch of my hands on your skin?" She tucked her fingers behind the column of his cock, tantalizing him with the potential of contact. "Or maybe it's something else?" Her fingers curled, delivering a haunting touch to the all-too-receptive skin. "Maybe you want something more?"

Any man would give a lot to have a woman look at him the way Lisa was eyeing him. Like he was a prime piece of beef. Like he was the icing on her cake. Like he was her dream come true. Damn it. It figured his conscience would choose that moment to pipe up. Catching her hand in his, he pressed her palm to his cock, holding them together.

"It's dangerous because of how much I want you."

The confusion he expected to see in her expression didn't appear.

"With your body or with your mind?"

"Both."

A tilt of her head sent her hair cascading over her shoulder in a hiss like fine silk on skin. "As a werewolf or as a man?"

That answered one question—she remembered his revelation. "You didn't blank that out."

She squeezed him gently, her smile rueful. "You and everything about you tends to linger in the forefront of my mind."

If he hadn't seen the betraying flicker of her eyelashes he might have believed her display of unconcern. With a graze of his thumb across the back of hers, he gave her a silent order to keep it put. He shoved his pants off his hips. His shaft sprang free onto the soft warmth of her palm. She held him gently, cushioning him through the transition.

She hitched up against the pillows as he took a step forward. Her hair parted, revealing his mark. There was no way she missed the response as his whole body tightened. The sheet slid farther, helped along by her encouraging shrug. She caught it just before it crested her nipple, her expression too innocent to be believed. He bit back a curse.

"See something you like?"

The challenge in her grin snuggled right up along his dominant side, coaxing it out to play. Power and passion, lust and laughter, she brought it all out in him, all at once.

"Yup." He kicked his feet free of his pants, letting the emotion swell over him. "You, wearing my mark."

Her hand clenched on the sheet, bunching it up against her chest. Her finger stretched up to touch the spot. It was a study in contrast, the shadow of his mark against the whiteness of her skin, dark to light, hard to soft. He leaned over the bed, trapping her within the prison of his arms, breathing in her scent. Anticipating how good all those curves were going to feel against him, he caught a fold in the sheet and tugged. It slid down, revealing those lush breasts topped with hard peaks. Her hands came around his neck. Her back arched. Damn, but he loved it when she did that, offering herself without reservation.

"Is this where I'm supposed to act all scared of the big, bad wolf?"

Actually, it was, and the fact that she wasn't worried him. He lowered his chest against hers, shuddering as her breasts melted, soft as down, against his muscle.

"No, this is where we talk."

His tone wasn't even. His hands weren't steady. He could never remember being so tempted to abandon his honor.

"You've got me naked, in bed, and all you want to do is talk?"

He couldn't believe it either. "Yes."

"I hope you know you're totally ruining my illusions about the sexual stamina of werewolves."

Contrary to her words, there was nothing disappointed in her expression. She looked like a woman on the verge of a good time. Her lids lowered over her eyes, the blue deepening with anticipation. Her lashes fluttered as she took a breath, held it. Shit. She was breathing him in.

He dropped his forehead to hers, his blood burning through his veins, his mind consumed with one thought—*mine.*

He groaned. "Do me a favor."

"What?"

"When this is over, appreciate my sacrifice."

She sighed, nodded, and then dropped back onto the pillow. "Fine, as long as you appreciate mine now."

"Done." He brushed a strand of hair off her cheek. "What's going on in your head, Lisa?"

"Nothing. Absolutely nothing."

"Why?"

"Because I can't handle any more." She dug the heels of her hands into her temples. "I haven't even accepted that you're my lover, and now you want me to except that you're something off the Sci Fi Channel."

"A werewolf."

"Yes."

"Say it."

"Why?"

"So I can at least believe you have a handle on the concept."

"Saying it won't make a difference."

"Then humor me. What am I?"

She glared at him. "A werewolf, okay?"

As soon as the words left her mouth, the sense of disorientation hit Lisa. Hard and fast. Devastating. A werewolf wasn't human. She couldn't have a relationship with something that wasn't human. She couldn't. She glanced down Donovan's body, over the swell of his pectorals, his flat abs, the faint jut of his hip bones, the prominent thrust of his heavy cock. Everything about him was aggressive. His size, his passion, his personality. So much so that she should feel very threatened right now. But she didn't.

She just felt . . . cherished. From the second she'd met him, she'd never felt less. He aggravated her, made her burn with anger and snap with frustration, but he never made her feel uneasy or threatened. And no matter what, she felt valued. There was a possible explanation. "Are werewolves telepathic?"

"Not all."

"Are you?"

"No."

She closed her eyes in deep relief. "Thank goodness."

"You'd have a problem if I were?"

She nodded. "That would just be too freaky."

His eyebrows rose and a hint of a smile alleviated some of the intensity in his expression. "But my ability to shape-shift is not?"

"Honestly?"

"Yes."

"I'd prefer we just keep that little exhibition on hold for a bit."

Understanding softened the edges of his profile. "You need time?"

"Yes. Probably a lot of it. Is that going to bother you?"

"No."

"Even if I deliberately pretend at times you're just a regular human like everyone else?"

"Are you going to make me wear condoms?"

"Can you give me a disease?" She held her breath for his answer.

"No."

"Get me pregnant?"

"Not unless you want to be."

Now there was a tidbit of information she'd have to explore later. "Then, no. And for the record, I don't want to be pregnant."

He had a charming smile, and when he tilted his head like that and arched his brow just so, it nearly melted her into a brainless puddle of need.

"Are you sure?"

Thank God for nearly. "I'm positive. I have enough on my plate with this inn, Robin's health, and now, Buddy."

Who was turning out to be a much bigger problem than she had anticipated. She sighed. "I should never have humiliated him like that."

"Your mistake was in letting him live."

That was a pleasant thought. "True. I should have crushed his throat."

"It would have been a surer thing for you to put the cue through his eye into his brain."

She started to laugh, but then something in his expression stopped her. "Good grief, you're serious!"

"Among my people, the price for touching a were female is death."

"Well, it's not among mine." Though there were times when she thought it should be.

"You should know that I won't tolerate a threat to you."

She blinked, once, twice, and then a third time simply because she didn't know what to say to that. "You can't kill someone just because you think I might be hurt."

"I'm wolf."

"And I'm human." God, it was bizarre just saying that. "If you want a relationship with me, it's going to take compromise on both sides, which means what's normal for me has to come into this somewhere."

"I'm a Protector. It's not my nature to be passive."

"What's a protector?"

There was a pause, which went on a shade too long. He was prevaricating. "The equivalent of your police."

He was a police officer of a people who had laws that dealt in absolutes, who imposed death sentences for infractions against their women. "I'm gathering your society is pretty male dominated."

"So is yours."

"A few remnants are hanging on, but we've made large strides. Can you say the same?"

After a moment he shook his head. "But it won't be an issue. We'll be living here."

"Shouldn't that be discussed?"

"We'll discuss it if there comes a time to leave."

She frowned, turning her cheek away from his touch. "That sounded like an order."

"Wolf women obey their men."

She propped herself up on her elbows. "Then you had better prepare yourself for a culture shock."

He laughed, angling a thigh over hers. Heavy and solid, it effectively pinned her lower body. "Consider me shocked."

He wasn't taking her seriously. "I don't have an obedient bone in my body."

He came over her again, his cock nudging her thigh, gliding up the side, landing on top—thick, hard, and ready. "But you do present a lovely challenge."

He had no idea. She tossed her hair back, a flair of something deeply feminine rising at his tone. "I'm not in the mood anymore."

It was a lie, but he didn't have to know that.

"Really? It doesn't matter."

She tilted up her chin. "Just going to climb on and do your thing?"

He cupped her breast in his hand. She glanced down. It was big enough to encompass her whole breast. The rough pad of his thumb swept the tip. She saw the caress before she felt it, but when the sensation came, it came in a burning rush.

"You could say that." He didn't miss a moment of her response—the shiver, the internal flinch. "You liked that."

"Not enough to obey."

"Ah, so that's the way you want to play?"

"Who's playing?"

"We are, seelie, a very old game, and the one thing you don't have to worry about is that you're caught between the sheets with a man who can't give you what you need."

Thirteen

SHE was going to challenge him in bed. Donovan ran his hands through Lisa's hair and gathered the mass into his fist at the nape of her neck. Desire pounded at his temples. Exhilaration fed his need. His canines stretched and ached. He could tell from the way her hand went to his mark that she felt the burn of his claim. He wanted to mark her again.

He slid down her body, stopping along the way to press kisses to her lashes, the end of her nose, that tempting, full mouth . . .

Her lips parted, distracting him with the essence of her taste. He indulged, growing drunk on the flavor of her, the scent of her, the promise of her. He eased his lips from hers. "Did anyone ever tell you it's dangerous to tease a wolf?"

"Yes."

Her nails raked the nape of his neck. The sharp sting drove straight to his groin, gathering in his balls, feeding the hunger.

Her mouth nibbled at his in hungry little bites. "They just never said why."

He drank in the sensuality in her face, the lack of fear. She might be having difficulty accepting the reality of his existence, but she wasn't afraid of him. He nipped her lip, took her gasp as his, and then soothed the wound with a stroke of his tongue before deepening the kiss. No fear was good. He worked his hand beneath her before giving her the explanation she was waiting for. "Because they can run wild."

"Are you going to go wild?

Neither her scent nor her voice carried any undertones of fear. But anticipation? That was a different story. Both were loaded with that.

The growl started deep, riding the surge of pure lust. The plumpness of her buttocks filled his hand. Soft, sweet, and welcoming. His fingers slipped between. Her gasp was sweeter as he delved deeper. He gave her an answer as his fingertip found the tight rosebud of her anus. "Yes."

He smiled against her neck as a shudder shook her from head to toe. She liked that.

"Oh, God."

He pressed gently. "Just me. Donovan."

The next shiver tightened her voice to a high-pitched thread of sound. "I think that's more than enough for me."

The softness of her breast beckoned. "It will be."

Her back arched as she struggled, temporarily drawing her nipple away from his trajectory. He growled his displeasure. The scent of her arousal intensified, nearly drugging him past coherent thought. He shifted his hips until his cock felt the kiss of her engorged clit.

"What does that mean?" she gasped.

His fingers slipped lower, bathing in slick feminine heat. He nudged her shoulder with his. She fell back, her hair fanning out across the pillows in a wanton lure. "It means I'm going to claim you tonight." He slipped just the tips of two fingers inside her tight channel. Delicate muscles clenched, parted, and then fluttered in temptation. The hard bud of her nipple brushed his cheek. He turned his head, capturing it between his lips, compressing lightly, giving her that little edge she liked with her loving. Her thighs fell wide, giving him back what he liked. Submission.

"No complaints here."

Her tongue flicked over her lips, seeking the lingering evidence of his kiss. He watched as she found it, watched as the blue of her eyes deepened as the aphrodisiac in his saliva seeped into her system, readying her. His cock throbbed with a feral hunger as the inner wildness she kept hidden flared to life, pulsed against his touch, compelling an answering hunger in him. He took a breath, trying to slow the spiral. He needed her very ready. He couldn't hurt her. He pushed his fingers deeper. The abbreviated husk of his name was his reward.

"Good."

Withdrawing his fingers, he moved them back down to her anus, circling lightly, scenting her interest. Feeling her hesitation.

"Donovan?"

"It's all right, Lisa." He pressed; she resisted with a quick clench. "Just give yourself to me tonight, the way I need."

She did, with an arch of her spine, a pull of her hands.

"Totally. Any way I want."

Her muscles parted in the tiniest of invitations. He accepted it gently, pulse pounding in his temples, breath coming hard and fast as she tightened around him. "Any way you need."

The tension in her built, transmitting to him through the resistance of her inner muscles.

"Okay?"

"I don't know. I've never . . ."

What she was saying was slow to sink through the haze of desire. He had her nipple in his mouth, her ass in his hand. Everything inside him said to hurry, that she was ready. And she was trying to tell him . . .

Ah damn, she was a virgin there. He held perfectly still, absorbing the reality, the knowledge that he would be the first. "We'll take it slow."

The softness of her chuckle eased a bit of his need. He needed her softness. Welcomed it.

"Why do we need to take it at all?"

"Because it's the were way." He sipped her nipple, drawing it into his mouth and pressing it against the roof, watching her expression as he did, applying pressure until expectation broke into pleasure. Perfect. His cock jerked. Precome dripped from the tip. Perfect. She was so perfect.

With the same slow deliberation, he withdrew his mouth from her breast. "And because you want it."

"I'm afraid."

"You won't be."

The fight came back into her expression. "How do you know?"

Her muscles weren't so tight around him now. In a steady glide, he gave her the first taste of what was to come. Her eyes flew wide, and her breath exploded in a little gasp before her attention centered inward at the new sensation. He kissed her softly, gentling her through the shock, before whispering in her ear, "That's why. I'll come into you just like that and the pleasure will be ten times as intense."

"I don't think I can take it."

"You can take everything I have to give." A kiss under her ear conjured goose bumps on her skin. He followed the trail downward. "My body." The hollow of her throat needed testing, nibbling, kissing. So did the hollow between her plump breasts. A space redolent with the richness of her scent, the one uniquely hers. The only one that mattered. He paused, breathing her in, before slicing open his palm, pressing it to her mark. "My heart."

A burning ache spread from his hand, whipping up his arm, sinking into his chest. She could never be lost to him now. Where she went, he went. Linked in life and in death. He whispered the vow against the beat of her heart. "My soul to yours, in this life and the next. We are bound."

Her back arched under the whip of sensation. "Donovan!"

He trailed a string of kisses down the center of her abdomen, the thin vertical line defining the muscle, his guide to the lushness beneath. "What?"

"What if I can't love you like that in return?"

He smiled, resting his chin on her pubic bone, staring up between her breasts to the worry in her expression. "You already do."

The shake of her head was more of a thrash as he blew gently across the engorged nub of her clitoris. "I don't know what I feel."

He rested his thumb against her sensitized clit and rubbed in a slow circle. He loved the way she shivered under his caress. The way her gaze clung to his as if he were the only thing solid in her world. "I can wait until you do."

"You seem . . . to be planning . . . on doing a lot of . . . waiting." The last syllable rose to a wail.

"I'm a hunter. It comes with the territory."

Her thighs stiffened. A flush rose from her chest to her cheeks. She was close.

He hitched down a bit more, the drag of the smooth comforter against his cock a pale substitute for the silken heat of her pussy. He wasn't going to last much longer, but he had to know she was ready. "Don't come yet."

Her heels dug into the mattress, driving his finger deeper.

"Then don't make me!" It was more of a scream than an order.

The emotion that inspired it, and the passionate nature that flavored it, made him smile. He removed his finger and cupped her ass in his palms. Pulling her down until her hips were at the edge of the bed, he angled first one shoulder and then the other under her thighs. Her head fell back as he visually feasted on the sight before him. A perfect little pussy—hot and wet, swollen with need, topped with the most receptive of garnishes—her equally sensitive, equally hungry clitoris.

"Mine."

She grabbed at his head, caught a few strands of hair, and tugged him forward. "Then stop torturing me and do something with it."

His chuckle blew across the receptive flesh. He watched the distinctly feminine muscles clench and flower, begging in their own way for what he was only too eager to give.

It took the slightest of shifts to center the hard little protrusion against his lips. "Ask me nicely."

"Oh, God."

Her grip tightened. "Not what I'm looking for."

"What do you want?"

He couldn't resist curling his tongue around the engorged flange, handling her carefully, knowing how sensitive she was, wanting to tease, not send her over the edge. Not yet. Not until she gave him what his wolf needed to hear. If she couldn't admit her love, he needed her to admit her desire and his control of it.

He laved her in small circles, keeping it light. "You."

Her calves tightened behind his head in a vain attempt to pull him in. "You've got me."

Her muscles were no match for his. He paused, flattened his tongue, and let her feel his denial as well as see it. "I've got your body."

"What else is there?"

Cream spilled from her body, moistening his hand. "Your surrender."

"You said you'd wait."

"For your heart, but here in bed, you need to submit."

"I don't know how."

Yes, she did. Her desire to do just that was in every line of her body, the way she opened to him unconditionally. It was just her mind that wouldn't let go. "Just stop fighting me."

"And what?" She gasped as he lifted her hips. "Just do what you say."

"Yes." That was exactly what he needed. "I need that to hold me until you find the words."

He suckled her softly while she debated, keeping the rhythm erratic, not falling into a pattern she could build an orgasm on. The spicy sweet taste of her filled his senses, flowing into his blood in a wild, molten surge. She wasn't the only one who was close.

"Give me what I need, seelie. Give me your surrender."

Her fingernails scraped across the sheets as his canines raked across her clit. He expected her to come. She didn't, just gripped the sheets and negotiated in one last desperate bid. "Tell me what that means first."

She was one stubborn woman. He growled the answer. "One forever bound to my heart."

"Oh, damn." The tremble started in her core, spreading outward in ever-growing strength until she was coming hard against his mouth, muscles clenching, body weeping with the joy he'd given her. The beauty of her response had him on the verge of coming, too. He gritted his teeth and held it back, the burn driving him as he reversed his path, sprinkling hard, biting kisses up her stomach, over her breasts, her throat, until he reached her mouth, prepared to take what he needed, only to find her kiss waiting. Expecting a fight when he took the kiss over, he found, instead, only acceptance in the searing immediacy of her response. Damn, he loved her.

He adjusted his stance. His cock fell naturally against her still-twitching pussy. She opened her eyes, her palms cradling his cheeks while the urgency pounded through him.

"I'm sorry."

His voice, when he found it, was a tight growl. "We'll work on it."

Against his cock head, her pussy clenched hard. He cocked a brow at her. She smiled back. "I lose all control when you do that. Can we work on that to?"

"No. I like that just the way it is."

"I bet you do." Her gaze searched his for a heartbeat and then her hips tipped up, nuzzling his shaft into the well of her vagina. "Donovan, I need you."

He needed her to. He braced himself up on his arms. She placed her hands on his chest, stopping him.

"For more than that."

For the rest of his very long life, he wouldn't forget the way she looked right then. Shyness mixed with passion, determination blended with an aching vulnerability as she tucked her knees up against his stomach and pushed. Watching her carefully, he stepped back. His wolf howled a protest, sensing the rejection coming. He set his jaw, battling instinct and decency. It was too much. He'd given her too much to deal with. She was withdrawing.

Shyness still clinging to her like an invisible blanket, she turned over and knelt on the bed. Her gorgeous heart-shaped ass wiggled like a red flag in front of a bull as she shifted position. With a flip of her hair she glanced over her shoulder and asked, "Is this how it's done?"

The look was sassy, the tone sexy, but in her eyes he saw the nervousness. She was afraid, but she was offering him this anyway. Because he'd asked for it. Because he needed it. Because she wanted to prove to him that he mattered by giving him what he needed.

"Sometimes." It was all he could do to get the word out.

"I haven't done this—"

"I know."

A step forward was all it took to wrap her in his embrace, to pull her back against his heart. To hold her small body beneath his, his cock nestled into her slick heat, her delicate ribs contracting and expanding against his chest while their combined scents wrapped around them. The nape of her neck was very white and so vulnerable. "You don't have to do this."

She turned her head. Her kiss landed awkwardly against his cheek. "This is not the part where you talk. This is the part where you take advantage before I lose my courage."

She was afraid of losing her courage. She who'd walked into a bar and taken on the man who had hurt her sister. His heart twisted. She who dared to take on a werewolf for a mate, was afraid of losing her courage. "You've given me everything I want, and someday, when you're not nervous, when you're not proving a point more to yourself than to me, you can give me this." A stroke of his hand over her buttock made her jump. "But for now, I want this."

"What's this?"

He nudged his cock forward, growling deep in his throat as he slid into her slick heat.

"You burning in my arms, offering me your trust and a future together."

She moaned and arched back, taking him deeper into her ultratight channel, milking him with muscles that rippled in delight as his cock jerked and throbbed with the same ecstasy, his balls aching, needing to come inside her, to mark her with his seed the way he'd marked her with his scent and teeth.

"You make it sound like a lot," she gasped.

He pulled out and plunged back in, forging deeper, needing to be deeper, so deep there'd be no telling where one ended and where the other began. So deep she'd feel his presence long after he left. So deep they'd always be one.

Stretching along her back, he set his teeth to the shadow of his mark, tasting her blood, their desire. Just before he bit down, he growled the truth. "It's everything to a wolf."

THE knock on the door came just before Lisa fell asleep.

"What is it?"

"It's Robin. Are you two coming down to supper?"

At the thought of food, her stomach rumbled. Behind her, Donovan laughed. His big hand opened over her abdomen as he inched closer. "I'd say that was a yes."

She couldn't get used to how easy he was with her body. "And you couldn't eat?"

His cock slipped between her butt cheeks, sliding along the crease, the fat head catching on her anus, inspiring a dark, forbidden hunger.

"I could eat food or you." The brush of a callus over her well-loved clit made her jump. "It's your choice."

There was a pause. Donovan was waiting. Robin was waiting. Clearing her throat, Lisa found her voice. "Maybe in a bit."

Her response had been more air than sound due to Donovan working that big cock along her crease as he milked her clit in an easy rhythm. It was doubtful that Robin heard. His shaft caught on her anus again, but this time it didn't move on. This time it stopped and pressed. Terrifyingly huge, impossibly tempting.

She gave up answering at all as desire exploded in her womb. Her whole body jerked as the repercussions shot outward in searing whips of hot sensation.

"Yes," he growled, pulsing against her. "Just like that, seelie. Welcome me just like that."

She didn't have a choice. Something deep inside her thrilled at the thought of giving herself to Donovan this way, wanted it, burned for it. She dug her nails into his hand, holding it against her stomach as she felt the tight ring relax that first little bit, felt his cock fill the shallow dent, take it over, demand more . . .

"We'll be out in a bit," Donovan called, his hand slipping lower.

"Oh, all right."

Even muffled by the door, Lisa could make out the wistful tone. It was so unfair that her sister had nothing, while she had everything. That Robin's only date had ended in a disaster and pain. That she could die without even knowing what it felt like to laugh with a man. She held Donovan's hand tighter as he leaned across her, reaching for the nightstand drawer, and blinked back tears.

"I wish Buddy hadn't been such a tool. I wish she'd gotten to experience at least a little thrill that comes with a first date."

The drawer closed with a soft click. Leaning in, he kissed her cheek. Out of the corner of her eye she could see the white tube of lubricant he'd retrieved.

"Don't worry, I've got someone in mind for her."

He did? "Who—?"

His finger circled her clit, pulling her nerves tight with expectancy. His breath wafted over her ear in an erotic prelude. "We'll talk about it later."

Kelon

One

YOU need to clean up."

Kelon took the pants Donovan handed him, feeling the bite of the wind against his sweat-slick skin now that he was out of his fur and in human form. "Any particular reason you felt compelled to jump on me with that as soon as I arrived?" he asked as he stepped into them.

"Yeah." Donovan frowned, tossing him a blue shirt. "You look like something the cat dragged in."

Kelon cocked an eyebrow at his twin as he zipped the jeans. "Worried I'm going to scare off your little human?"

To his surprise, Donovan smiled. A genuine smile. "Lisa's more the type to hand you your balls for breakfast than to run in fear." He handed him socks and boots. "But you can try to scare her off if you'd like."

There was only one reason Donovan would encourage him to be anything but welcoming to his mate. "She's the type to stick like a burr if told to 'beat it,' isn't she?"

Donovan's smile spread. "Yup."

Kelon stomped the right boot on and slid on the second. "If

she's your mate, why are you looking for ways to make her stay?"

"She's human. Commitment for them is more of a process than an instinctive recognition. I'm for anything that will speed up the process."

Kelon stomped the second boot. "Which translates into . . . ?"

"She hasn't accepted with her mind what she's already committed to with her body."

"That's got to gnaw at you."

Donovan tossed him a down parka. "A bit. But she'll work up to it."

Kelon shrugged into it. "Since when did you become an optimist?"

Glancing toward the big Victorian house in the middle of the clearing surrounded by heavy-limbed, towering pines, he smiled. "Since about four days ago."

Kelon had to admit it was a very picturesque image, with the French windows casting patterns of mellow light over the new snow and the gingerbread trim framing those shadows with the illusion of lace, but it wouldn't make him smile like a sap.

"Uh-huh." Now probably wasn't the time to bring up the possibility it might not be a true mating. Kelon raked his hand through his long black hair, jerking when he hit a knot too thick to be called a snarl. Maybe Donovan was right. Maybe he could use some cleaning up. "It could just be lust, you know."

He wanted it to be lust. He didn't want to lose his brother.

Donovan cocked an eyebrow at him. "It could just be the real thing, too."

The cold wind blew down off the mountain, kicking up curls of snow between them, circling Kelon in a chill of foreboding. When Donovan got that expression on his face, it meant he'd made up his mind and it didn't matter if he was looking at fact or fiction. Donovan was one stubborn bastard when he decided on something. Kelon pulled the shirt closed and buttoned it with efficient movements. "What makes you so sure?"

"She took my mark, Kelon."

Shit. No wonder Donovan looked like a man who had the world at his feet. A woman taking a man's mark was proof positive the mating was solid. "Congratulations."

"You could try putting a little more enthusiasm behind your congrats."

"It's hard to be enthusiastic, knowing the price you'll be paying." Donovan met his glare calmly, none of Kelon's frustration showing in his expression. And why shouldn't he? He'd had days to adjust while Kelon had only a matter of a few hours to absorb the reality, thanks to Wyatt's waiting until last night to drop the bomb that Donovan had found a human mate. He raked his hand through his hair again. "Goddamn, Donovan. She's going to cost you everything. You'll be packless. Shunned. Alone in the world."

"No, he won't."

Conviction, anger, and aggression snapped out of the bushes behind and to the right of Donovan. A small woman with light brown hair, big blue eyes, and a nicely rounded figured stepped into view. Her scent and her manner marked her as human. Unlike a wolf female, she didn't drop her gaze from his, just squared those slender shoulders, notched up her chin, and took a position just in front of Donovan. As if her fragile human body was a barrier to anything.

"He'll have me."

Donovan caught the woman's hand and tugged her back, frowning down at her.

"I thought I gave you orders to stay inside."

"Technically, you told me to stay put until your brother arrived." She shrugged. "Not only did I wait until he arrived, I waited until he was dressed. Is this your brother?"

"Yes." He tucked the woman under his shoulder. "Kelon, this is my mate, Lisa Delaney."

Lisa looked between them and frowned. "I thought you said he was your twin?"

"Under that hair and beard, he is."

She narrowed her eyes. A germ under a microscope had never been so minutely analyzed. Then, she shook her head. "You have to find someone else. Robin will never go for him."

It was a new experience, being found lacking by a woman. Kelon leaned against the tree trunk. "Who's Robin?"

Neither Donovan nor Lisa paid him any mind.

"She needs someone handsome and kind. Not rasty and angry."

"Trust me, he cleans up well."

"Will a bath clean up his attitude?"

"Probably not. He's not big on humans."

"He doesn't like humans?"

"He doesn't like anyone."

Lisa slammed her hands down on her hips. "And that's a recommendation?"

"Recommendation for what?" Kelon asked.

Lisa barely spared him a glance as she snapped, "To date my sister."

I came here to kick some ass, not court it," Kelon interjected, just in case that fact mattered to anyone. It didn't appear that it did.

"I told you to let me handle it," Donovan drawled, lifting Lisa's face to his with a finger under her chin.

"That was back when I thought you had taste." The look she cast Kelon was eloquent.

Donovan growled his displeasure at the challenge to his authority. Lisa jumped and her chin lost a little of its elevation as the air sweetened with her response, but by no stretch of the imagination could anyone call her cowed. His brother's mate was more fire than water and clearly had yet to be educated in proper pack behavior, the number one rule being females did not challenge males. There were sound reasons for the rule. Male wolves were aggressive and dominant. While law demanded they keep that side of their personalities under control while around their females, there was always the danger they wouldn't. Since the penalty for hurting a female was death, a female's compliance was necessary for harmony to be maintained within the pack.

Something Lisa obviously didn't believe in as she matched her mate glare for glare. Finally, Donovan sighed, cupped her cheek in his hand, and shook his head.

"You're reckless."

The softness in the reprimand was more telling to Kelon than a thousand words. His hard-as-nails, just-as-soon-kill-you-as-look-at-you brother was in love. With the forbidden—a human.

Oblivious to the cultural concession his brother was making, Lisa shrugged. "You like it."

"In bed, yes. Out of it, no."

This time the glance she cut Kelon was horrified. "Donovan!"

It was a purely feminine cry of distress. His brother's reaction was predictably wolf. He laughed and tugged her against his chest. She went with no resistance, her manner implying complete trust. While Donovan—well, Kelon had never seen Donovan smile like that. As if the world was right. As if peace had found him.

He sighed as the grim reality settled in. Donovan wasn't coming back. He'd found his mate, and the pack would just have to accept it and move on. Hell, he was going to have to accept it. His partner, his brother, from here on out would be ostracized. Shit, it was his duty as Protector to ostracize him. Kelon pushed away from the tree, anger and loss whirling inside him, demanding an outlet. "Did you call me here to kill someone or to watch you make goo-goo eyes at each other?"

"Which would you prefer?" Donovan asked.

"To kill someone."

Lisa gasped. "You can't just decide to kill someone."

Kelon cocked an eyebrow at her. "Actually, I can."

Crossing her arms over her chest, she shook her head at Donovan.

"He's *so* not going to do for Robin. She doesn't even believe in killing spiders!"

Kelon had to agree. Donovan must have lost his mind. "And you want *me* to take her out?"

"Not only that, I want you to show her magic."

Magic wasn't in his repertoire. "I think I'll just go back to the mountains."

He didn't begrudge his brother his happiness, but he was a Protector to his bones. And with Donovan out of the running, the responsibility to guard the pack, to uphold pack law, and to continue his line fell on him. Dating humans too unsocial to get a partner among their own kind was not in his job description.

Donovan motioned toward the house. "You might want to meet her before you make such blanket statements."

From here, Kelon could make out a small silhouette standing in the doorway, staring out into the darkness. The woman must be as ugly as sin if no human would date her. "Why?"

"I don't think she's quite what you're imagining."

What he was imagining wasn't pretty. "Hell, I hope not."

Two

SHE wasn't ugly. Far from it. As a matter of fact, Robin Delaney was the softest thing Kelon had ever seen. Soft scent, soft mouth, softly rounded figure, so far from wolf as to be the opposite. She stood in the doorway of the big Victorian, light from the interior framing her in a golden halo, and summoned his soul from his body with the wistful smile that touched her mouth as she observed Donovan and Lisa's linked hands. He wanted to kiss the sadness from her lips, wrap himself in the nectar of her scent, deliver happiness to her eyes. Instinct pushed him back into the shadows as her impact rolled over him. Danger. Heaven. Death. Life.

He studied her, looking for the source of the threat, finding instead more details that pleased. From this distance, he couldn't make out the color of her eyes, but her long hair was brown, without a hint of wave, her nose small, her chin pointed, and her lips beautifully full and shaped in a plump bow. He couldn't take his eyes off her, and stayed out of sight until the last possible moment, studying her, memorizing her, imprinting every detail in his mind. There was something fascinating about the way she moved, a graceful femininity that made his palm itch to test the curve of her shoulder, her breast, her thigh . . .

She stepped aside, smiling at something Donovan said as he climbed the porch steps. The light caressed her cheek, highlighting the yellow green residue of a bruise. A snarl rumbled in his chest. Someone had dared to touch her, mark her with violence. His claws extended. Bloodlust rose.

The woman spun around, peering into the darkness. "Who's there?"

Her voice stroked along his libido, the little husk in the depths catching on his interest, heightening it. The touch of fear pulled him forward with the need to soothe it.

Lisa glanced behind, frowning when she didn't immediately find him, and cast a questioning a look at Donovan. He merely shrugged. "We were just showing Kelon the property."

"In the dark?"

"He's impatient." Lisa shielded her eyes from the porch light. "Kelon?"

"Who's Kelon?"

"My brother. He stopped to look at something."

"Stopped to look at what?"

Kelon stepped out of the shadows into the light, not taking his eyes off Robin's face. He needed to know the color of her eyes. "It was more like I was trying to avoid being a voyeur. These two definitely have a problem keeping their hands off each other."

The woman stared at him, making him aware of his beard and his uncombed hair. She took a step back. The welcome faded from her smile. Fear scented the air.

It was wrong that she feared him. Kelon took one step, and then another, drawn forward by an intriguing element to her scent. An element he'd never smelled before but recognized anyway. Way down deep in a part of him that had given up hope, he recognized that fragrance.

For every step he took forward, Robin took one back, but her steps were smaller than his. *She* was much smaller than him. Small, fragile, and intriguing. Her face was rounded, maybe a little more than was fashionable. Her figure definitely was. She had full breasts that pressed heavily against the soft material of her scooped-neck shirt. Breasts that would fill a man's hands no matter how big they were. Her hips flared in a lush curve from the bottom hem of her shirt, blending into thighs that were also deliciously rounded, tempting, perfect to take a wolf's bite. And her eyes. He drew in her scent, holding it in his lungs as he got close enough to see her eyes.

Her eyes were a bright sky blue, with darker flecks in the middle. The bottom step creaked under his weight. She gasped and backed up against the doorjamb. Donovan cut him a warning glare. Kelon didn't care. No warning look could keep him away from the secret she kept. No way anything could keep him from her. He was wolf, a Protector, and she was . . . She was unique.

He started to touch the brim of his hat before he remembered he wasn't wearing one. "It's nice to meet you, Robin."

The words came automatically, a knee-jerk conditioning, when in reality his focus was on the feedback from his senses, the scratch of her nails along her jeans, the increased rate of her respiration, the taint of fear. His wolf cataloged everything about her that called out to the primitive within him, pausing as something new entered the maelstrom. Recognition. The knowledge slammed through him. He recognized her.

With her back against the wall, she came out fighting. Her chin went up a notch and she took a step forward. Closer.

"It's nice to meet you, too."

Her voice flowed over him like honey, a touch of accent drawing out the "you." He could only stare at her as the enormity of what he was looking at pounded into his psyche. His mate. He had a mate.

Glare from the porch light reflected off the trepidation in her eyes and the highlights in her hair. He would have expected red streaks to match her sister's, but it was strands of blonde, glowing like touches of sunlight that framed her intriguing face. A face that wore a bruise. His wolf snarled. His hands clenched as he cleared the last step. "Who did this to you?"

Donovan stepped into the periphery of his vision. Robin shook her head, her gaze darting right and left. She had nowhere to go. The building was behind her and he was in front of her. There was nowhere she could run that he wouldn't find her.

Donovan stepped between them, elbowing Kelon back. "I apologize for my brother. He can be single-minded."

"It's all right." The tremble in her voice said it was anything but.

"Donovan?" Lisa called.

"I've got it."

Kelon's reaction to the threat was immediate. He snarled.

In a voice so low none but another were could hear, Donovan said, "Get hold of yourself."

"Stay away from her." No other male should be near her.

Donovan's jaw set. "You're scaring her. Stand back."

"No." If anything, he needed to be closer.

"Your lust is clouding your brain."

No, it wasn't. For the first time ever, Kelon's mind was perfectly clear. He knew exactly what he had to do. Exactly what he wanted. Saw clearly where he was going. That all paths led to her.

Donovan edged him back with a shoulder to his chest. To an outsider it might look like two brothers sharing a joke, but in reality the only thing keeping him from snatching Robin up was Donovan's determination.

"Keep scaring her and she'll run," Donovan grunted, tossing a smile over his shoulder at Lisa.

"Then I'll catch her."

"Your suit would go a lot smoother if you'd just court her."

The rumbling in Donovan's chest reminded Kelon that, by pack law, Robin was under Donovan's protection. That was going to complicate things. Donovan took his responsibilities seriously, and no male, not even a brother, would get around his Protector's dedication to duty.

Kelon took one breath, then two, scenting Donovan's aggressive determination, scenting Lisa's nervousness and Robin's apprehension. The scent he clung to was Robin's. His true mate.

A little of the wildness settled as thought took over from instinct. He'd found her. She was his gift, presented to him by destiny. Her value was immeasurable, and she had the right to have her worth proven through courtship.

With a jerk of his chin, Kelon nodded his acceptance. He would court her. Donovan didn't immediately relax. That happened over the span of several seconds. Finally, Donovan stepped aside, but he watched him.

He didn't have to worry. His mind wrapped around his purpose, Kelon was back in control. Putting a smile on his face, mentally running movie dialogue through his head for an appropriate line that would please a human female, he extended his hand. "I've been out in the wilderness too long. My manners are lacking. I didn't mean to scare you."

A were female would have followed her first instinct and stayed away from him, but Robin wasn't wolf, she was human, and apparently humans followed their hearts over their heads. He made a note of the tendency as she placed her hand in his. He also made a note of the way Lisa watched warily. Lisa's opposition wouldn't change anything, but her interference could delay the inevitable conclusion to his courting.

"No harm done."

"I was rude"—he didn't let go of her hand—"and seeing you standing here so sweetly knocked the sense from my head."

Behind him Donovan groaned. Lisa rolled her eyes. Robin blinked, but she didn't look away and she didn't tug at her hand.

"I'd like to make it up to you by cooking supper. Unless you've already eaten?"

He was reasonably sure they hadn't since there were no smells of dinner in the house. To a were female he would have brought a symbolic fresh kill to indicate his interest. For Robin he would cook dinner. Same idea, less messy. He steered her through the door. She glanced over her shoulder to Donovan.

"I'm not sure . . . ?"

"Hell, if Kelon's cooking, you just want to sit down and let your taste buds anticipate the paradise coming your way."

This time Kelon's smile was genuine. He always could rely on Donovan's appetite to swing things to his side of a point.

"You can cook?" Robin made it sound like he'd said he could walk on water.

"I like the creative aspect." And the dexterity exercise when it came to the knives and chopping.

She relaxed slightly. Another glance over her shoulder at Donovan, and then she relaxed completely, gracing him with her first smile. "How creative? You don't make it too outlandish to eat do you?"

"Show me the way to the kitchen, and I'll give you a taste of what I can do."

She paused in the middle of the old-fashioned parlor, looking completely at home amidst its antique furniture. There was a graciousness in the way she held herself that reminded him of women from a century past. A woman of hearth and home. A woman to come home to.

"Do you want to clean up first?"

The way she kept staring at his beard and then quickly looking away told him that might be a good idea.

"I'd love a shower and shave, but first let me get you something to tide you over, okay?"

"Do we get some, too?" Donovan asked.

Kelon caught Robin's gaze. "Do you want to share with them?"

"Of course."

"You don't have to. I know my brother's intimidating, but I can take him."

He ignored Donovan's "In your dreams" and focused on the budding understanding in Robin's eyes. It was just dawning on her that he was interested in her. What in hell was wrong with human men? A woman this sweet was a treasure. He rubbed his thumb across the back of her hand. The softness of her skin sank to his bones. His cock ached with the need to feel all that creaminess against him.

Her gaze dropped to his groin. The red-hot blush that immediately stained her cheeks let him know she'd noted his arousal. A hard thing to hide for any wolf. More so for him.

He caught her gaze, not allowing her to look away, letting her feel a hint of the wildness prowling inside, letting it draw her to him. "If you want it all, I'd be happy to give it to you."

Her eyes were a brilliant blue against the red of her cheeks, but embarrassed or not, she didn't back down, just gave him a smile that set his blood to pumping and said, "Maybe I should wait and see how you handle dinner before I answer that question."

"It's a standing invitation."

More color hit her cheeks, and along with it came his first scent of her arousal. Clean, earthy, and spiced with a unique feminine tang, it was just as endearing as she was. His pleasure with the bit of intimate knowledge rumbled out of him on a low growl. Donovan slapped him on the back, cutting off the betraying noise.

"No fair unduly influencing the decision by flirting."

"Who's flirting?"

Another slap on his back, harder this time. "You are."

Robin's smile was cautious and maybe hedged with a bit of hopeful awareness? "Don't stop on my account."

Kelon flicked his finger down her cheek, trying for lightness when everything in him was heavy and dark. "I won't."

Her gaze clung to his. He didn't like the dark circles under her eyes, nor the something he could detect in her scent that wasn't quite right.

Her "Good" was breathless, her smile brighter as she stepped back. Letting her go was the hardest thing he'd done in a long time.

"The kitchen's this way."

He studied her as she walked ahead of him, his focus only partially on the delectable fullness of her rear. He was more concerned with the weakness that was revealed in her scent. Now that he was paying attention, her footsteps were a little heavier than normal and she had a way of resting her hands on flat surfaces as she passed, as if she was steadying herself. She wasn't well. Standing in the doorway, she motioned him into the kitchen.

It wasn't an accident that his shoulder brushed hers. The little gasp she released was music to his ears. Even better was the grin she shared with him during the moment of awareness before he entered the room. She was shy, but not fearful, and definitely open to his pursuit.

A quick glance around the kitchen revealed any pot he could possibly need hanging from the rack in the center of the spacious room. The refrigerator and the stove were placed for efficiency of use. He was glad to see the latter was gas. Opening the refrigerator showed it was well stocked. He looked up. Robin was still standing across the way, leaning against the doorjamb.

Rifling through the cupboards, he grabbed the ingredients he needed and tossed them on the cutting board. Robin watched every move with the same fascination that he watched her. Floorboards creaked in the hall. No doubt Lisa and Donovan catching up. Robin smiled over her shoulder at their approach. The iron skillet clattered on the metal stove, obscuring Donovan's voice. Robin froze and then stiffened.

He waved to the stools on the other side of the counter. "Come keep me company."

She approached cautiously, her once open smile now stiff. He didn't know what she'd overheard Donovan saying, but he did know one thing: he was going to kick his ass for whatever Donovan had said to take the joy from her face.

"I'm really not that hungry."

Rolling up his sleeves, he pretended he hadn't noticed the change in her demeanor. Snagging a glass from the drying rack, he poured her some juice. "You can keep me company then."

"There's no need for you to cook for me."

"It'd be my pleasure, and anything you don't want, you can throw to Donovan. He can always eat."

"So can Lisa."

"Really?" He watched as she crossed the room. "A body couldn't tell from looking at her."

The smile faded from Robin's face. "She can eat anything and not gain a pound."

She wrapped her fingers around the glass and sighed. It wasn't hard to see where her mind was going. He knew the plumpness of her figure was not popular among humans. But he wasn't human. He was wolf. And wolf women tended to be lean and muscular, very fit. Stunningly beautiful, but for a man who craved softness, not his ideal.

"I suppose, if the man is into that type, that would be a good thing. But . . ." He waited until had her attention, and then he let his gaze slide slowly, deliberately over her rounded shoulders, plump breasts, and full hips. "Every man's different."

Robin shifted uncomfortably in her chair and her flush returned, along with the sweet spice of her arousal.

"Where do you keep the flour?"

"In the canister on the counter," Lisa said, giving him a cautious look and pulling up a chair beside Robin. Donovan settled himself on Robin's other side.

"What are you making?"

"Don't question the cook." He motioned to the glass in front of Robin. "Drink."

Her head dropped down, and he had a glimpse of her lips set in a straight line before her hair fell forward, obscuring his view.

Donovan shifted in his chair. The wooden legs creaked in protest.

"Just ignore him when he starts spouting orders, Robin. That's what the rest of us do."

Her head came up and she cut a glance at him out of the corner of her eye. "Does he always give orders?"

"When he thinks he knows what's best, yes."

She tilted her head to the side. "And you think I need this juice?"

"Yes."

He measured flour, salt, and baking powder into the bowl. He spooned in shortening.

"Why?"

He mixed the shortening in with his fingers, working it down to fine crumbs. "From the way your words stick when you talk, and from the dryness of your lips, I can tell you're dehydrated. I'm guessing from the way you keep a steadying hand on the furniture around you that you feel a little light-headed." He motioned to the glass. "Juice has fructose for your dizziness and liquid for your dehydration."

For a heartbeat she stared at him. "You noticed all that in the few minutes you've been talking to me?"

He set the bowl aside. "Yes."

Another pause, during which she just stared at him, no change in her expression, and then she grinned, revealing the mischief in her soul. Damn, he loved a woman who liked mischief.

"I bet you like to do puzzles."

It was his turn to stare. Not many people knew that about him. "I do, but only the three-dimensional ones. The flat ones are too easy."

She ran her fingers up and down the side of the glass, catching the condensation on the tips and spreading it around. It was all too easy to imagine those fingers on his cock, doing the same. It was a unique experience. He'd never been jealous of a juice glass before.

He added enough water to make the dough elastic.

"I like the three-dimensional ones, too."

It was the most awkward opening a woman had tossed his way in a long time. It was also the most endearing, and the way she blushed and held his gaze in the aftermath as she waited for rejection raised every one of his protective instincts.

"If you've got one around, we can work on it after supper."

The flush on her cheeks blossomed to crimson and then scarlet when Lisa jumped on the opening.

"I think that's a wonderful idea. It'll be fun for you to have someone to do the puzzles with. They've just been sitting around since Heather went back to work."

Kelon winced internally. It couldn't be more obvious that Lisa thought he'd have to be forced to spend time with Robin. And there wasn't a damn thing he could do to counter the impression right now.

Caught between a rock and a hard place, Robin didn't look the least enthusiastic anymore. Kelon had to give her points for managing to hold on to her smile.

"Yes, it will."

"As a matter of fact—" Lisa began. Donovan grabbed her hand.

"Seelie?"

"What?"

"Shut up."

She looked around, saw Robin's expression, and gasped. "Oh heck, that came out wrong. I didn't mean that at all the way it sounded. I'm sure—"

This time Kelon cut her off. "That I was thrilled Robin beat me to the punch and offered an opportunity for me to get to know her better?"

"Um, yes."

"Then you'd be right, but in the hope that Robin will stop blushing before she turns into ash, could we drop the subject?" After separating the ball of dough into three equal parts and tossing a section of paper towel to the people in front him, he gave them each a ball of dough. "Make those into one-inch balls for me."

Donovan looked over as Lisa rolled hers in response to the directive. "See, even when he's being polite, he's giving orders."

To Kelon's surprise, Robin leapt to his defense. "Just like someone else I know."

For a man as bossy as all get-out, Donovan could put on a damn good act of looking innocent. "And who would that be?"

"As if you didn't know." Rolling eyes was apparently a family habit, but in Kelon's opinion, Robin did it a lot cuter than her sister. Looking over at Donovan, she plopped a ball of dough on the board in front of him.

"Is that good?" she leaned in, comparing her ball of dough to those Kelon had made. Leaning over provided him with a peek down the front of her shirt. If she was trying to seduce him with her cleavage, he was there. The deep valley was redolent with her scent, tempting in the erotic possibilities it presented.

"Perfect."

Her gaze followed his. With a little gasp she slapped her hand on her chest. Even her hand turned him on, half the size of his without the hard calluses and even the harder memories that tainted it. And lying where it was, he could think of all sorts of ways she could titillate herself while he undressed.

Donovan cleared his throat. Kelon swore under his breath. He was coming on too strong. Likely there was no instant recognition for her. Humans didn't think like wolves.

For the first time since he'd walked in the door, reality sank in. Like his brother, he might have found his mate, but she was human. If he pursued his interest, he was going to have to restructure everything in life he held dear. Likely give it all up. To do . . . what?

Robin sat back, reminding him she was waiting on his verdict.

"Hmm, perfect." He took a dough ball and rapidly flattened it into a thin pancake and tossed it in the oil. It cooked with a slow sizzle. After a couple seconds, he turned it over. When it was done he put it on paper towels to drain. He reached for another ball, only to find Robin efficiently fielding the ones Donovan and Lisa were tossing her.

Passing him one, Robin asked, "Can I ask what you're making?"

"I figured I'd make quesadillas to tide you over until supper is ready."

"You don't even know what we have to make supper with."

He shrugged. "I can come up with something. I'm good in the kitchen."

She didn't catch the next two balls. They flew by like Frisbees. She slid off her stool and darted around the counter just as they slipped over the edge. He reached for them at the same time. His reflexes were faster and he got there first. When she swayed as she started to stand, he wrapped his arm around her waist and steadied her. A glance at the table confirmed his suspicion. "You didn't finish your juice."

"I know."

The hands she raised to her brow were shaking. Both Donovan and Lisa were staring at her with concern, but not shock. Kelon got a sick feeling in his gut. There was more going on here than he'd suspected. He took the tortillas off the heat and led her back to her chair. "You all right?"

She nodded. "I just got a little dizzy there for a moment."

As soon as things were more settled between them, they were going to have a talk about her tendency to lie.

He pushed the juice toward her. Her bruised cheek caught his attention, and his fingers burned to touch the damaged skin. The glands under his tongue swelled with the need to heal her. He clenched his teeth against the urge. He wasn't an impulsive man, but around her he seemed to be more instinct than thought. He didn't like the feeling. He was much more comfortable with calm logic.

It didn't help his temper one bit that Donovan noticed his discomfort and was amused by it. If he didn't have more pressing things to deal with, he'd take his twin out back and wipe that gloating grin off his face. Or at least try. Truth was, they were pretty evenly matched.

"Drink the juice."

That got a rise of Robin's eyebrow, but no drink. He waited until she took a sip, and then finished up the appetizer, every few minutes motioning for her to take another sip until the glass was empty.

"If someone can show me the way to the shower, I'll clean up, then get started on our supper."

"I can make supper," Robin said. He caught her gaze and shook his head.

"You don't have to do anything but relax. I'll take care of things."

His "From here on out" was a silent addition in his own head.

Lisa glanced between him and Robin and the confused look on her face quickly turned to suspicion. "Your taking over wasn't part of the deal."

"What deal?" Robin asked.

Kelon shook his head, keeping his eye on Lisa. He didn't need her spilling the beans about she and Donovan asking him to date Robin. There was no way Robin wouldn't be hurt. "Nothing that needs to concern you."

"Some things can't be controlled," Donovan added, helping himself to a slice of quesadilla.

Like where a man loved, Kelon realized, understanding Donovan's choice so much better now. Unless Kelon chose to ignore his destiny, everything Robin did would concern him. And everything he did would involve her, including pack justice, whether he was administering it, or if it came looking for them.

He washed his hands and wiped them on a paper towel, before running a hand over his beard. At least there was *something* he could control. "If you all don't mind, I'll go clean up now."

"I don't mind at all."

The potential for a double entendre in Robin's response kept him smiling all the way to the shower.

Three

HE cleaned up well.

Robin almost swallowed her tongue when she saw Kelon standing in the doorway of the game room, clean shaven, his long black hair falling about his shoulders, highlighting the sharp lines of his features and the wildness that was so much a part of him. That beard had been hiding finely sculpted lips, a square chin, high cheekbones, and a sharp blade of a nose. Aggressive features that came together in a clear statement: This was not a safe man. This was not the kind of gentle soul who spent evenings at home. Yet he was here, prepared to do just that.

He leaned his shoulder against the jamb. "I missed you at dinner."

"I was full from the appetizer." The real truth was she'd been horrified to overhear Donovan and her sister talking about how they'd singled out Kelon to take her on a date. Embarrassment had kept her from dinner. Along with the persistent nausea that plagued her.

"I could have tempted you with something special."

He sounded a little put out that she hadn't been there. "Do you really like to cook?"

He shrugged and pushed off the doorjamb. "It relaxes me."

If this was relaxed, she'd hate to see him revved up. She looked at the puzzle in front of her and felt stupid for even mentioning it. Doing puzzles just screamed old maid, and for this man she'd love to be a femme fatale. Like that was ever going to happen.

"You don't have to do this," she told him as he came into the room with that easy, rolling walk that somehow made her think of an animal on the prowl.

"But what if I want to?"

"You don't."

"How do you know?"

He had muscle piled up on top of muscle. "I just do."

Energy poured from him in a wave. Not for the first time, she wished she were healthy. At least for one day. She had a feeling an affair with a man like this would be one a woman would remember for a lifetime. No matter how long that life lasted.

Picking up the box cover, Kelon looked at the picture. "The Eiffel Tower? Not too ambitious, are we?"

She was only a quarter of the way through, and she'd been working on it for a month. She'd gotten a little spoiled while in the hospital. One of her sisters had always worked with her. Building puzzles had been a social thing and bringing it back to a solitary pursuit just wasn't cutting it for her. Something Lisa didn't understand. Lisa had never been sick in her life and couldn't understand the total dependency that came from being bedridden, or how the sick person had to utilize external methods to hold the interest of the active, healthy people around them. And she hoped she never would. "I enjoy the challenge."

He was standing right in front of her, vitality and sexuality pouring off him in rhythmic waves that swept over her in an even ebb and flow. She might have led a sheltered life and she might be dying, but she was still female, and though she'd been drawn to Kelon when his face had been obscured by his beard, seeing him cleaned up was definitely knocking her hormones off-kilter, because she was seriously contemplating throwing him down on the coffee table and climbing on board.

She dropped the puzzle piece she'd been trying to fit to the left side.

"Frustrated?"

He had no idea. "For the moment."

"And you will tell yourself what, in this moment?"

The formal phrasing startled her. She looked at him again, that same sense that told her Donovan was more than he seemed was working overtime with Kelon.

"I'll tell myself tomorrow is another day, that a good night's sleep makes everything look better." She shrugged and smiled ruefully. "And any other cliché I can come up with to keep me going."

"You're an optimist."

There were four chairs at the table. He would have to choose to sit on the side facing her bruised cheek. She knew how ugly it looked, knew the speculation he was probably indulging in. Embarrassment rose. She'd been so stupid. She pretended to sort through the puzzle pieces. "I'm not going to talk about it, so if the bruise bothers you, you might want to sit on the other side." She glanced over, noting the width of his shoulders, the easy confidence with which he carried himself. He was sexy, gorgeous, and way out of her league.

Kelon reached out and touched her cheek briefly, gently. The spot tingled. "I would take the pain from you."

"It's probably just as well that it's there. Sometimes I need reminding that the world isn't a fairy tale."

He stilled, the deep black of his eyes taking on a gleam that compelled her attention. Not allowing her to look away, not even allowing her to breathe, except she had to breathe because there was something deeply compelling about the way he smelled. Like chocolate cake on steroids. Like the tease of memory she hadn't wanted to forget.

His hand came back. This time he cradled her cheek in his big palm, the touch so tender she couldn't equate it with the man in front of her. A man so hard that he looked as if he could take on demons and walk away smiling. "Fairy tales often end badly for those not protected."

It was a struggle, but she regained her senses. "I don't need protection."

He freed her from the prison of his gaze. Picking up a piece, he studied the puzzle. "I don't agree."

She pushed her hair out of her face, not entirely surprised, considering the mess she'd gotten herself into. Weariness settled over her. "Donovan brought you here to help with Buddy and his friends, didn't he?"

"Yes."

That made sense. He looked the type to welcome trouble. "You don't have to."

Another glance at her cheek. "Dealing with Buddy will be my pleasure."

She kind of liked the old-speak that slipped into his phrasing. "It's worse than you're thinking it is."

She didn't want him to get hurt.

He added his piece of puzzle to the base. "In what way?"

"A couple of Buddy's friends have a bad history. They tried to run Lisa off a cliff. They thought it was Donovan, but it wasn't." In case he didn't understand the seriousness of the issue, she added, "Donovan could have been badly hurt."

Kelon didn't even flinch. He sorted through the pieces on the table. "You think those two, at least, are playing for keeps?"

He didn't seem the least disturbed by the possibility that kept her up nights. "Yes."

A ghost of a smile flitted across his lips. He dropped the piece and searched for another. "Good."

"You scare me." The confession just popped out. He didn't even glance up from his sorting.

"I know."

He knew? That was all he had to say? She wished she had more experience dating so she'd know how to handle this. Then again, she decided, sneaking a peek at Kelon from under her lashes, there probably wasn't any way for a woman to prepare for a man like him. Which meant she probably ought to end the game here and now. Especially as she was never going to be able to finish it.

"I know why you're here."

He did look up at that. "I thought we'd already established that."

"I mean, here. Tonight."

He gave her his full attention. Her tongue stumbled on the words.

"I know your brother asked you to . . ." This was so embarrassing, humiliating. She licked her lips. It was a pointless effort. Her mouth was as dry as dust. It just wasn't fair to have so much masculinity thrown her way then be given the knowledge that he was there out of a sense of pity. Sighing, she found her voice.

"Donovan has an overly developed sense of responsibility. You don't have to spend time with me after tonight."

"But you want tonight?"

Good grief, couldn't Donovan and Lisa have just hired a gigolo? That would have been a lot less complicated and probably a lot less embarrassing. She gritted her teeth in mortification and plunged on.

"If you stay an hour, Donovan will be satisfied. He'll let go of the idea of finding me a decent date."

Kelon fit the piece he'd just picked up into the puzzle. That was two in ten minutes. How did he do that?

"But what if I'm not?"

She frowned. "Not what?"

His hand came under her chin, rough with calluses, strong,

undeniable. Her body reacted instinctively to the purely masculine gesture, a silent command to look at him. She raised her gaze to his.

"What if I'm not satisfied?"

Fear—cold, dark, and suffocating—stirred inside her. She tried to jerk her chin free.

"No." His thumb stroked over her lips in a surprisingly erotic caress. "You have no reason to fear me, little one. I only meant what if 'only now' isn't enough for me?"

She rolled her eyes. How naive did he think she was?

"Please, I'm a woman who does puzzles for entertainment and you're man who does"—she waved her hand to encompass the whole of him, the deadly intent, the barely restrained energy—"the man who thinks playing for keeps is a good thing, for goodness' sake!"

"It's true that Donovan intended for me to date you."

It hurt hearing it. Even if everyone had set this up for her own good, it really, really hurt to hear Kelon say it. She jerked her chin. She did not want this man to see the tears burning in her eyes. Since she couldn't get free without betraying more than she wanted, she closed her eyes, blocking out the pity she knew she'd see in his gaze. This nightmare was easily the most embarrassing time of her life, even more humiliating than the first time she'd had to submit to a gynecological examination.

"Robin, open your eyes and look at me."

The order brooked no denial.

It felt good to ignore him, to show she was in charge of something. "No, this is too humiliating."

"You're upset because you think I'm here because Donovan asked it of me."

"I don't think it. I know it."

His amusement vibrated down his arm to his hand, transferring to her face, shaking up her conviction. "Do you really think anyone can tell me what to do?"

"Family can make family do anything."

His voice sounded closer, his scent was stronger, ferreting out her libido, bringing it to life. Oh, what she wouldn't give to have an affair with this man.

"No, they can't. Open your eyes, little one."

"Why?"

"Because I want you to know who's kissing you this time."

Four

As if she wouldn't know who kissed her. Kelon was a force all by himself. Dark, dangerous, and hot. Very, very hot. The type of man who took a woman right on past her inhibitions and, laughing, tossed her into the fire beyond. And yet, he was touching her as if she were made of spun glass, nibbling at the corner of her mouth, touching his tongue to the curve of her bottom lip, brushing his nose over hers.

"I thought you were going to kiss me."

His laughter buffeted her cheek. "I'm letting you warm up to the idea."

"I'm warm. Do your worst."

"Warm enough to open your eyes?"

Probably, but she didn't want to, for the same reason her hands were still fisted tightly in her lap. Because if she changed anything, if she moved, this moment might shatter. Or worse, she might say something really stupid and careless. She didn't want to do that. Not when this moment was the kind she'd dreamed about for so many years.

"It's better this way."

"Not for me."

"But I thought tonight was supposed to be all about me?"

"It will be."

She tilted her head to the side, facilitating the kiss he placed under her ear. It should be impossible for such a simple caress to have such far-reaching effects, but the shiver that started in her neck gained momentum as it spread downward, catching on nerve endings as it went, snapping them into vibrant life, fanning tiny waiting embers into flames. "Do that again."

His low laugh stroked over her skin. "You liked that?"

It would be stupid to deny it. "I think when it comes to you, I'm pretty much going to like everything."

"You won't find me complaining."

"Men never complain with an easy woman."

His fingers stilled on her cheek. "You think I think you're easy because you respond to me?" His lips brushed over her bruise. "Silly, baby. You're supposed to respond to me. Only me."

Another brush of his lips, this time parted, and then the wet heat of his tongue. On her skin. It should have felt gross. It didn't. It was scintillating, forbidden . . . tempting.

"Are you going to kiss me now?" she gasped.

"Not yet." Everywhere his tongue touched, her face warmed. She shifted, trying to turn into the caress. He wouldn't let her, just held her still to his desire, making her endure the spreading heat with no relief. "Shh, first you heal, then we love."

"Heal?"

His "Yes" was a muffled sigh. When he finally tilted her face up to his, she was breathless, hungry, uncertain. And her face didn't hurt anymore. His dark gaze searched hers. "What?"

She couldn't hold his gaze, because it suddenly occurred to her how pathetic she must look. A woman who went wild when a man did nothing more than kiss her cheek. And the only reason she could imagine he was delaying so long was because he hadn't been planning on her being this eager. He'd probably only meant to kiss her cheek all along, to "court her a little," give the lonely woman a thrill, but she'd reacted like the sex-starved virgin she was, and now he didn't know how to get himself out of this mess.

She forced her hands open and placed them against his chest, pushing him back. "You don't have to kiss me if you don't want to."

Kelon blinked, the rejection reaching where words couldn't. Through the haze of his lust, he saw the hesitation in Robin's eyes. The uncertainty. He shook his head to clear his mind. Damn it. He had to slow down. The last time she'd been with a man she'd been hurt—he knew that. He didn't want to hurt her, but she made it so hard. *Him* so hard. He had her in his arms, her scent in his blood. She was ready, eager. All he had to do was reach out and take her. But she was afraid.

"I want to kiss you."

Damn, that sounded more animal than man.

He took another breath, his pulse pounding in his head as the sweet scent of her arousal poured through him. "I want to start here." He pressed a kiss on her hair. "And end at your toes." He rested his forehead against hers. "And I don't want to miss an inch in between."

She shuddered as if he'd sent an electric shock to her. "Oh, yes."

"But not tonight."

Her fingers clenched in his shirt. "Why not?"

"Do *not* tempt me. I'm trying to do things your way."

"My way?"

"Yes. You have a right to a courtship."

"Who said anything about courting? Courting takes time, implies things."

He eased her forward until she leaned against his chest. Her face pressed into his throat. She felt right in his arms. Womanly. Soft. Perfect. His cock, his body, his soul ached for her.

"Well, we could always do things my way."

"Does your way get to the good stuff sooner?"

Maybe Donovan was wrong. Maybe not all humans required courting. "Yes."

"Then your way will be fine."

"Are you sure?"

She palmed his chest, licked her lips, and nodded. Her desire perfumed the air. "Yes."

"Put your arms around my neck."

She did—with a trust that humbled. Sliding his hands down her back, under her hips, beneath her thighs, he lifted her up and brought her to his lap. Her groin snuggled up to his. He could feel the heat and moisture waiting for him as her ankles hooked around the legs of the chair. A satisfied growl rumbled in his chest. Robin wiggled in response. His cock throbbed and stretched.

"Do that again."

It was an easy request to fulfill as the next shift of her hips pulled a more aggressive growl from his lips. "It's not wise to tease a wolf."

"It's not smart to tease a sex-starved virgin." Her hands went to his shirt, popping buttons faster than he could process what she'd said.

"This is your first time?"

The admission was shrugged aside as if it didn't matter. "It was a lack of opportunity thing."

She shoved the lapels of his shirt aside and then just froze, looking up at him, with wonder in her eyes. "Do you know how beautiful you are?"

He paid attention to how she touched him, saw the hesitation, the resolution. "I'm glad you find me appealing."

"Good lord, there isn't a woman alive who wouldn't find you appealing."

She reached for the button of his jeans. The hairs on the back of his neck prickled a warning. Something was wrong. She desired him, but beneath the desire there was something else. Her hands fumbled with the button fly.

As her gaze flashed to his, he caught it. Desperation. His hand covered hers.

"Robin, look at me."

"Trust me, I'm looking my heart out."

The bold-as-brass statement made him smile. The evasion did not.

"Look at me."

She did, slowly. And alongside the desperation he saw a new emotion. One that twisted something in his chest—fear. She was afraid of being hurt.

"I won't hurt you, seelie."

"I know."

He didn't think she did. "I won't hurt you like this." He touched her cheek. He moved his hand down and cupped her breast. "And I won't hurt your heart."

She shook her head. Tears gathered in her eyes, heightening the blue. "I think I'm just one of those women."

"Excuse me?"

She swiped at her cheeks. "You know, women who fall in love with anyone who pays them any attention, regardless of who they are. First Buddy, and now you."

"Buddy is the one who did this."

"Yes. Not a shining moment in my love life."

He caught a tear on the edge of his finger. "You will stop crying for him."

"I'm not crying for him. I'd like to kick him in the nuts."

"Then why are you crying?"

"Frustration. I'm crying because I'm frustrated." She slapped his chest. "I want sex and you won't give it to me."

"You're not a woman a man has sex with."

"Oh, please."

"You're a woman who should be savored, cherished by her mate."

She cut him off. "I don't want to be savored. I want to be fucked."

"You wouldn't enjoy being fucked as much as you'd enjoy being loved."

"Try me and find out."

"No."

She slid out of his lap. He stood beside her, keeping her against him as she lost her balance. "Why?"

He didn't like that she was so weak. It was more than hunger. More than tiredness. "I'm on guard duty tonight."

She twisted out of his arms and shoved her hair out of her eyes. It fell right back forward, framing her gentle face in a soft brown. Everything about her was soft. Especially, he suspected, her heart.

"However, things might be different tomorrow night."

"Tomorrow night? What's tomorrow night?"

"Our date."

Five

DONOVAN was sitting in the kitchen when Kelon found him. He didn't hesitate, just walked up to him and decked him. The chair crashed over. Donovan came up with a snarl, fists clenched. "What in hell was that for?"

"For Robin."

He drew back his fist again. With reflexes and strength that matched his own, Donovan caught it. "What about Robin?"

"She knows you asked me to entertain her."

"Shit."

"Yeah." Kelon yanked his hand free. "Shit. She thinks I pity her."

"And you don't?"

"No." His claws cut into his palm.

"Did you scare her?"

"Not nearly as much as she scared me."

Donovan righted the chair. "What do you mean?"

"I'm a Protector, Donovan. It's all I've ever been."

"So am I."

"I'm damn good at it."

"The best there's ever been."

"I'd be a lousy mate."

The two-beat hesitation before Donovan answered was telling.

"Not necessarily."

"Yeah. That's what I thought, too."

Donovan put the pieces together.

"Robin is your mate?"

"No need to sound so horrified."

Donovan walked over to the cabinet and pulled out a bottle of whiskey and hooked two glasses out of the dishwasher. "Damn, Kelon, I'm sorry."

"Sorry about what?"

He opened his mouth and shut it. "Nothing."

"Like hell, nothing."

The only time Donovan touched whiskey was when there was bad news. Kelon took the glass and pulled up a chair at the end of the table. "Spill it."

"It's not my secret to tell."

"She's my mate."

Donovan shook his head and picked up his glass. "She hasn't accepted your mark. Until then, she's under my protection. And that means her secrets, too."

"Then protect her. Tell me what threatens her."

"Right now, the two wild cards in Buddy's entourage."

"Not Buddy?" Buddy of the heavy fists. "Did he rape her?"

"Best I can figure, no."

"What do you mean, 'best you can figure'?"

"She doesn't talk about it. Just wants it buried. But Lisa says no. Buddy only roughed her up."

"What's your impression?"

"That he's a little boy who lashes out when he doesn't get what he wants."

"And he wanted her."

"Yes."

"What did she want?" Jealousy ripped through him at the thought of another man feeling those soft arms come around his neck, at feeling the way those full breasts melted into his chest as her breath sighed against his throat.

Donovan took a sip of his whiskey. "*That* you're going to have to ask her."

"I'm your brother."

"And she's sister to my mate with no one to stand for her but me. I won't betray her trust."

Kelon wanted to tear into something—his brother, Buddy, Buddy's friends, it didn't matter. He needed to do something to release the anger. "I'm her mate."

"Then you have two choices. Get her to accept your mark, or get her to talk."

"There is a third choice." Kelon took a too-casual drink. "I could just beat a confession out of you."

Donovan leaned back. "I might have mated human, but I'm the same son of a bitch you've been cursing for years. There's no way in hell you can make me do anything."

No, there wasn't. Like him, Donovan had a strict code of honor, and he took his responsibilities to the women in his care seriously. He would die before betraying Robin's trust. "You know it was only pure luck that got you the assignment of fetching Wyatt."

"The luck of being firstborn."

"At some point you'll have to stop lording that ten minutes over me."

"Not likely." Donovan tossed back the last of his whiskey. "Not when it works so well."

Kelon supposed not. He looked through the black window to the moonlit yard beyond. "Has there been any sign of activity?"

"Not since they tried to run Lisa off the cliff."

"I can't believe you let them live."

"It wasn't by choice. The women's safety comes first."

Kelon ran his fingers through his hair, feeling the coarser strands, remembering how soft Robin's was to the touch. He wouldn't be bedding Robin tonight, but there was no reason Donovan had to suffer. "Go find Lisa. I'll keep guard."

"You sure?"

"Yes."

He headed for the door and stopped. "Kelon?"

"What?"

"I will sanction the mating if, after you have all the facts, you choose to proceed."

"Facts won't keep me from her."

Donovan nodded. His "I know" was weary in a way that had nothing to do with lack of sleep, leaving Kelon with a restlessness he couldn't shake.

THE cold air embraced Kelon as soon as he stepped out into the moonlight. The night welcomed him with the utter stillness of a predator's playground. He scanned with his senses, listening to the wind blow through the trees, feeling the heaviness of the air, the warning in the creak of branches rubbing together. Something wasn't right.

He made a mental check of what he knew of the terrain, looking back at the house, checking the position of the road. From the lack of scent in the wind, he knew where they were. He dropped his leather jacket into the snow. Leather made too much noise for a hunting wolf. He slipped into the woods, dressing himself in shadow, skimming the snow, avoiding the betraying snap of twigs. From ahead and to the right came the scent of cigarette smoke. Apparently, Buddy's friends weren't hunters, or they would know the scent of cigarettes carried for miles. A clear warning to prey and predator alike that humans lurked here.

He followed the scent trail up the hill that rose behind the house. The cigarette smoke was stale, likely meaning the person was no longer there, but he would have left clues. Maybe important ones. It wasn't hard to find the spot were the intruder had made his stand. The ground was littered with cigarette butts.

Kelon knelt on one knee and checked the footprints left in the snow. There were surprisingly few. The man who'd come here had done so with a purpose. He'd set up and watched. The question was, what? The answer lay in the trajectory.

From here, the back of the house was visible, with a clear view of the turret wing—the game room on the first floor and the women's bedrooms on the two floors above. This wasn't a random person looking for revenge for a fight in a bar. This was someone with a target in mind. He placed his fingers in the three holes that formed a triangle. A tripod had sat here supporting something heavy. The tripod could have supported a camera. An arm resting on the camera could have increased the imprint. He brought up his binoculars. It was a clear view, clear enough for a camera shot. Clear enough for a gunshot. As Kelon watched; he could see shadows of bodies moving behind the shade in the third-floor bedroom. Donovan passed by first, his shadow much bigger and bulkier. It was quickly followed by a smaller silhouette. Lisa. The shadows came together. His finger drew on an imaginary trigger. Easy targets.

He lowered the binoculars past the other second-story bedroom—Robin's room—to the game room below. All the lights were on. Robin was still on the chair in front of the coffee table, her head in her hand. The tall windows gave a sniper a wonderful shot. Kelon ran a mental diagram of how the game room was laid out. There were no nooks and crannies. It was a fishbowl, plain and simple. All anyone would have to do to take out everybody would be to pump enough bullets into the wide-open space fast enough.

Shit.

Picking up one of the cigarette butts, he held it to his nose. He wanted the scent of the bastard who hunted his mate. He found just a trace. Maybe enough to recognize, maybe not. But it was a start. He noted the brand of cigarettes and checked around to see if there was any more evidence. There wasn't.

He backtracked the sniper's trail up the hill. From the size of the man's footprints, the length of his stride, and the depth of the imprint, he was looking for someone under six feet tall. A man with a tripod and a gun, and a hell of an axe to grind. Those weren't the kinds of clues that sat easily on a man's nerves. When he reached level ground he stopped, noticing something different about the tracks. The tread of the boot was very distinct. The kind usually only found on designer footwear. Nothing anyone in this poverty-stricken, dying town was likely to have the cash to buy, which meant his hunter probably wasn't local. Which added a whole other twist to the story. The threat to the women was apparently twofold.

Shit didn't begin to cover it.

Kelon continued up the hill, covering the ground in an easy lope, senses flaring outward, cataloging everything around him. There were no sounds that shouldn't be there. No disturbances. An owl hooted, branches rustled, and trees popped a protest against the cold, but nowhere, except around him, was there an unnatural stillness that would indicate the presence of death. He paused at the road at the top of the hill. Tire marks were clear in the snow. No distinctive side wear. No distinctive tread. From the distance between the wheels, he was looking at an SUV or a truck, but those were a dime a dozen up here. His prey was gone. The trail was cold, but the threat remained.

Donovan was not going to be pleased. Kelon stood and brushed the snow from his hands. Worse for the ones hunting his family, neither was he.

ARE you sure?"

Kelon leaned against the porch rail and checked the sight on his rifle. "Unfortunately, yes."

Donovan slid his knife into its sheath. "What the hell is a city slicker doing up here hunting our women?"

"That would probably be a good question to ask the women."

"Are you sure it wasn't Buddy?"

Kelon pulled the cigarette butt out of his pocket and handed it to Donovan. Donovan took a sniff and shook his head.

Kelon sighed. "I didn't think so, which means we're back to the women."

"You were there. They don't know any more than we do."

"Did you get the sense they were lying?"

Being mated to Lisa, Donovan would have a much better sense of whether she was telling the truth.

"Lisa doesn't have a clue. Robin just looked mystified."

And terrified. She covered it well, but she was terrified. And who wouldn't be? They'd come out here to start over, and now they were being hunted from all angles. Women who had been fighting for so long deserved peace. They didn't deserve this.

"How do you want to handle it?"

"I think we should split the women up. Force the hunter into the open."

Donovan cocked an eyebrow at him. "You wouldn't be seeing this as an opportunity to get Robin to yourself, would you?"

He checked the ammo. "There is that upside."

"I could just send Lisa with you."

"But you won't."

Donovan picked up a revolver. "Only because I trust you and

because it's a good way to force the hunter out into the open."

"You sure you want to trust me?"

Donovan smiled that hard-edged smile of his. "It's the best way I know to tie your hands."

"I could have lost all sense of honor."

"I don't think so."

"What makes you so sure?"

Donovan closed the chamber on the revolver. "You're still breathing."

Six

I thought we were running away, not going on a picnic," Robin said, fastening the snowmobile helmet. Kelon handed her the picnic basket.

"I promised you a date tonight."

"So this is kind of a running date?"

"You could call it that." He checked the gas can on the back of the snowmobile, making sure it was full and the sled carrying the supplies was tied securely. Then he turned to check that her snowsuit was zipped tightly and her boots and gloves were good quality. He checked the helmet. It was a little loose, so he fixed it while she watched him patiently.

"I do know how to dress myself."

"I'm just cautious."

"So you keep telling me, but even though somebody's trying to kill me—somebody we don't know—we're going out into the wilderness on the date." Putting her hands on her hips, she demanded, "You tell me how that correlates."

He wasn't going to tell her a damn thing. He held the helmet in his hands, keeping her head at the angle he wanted before pressing his mouth to hers. Her lips parted in a gasp. He took advantage, deepening the kiss, stroking his tongue along hers, tucking her between his thighs. They had too many clothes on to feel each other, but he could imagine the touch of her breasts, her supple thighs . . . He could imagine her naked very easily. Wanted her naked.

He liked the way she clung to him after his kiss, liked the way she didn't hide how he made her feel. He especially liked the way she licked her lips, swallowed hard, and then sighed.

"Has anybody ever told you that you can really kiss?"

"Nobody that mattered."

She frowned. "That's a horrible thing to say."

"Why?"

"People you kiss should matter."

"In my family, there's only one woman who matters."

"So all the others are discarded like so much debris?"

"No, they weren't debris. They just weren't the one."

She considered that for a second. "If you weren't packing those guns strapped crossed your chest, I'd call you a romantic."

A romantic wolf? He didn't think so. He'd be the butt of pack jokes for a decade. Stroking his thumb over the corner of her mouth, he removed the last touches of his kiss, sadness mixing with desire. If he mated with Robin, there'd be no pack to worry about. Donovan thought Wyatt could work miracles, but Kelon had his doubts. The Carmichael Pack was steeped deep in tradition, racked with superstition, and believed salvation would come to them through following the old ways. That kind of mind-set left them vulnerable, in need of their Protectors. And he was going to walk away. His mate or his pack. Both needed him. He wanted both. He could have only one.

"You don't have to do this," Robin said for the fourth time. "I'm sure whoever was out there was probably just up on the ridge shooting for a magazine. There are a lot of photographers around here and the house is very photogenic."

He glanced up at the ridge. He would like to believe it was just an innocent photographer, but his gut said no. "Maybe."

"Honestly, nobody has any reason to hurt me. I've barely left my home in the last twenty years. Nobody even knows me. How can they possibly want to kill me?"

"We'll talk about it when we get to our destination."

"About why somebody would want to kill me? That will be a very short conversation." She slid her leg over the back of the snowmobile and wrapped her arms around his waist.

"Then maybe we'll talk about why nobody knows who you are."

"And maybe we won't."

He opened the throttle. "We definitely will."

Robin was nervous. Kelon hefted the backpack of supplies and watched her hesitate at the entrance to the cave. She was nervous but game. There weren't many women he knew who would take the news that someone was trying to kill them with a fatalistic shrug and the complete trust that he could keep her safe.

"It's too cold for snakes."

She looked over her shoulder at him, a smile hovering at the corner of her mouth. "Is it too cold for bears?"

He smiled and chided, "City girl."

"You say that like it's a bad thing," she said, coming back to stand beside him. He handed her a sleeping bag.

"It's just different."

She followed him into the cave. "You never dated a city girl before?"

"Nope. I haven't spent a lot of time in cities."

He opened the sleeping foam and rolled it out on the floor. She came up beside him and looked at the thin mattress. "I'm going to sleep on that?"

"No." He rolled out a slightly thicker mattress. "You're going to sleep on this one."

She eyed it dubiously. "Thanks." He motioned to the sleeping bag in her hand. "Want to get that set up while I go get the food?"

"Food?"

"Can't have a picnic without food."

Robin stared after Kelon. They were really having a picnic? He ducked and exited the cave, and she was left looking at the vastness of the landscape. It was a beautiful view. She just wished she could enjoy it. Heck, she wished she could enjoy Kelon, but somehow, thinking someone was out there somewhere with a gun pointed at her head took the fun out of everyday things.

She dropped the sleeping bag on the ground. Despite what she'd told Kelon, she was worried. Crossing her arms over her chest, she rubbed her arms through her coat. She just couldn't figure out why anyone would want to kill her. Or worse, Lisa. She heard Kelon reenter the cave. Turning around was out of the question. She didn't want him to see the fear on her face. He was a man who respected strength; she was a woman who didn't have any right now.

His arms came around her from behind and pulled her back against his chest. She always felt so small in his arms, so protected. Which was stupid. She didn't even know him. For all she knew, he could have made up the whole story.

"Are you a liar, Kelon?"

He turned her in his arms, his fingers sliding through her hair, pulling gently, tilting her head back. The little stings in her scalp popped like sparks in her blood.

"Do you need me to be?"

His gaze met hers steadily and against her stomach she could feel the press of his cock—a solid statement. In his eyes, she could see the desire burning. Maybe she was the reason he was aroused. Maybe not. He could just be the type who got hard whenever he was close to a woman. "Yes."

"What do want me to tell you?"

"Tell me you can handle this."

"I can handle this."

"Tell me you want me."

The black fire that seemed to light his eyes from within intensified. "I want you."

She unzipped his parka. His body heat spread between them, carrying his scent with it. "You always smell so good."

His fingers worked faster than hers, opening his shirt. Pressure from his hand brought her mouth to his chest. "You should see how I taste."

She placed her finger to her mouth, then to his skin, linking them, but maintaining that critical distance. He was a man. He wanted sex. *She* wanted sex. There was no reason to make anything more of this. People did it all the time, made love and kept secrets. She glanced up into Kelon's eyes again and knew she wasn't one of them. Not with him. Not when he looked at her as if he was serious, as if she was something special. Not when he looked at her as if he saw his future.

And there just wasn't going to be one. "Oh God."

The hard desire in his eyes softened. "What is it, seelie?"

"This can't be more than tonight, Kelon."

His lids lowered the way they always did when he saw something as a challenge. "It can be whatever we choose for it to be."

She wished that were so. "No, it can't."

She reached up and touched the hard edge of his cheekbone. How did one tell someone that they were dying? That she didn't know how much time she was going to have. Her kidney could fail tomorrow. The drugs they were giving her to stop the rejection could cause a complication today. And she wasn't going back on dialysis. She already knew that. While she debated, she discovered how. She just . . . said it.

"I'm dying."

At first she didn't think he'd heard her. Nothing in his expression changed. Then his jaw tensed. "What makes you think that?"

Denial. Everyone always denied the reality, and then they wanted to fight it. But there was no more fighting. She'd spoken to the doctor, forced him to be blunt. Her kidney was being rejected. The drugs weren't slowing it. Even if she went on dialysis, she probably wouldn't make it until another donor came up. She was a hard match. "I had a kidney transplant. It's failing."

His hold gentled even more. "Then we'll get you a new one."

"It's not that easy. This is my second one."

"We'll make it that easy."

She should have known he would take it this way. The man was a warrior. She palmed his cheek, tying to soften the reality through touch. He couldn't fight this. "You see why I'm okay with just a good time?"

"You can't just give up."

"I've been fighting my whole life, Kelon. I'm tired."

His expression turned fierce, almost feral. "I'm not."

The air around them thickened with tension. "This isn't something you can fight for me."

"Then I'll fight with you."

He meant it. There was no doubting that. Rising up on her toes, she replaced her fingers with her lips, pressing a kiss to the hair-roughened flesh, stealing a taste of his skin, closing her eyes as his salty flavor rolled through her mouth like ambrosia. She put her arms around him, hugging him as tightly as she could, blinking back tears because it was so unfair that she met him now, like this. When nothing could come of it. "You can't."

She shook her head and stepped back, blinking fast. She made it as far as the length of his arm. "I just want a night, Kelon. Just one night to pretend that magic happens. One night to feel like a woman, not a fragile doll, but a real red-blooded woman desired by a real red-blooded man. That's all. Not forever. Just that."

"And you've picked me."

"Don't read too much into it. I chose Buddy, too, in case you forgot."

He brushed her hair off her cheek, making her aware of how it must look. Helmet head on top, rat's nest on the bottom.

"Because he was shallow and wouldn't be hurt."

How had he known that? "Yes. I knew he'd walk away."

"I won't."

She was afraid of that. "That's going to be a problem."

"Why?"

He stood there, every woman's dream, a strong man not afraid of going after what he wanted, not afraid of adversity, who'd shown up on her last days, and he asked why?

A knot lodged in her throat, swelled until she couldn't get words past it. The damn tears wouldn't stop coming. No matter how hard she blinked, no matter how often she swallowed, she couldn't fight them back. "Damn you."

He didn't look the least apologetic. "You said you wanted to do things my way. And my way involves love at first sight."

"You can't love me."

"Why?"

"Because there's no future in it."

"It is all the future I will have."

He was back to talking in that formal way of his. "Don't love me, Kelon."

"It's too late." He bent and scooped her into his arms.

She linked her hands behind his neck, clinging, because she was afraid of falling. "Loving me just means you have to say good-bye."

"I'm not big on good-byes."

He let her thighs slide down his until her feet touched the floor.

It was too short a drop, too brief a contact. It was as if her hormones had waited all through time for this moment, this man.

The pain cut deep. She nodded. "I understand."

He cupped her chin in his palm. "No, you don't, but you will after tonight."

"I will what?"

His head lowered. "Understand how my way works."

It took her a second to remember that she'd agreed they'd be doing things his way. "You're determined to do this."

"I'm aching to do this."

"You won't let yourself get hurt?"

"You can't hurt me."

She clutched his shoulders. "Promise!"

His hand slid down the length of her hair. He seemed to like her hair, always wrapping his hands in it, sliding his fingers through it. "I promise."

"Then what are we waiting for?"

"For you to relax enough for us to proceed."

"What about the bad guys?"

"The bad guys can't get within one hundred yards of here without me knowing."

"You're that good?"

"I'm that good." He angled her down toward the mattress.

As much as she wanted to go, she couldn't get her knees to bend. "Are you as good at this as you are at cooking?"

"Better."

She blinked. Lisa had been raving about that dinner since he'd cooked it.

"I find that hard to believe."

"Unlock those knees and find out."

She dropped her head against his chest. "This is going to sound crazy."

"I doubt it."

"I can't."

"Can't what?'

She shook her head and accepted the truth. No way was she getting through this without totally humiliating herself. "Bend my knees."

He laughed. "Nervous?"

She grabbed his shoulders and dug her nails into the thick leather of his coat. "I'd planned on starting out with someone with more ego than goals."

His fingers went to work on the zipper of her coat. "Doesn't sound like much of a plan."

"It was an excellent plan." Her head naturally fell back into his palm as his lips brushed her ear and then moved to the small hollow beneath. "Egomaniacs are inclined to see it as being all about them."

"Doesn't seem like that would be much fun for you."

"I wasn't planning on fun the first time," she gasped. "That was for education. I don't want to be laughed at."

Ah God, if he didn't stop nibbling there she was going to lose her mind.

"Interesting plan." He found the cord of her neck and continued nibbling his way along. "But mine's better."

She thought that would be better. It was worse. Each graze of his teeth, every soft nibble or suction stroked a nerve connected with her very core, tuning it to the sound of his breath, the anticipation of his kiss, the rhythm of his pulse, until all she could do was cling to his shoulders or fall to the ground. "What's yours?"

"I thought I'd just seduce you. Any complaints?"

"No," she gasped as he buried his mouth at the point where her neck met her shoulder. "Not a one."

His growl rumbled along her sensitized nerves, sinking deep into the embers of her arousal. His mouth opened, hot and moist. Her knees buckled. He followed her down, his hand cushioning her tumble to the surprisingly resilient foam cushions.

"Guess that takes care of your knee problem," he drawled as

his fingers worked at the buttons on her shirt. First one button, then two, three, four. They all gave up the battle with the same amazing lack of resistance that she had shown.

"Kelon." The prick of his teeth popped her eyes open. "Are you biting me?"

"Not yet." His head dropped to her collarbone and his breath sucked into his lungs in a ragged pull. "God, not yet."

"But you will?" She sank her fingers into the smooth coolness of his hair, holding him close as he struggled with whatever it was.

"Yes."

She shivered. "That's almost as hot as your growl."

His big body shook above her. His next growl sounded a bit like a laugh.

"What?"

"I'm trying to go slow, Robin."

She'd said something stupid. She'd just known she was going to do something stupid. "I should have gone back to Buddy first."

"Like hell." He propped himself up on his elbow. "You're right where you belong."

He really did say the sweetest things. She wiggled until she got her hips under his. "Not quite."

A hand on her hip tucked her the rest of the way in, and then, for the first time ever, she felt the delicious weight of a man's body on hers, felt the pressure of his cock between her thighs, the potential threat of all that muscle, the protective restraint that kept him from crushing her. It made her feel soft, feminine, hot. She arched into the feeling, pressing the hard ridge of his cock along her aching cleft. All the clothing in the world couldn't suppress the feeling. Oh God, so hot. "I think I'm going to come."

She wanted the words back as soon as she said them, but of course there was no more chance of taking them back than there was of stopping her body's headlong rush toward satisfaction.

There was nothing to do but brazen it out. "I'm sorry, it's just all so new."

His smile was gentle. “And you want to come.”

“I’ve waited a long time for it.”

He paused, his eyes seeming to glow, his chest barely moving. “You’ve never come, not even by your own hand?”

“I decided it would be cheating.”

“Pleasure is pleasure, baby.”

She worked her hand between them. “So you’d rather be touching yourself than have me touching you?”

“Hell no!”

“Well, I decided I’d rather come from a lover my first time than by my own hand.” With her free hand, she touched the strain lines at the corners of his mouth, watched as wonder spread across his expression, traced the set of his jaw, and knew, just knew, why she’d always felt she had to wait. Why it had never felt right before. “I didn’t know it at the time, but I think I saved myself for you.”

Seven

I saved myself for you.

The simple truth ripped through Kelon with the lethal efficiency of a blade, severing the tight hold he had on his control, bringing forth the wildness he was trying to restrain. His. She would be completely his. The only pleasure she would ever know would be what he delivered. All of her firsts would come from him—her gasps, her cries, her screams. He looked down into her bold-as-brass gaze above that tentative smile. Oh yes, he really wanted to hear her scream. He brushed the hair off her cheek. His fingers lingered on the smooth white skin, tracing the line of her jaw. She was such a mix of contrasts—innocent and bold, soft yet strong, sweet and yet incredibly sexy. And she was his. He rested his thumb on her lips, admiring the way passion sculpted her face into pure beauty. "You might as well give it up."

She blinked. "What?"

He tucked her a little farther under him. "Trying to hold on to control."

"Why?"

He could tell she liked being pinned beneath him. Every time he moved, every time he breathed, she flinched in surprise and shifted, encouraging more of the same. "Because I'm not going to leave you any."

"Why?"

He unbuttoned the last few buttons on her shirt. "Because I've been waiting for you, too."

Her eyes went wide. "Really?"

He spread the lapels. She wore a black lace bra. One that was more lace than support and guaranteed to send a man's blood pressure sky-high. "Did you wear this for me, baby?"

She nodded, a blush riding her cheeks. "Do you like it?"

Her nipples peeked at him through the lace. Shell pink nubs of temptation that made his mouth water. His cock throbbed to take, his nature to dominate. He had to suppress the inclination. Robin wasn't wolf. She wasn't built for violence and wouldn't understand it. This was her first time. She needed careful handling and gentleness. Damn it, there had to be gentleness in him somewhere. "Definitely."

She touched his cheek again. "Am I doing something wrong?"

"Why do you ask?"

"You look upset."

She was more attuned to him than he'd thought. He tugged her arms free of the shirt and then hooked them behind his neck, easing that sexy bra and those gorgeous breasts into his chest with a hand at the small of her back. "I'm not a gentle man."

The admission jostled a smile from her frown. She cocked her head to the side. "And you consider that a news flash, why?"

"I don't want to hurt you."

"You won't."

"First times can be tricky."

"I'm prepared for it."

He didn't want her prepared. He wanted her wild. He wanted to go wild with her. He wanted to give her passion and beauty. He was only schooled in violence and mayhem. The tension entering her muscles said she was aware of both. "Ah, baby, no."

"No what?"

"Don't tense up. I might not have a lot of experience with gentle, but I can learn."

She paused, her face buried in his neck, and then all that sweet softness relaxed against him and her head tipped back and her smile spread over him in a flash of warmth. "So, we'll be learning together?"

He could tell she liked that idea. "Yes."

"Good."

It was good. Very good. Feeling her relax beneath him, experiencing her trust as she arched into his palm, there was nothing better in the world.

She tugged on the collar of his shirt. "You have too many clothes on."

He braced himself on his elbows above her. "Funny, I was going to say the same thing about you."

"You first."

"No. You."

Her head cocked to the side as mischief entered her gaze. "I've been waiting longer."

He cut the front of her shirt with his claw, keeping her distracted with light kisses on her face and throat. "I'm hungrier."

Immediately, she shook her head, pushing at his coat. "Not possible."

He went to work on her jeans, stripping them from her with neat efficiency, leaving her in nothing more than sheer lace panties that taunted his wolf with the tiny bit they covered. He growled in appreciation. "I know what I'm missing."

She didn't miss a beat as he shrugged out of his coat, unbuttoning his shirt from the bottom up, those hungry eyes locked firmly on the solid ridge of his cock straining behind thick denim.

"I've been imagining what I'm missing." She licked her lips as one hand dropped down to explore his length. "And everyone knows nothing beats a good imagination."

His hips bucked under the gentle touch. Too gentle to give him what he needed, but packing an erotic punch with the wonder with which she explored.

"Baby."

Her eyes met his. "I like the way you say that, kind of soft and sexy, yet with that growly undertone, as if you think I'm hot."

She was a talker. He smiled. He could work with that. "There isn't anything hotter than you naked, hungry for me."

She glanced down. Tension entered her muscles immediately. He knew why. He stopped her before she could cover the scar. "No."

"But . . ."

He met her gaze. "I've seen it. It means nothing. Diminishes nothing."

"Actually"—she frowned and there was a distinct grumble in her tone that matched the impatient yank on her hand—"I was covering my potbelly."

It was his turn to blink. She thought that delightfully rounded belly of hers repulsed him? "Then you've definitely got the wrong idea of what turns me on."

"I do?"

Splaying his hand over her navel he held her gaze as he slid his fingers back and forth. "This, I like. I want to feel it against me. I want to feel it cushioning my cock as I kiss this sweet mouth."

"But you're so fit . . ."

"And you're so soft and welcoming, so different from me, so absolutely feminine." He slid down her body, noted the goose bumps on her skin, grabbed one of the sleeping bags, and threw it over them. "I'm sucker punched every time I look at you," he drawled against her throat, dragging the words with him as he angled kisses southward.

A gasp greeted his arrival at her plump breasts. A shudder encouraged the exploration of all that tempting flesh, and when he unfastened the front clasp of her bra, she arched on a "Please."

She might be shy out of bed, but in the throes of passion she was articulate, guiding him with her hands, her moans, teaching him what she liked, what she'd dreamed of, frowning in surprise when he finally reached the tip.

"What?"

She shook her head, her fingers clenching in his hair. "It's just . . ."

"You thought it would feel differently?"

She bit her lips as he took the tip just as gently into his mouth again.

"I thought it would feel more . . ."

He brushed the lacy cups aside, holding her gaze. "And you want to feel more?"

She nodded, hope in her eyes. "It's just that this might be the only—" She stopped and then finished with a breathy "Yes."

She'd been going to say this might be the only time she got to make love. His wolf snarled a protest. He wouldn't believe that. Her human doctors would fix what was wrong. Stop the rejection. He would not find her just to lose her. He would not. Anger championed desire, adding an edge to the gentleness he was striving to maintain.

"Just relax then, and let me work my magic."

She held his hair back from his face, her smile shaky. "You have magic?"

That smile tore at his heart harder than any words. "Special magic, just for you."

"I'm honored."

No, he was the one who was honored. Honored that she had been given to him, honored that she trusted him, honored that she had chosen him for her firsts. He kissed her pouting little nipple, smiling at her frown. She had no idea what he could do for her. The aphrodisiac in his saliva guaranteed any woman a good time. The mating hunger between them guaranteed an experience beyond her wildest dreams. "I'd prefer you eager."

"I'm trying, it's just—"

He gave in to his natural urges and nipped her, remembering at the last second to cover his teeth with his lips. She almost came off the bed.

Her hands wrenched his hair, yanking him backward as the sensation shot through her, and then she pulled him back as it began to retreat. "Oh my God!"

Under the tent of the sleeping bag, the scent of her arousal blended with his, making him drunk with need. "You like that?"

"Yes, oh yes." He did it again, this time holding her still as the sensation speared through her, waiting until she was strung tight on the pleasure before taking her nipple into his mouth. He sucked lightly at first and then harder until he found the pressure that had her shaking like a leaf suspended in his hands, with her own anticipation, her broken cries of "Yes," spurring him on.

He switched his attention to her other breast, bringing her up the same way with increasingly harder nips and strong suction, knowing the aphrodisiac in his saliva was sinking through her skin into her blood, readying her even more.

He released her nipple with a soft pop and leaned back to admire her as she strained upward, offering him her breasts. Breasts that quivered with her rapid breaths. Breasts topped with tight little nipples, swollen and red from his attention.

He brought his finger to one moist point. "Damn, that's pretty."

She cried out as he pressed downward, his finger sinking into the full flesh, creating a hollow that begged to be filled. His cock throbbed. She had perfect breasts for fucking.

"Oh God, Kelon." Her hands tore at his fly. "I need you."

Not yet, she didn't. Not enough. "Soon, baby."

She didn't want to be soothed. The impatient rake of her nails over his lower abdomen as she thrust her hand inside his pants sent bolts of hot lust straight to his aching balls. She didn't want him any more than he wanted her, but she had to be ready. He had to make her ready.

She pushed his jeans off his hips, catching his cock on her palm as it sprang free.

"Oh, my."

He ground his teeth and closed his eyes. She was a virgin, and he was bigger than most men. "It's all right. I won't hurt you."

"Are you under the impression this bad boy is giving me the freaks?" She gave his cock an appreciative squeeze.

"It's not?"

"I've read enough to know when I've hit the mother lode and to be appreciative of it."

He laughed. He couldn't help himself. She was so unlike what he thought a virgin would be, a human would be. The fire danced shadows over her face, playing hide-and-seek with her expression, but her hands didn't stop petting him with light strokes that teased and tormented. His hips thrust helplessly.

"Does this mean you don't want me to cater to your maidenly modesty?"

She snorted, a distinctly unladylike sound, but one that fed the laughter. "Hardly. I want the whole shebang."

Growling the way she liked, feeling her subsequent shiver, he laughed. He'd never made love with laughter before, but surprisingly, it didn't lessen the experience, just took it deeper. "Then prepare yourself to be shebanged."

She wiggled. "That sounds kinky."

He knelt, straddling her thighs. "Do you like kinky?"

Her eyes darkened to a deep blue and the sexiest of smiles ghosted her lips as she cradled his cock in her hands. "I'm thinking I might."

He couldn't look away as she tugged him forward. Still holding his gaze, she brought his shaft down until it rested against her stomach.

As bold as the move was, he didn't miss the nervous flick of her tongue over her lips as she cuddled him close. Damn, she was soft. So incredibly soft.

"Do you like that?"

His claws extended on a torrent of need. He drove them into the foam to keep them away from her skin. He shook his head.

Her face fell. Her hands let go. He caught and pinned them against his cock. "No, just give me a minute."

Despite the fact that his voice was a hoarse grate of sound, she smiled as if he'd given her a pile of jewelry.

"You liked that."

"Too much."

Her head cocked to the side. She looked down at his cock, throbbing hard and dark in her hand. Her fingers stroked slowly along the length and that tongue, that sweet tongue he'd kill to have on his flesh glided over her lips again. "Could you come if you wanted to?"

He'd been able to come from the moment he'd met her. "Yes."

Her gaze met his. "I think I'd like to see that."

His cock jerked in her grasp, all too eager to give her what she wanted. "Shit!"

She blinked way too innocently for a woman who was lovingly stroking the cock in her hands. "What?"

"This is supposed to be about you."

"And I can't give pleasure, too?"

She could give all the pleasure she wanted, but this first time round, there were some things she'd be better off dreaming about. "You give me pleasure with every breath."

She blinked rapidly, but not fast enough to hide the sheen of tears. Hell, he'd shoot himself if he'd hurt her feelings. She'd built this moment up so much in her mind. For all he knew she'd choreographed it. "Baby, there are some things you need to build up to."

"It's not that." She scooted up from under him. The sleeping bag slid off his back.

"It's just . . . you say the sweetest things sometimes," she whispered, staring at the blunt tip of his cock, that pink tongue touching her lips and then lingering as if she could taste him on the air.

The cooler air chased a shiver down his spine. He ignored it. A glacier could have dropped on him right then and he doubted he would have felt it. She hunched forward, or maybe he moved forward. He didn't know, didn't care. His world consisted of this moment as her lips closed around his cock, hesitant yet determined, suckling gently, as if she was afraid she'd hurt him while his nerve endings raged for the hard pressure that would give him the ultimate satisfaction. He cupped her head in his hands, and when she quivered, slid another behind her back, holding her to him, letting her deliver his pleasure any way she wanted. She kept shivering. In a far-off corner of his mind he realized she must be cold.

She took him deeper, working that hot mouth down his shaft. His cock jerked; his hips pulsed. His cock head hit the back of her throat. She gagged. He swore. She apologized with a kiss. Pre-come leaked past his control. Her eyes widened. He expected her to be shocked, maybe even repulsed. He did not expect the eager flare of excitement, or for her to lick her lips again before taking his seed inside her mouth and drawing hard. Nor did he expect her exotic cry as his taste filled her mouth again.

"Kelon."

"Goddamn, baby." He dragged her forward, at the last minute remembering to check his strength. She tumbled across his chest. Yanking the sleeping bag from behind him, he threw it over her, cocooning her between his hardness and the material's softness.

Her smile was as big as the outdoors as she knelt above him. "I get to be in charge?"

"Yes." It would be safer that way. If she were on top, he couldn't forget and thrust too hard.

"This is going to be fun."

It was going to be hell, but he'd kill anyone who stopped her. He wanted that hot mouth like hell on fire. She didn't make him wait, just kissed a direct path down his torso, letting him feel her smile and the edge of her teeth. He shook like a green boy. Foam ripped under his claws as she babied the tip of his cock, nuzzled it with her lips, kissed it, lapped the pre-come that spilled past his control, and hummed with satisfaction as she took it within her mouth.

"Robin," he warned.

"What?"

"I can't take much more of this teasing."

She rolled her eyes, lifted his cock, and studied the underside. "Suck it up. I've been waiting a long time to do this."

Fire seared his spine as she traced the path her eyes had taken with one sharp nail.

"If you'd start sucking and stop playing, we'd both be having a good time."

She raised her brows at him. "Who says I'm playing?"

"I do."

He growled. She laughed and nipped his stomach, watching him from under her lashes. "I'm glad I waited for you, Kelon."

He caught her head, holding her to him. "Why?"

She obliged the silent order, biting him again, harder, and damn if she didn't laugh when he bucked. This time his growl was serious. Females did not challenge males. Especially in bed.

"Because I can be myself with you."

The confession stole the aggression from his desire. Her mouth, the breath from his lungs. She took him hard and fast, working him to the back of her throat before releasing him in a searing glide, driving him closer and closer to the edge of his control with lightning flicks of her tongue and long pulls from her mouth. His breath came in growls, her laughter in muffled spurts. And she watched him the whole time, joy in her eyes, love in her touch.

Again the knowledge rang in his head, settled deep, and filled the empty part of him that had always longed. *His.*

With a snarl he flipped her over, his body protesting the loss.

Her palms slapped the ground. Her feet tucked under her in an instinctive reaction of which he took full advantage. Grabbing her ankles, he slowly, deliberately slid his arms beneath and walked up her body, spreading her thighs, opening her for his perusal, his hunger. She squeaked at the touch of his mouth on her pussy, an incoherent sound—half fear, half shock. Her hips bucked under the first touch of his tongue.

"Hold still."

The order was barely coherent. *He* was barely coherent. He'd waited so long for her and she was here, offering herself to him. Near drunk with lust on her scent, reeling from the honey-sweet taste of her desire, there was little left of his thought processes except instinct. Dangerous, violent instinct. He feasted on her, lapping and nibbling, taking her cries as incentive, needing to give her more, to give her everything, and even when her cries fell quiet, he couldn't stop, needing to take her to the next level, the next extreme of pleasure. He caught her clit between his teeth, slid one finger into the ultratight channel below, then another. Her tired body rose one more time to his command, giving him the orgasm he demanded, before collapsing back on the makeshift bed in breathless sobs. He couldn't wait any longer. Tearing his mouth from her pussy, he moved his hands up her body, letting the pressure on her legs tilt her hips up.

Mine. Mine. Mine. With every beat of his heart, the knowledge pounded through him. She was his. No one else's. His cock dropped to her swollen labia, bathing him in liquid heat.

His "Yes" was a snarl of satisfaction.

"Kelon, please."

He became aware of her hands pounding on his chest, of her body twisting to get away, worse—of the fear in her eyes as she battled to get away.

She was scared. *He* was scaring her. A small part of his mind absorbed the information; the larger part didn't care. It just wanted to fuck her, mark her, brand her with his teeth and his seed.

Robin said his name again. Her voice, which had started so full of laughter, now hoarse and trembling with trepidation. He'd done that to her, would do worse if she didn't get away. He closed his eyes, battled back his beast, gained a split second of reason, and shoved her out from beneath him. "Run."

Eight

SHE didn't move, probably too much in shock to do anything. And as she sat there, the focus of his need, everything in him said pull her back. His canines threatened to extend along with his claws. Passion and need rose to insurmountable levels, forcing the change. He'd never keep himself off her if he changed. "Damn it, Robin. Run."

She didn't run, just sat there, arms braced behind her, staring at him. And then she did the most astounding thing. She knelt, put her arms around his chest, laid her cheek between his shoulder blades, and simply said, "No."

He wanted to throw his head back and howl. He wanted to rage, but then she did something even more shocking. She leaned over and kissed his cheek, offering him all the compassion in her generous heart. To him. The man who'd almost raped her.

"It's okay, Kelon."

Ah damn. He grabbed her and crushed her against him, barely remembering to keep his claws from her skin, burying his face in her hair, breathing deep of her scent laced with the melon-scented shampoo she used, rediscovering his humanity as she stroked his back and offered him absolution for no other reason than that's who she was. When his canines had retracted and his claws pulled back, he wrapped her in the sleeping bag, a task made more complicated because she wouldn't let go of his neck.

"I guess I'd better work on my gentle."

"Or maybe I have to work on being less of a coward."

"No, it's definitely a case of my having to work on gentle."

She worked her hand free of the sleeping bag and touched her fingers to his.

"What happened?"

He flipped his hand over and left it open beside him, a lure. "You went to my head."

"You weren't trying to punish me for being too forward?"

"No." Her fingers sneaked into his, hesitating on the edge, as if she worried he'd reject her. There wasn't a chance in hell of that happening. He carefully closed his fingers around hers, giving her ample time to pull away. She didn't. Her hand was so small in his, so white. The bones delicate. He looked up to catch her smiling.

"You don't have much in the way of survival instincts do you?"

"When it comes to you?" She shrugged philosophically. "Pretty much none."

He rubbed his thumb against the back of her hand. He'd ruined her special night, turned magic to nightmare. Donovan would gut him. And he'd stand there and let him. He knew she wasn't were, knew she wasn't experienced, and still he'd come at her like she was both.

"I got carried away. I'm sorry."

She frowned and pushed her hair off her face. He got a glance at her watch. An hour. Son of a bitch, he'd been at her for an hour. No wonder she looked pale and shell-shocked. No wonder she flinched as she shifted position. A tear gathered in her eye.

"Son of a bitch. Don't cry."

"I won't."

The tear fell. He couldn't look away as it slipped over her cheek to plop to the back of their joined hands. He should be horsewhipped. "What do you need, Robin? Whatever you want, it's yours."

"I want you to hold me."

He blinked.

"Can you do that?"

He very carefully put his arms around her, unable to believe she wanted him to touch her. His cock leapt with hope. He ignored it. "Yeah. I can do that."

She leaned against him for several heartbeats. When she struggled within the sleeping bag, he helped her get her arms free.

"Better?"

She nodded. "Yes."

She shoved the material down, a blush riding up her chest as her breasts swung free. She took their linked hands and brought the back of his to the ultrasoft skin on the underside of her breast. Turning his hand, she offered him the full curve. "Can you make love to me now?"

He stared at her, a "No" springing to his lips. He, a man who'd never known fear, terrified to lose control, to be the one to hurt her. "You really don't have any survival instincts."

Her chin came up. "Is that a no?"

He cupped her jaw, sliding his fingers down to her chin. "I don't trust myself around you."

"Men usually say that as a cop-out."

"I'm saying it because it's the truth."

"I did too much, didn't I? I read about men getting to a point of no return and how it can—"

He put his finger over her mouth, cutting off the justification. "You did everything right and nothing wrong. You just went to my head. I touch you and I lose all rational thought."

Her smile returned, like the sun breaking out of the clouds. "You want me that much?"

He frowned at her. "It's not a good thing."

"It's a pretty wonderful thing." She pushed the material the rest of the way off and practically launched herself into his arms. He caught her, taking her weight easily. She let her head fall back. "I've always fantasized a man would want me that much."

She had no idea how much he wanted her. "I'm a wolf. Do you want me now?"

With a shake of her head, she sent her hair whipping across the top of his thighs. He clenched his teeth against the silken sting.

"I'm a virgin with no bed skills at all—do you still want me?"

"With every breath I take."

She dropped back on the mattress in a wanton sprawl, the mischief in her smile not totally disguising the lingering uncertainty in her eyes.

"What are you doing, seelie?"

Her smile faded. Her expression turned serious. "I'm trusting you."

She was going to tear the heart from his chest before this was over. He came down over her, slowly, so as not to scare her. "Why?"

"Because I can." She cocked her head to the side. "Is that a mistake?"

"No." He jumped as she tucked her cold feet inside his calves. "I promise. I won't lose control again."

"Let's not get drastic. It's not like it wasn't fun—it just got scary there at the end. I didn't know who I was, what I was doing, but . . ."

His cock lined up with her pussy, falling naturally into the distinctly feminine crevice. "You wanted me."

Her arms came around his neck. "I still do."

Her lips were swollen and red from his kisses and the press of her teeth. Irresistibly so. He leaned in. She rose, meeting him halfway, those lips parted, eager for the union. It was a long kiss, a thorough kiss, and when it was over, she was breathing as hard as he was.

"Good." It was more than good. And he wouldn't fail her this time. He wouldn't lose control. He would give her what she dreamed of. A night to remember.

Her eyebrows rose. "Then what are we waiting for?"

"Not a damn thing." He worked his hand between them, sliding his thumb over her slick clitoris. She flinched. Her eyes flared open with alarm.

"Easy. It's not going to be like before."

"I'm sorry."

"You're doing fine. Just relax for me."

She was tight with a virgin's fear, wet with a woman's knowledge. He made another pass of his thumb over her clit, softer, more gently than he'd ever touched a woman before. She responded with a gasp and a relaxing of her inner muscles. His cock inched forward.

Two sets of nails bit into his neck. "Oh."

He paused. She just had the head. "Too much?"

She shook her head. "Not enough."

"Good."

It was too abrupt, too blunt, but it was all he could get out as her body accepted his in small increments. He kept a steady caress going on her clit, judging by the internal contractions what pattern pleased her most, pressing his advantage when her muscles relaxed, holding steady when they clenched as tight as a fist. He was breathing as heavily as she was when he reached the barrier of her virginity. This time there was no mistaking the pain that accented his name. "Kelon!"

"Right here, baby."

Her head thrashed from side to side, caught between the pleasure she wanted and the pain she feared.

"We're good." He backed off that crucial inch, retracing his steps to forge back again, tasting her gasps of wonder and pleasure.

He closed his eyes against the need to thrust hard and deep, against the need to come. "This is good."

And it was, in a very different sort of way. He'd never cherished a woman before, but he was cherishing her, one inch at a time, one gasp at a time, finding a softness in himself he hadn't known existed, sharing it with her. Only her.

"Yes," she gasped. "Very good."

A fine trembling began in her stomach and spread, along with a flush, across her chest. Her gaze became unfocused, her attention centered inward. He wanted this for her. Pulling out slow and easy, stopping just short of a full withdrawal, he whispered, "Just let go, Robin. Let go for me."

"I can't."

He surged back in, rubbing her slick little clit a bit harder, a touch faster. "Yes, you can. I won't let you fall."

Her gaze locked on his. "Promise me?"

He worked his hand under her head, supporting her. "I promise."

She bit her lip. Her breath caught. He needed her attention a moment longer.

"Do you accept me, Robin?"

"Yes."

"Then, come for me."

With a thrust of his hips, and a stoke of his thumb, he threw her over the edge, his shout joining hers as her internal muscles milked his cock with the strength of her climax. Drawing him deeper than before, past the barrier of her virginity, past the point of no return, taking him to the hilt, taking him until there was nothing left to block them. Until there was only him and her. As one.

Until peace found its way between them in a simple truth.

"Mine."

"Yes."

He hiked his hand behind her head and pulled her mouth to

his, catching her gasp and the last of her pleasure in a kiss that seared him to his soul. She was human, fragile, forbidden. And completely his, for as long as she lived. Denial raged through him in a pointless, empty howl. A were bite wouldn't cure an existing illness. It only worked against subsequent illness. Mating with Robin wouldn't change her destiny. She would still die. She was still living on borrowed time.

As if reading his thoughts, she gathered his hair and held it behind his head. Her free hand came back to his cheek, cradling it as if she hoped to protect him. "I wish we had more time."

He stared down into her eyes, seeing the history of her "I wishes" and "if onlys" written there. They were still joined, yet she was distancing herself from him, from any potential of a happy ending.

"The game's not over yet."

She gave him a weary smile. "No, it's not."

She was humoring him. She didn't really believe it. He wiped away the tear that leaked from the corner of her eye with a swipe of his thumb. She wrapped her fingers around his wrist, stilling the motion, claiming his attention.

"I'm sorry I can't be what you need."

"You already are."

"You'll find someone, someday."

"I already have." He pushed the soft brown strands of hair from her face, accepting what he'd known all along. When she left this world, she wouldn't go alone, defenseless against what waited on the other side. He followed the track of the tear over the smooth skin of her cheek, the warmth of her throat, finding the beat of her pulse, riding it to the base of her neck, gliding along the curve to the soft pad of muscle to the right and above her collarbone. His canines elongated in a grinding ache. Anticipation and joy laced the bittersweet moment that should mean "forever" but instead only meant "until."

He pierced her that first bit, the marking hormones flooding his mouth, mixing with her blood, her ecstatic cry. His cock hardened within her, the eroticism of the bite blending with the poignancy of the moment.

He bit deeper, thrusting slow and sure, maximizing her pleasure, wanting her to remember.

She came in a slow ripple. As she pulsed around him, he cut his palm with his claw and placed the cut over the mark, summoning the ritual as old as time as their blood mingled.

"My soul to yours, in this life and the next. We are bound."

His palm burned, the ache spread up his arm, entered his chest, his head, his extremities. His cock ached and throbbed. His balls burned. His orgasm rolled over him, white-hot and intense as Robin gasped, her back arching. He held her down until the burn faded to a deep warmth, then met her gaze. "It is done."

Nine

THE rejection was happening faster than she'd thought. Robin held the bottle of pills in her hand. In the last three days they'd been in their love nest, as Robin had dubbed the cave, it had gotten to the point where taking the medicines to stop the rejection was worse than the symptoms of the rejection itself. She glanced over to where Kelon was measuring coffee into the pot. She put the pills back in the container. This time was special. She didn't want to waste a minute of it.

Kelon glanced up, concern and warmth in his gaze. "Feeling better this morning?"

She screwed the cap on the bottle. "Yup."

She stood and crossed to his side, her steps a little awkward, thanks to the rawness of the flesh between her thighs. The mark on her shoulder, where he'd bitten her, took on a feverish warmth when she got near him. He reached out. Giving him her hand, she let him draw her in.

"You're walking funny."

She snuggled into his side, breathing deeply of his scent. She always felt better when she was near him. "Whose fault is that?"

The grin that question inspired was beyond pleased. "Mine."

He eased her back. She was only wearing his shirt, the cave having heated up nicely the last few days. "Then maybe I'd better do something about it."

She couldn't help it, she blushed. The images that came into her head from the last time he'd "done something about it" were too vivid. His hands under her hips, his tongue hot as a brand on her flesh. He chuckled and lifted the edge of his shirt, exposing her scar and her abdomen. As always he kissed both, a kind of homage she found so sweet, before turning his attention lower.

"Kelon, no."

"You're hurt. It's my duty to soothe you."

The way he talked sometimes was so sweetly old-fashioned and yet so sexy at the same time. It gave her goose bumps. "That's how I got sore this time. Your soothing always leads to more."

His right eyebrow cocked up. He blew a breath over her pussy, smiling when she shuddered. "Is that a complaint?"

No. Yes. She couldn't decide. Her stomach rumbled loudly and she remembered why she'd vowed to stand strong this morning.

"Yes," she gasped, working her fingers between his mouth and her flesh. "You might be able to live on love, but I'm starving."

"So I hear." He kissed the back of her hand, tugged the shirt down, and then, with a hand at the back of her neck, tugged her up into his kiss. She sighed and relaxed against him. The man did know how to kiss. The power and passion with which he took her mouth always made her feel completely claimed and totally cherished at the same time.

"You're a hundred percent sure you don't need to be soothed?"

Her stomach answered for her, rumbling again.

"Apparently so."

He let her down gently, those dark eyes of his not missing a thing, waiting until he was sure she had her balance before letting her go. It didn't matter that he took his hand away, she still felt connected to him. He headed over to the side of the cave where he'd left his weapons.

"Can I come with you?"

Sitting in the cave was extremely boring.

He shoved his knife into the top of his boot. He reached for his rifle. "Baby, I'm going rabbit hunting. Do you really want to be there when I kill Thumper?"

Her stomach rolled at the thought. "Maybe I do need soothing after all."

He shook his head, his long hair sliding over his shoulder, framing his dark face in stark relief and highlighting the sharp angles, giving him a distinctly dangerous look. "Or maybe you just have a weak stomach."

He was onto her. "Well, this time, do me a favor and skin it before you bring it back."

"I learned my lesson last time. Still can't get the smell out of my boots."

She felt bad about that but when he'd held the bloody carcasses up, showing her the catch, obviously caveman proud at having provided for her, instead of anticipating the wonders he would create with the fresh meat—the man was a phenomenal cook capable of making miracles of nothing—she'd promptly vomited. All over his boots.

She tugged his shirt down. It still embarrassed her. "It was your own fault."

"Do I look like I'm arguing?"

She cocked her head to the side. "A little. Around the eyes."

He came over, a big, mean-looking man who made her feel more precious than diamonds. His hair fanned out beneath his Stetson as he approached. His smile teased. His hand cupped her chin. "Well, I'm not."

A stroke of his thumb across her lips was all it took for her libido to perk right up. "You stay inside the cave while I'm gone.

And stay away from the entrance. I don't want you caught in the traps I set."

Something cold and hard pressed into her hand. She wrapped her fingers around it. "A gun? You've got the place rigged with more booby traps than a scene in a Rambo movie, and you think I'm going to need a gun?"

From the way his expression didn't change, he didn't share her skepticism. "Anyone comes through the entrance, turn off the safety and start firing."

As if anyone would be dropping in way out here. "You worry too much."

"Nah." He tipped her face up and brushed his mouth over hers. "I'm just cautious."

THE fire was dying. Kelon wasn't back yet, and the temperature was dropping outside. She was also low on water. Robin walked to the opening of the cave and looked out. Dusk was falling, casting the dramatic landscape that fell away from the cave entrance in stark relief. Rocks stuck out at sharp angles, and trees created a home for themselves in whatever viable space they could, clinging to the hillside against the odds. Amidst the flourishing trees were ones who hadn't made it. Skeletons of dead hope.

She rubbed her hands up and down her arms. She didn't want any reminders that her time was short. She also didn't want anything spoiling this day. Kelon coming back to a cold cave, dead fire, and dehydrated girlfriend would upset him. He was a natural caretaker, and for all that he had that dangerous edge, not the least afraid to show it. At least when it came to her.

She shook her head, her hand going up to the place where he'd bitten her, a smile playing around her lips. Kelon didn't like her calling herself his girlfriend. He made that growly sound in his throat every time she did, which, of course, had the effect of making her say it more. She liked it when he growled, the same way she liked it when he bit, which just went to show the kinky side she'd always suspected she harbored was alive and well.

And flourishing under Kelon's care. The last sparked a rueful grin. The man was inexhaustible and creative. And he loved to hear her scream, would hold off his own tremendous need until she came however many times he deemed sufficient. Only then would he come for her, growling her name and calling her *seelie*, holding on to her as if she was all that mattered, sheltering her from his weight and the violence she could feel rising inside him, holding her until the fury died and his muscles relaxed. Holding her until he found peace. The only time she saw him that relaxed was in her arms. She was glad she could bring him peace. She owed him so much.

She scanned the area below. There was no sign of movement, human or animal. There was actually no sign of life for as far as she could see, and a tiny niggle of concern wormed its way into her complacency. What if something had happened to Kelon? He was never gone this long. How would she find him?

The fear lingered, digging into her confidence, snuggling into her worry. Once lodged, it wouldn't go away. She palmed the mark on her neck from where he'd bitten her. Nothing could happen to Kelon. The only thing that made her dying bearable was the knowledge that he would live, and the illusion that a bit of her would carry on in his memory.

But for that to happen, he had to survive. The beauty of the vast landscape suddenly took on a sinister quality. Kelon could be anywhere. He could have fallen into a valley, be caught in a crevice. Tripped on his knife.

The last make her laugh. She was being crazy. Kelon was very at home with his weapons. Very at home in the wilderness. He was fine, which left her with the original problem. Wood, water, and boredom.

The stream was down and to the right, not more than one

hundred yards. One hundred open yards. There was wood galore around the stream. Maybe not all of it dry, but Kelon had told her how to find the drier wood. Not showed her, because in the interest of his cautious nature, he hadn't wanted to risk her being seen. She looked again at the desolate landscape. Seen by what? Squirrels? Assuming any of those were even out. The wind smelled of cold and storm. They were going to need the wood and water if the storm was a large one.

She pulled her coat around her, the revolver in the pocket adding a lopsided weight, feeling foolish for the nervousness that hit when she stepped outside the cave. Kelon's overly developed sense of caution was affecting her. As if she had anything to be cautious about. Being eaten by a bear was probably preferable to going the way she was going. She wasn't sure, though. She hadn't done the research. During one of her more depressed moments, she'd explored the possibilities. It hadn't taken her long to decide there were some things that were better off being a surprise.

Her foot slipped on an icy patch as she carefully made her way down the incline. Grabbing a tree, she caught her balance. The world spun as she sat. She stayed there until the wave of dizziness passed. She looked back up the hill. The cave looked a long way away when she was at the bottom of the climb. She took a breath and got carefully to her feet. The dizziness didn't return, but the short walk down the hill had left her more tired than she'd anticipated.

She filled the large drink cooler with water, beat her hands against her thighs to get the feeling back in them, put her gloves back on, and gathered some wood in the sling. It was only half-full when she realized she couldn't carry any more. It would take several trips before she had enough to make a dent in their need. Well, hell. Now Kelon was going to yell and she wouldn't have the satisfaction of silencing him with a job well-done.

"Hello, Miss Delaney."

It was a perfectly civil greeting given in a perfectly normal voice. It froze her blood. No way in heck should she be receiving it out here in the middle of nowhere.

She turned. The man wasn't overly tall, overly handsome, overly heavy, overly anything. He wasn't even overly scary except for the fact he'd tracked her down in the back of beyond. And the fact that he had a very ugly gun in one hand and a red and white cooler in the other.

"Do I know you?"

"You knew my sister."

She racked her memory for any acquaintance who had the sharp features, brown eyes, and dark hair of this man. She came up zero. "What is her name?"

"Evelyn Shapiro."

The name sounded familiar but she couldn't put a face with it, and it wasn't like she had that many outside acquaintances. He was staring at her as if he expected recognition to occur immediately. She took a step backward. "I'm sorry, I don't recognize the name."

"She saved your life, and you don't remember her?"

She'd had a teacher who used to respond to incorrect answers to test questions with just that level of controlled disappointment. She'd hated that teacher.

She tightened her grip on the water jug and the wood. "I'm sorry. No."

He nodded as if she'd just confirmed a suspicion. "I told them it wasn't right." He took a step forward. "Evelyn should be allowed to rest in peace."

"She's dead?"

"As if you didn't know." He motioned up the hill. "We need to return to the cave."

"Why?"

He held up the cooler. "I need room to work."

How could a cooler look so sinister?

"I'm sorry." She took another step back. "Kelon doesn't allow me to entertain when he's not home."

His brows rose in polite inquiry. "The man with you?"

She nodded.

He smiled. "Kelon will never know."

She would give anything for Kelon to know. "It's not my nature to lie."

"Now, we both know that's not true." He motioned with the muzzle. "Get climbing."

Climbing meant she had to turn her back on him. "I'm pretty tired. Maybe we could just talk here."

The gun came up, centered on her chest. "No."

The simple answer didn't give her anything to work with. She turned her back, fear rising in a choking wave.

"Move."

She did, putting one foot in front of the other, every nerve ending in her back dancing as if possessed with St. Elmo's fire. The revolver Kelon had given her, safely zipped in her pocket, felt like lead. A quarter of the way up her strength gave out. "I have to take a break."

"No."

She glanced over her shoulder. Her arms ached, her lungs burned, and there was no way she was going to be able to lift her leg another step. "It wasn't a question."

He brought the gun up. "Walk."

"I can't."

His lip lifted in a snarl. "I can't believe they gave part of Evelyn to a weakling like you."

The light dawned. *Part of Evelyn.* Evelyn Shapiro had been the woman who'd donated her kidney.

"I'm not weak. Just sick."

"You're weak."

He poked her in the back with the muzzle. It hurt a lot more than she thought it would. She stumbled forward and stopped.

"Keep moving."

She understood now the stories of people and animals that just lay down and accepted their fate when they were hunted. Weariness could be more powerful than fear. She dropped the wood but held on to the jug. It might work as a weapon. "Why?"

"Because Evelyn needs to rest in peace."

She looked over at him, at his eerily composed expression, his dilated pupils. "What's stopping her?"

"You are. You're the last one."

That did not sound good. "Last one of what?"

He glanced at the sky and jerked the gun up the hill. "You're wasting time."

"I'm catching my breath."

She strained with her ears, her eyes, her mind. Where was Kelon?

"Your companion won't be coming back."

That whipped her attention back. "What?"

He shrugged humbly. "I'm very good with a high-powered rifle."

She could picture him with a calculator, but a high-powered rifle? "You don't look the type."

He frowned. "Not all sports require muscle."

The only way Kelon wasn't coming back was if this lunatic had shot him. "No." She could barely get her lips around the words. Oh God. Kelon! "They don't."

Rage and loss battled for supremacy within her. She reached up and slid her hand under her coat, covering the place where he'd bitten, struggling to keep her expression passive while inside she screamed for him, for the loss that wasn't supposed to happen. The spot burned against her palm, or maybe it was her rage she felt reflected back at her.

She turned slowly, her muscles so tight movement was awkward. She needed to know. "You killed him?"

He raised the gun. "Yes."

She took a step forward. "Why?"

"I couldn't risk his interference. You're the last one."

She took another step forward.

"Stay right there."

She ignored the order. Her attention focused on his face, memorizing it along with his feel. If he killed her before she killed him, she was going to haunt him. And she wanted to remember exactly how he looked and felt so that even from the hereafter, she could find him and make him sorry. "You keep saying I'm the last one, but not of what."

"Evelyn can't ascend to the resurrection if her body is not complete."

"That doesn't make sense."

"It does for our beliefs."

She took another step forward, tightening her grip on the jug and reaching for the zipper on her pocket. He was a very sick man. And he'd killed Kelon. Because he had some idea that, if he put his sister back together, he could somehow control what happened in the future. A mental case.

"Your sister signed an organ donor card. That means she gave her permission for me to use her kidney. And you know what? I'm keeping it."

She probably should have been worried by the fact that he didn't tell her to stop or step back, but she was beyond that. Kelon was dead. This man had killed him. She couldn't think beyond that.

On her next step, the man lunged, wrapping his fingers around her arm, yanking her forward. She swung with the jug. It bounced off his shoulder. He swore, but didn't release her, surprisingly strong for somebody who looked so thin. Maybe insanity gave him extra strength, or maybe she was just extra weak. She yanked on the pocket zipper. They made it look so easy on the cop shows. In reality, fighting with somebody while trying to get a gun out of a pocket was next to impossible. It caught halfway, remaining trapped in her pocket. She couldn't get her hand in far enough to work the trigger. She couldn't get free.

Robin did the only thing she could as she battled. She screamed—loudly. It was pointless and useless, but it was all she had. It wasn't until the man slapped her and said, "He can't help you," that she realized it was Kelon's name she was screaming. The spot on her shoulder burned like fire. Around her there was an echo of a snarl. She looked up. Nothing moved and the man was still staring at her. The hairs on the back of her neck stood on end and the sense of danger increased.

She closed her eyes. Kelon couldn't be dead. She wouldn't believe it. She pictured his face, recreating it to the smallest detail. Everything inside her screamed for him. Yearned for him. So much so that she thought she felt him coming. So much wishful thinking. Oh damn. *Kelon!*

Pain blossomed in her shoulder. She opened her eyes and looked down at the syringe sticking out of her shoulder, at the thumb depressing the plunger, felt the burning intrusion. Horror followed. He'd injected her with something. She could feel it creeping through her system, cold, burning. Relentless. She screamed again for a whole different reason.

Numbness spread outward from the injection, taking strength and will with it. Her legs buckled. He caught her, his grip almost gentle as he lowered her to the ground. "I was going to do this in the comfort of the cave, but you had to be difficult."

Of course she was difficult. He was trying to kill her. Her lips wouldn't shape the words. She was paralyzed. The man took out a thin stainless steel knife. A scalpel. The kind used for surgery. Oh God! She glanced from the knife to his none-too-sane eyes. Oh God!

She needed to get out of there. She needed to get up and move, damn it. She told her legs to move, but nothing happened. Small grunts came from her throat. Pathetic. Useless.

"Don't worry, the paralysis will wear off in an hour."

If he succeeded in what he was doing, she wouldn't be alive in an hour.

The man opened her coat. Cold pricked goose bumps over her stomach as he spread her shirt. He brought the knife up.

No. No. No. She couldn't stop chanting that one word. She'd known for weeks she was dying, but she didn't want to go this way. He patted her shoulder. "Don't worry, it won't take long. I know it would be kinder to kill you first. I'm not a cruel man, but the organ has to be taken from a living body. As it was taken from hers."

Dear God, he was insane. Worse, she couldn't open her mouth to tell him so. Not that it would make a difference, but it would feel better to do something. Scream, holler, swear, curse, anything but lie here as a man put a scalpel to her abdomen and began to cut.

He really was going to cut the kidney from her while she was still alive.

A burning agony spread from one side of her lower abdomen to the other.

"Just marking my place. Don't worry, it'll be over soon."

It felt like she was breathing in heavy pants, but she couldn't tell. It also felt like she wasn't getting enough air. Had he given her too much anesthesia? If he did, please let it take effect before he got to the serious cutting.

She was so scared she couldn't even close her eyes so she wouldn't have to see his sick, twisted, strangely calm face as it did this disgusting surgery.

Kelon!

She rebuilt his image in her mind, paying attention to every detail—the shape of his face, the set of his brow, the deep brown of his eyes, the sculpted beauty of his mouth. Perfect, everything had to be perfect, right down to the smallest scar. The last made her stop and think. Did he even have a scar? She couldn't remember one. He really had been perfect, and he'd died. Because of her. Protecting her. This was just too sick.

The scalpel flashed in the fading light as the man held it up, muttering some prayer in a language she didn't understand, giving religious overtones to such a heinous act she couldn't stop, prevent.

She hoped he hid her body really well when he was done. She didn't want her sisters to find it and know how she had died. No one should have to live with that knowledge. The scalpel came down. She held tighter to Kelon's image. Steel touched her flesh.

Kelon! The scream came from her heart. The bushes to the right exploded with a roar that drowned out her scream. A black form leapt into her line of sight, colliding with the man. His arm flew up; the knife flashed down. The beast didn't even flinch. Horrible snarls filled the clearing. A man's hideous scream cut across the cacophony. The scream died as abruptly as it began, and then there was silence.

Robin strained, tried to turn her eyes to the corner to get a view. A black form came near, taking shape. A wolf. It was a wolf. The biggest wolf she'd ever seen. Blood darkened the fur by its mouth. Drawing back its lip, it showed her vicious white teeth. She stopped breathing altogether.

Dear Lord, she prayed, *if I have to go this way, could you take me now?*

She didn't expire. The wolf lowered its massive head. Her scream was a tiny gasp of breath. Its cold, moist nose touched her cheek, her forehead, her jaw, before sliding down inside her coat and sniffing the spot on her shoulder that burned. She couldn't turn her head. She couldn't do anything but wait for the bite that would end her life.

The animal growled low in its throat, and everything inside her paused. She knew that growl. It was impossible, but she knew that growl. The wolf sniffed down her body, finding the blood on her abdomen. This time it snarled. Its head turned to the right and delivered a vicious snap at the feet of the dead man. Inside, she whimpered. Outside she just lay like an inflatable doll waiting for whomever, whatever, to do with her as they willed.

The wolf whimpered. The sound was as sad as the one she wanted to make.

It sat on its haunches, tilted its big head back, and howled. The sound bounced off the mountaintops. Before the echo faded there came an answering howl in a different timbre. Had he called in reinforcements? Why? How much of a threat could she be?

With a last touch of his nose to her abdomen, the wolf whimpered and walked out of her sight. She heard a splash as it entered the stream. There were a lot more splashes, and the unmistakable sound of an animal shaking off. Icy pellets of water splattered on her cheeks. As if the animal felt her start, it came back over. Its nose touched her cheek again, and then the wolf, holding her gaze with its eerie one, stepped back.

Its image obscured, distorted. She blinked. What she was seeing didn't change. The wolf was morphing, stretching, elongating. Bones crackled and fur disappeared in a rapid blur until there was nothing left of the wolf, and standing its place was . . . Kelon.

That was impossible. The drug must be affecting her brain. Kelon knelt beside her. His hand cupped her cheek. For an illusion, he felt very familiar. "Ah baby, what happened?"

The tears she'd been holding back spilled over. She had a feeling that should be her question.

Ten

WHAT did you do with the body?"

Robin sat on the bed with her back against the headboard. Of all the questions in her mind, that seemed the safest to ask. And, six hours after the incident, two hours since the paralyzing agent had worn off, those were the first words she'd spoken. Kelon, sitting in the chair by the bed, didn't even look surprised.

"Going with the lesser of the evils?"

"I'm not sure I'm going to go any higher." She cut him a glare. "Ever."

She could not cope with a man who changed into a wolf. Not right now.

He stood, a strange energy vibrating off him. She held up her hand. "You can answer me from over there."

"Ignoring what you know isn't going to change anything."

She threw a pillow at him. "You don't get to tell me how I get to deal."

He caught the pillow. "Does this mean you intend to deal?"

"With what?"

He tucked the pillow behind her. "With the fact that you saw me change from a wolf to a man."

"That was an hallucination brought on by the drug that awful man gave me."

It had to be.

"You know what you saw, Robin."

"What I saw was impossible."

"No." He brushed the back of his fingers down her cheek. "It wasn't."

She stared straight ahead, ignoring the contradiction. "What did you do with the body?"

"Donovan went back and took care of it."

"Not the law?"

"We are the law. He touched you." Claws scraped down the pillow. "Justice was delivered."

She had never seen him like this—hard, angry, lethal. "I've decided you're a very scary man."

"Never to you."

She recalled the wolf, the screams, the moment he had changed. "I've got a news flash for you. Even to me."

He lifted the covers and put his hand on the healed wound where Evelyn's brother had cut her. The wound he'd healed. "I thought I was too late, Robin."

She didn't allow herself to believe the anguish in his voice.

"You almost were. Another few seconds and no one would have to worry about trying to explain anything to me. The joke would have ended right there."

"What joke?"

"The one that started out of pity. The one that had me believing that someone like you would really be interested in someone like me."

She ignored his growl. The doubt that had been gnawing at her since the first day she'd met him surged, refusing to stay suppressed any longer. "It's my fault, really." She plucked at the covers. This didn't paint a pretty picture of her personality. "I was willing to play along, since I'm living on borrowed time and it got me what I wanted—a red-hot affair before time ran out, but somehow it's all different knowing what I know."

"And what exactly do you know?"

She knew she couldn't live on pretense anymore. She glanced up. His lips were set in a straight line of displeasure.

She pleated a tuck in the quilt between her fingers, avoiding his gaze. It hurt to say this. "You've never made any secret that your people have set ideas about women. You take care of them. You did a really good job taking care of me, kept your promise to Donovan to show me a good time, but it's time to end it."

"I made a promise to you, too."

He'd promised not to hurt her, physically or mentally. He'd kept that promise. She was the one who'd gotten "now" mixed up with "forever."

"I can't pretend anymore, Kelon. I've run out of imagination."

His fingers left off playing with her hair to cradle the nape of her neck. His thumb under her chin tipped her face up. His eyes were very dark, darker than the night beyond the window. "Wolves play for keeps."

"I don't know what that means."

"It means you're mine."

"What if I don't want to be?"

"It doesn't matter." He moved her nightgown to the side and placed his hand over the spot where he'd bitten her on her shoulder. The wound burned, pulsed in recognition, sending streamers of desire flowing through her shell-shocked body. "We are bound."

The words were familiar.

We are bound.

The streamers flowed with the internal echo into her core, releasing the need that always rose for him. She shifted on the bed, trying to suppress the response. "What does that mean?" Kelon's eyes narrowed and his nostrils flared. When his gaze dropped to her groin she knew her efforts were for nothing. There were some things she could never keep from Kelon. Desire was one of them.

"It means by wolf law, we're mated."

No matter how matter-of-factly he said that, it sounded bizarre. A body just couldn't say *werewolf* and *mated* in the same breath and expect to be taken seriously. "Werewolf law?"

"Yes."

"There's such a thing?"

His lips twitched. His touch gentled. "Yes there is."

Another thought pushed forward out of the chaos in her mind. "You bit me; does that make me a werewolf, too?" Every scene from every horror movie she'd ever seen—and she'd seen a lot—flashed through her mind. "Because I have to tell you, that's not going to help my self-image."

He shook his head, his hair sliding over his shoulder in a sheen of black. She loved his hair. She just didn't know if she should anymore.

"Werewolves are born, not made."

"Will your bite heal me?"

The hope that came with that thought was staggering. The disappointment at the answer debilitating.

"No." The tips of his fingers grazed her cheek. "We can't cure existing illness. Our bite merely gives you antibodies that protect the flesh against future illnesses."

She sighed under the weight of understanding. "So I'm still dying."

"Yes." His palm flattened against her cheek, holding her face to his shoulder, as if through sheer force of will he could keep her safe, and suddenly, it didn't seem so important what he was. Just that he was. "But when your time comes, you won't be alone."

He was saying he would be with her. He'd watch her die. She'd leave this world with his sadness in her soul. She tilted her head back, not pulling her punches. She hadn't been able to live on her own terms, but she could damn well die the way she wanted. He was her happy memory. She needed him to stay that way. "I don't want to leave this world with your sadness as my last memory."

She'd had enough of sadness.

He opened his mouth, but she cut him off by simply placing her hand over his lips. His five o'clock shadow tickled her palm. Another memory to store and treasure.

"Promise me."

His eyes narrowed. Grief entered his gaze. Kissing her palm, he brought her hand to his chest. His heart beat with a strong rhythm. Steady. Like him. "I can't make you that promise, seelie. I'm a Protector. You're my mate. I cannot let you leave this world alone."

She wasn't going to change his mind. She was both appalled and comforted. Dying was scary no matter how much she tried to prepare herself for it. As much as she didn't want to burden her loved ones, part of her was relieved that she wouldn't be alone at the end. "It might not be pretty."

His jaw set. "You will not be alone."

And that was that. She sat for a minute, feeling his heart beat, feeling his determination. Borrowing some of his strength. "What does *seelie* mean?"

The change of subject didn't even make him blink. Her scalp tickled where his lips brushed over her hair. "*Seelie* is an endearment that a wolf gives to the woman who holds his soul. It literally means 'bound to my soul.' "

"That's beautiful."

"Yes, it is."

With that easy strength that always thrilled her, he lifted her, tugging the covers from under her hips. "Put your legs around my waist."

She did, but only because it made it easier for her to snuggle into his heat. She needed to feel him. It was only hours ago she'd thought she'd lost him. She pressed her cheek over the bullet wound. Nothing more than a scar now. He'd healed himself and her. He had to be tired. He wouldn't let her hide, wouldn't let her pretend. His palms were rough against her cheeks as he cupped her face and held her gaze to his dark one. Curving her palms over the arc of his shoulders, she sighed. Her eyes burned. She was going to miss him so much.

"You were never a joke to me, seelie. You were never a pity date." His thumbs stroked the tears she couldn't contain from her cheeks. Her fingers stretched to encompass all of his power.

"You were never other than the one who holds my heart. From the moment I saw you, from the moment I took your scent, I knew you were the one I'd been waiting for."

"But I'm dying."

There was no getting around that fact.

He shook his head as if she was missing his point. His hair slid across the back of his hands in a stroke of cool satin. "Which only makes me glad that I didn't miss you this lifetime."

This lifetime? At last a fragment of hope. "There might be other lifetimes?" she asked. "I might come back again?"

"There are no guarantees."

She pressed his hair back from his face, needing to see his expression. "But there's a chance?"

His lips thinned. "Yes."

"You don't believe in it, do you?"

"Not entirely."

She just needed him to believe a little, to give her something to hold on to for the time they had left.

"Then let's believe that, okay?" She blinked back the inevitable tears. "When the time comes, no saying good-bye, just 'until we meet again.' "

Maybe if she died believing she could be reincarnated, it would influence whatever determined these things and she'd come back sooner. So he wouldn't have to wait so long. Oh, God, how selfish could she be? She was making him promise to wait for her no matter how many lifetimes it took.

"I'm sorry. Don't promise that. That wasn't fair."

It was just so hard to say good-bye to him, to what they had together. That they could have had. His fingers under her chin tipped her face up. Fire glowed in his eyes.

"I don't need fair. No wolf needs fair. All we need is this." Her head fell back into his shoulders as he pressed his mouth over hers in a hauntingly tender kiss. "For one day, one month, or a lifetime, the length of time I have to know you doesn't matter," he whispered into her mouth. "It only matters that I found you."

She slapped his shoulder halfheartedly, tucking her face into his neck, unable to bear the intimacy of breathing the promise of his words. It made her hunger. "You're going to make me cry."

His head canted to the side. His beautiful mouth tilted in a gentle smile. "I'd rather make you sigh with pleasure."

That sounded so much better than sobbing over that which couldn't be changed. "I wish you would, too."

"Then why don't I give it a try."

Dropping his shoulder, he tipped her off balance. She had no choice but to fall back on the bed. Kelon came down over her, a dark shadow, inhuman, different, but everything she'd ever wanted. Her hands slid over his shoulder as naturally as her next breath entered her lungs. As if he could read her mind, he asked, "Does it really matter that I'm different?"

She linked her fingers behind his neck. "Does it really not matter that I'm dying?"

He shook his head. "Not when I have today."

She liked that philosophy. Focusing on today meant she didn't have to worry about where this was leading, didn't have to worry about anything beyond making this moment work with this man in this time. She could live like that. "I like that philosophy."

"Good, because there's something else we have to talk about."

The gentleness left his expression. Now she could identify the thread of energy that had been teasing the edges of her consciousness since she'd addressed him. Anger.

His hand covered her abdomen where the wound had been. "I believe I told you to stay in the cave."

She should have known she wasn't going to get away without a lecture on this. "I just went to the stream."

"You just went into the open unprotected with no way to defend yourself."

"I had the gun."

"Zippered in your pocket so you couldn't get to it."

What could she say? He was right. "Okay, so I never figured on some weirdo running around trying to cut the donated kidney out of me because he believed putting his sister's corpse back together would guarantee her resurrection." She shrugged. "Sue me."

His eyes took on a dangerous edge, his touch a forewarning tension. "I'm more interested in obedience than money."

Robin wiggled back, not liking that tone in his voice. "Trust me, you'd be more satisfied with the money."

"I don't think so."

The utter calmness of the statement sent a frission of alarm through her as his hand locked on her thigh. She had a glimpse of his expression, the determination setting his mouth, the unnamed emotion darkening his eyes before she was flipped over. Too fast. Dizziness warred with nausea.

"Ugh."

His hand rested on her rear. Heavy and ominous. "What?"

"I think I'm going to puke."

The hand immediately left her buttocks to stroke over her back, pressing into the tense muscle between her shoulder blades, rubbing gently until she relaxed and the nausea subsided. The man was not cut out to be a disciplinarian, but he was a heck of a masseuse. As Robin sank into the mattress, honesty forced her to admit, "I was wrong not to listen to you."

"Yes, you were."

He didn't have to sound so arrogant about it. She was apologizing after all. As a result, her "I'll try to do better in the future" wasn't nearly as conciliatory as she'd intended.

"I know you will."

She didn't like the way he said that. "Kelon . . . ?"

"Stay where you are, seelie."

The hand in the middle of her back assured her she had no choice.

"What are you going to do?"

"You disobeyed your mate. Put yourself in danger. I am obligated as your Protector and mate to discipline you."

His hand ghosted over her buttock. She screamed as if he'd beaten her, and then immediately felt embarrassed for the overreaction. Pushing hard with her arms, she struggled to get upright. The next little swat sank like hot butter to her core, melting over her resistance, coating it with an illicit thrill. A questing touch between her legs spurred a soft, purely masculine chuckle.

How could she be turned on by something like this? "You are *so* not spanking me like a child."

"No." The silk of her gown pooled in the middle of her back. The bunching of the fabric took on the weight of what it signified. Vulnerability. Submission. Excitement. The warmth of his fingers shaped to the curve of her buttock. "I'll be disciplining you as a woman who needlessly risked the thing most precious to me. Her life."

She strained to catch his eye over her shoulder. All she got a view of was his shoulder and the flex of muscle as he raised his hand again. She kicked out. "Like hell you will."

"It is my duty."

There was a note in his voice that had nothing to do with anger. A dark, sexy resonance that tugged on her senses. A hint that punishment was not the main point of this exercise. And if punishment wasn't the man's goal, that only left one other: pleasure. Her inner tension relaxed. Kelon was very good at delivering pleasure.

The next tap held a slight sting. As much as she wanted to be outraged, there was an element of excitement in the moment, a hint of delight in the stimulus, a certain sensuality in the delivery. "Duty?"

"Yes. It is wolf law."

His fingers, now in the middle of her spine, massaged gently.

"And you always follow the law?" she gasped as he found a spot that flashed a shiver outward.

His fingers pressed, steadying her through the burst of heat. "To the letter."

That was definitely humor in his voice, along with a deep, sexy promise. The next of those teasing swats went straight to her womb, creating havoc and confusion in its wake. How could something so wrong feel so good? Another swat, another hot bite of pleasure. Her legs parted, her hips arched as the previous was quickly followed by another and another, light spanks that didn't exactly hurt, but stung in a way that had her squirming, to the point she didn't realize Kelon wasn't holding her down anymore. Her hands were buried in the comforter, and she was pushing back into each smack, willing him to do it harder, to give her more, to make her burn the way she sensed she could.

"Kelon?"

"What?"

"Do it right!"

She didn't know what right was, but instinct told her he did.

His rumbling chuckle was just one more bit of stimulation amidst an overabundance. "Are you asking to be disciplined, Robin?"

She curved her spine and bit his thigh, hard, hearing his growl, shuddering as the timbre hit her ears just right, sending a delicious pulse of desire rolling down her back, flowing naturally into her center, down her thighs. "Yes."

His palm cupped the lingering sting from the last swat, sheltering it, nurturing it. "Are you asking for me to spank this sweet ass?"

He was pushing it. "If I remember correctly, you weren't giving me a choice."

"A man has his duty."

The smile in his voice was easy to detect. "Then do it right!"

His hand lifted out of her line of vision, flashed back in as it came down. She heard the contact before she felt it. Harder than before, edging the dark pleasure with hot pain, dragging part of her she'd only suspected she harbored to the fore.

"Are you repentant?"

"Damn you, yes!"

"Good."

He started slow, teasing her with random spanks that snagged her breath and pulled her nerve endings to knots of volatile expectation. If only she could catch the pattern, predict the sensation . . .

He didn't let her, changing the pattern, varying the force, keeping her on the edge, trapping her between pleasure and pain, agony and ecstasy. She clawed at the quilt, swore, screamed. Once, twice, three times. The spanking stopped. She screamed again for a different reason. He couldn't leave her like this. He couldn't.

"Kelon!" The snarl was more threat than plea.

He just growled right back. "Lift up."

It took her a second to process the order, but when she did, she obeyed, without thinking, just hoping.

He delivered on that hope, his fingers tucking between her thighs, the middle one resting directly on her engorged clitoris. "Oh God!"

She bore down, grinding against the digit as he started up again, not with the firm swats she wanted, but with those light, teasing spanks she'd outgrown five minutes ago.

"Kelon, I'm going to kill you if you don't get serious."

He had the gall to laugh and continue teasing her with the

same elusive pressure on her clit as he was delivering to her rear. In the far corner of her mind she recognized the disturbance at the bedroom door, recognized Donovan's voice, Lisa's outrage, but it was all so far away. All that mattered was the sweet agony swelling in her center, spreading outward. She kicked with her feet, twisted. Kelon snarled. His finger stroked once, twice. She shuddered as the joy spiked deep; her gasp escalated to a moan as he did it again, the same way, same rhythm. Against her rear, his palm fell with the same regularity, the force increasing incrementally with each blow, predictably, wonderfully. Her climax shimmered just out of her reach, beautiful, hot, just waiting.

"Damn it, Donovan, he's hurting her."

The door swung open. Robin had one split second to absorb the impression of Lisa's horrified expression and then Donovan's amused one before Kelon pinched her clit between his fingers, squeezing and releasing in a rapid pattern that echoed the blistering, fast swats that sent her hurtling over into the violence of her climax, where nothing mattered except the ferocious spasms that jackknifed her into the bed. She reached out, terrified. "Kelon."

He was there, gathering her up, pressing her against him, letting his big body absorb the aftershocks, supporting her through the residual power of her orgasm. From far away she heard Lisa's voice.

"He's not hurting her?"

"No. He's disciplining her."

Robin buried her face in Kelon's throat, breathing deeply of his scent, knowing mortification was coming, not caring, simply floating on the residual bliss. The door closed with a decisive click. Through the wooden barrier she heard a muffled, "Well, heck. How come you never discipline me?"

"Give me a reason."

Kelon chuckled, bouncing her against him. Robin slapped his shoulder. "I'm never going to live this down."

"Nor should you. Lessons should stay learned."

She leaned back, not worrying about falling. Kelon would catch her. He always did. She settled into the curve of his arm, hitching her hip up so her buttocks cradled his rock-hard cock. "So you're telling me that every time I disobey you'll make me come so hard I lose track of everything except the pleasure?"

His lips brushed her hairline. "Pretty much."

"And that's discipline?"

He shrugged and his gaze didn't quite meet hers. "Apparently the only kind I can bring myself to administer."

He sounded a bit disappointed in himself. She preferred him amused. She stroked his cheek and smiled before putting the back of her hand against her forehead and dropping back over his arm with dramatic flare. "Brace yourself, I feel another bout of disobedience coming on."

He hauled her back up with a flex of muscle. "Imp."

She wrapped her arms around his neck and tickled his ear. "Your imp, though."

"Yeah." His smile was beautiful to see. Slow coming, slow spreading, but when it arrived, all encompassing. "Mine." He touched the corner of her mouth, his finger lingering on the crease of her laughter, as if he wanted to capture it. "Donovan's going to rib me to no end."

"Why?"

Patting her thigh, he confessed, "When it comes to you I lack the proper diligence."

She wiggled her butt. "I'm not complaining."

"You should be. I have a responsibility as your mate."

He really sounded like he thought he'd let her down. "Which you fulfilled beautifully. That was kinky, and I liked it."

His smile canted to that sexy grin. "So did I."

Only up to a point. He hadn't come, and that was her responsibility. "As your mate, don't I have responsibilities, too?"

"Yes. To live."

She rolled her eyes. The man could be too fixated sometimes. She caught his gaze, held it, licking her lips as she slid off his lap. "And nothing else?"

His big hand fell naturally to her head. Fine lines fanned out from the corner of his fascinating eyes. "And to please your mate."

She unbuttoned his fly, unzipped his pants, leaning forward as his fingers pressed against the back of her skull, teasing him with her breath through his jeans. "I knew you had a selfish bone in you."

"It's not a good thing."

She shook her head. "On the contrary, I think it's a very healthy thing. It guarantees you get what you need from me."

His cock was too big just to pull out of his pants.

Anticipating her needs, he lifted up. "Just having you is enough."

Rolling her eyes, she shook her head. "Honestly, Kelon. That is just so much bull, and if there was any chance of this being a long-term relationship, we'd have to have a long talk."

His thumb slipped into the corner of her mouth, pressed, parting her teeth. "Are you going to lecture me or pleasure me?"

"Would taking you in my mouth give you pleasure?"

He growled deep in his throat. His cock jerked in her hand. A bead of pre-come coated the tip. A shiver when down her spine. It did wondrous things to her libido when he went all primitive on her. "I'll take that as a yes."

She gathered the salty bead on her tongue, knowing he was watching her savor the taste, the texture. His hands fisted in her hair and another growl followed the first.

"Swallow."

She did, slowly, elaborately, tipping her head back, smiling into his eyes as her throat worked, licking her lips in the aftermath.

His hair fell forward, shadowing his face as he leaned over her, his hands almost convulsively jerking her toward his cock. "Seelie, baby, it's dangerous to tease me."

"Why? Because you'll go wild?"

He groaned. "Yes." With a pulse of his hips, he pressed his cock against her lips. "Open."

It didn't surprise her that he couldn't remain passive. She cuddled into the hollow created by his thighs. "Make me."

"Robin . . ."

Running her fingers up and down his shaft, she arched her brow at him. "I dare you."

"Robin . . ."

"I love it when you growl." She touched him with her tongue. "Tell you what, I'll even double dare you. Will that do the trick?"

Apparently so, because the hands that had been cradling her face moved, gathered purchase, pulled her face in, spearing his cock past the barrier of her lips, over the edge of her teeth, until he reached the back of her throat. His eyes were wild, brilliant with an inner glow, hot with hunger. For her.

It was more than she'd expected. Robin gagged, and grabbed for his thighs, catching her breath as he pulled back until only the fat head rested on her tongue.

There was no mistaking why he paused. He was fighting himself, fighting the instinct she'd aroused in him. She didn't want that. She didn't want him holding back. She shook her head and grabbed his cock with both hands. Leaning in, she took him the same way, hard and fast, relaxing her jaw as his cock surged in, holding him at the back of her throat, wrestling with the urge to gag. His cock jerked, and a salty flavor spread through her mouth. She closed her eyes and swallowed. The urge to gag abated for a second.

"Yes, just like that. Take me."

She looked up, blinking, words impossible.

His cock dragged over her tongue as he withdrew. Wanting to give him the same joy he gave her, she sucked hard, laving the underside with her tongue.

His hips bucked and his cock speared back in, gliding over her lips, tickling the nerve endings there, sending licks of fire coursing through her. She clenched her thighs on the dash of joy that flavored the uniqueness of the moment. His cock hit her throat again. She swallowed fast. His head fell back, and his cock leapt in a sporadic jerks as he forged in, demanding more even as his fist closed around the base of the thick shaft, restricting his own want. For her. He was always thinking about her. She didn't want worry between them; she wanted passion, joy, and freedom. For him to ask for what he wanted. For her to know so she could give it. With a soft stroke of her fingers down the inside of his thighs, she gentled his tension. With a cupping of her fingers around his balls, she stole his control. With a firm grasp, she removed his hand.

Immediately he sat up. "Not smart, baby."

Sometimes his protectiveness got in the way. "I'm not a baby. I'm your woman and I think you need to settle that in your mind."

"I know who you are."

Putting his hand on his thigh, she said, "Then prove it. Let me do what *I* want."

"You don't understand how it is with a wolf."

She met his gaze, not flinching from the fire she saw there. "I know how it is with us."

"And how is that?"

Cradling the heavy weight of his balls in her palms, she whispered, "We're right together, Kelon. Either you trust that or you don't."

His fingers tangled in her hair. His chest expanded on a deep breath. "I don't want to hurt you."

"You can't."

"It would be so easy."

His balls were heavy, taut with a need he wouldn't let loose. That was going to have to change. "Maybe for another, but never for you."

"You have too much faith in me." The accusation rumbled out

of his deep chest, ending on a higher note as her thumb pressed against the heavy vein at the underside of his penis.

She squeezed his balls lightly in a slow enticement. "Maybe you just don't have enough."

He opened his mouth. It was a simple process to shut him up. All it took was the slow glide of her mouth down his thick cock, an equally slow retreat, a delicate nibble on the mushroom head. He groaned and she smiled, taking him again, deeper this time, holding him longer, absorbing his thrusts and wildness, glorying in his pleasure, repeating the process over and over, knowing he was getting close when his muscles stiffened and his cock swelled to impossible proportions.

She grabbed his hips when he went to pull back, snarling at him. This was her gift. She'd deliver the way she wanted.

"Baby, I can't hold back."

She didn't want him holding back. She wanted to know how it felt to please him like this, to feed the dominant side of his personality the way he fed the submissive side of hers. She shook her head. He grabbed her hair. She shuddered as tiny pings of pleasure sparked through her at the hard tug.

Come for me.

The thought lingered in her mind, riding her passion, centering her focus. She wanted him to come like this—wild, dominant, crazy with the pleasure she offered. His cock pushed deep. She couldn't breathe, but she didn't struggle, trusting him. His fingers lingered on her cheek, riding the bulge of his cock.

"You want me, baby?" A tiny pulse of his hips gave her a fraction more. "Like this?"

Before she ran out of air, before she could even think to panic, he withdrew. She took a deep breath through her nose and smiled with her eyes.

"Hold on then. This is going to get a little wild, because truth be told, your mouth drives me crazy."

She gave him a little nod, and he gave her what she wanted. Him the way he wanted to be with her. Wild, forceful, but never hurting. And she gave him what he wanted—her acceptance of him as he was, as he needed to be. Cupping his heavy balls in her hand, she squeezed. His control shattered, and she watched it happen. The fissure started in his eyes, tore along the sharp edges of his expression, snaked through his arms before finally transferring to his hold. His hips bucked sharply, once, twice. His cock head hit the back of her throat, and then went farther. She swallowed desperately against the urge to gag, not wanting to fail him now, needing to give him this, struggling to adjust to his roughness, succeeding. Then he was giving her all he had and she took it, cradling his softness, nurturing his wildness, needing him as much as she needed to breathe. And when the first flush of wildness was over, he was looking down at her, regret in his eyes.

"Ah damn, Robin."

The same regret was in his voice, in the hands that eased her back. His cock slipped from her lips. Her moue of protest was instinctive. She relaxed into his hold, lifting his cock back, taking him back into her mouth, milking the last of his pleasure from him, leaning against his thigh. He shuddered one last time, pulsed one last time. His cock softened slightly. Fascinating.

He slid off the bed, gathering her into his arms, holding her the way he always did, as if there wasn't anything more valued anywhere. Brushing his lips across her hair, he released his breath on a ragged sigh. "You're going to lead me a merry dance, aren't you?"

She turned into his embrace, snuggling into his thigh, not fighting him when he cupped her throat in his hand. "That's my plan."

"Are you okay?"

"I'm fine." She couldn't keep the pride out of her voice. Nor the hoarseness.

Leaning back, he eyed her critically. "I was too rough. Damn it."

Before she could blink he had her stretched out on the floor. She slapped his hands away.

"Stop messing with my postcoital bliss."

"I hurt you."

"No, you didn't, but you are seriously ruining my rosy glow."

He paused, sensuality edging out the concern. "Rosy glow?"

Following his gaze, it wasn't hard to see why. Her nightgown was twisted around her waist and hanging half off her torso, leaving her right breast fully exposed.

She arched her back, thrusting her breast up. "Definitely."

His eyes didn't leave her chest. "I suppose you think it's my responsibility to bring it back?"

"Yup."

Centering her nipple in the middle of his palm, he closed his fingers over her breast. "I suppose I can be persuaded to see things your way."

She notched her pussy to the thrust of his rehardening cock. "And what form would this persuading take?"

"Your promise to behave."

She wrinkled her nose at him. "You worry too much."

He lowered his mouth to hers. "Nah. I'm just cautious."

Eleven

THIS isn't good."

"What isn't?" Kelon asked Donovan, coming into the kitchen. He nodded to Lisa standing in front of the stove. She flinched, blushed, and then glared at him. He cocked an eyebrow at Donovan.

He shrugged. "She's mad because I won't discipline her."

Lisa snorted and stirred the pot of oatmeal on the stove. "Oh please. Like I couldn't get a spanking if I wanted one."

Donovan's mouth twitched into a smile Lisa couldn't see. He winked at Kelon before he took a sip of coffee. "So you say."

Another snort from Lisa. Donovan glanced at her fondly and then he turned back to Kelon. His expression sobered. "How's Robin?"

"No worse for wear." Determined to eek out every bit of excitement she could from the time they had left. Rushing hurdles faster than with what he was comfortable. "She's sleeping."

Because he'd exhausted her. And despite the satisfied smile on her lips when he'd left her, he couldn't help but feel guilty about how little he was able to resist her. A Protector ought to have better self-control.

"How's she handling the fact that you're a werewolf?" Lisa asked.

"She was more concerned about whether my dating her was an act of pity."

Lisa rapped the spoon on the side of the pot, put it on the stove top, and came over. "Was it?"

Donovan caught her hand and pulled her into his side. "Wolves don't work that way."

"We're more all or nothing," Kelon supplied, taking a sip of his coffee. It was strong and rich. Donovan couldn't cook worth a damn, but he made good coffee.

Lisa looked between them. "Yeah, I'm beginning to get that."

Kelon motioned to the stove. "The oatmeal's burning."

"Shoot."

"What isn't good?" Kelon asked Donovan again.

"I can't get through to Wyatt."

There were any number of reasons why Wyatt might not be answering his phone, all of them sensible. None of them as likely as the suspicion that had the lights glowing in Donovan's eyes.

"Without anyone to watch his back, he'll be vulnerable to challenge."

"I'd thought of that."

"Of course, his phone could just be out."

"Yes, it could."

Donovan didn't sound any more convinced than he did.

"Whose phone might be out?"

Robin stood in the door. She was pale, but smiling. The welcome in her eyes rolled over him like summer heat. "You're supposed to be sleeping."

"I'm hungry."

"I've got oatmeal ready," Lisa called.

"Good."

Robin didn't want oatmeal. Kelon could read it in her face, but she'd never tell her sister that. He tucked her into his side. Under the pretext of kissing her he whispered, "Want me to mess with your oatmeal?"

"Can you?"

"It'll cost you."

"I'll pay whatever you want."

His right eyebrow cocked up. "A blank check?"

"Yes."

"You're on."

"What are you whispering about?" Lisa asked.

"I'm negotiating," Robin answered.

Lisa glanced at the oatmeal. "Breakfast?"

"Yup."

Lisa held out the spoon to Kelon. "Whatever she offered, I'll double."

"The hell you will!" With a wolf's hearing, Donovan knew exactly what Robin had offered.

Kelon laughed, sat Robin in a chair, and took the spoon from Lisa. "How about I just take over?"

Without a qualm, Lisa relinquished the spoon. "Works for me." Folding her arms across her chest she asked, "Wyatt's in trouble, isn't he?"

Kelon glanced at Donovan, who shook his head. "Not necessarily."

He grabbed brown sugar and cinnamon from the cupboard.

Unfortunately, Robin could see the look Lisa couldn't. "He's in trouble because you're here with us?"

Damn, the women were quick. "Maybe."

"You have to help him."

"No."

"He's your cousin," Lisa snapped.

"And we're their mates," Robin interjected. "They won't leave us here."

"Since when are you an authority on all things wolfie?"

"Since I married her," Kelon growled, crumbling brown sugar into the mixture.

Lisa spun toward him, rapping Donovan in his face with her elbow. "You married her? When? How?"

"The same way you married Donovan."

"Without permission?"

Donovan pulled her back. "I gave my permission, seelie."

Robin sat up straight. "We're married? Did I sleep through the ceremony?"

"Tapping the spoon against the rim of the pot, Kelon caught Robin's eye. "More like you screamed your way through it."

Color flooded her face in a tide of red.

Lisa snorted. "An orgasm does not a marriage make."

"It does for a wolf."

Robin recovered her voice. "I'm not wolf."

"But you are mine."

For that, she didn't have an argument. Lisa did, flashing him a glare, clearly protective of her sister. "I still don't understand why you have to stay here. The bad guy is dead, or did I misread Donovan's sudden trip into the woods?"

"Buddy and friends are still around," Donovan rumbled.

Lisa threw up her hands. "The ones who ran us off the road fled, and without them, Buddy is harmless."

"You can't hope to convince me of that, so don't even try."

"The only solution is for us to go with you," Robin interjected as if she were the sensible one.

Donovan's "No" synched with Kelon's "Hell, no."

"It's the only solution," Lisa pointed out with perfect reason. "You can't leave Wyatt unprotected in a hostile pack. You're Protectors."

And there was the catch gnawing on Kelon's conscience. "No."

"The pack must be civilized."

"What makes you think that?" Donovan asked, hitting the Send button on the satellite phone again.

Lisa wasn't one for giving up. "You're the most civilized men I know. It stands to reason you came from a civilized society."

"You're human. Werewolf law doesn't apply to you."

"It applies to you, and I can't see anyone bothering someone under your protection," Robin added.

"She's got a point." Donovan hung up the phone and met Kelon's gaze. "Went directly to voice mail."

Kelon got that same sick feeling in his gut he'd gotten when he'd seen Robin lying beneath the maniac with the knife in his hand. "Wyatt's never been out of communication this long."

"I know."

"He's in trouble."

Robin pushed her chair back. "I'll start packing right after breakfast."

Lisa put her coffee cup down. "I'll help."

Kelon added three sugars to Robin's coffee, suppressing a shudder at the amount. The women's enthusiastic assumption was only going to meet with disappointment. Neither were going anywhere near the pack. "Nothing's been decided."

"I know." Robin shrugged and took the cup he handed her. The smile she gave him was sweeter than her coffee. "We'll get ready just in case."

"It's a rough trip, and you're sick."

Her smile didn't falter. "You'll take care of me."

This from the woman who was always saying she didn't need to be taken care of. The shake of his head was a warning. She was too excited about seeing his home to pay heed. "Robin—"

"What?" she asked. "Can I help it if I'm excited about seeing where you grew up, about meeting a whole new society?"

"Robin, it's not going to be the 'welcome home' you're expecting."

His home was nothing like a human one. Politics and battles for position were the constants.

"Then you'll need me there to make you feel better at the end of the day."

"You might as well give it up." Donovan sighed. "They're right and they know it. Unless we're going to abandon Wyatt, we don't have any choice but to bring the two of them with us."

Lisa glanced out the window. "Make that the three of us."

Kelon turned off the flame under the oatmeal and leaned over to see out the window. A slender woman dressed in a business suit was getting out of a gold sedan. There was a similarity in her coloring and facial features to those of Robin and Lisa. Her movements were smooth, quick, and efficient.

"Our sister, Heather," Lisa explained as the woman approached the house at a brisk pace.

"We'd better think of a story fast if you don't want her to know you're a werewolf."

Kelon smiled. It was easy to see the woman intimidated her younger sisters. "I think we can handle the visit of one overprotective sister."

Lisa shook her head. Robin patted Donovan's shoulder. "You don't know Heather."

Donovan patted her shoulder right back. "You don't know werewolves."

One

THERE'S no such thing as werewolves."

Her sisters, Lisa and Robin, just stared at Heather as if she had a great realization coming. One of the men, Kelon, she believed he was called, put a bowl of oatmeal in front of her. It smelled wonderful, like cinnamon blueberry muffins.

"Everyone says that at first."

She picked up the small pitcher of cream and poured for the count of two, which should be roughly a fourth of a cup. "You run around telling everyone you're werewolves?"

Donovan leaned back in his chair. She caught her breath, half expecting it to collapse under his muscular frame. The men her sisters had taken up with were as big as mountains. Yet another worry to add to her growing pile.

"No. That would invite too much speculation."

Not to mention frequent visits from men in white suits who worked at the funny farm, she bet.

"Oh." She took a bite of her oatmeal. It tasted divine. She forced herself to swallow past the tension knotting her throat. "At least you had the good sense to take up with men who cook."

Too late, she remembered to smile.

Lisa frowned. "Donovan doesn't cook."

"Oh." She put the spoon down. For the life of her, she couldn't come up with anything more diplomatic to say.

Which pretty much left her sitting on one side of the table and her sisters and their self-proclaimed werewolf "mates" sitting on the other. Her sisters' expressions were easy to read. Defiance because they knew she wasn't going to believe them, combined with an unreasonable, predictably stubborn determination that she would. The men's expressions were not so clear. They just stared at her, waiting, their faces blank of anything except calm patience. She had a feeling they were very good at waiting. Patience wouldn't do them any good. They could sit there until the cows came home and she still wasn't going to have a hallelujah moment. There were no such things as werewolves.

Along with being big, both men had similar dark hair, dark eyes, and sharp features. Obviously twins. It was easy to see why Lisa and Robin were interested in them. Any woman with an active red corpuscle would be. They radiated sex appeal and danger. A classic bad-boy combination. The kind that always drew Lisa like a magnet.

Robin didn't have a type, but her youngest sister always followed Lisa's lead, and Robin's health problems had left her vulnerable, especially after that bastard Buddy had nearly raped her. It wasn't so clear why the men were interested in her sisters. Maybe they just needed women who were willing to believe in their delusion?

She sighed internally. If her sisters had to take up with lunatics, why couldn't they have picked ones with less muscle and less of a threat factor? Men that didn't make her feel so aware of her own lack of strength? Both Donovan and Kelon radiated an edge that made her think in terms of *scalpel.* Edgy, potentially lethal, and ready to cut at the slightest mistake.

"Have you ever been in prison, Donovan?"

He didn't bat an eyelash. "No, but I've put a few people behind bars."

That explained a lot. Cops often shared the hard edge common to criminals. "What division of law enforcement are you in?"

"I'm a Protector."

The dull throb behind her eyes increased. This was like pulling teeth. She pinched the bridge of her nose. She hadn't become an ER nurse by not being able to handle stress. It was just that after the last year and a half, the depressing news about Robin's prognosis, and Lisa's call about Robin being attacked, her quota was full. "And just what does a Protector do?"

Amusement lurked around the perimeter of his expression. "I enforce the laws of my people, deliver justice, and protect."

He was humoring her. She hated to be humored. She rapped her fingernails on the table. "Obviously, you're not tops in your field, or I wouldn't be here."

That took the patience out of Lisa's wait. "That was uncalled for."

Probably, but she didn't care. "Pardon me, I'm trying to convince myself that both of you haven't lost your minds and taken these two right along with you."

"How's that working?" Donovan asked.

She looked at him from under her hand and smiled coldly. "It's not going well for you."

Lisa elbowed the man beside her. "Stop provoking her, Donovan."

Kelon's chair creaked as he shifted position. "Provoking people comes naturally to Donovan."

She really wished the damn chair would break. That much arrogance begged to be landed on its butt on the floor. Heather gave him the same teeth-baring grin she'd given Donovan. "I believe you, and if I was in a better mood, I might even humor you, but right now I'm tired. My patience is shot, and I really do not have time to indulge your little delusion, so if you have any proof of werewolfism, show it. Otherwise, stop insulting my intelligence. I'm not finding this joke funny."

"What kind of proof are you looking for?" Donovan asked, as if she'd just asked to see his financial prospectus.

Heather leaned back in her chair. "Werewolves are supposed to be shape-shifters, aren't they?" She waved her fingers at him. "So shift."

He glanced at Lisa. "I can't."

Just as she thought. "I guess that settles that."

"I can," Kelon offered.

She wondered how long it took to implant a delusion so deep that a man could say that with a straight face. Wrapping her fingers around the spoon handle, she squeezed. Hard. "How come you can shift, and he can't?"

"Because I didn't promise not to."

This was just getting more and more bizarre. "Promised who?"

Lisa slammed her cup on the table. "Me, okay? Donovan promised me he wouldn't shift because, quite frankly, I can't handle any more right now, either."

Welcome to my world. Heather turned to Kelon. "But you didn't promise anybody?"

He was still watching her with that same calm patience that made her feel like a bug under a microscope. "No."

"Then shift and let's just get this over with."

"Bossy, aren't you?"

Robin leaned into his side, and rested her palm on his admittedly very impressive chest. "She always has been."

The shift in Kelon's demeanor was subtle, but with the touch of Robin's hand, that hard energy around him seemed to soften. Delusional or not, he cared for her sister. Kelon put his arm around Robin's shoulder. It was a very possessive gesture. It was also disconcertingly tender.

"Do you wish me to give your sister proof?"

Robin's fingers looked so fragile against the strength of Kelon's. She *was* fragile, always had been, but there was nothing fragile in her glance when she looked up. "No."

Beyond an arch of an eyebrow, Kelon didn't question the statement. That was left up to her. Robin didn't hesitate to answer.

"Because it should be enough that I said it. It should be enough that I told you, Heather."

There were limits to "should." "You're asking me to believe in the impossible."

"But the fact that it's me asking you to should count for something."

She blew her bangs off her forehead. "I'm sitting here discussing the matter, aren't I?"

"No, you're sitting here dissecting everything we say, looking to punch holes in it, looking to prove your theory that we've been duped and we've lost our minds."

This was so unlike Robin. Robin never argued. She'd always been the buffer between Lisa and herself. The peacemaker. "What do you expect me to do?"

"I expect you to believe me. I expect you to give Kelon your support and welcome him to the family."

"Seelie—"

"Don't interfere, Kelon."

"You can't expect your sister to believe without proof."

Great, now she had a man who thought he was werewolf on her side in an altercation with her sister about something that wasn't possible. It only went to show how tired she was that she couldn't tell if that was a plus or minus to her side of the argument.

"Actually, I can."

"Robin—" Heather began, unsure where she was going but needing to go somewhere.

Robin cut her off. "I've always given you my complete faith. When you asked me to have the second transplant, when you told me it was going to work and to give it another shot, I did. I went through it because you asked me to, because I trusted in your faith, but now it's my turn. I'm asking you to believe me this time."

"What you're asking me is pretty incredible."

"So was your statement that the second time was the charm when it came to a kidney transplant."

And it hadn't been. Robin had gone through the months of dialysis, the painful operation, the false hope—she'd gone through all of it because Heather had asked her to, and it had all been for nothing. Damn! When had Robin learned to fight so mean?

"It's totally illogical."

"I know."

"I don't do illogical well."

Her sister leaned forward, her eyes and posture backing the plea in her voice. "But you do love well, and I'm asking you to love me enough to believe what I'm saying. Please, Heather. I need this."

The question was why. Heather opened her mouth, not sure what was going to come out but knowing what Robin needed her to say.

Kelon tucked Robin into his side. "Baby, even I know that's too much to spring on someone and expect them to digest it right away."

There was a world of tenderness in the way the man held her sister, and an overt message conveyed by the protective way his body sheltered hers. *Mine.*

Robin looked up at him, her heart in her eyes. "I need this, Kelon."

He touched his finger to the corner of her eye, catching a tear before it could fall. He might be nuts, but he loved her sister. Jealousy, unexpected, painful, thrust sharp and deep as the Cinderella dreams Heather had thought dead and buried rose to the surface.

"And if it was in my power, I'd give it to you."

It was in Heather's power. Maybe. Barely. But . . . Heather sighed, poking at the oatmeal in her bowl with her spoon. She'd been starving right up until she'd come in and found the two examples of sex on the hoof ensconced with her sisters. Now, her stomach was churning too much to eat anything. "Couldn't you ask me to believe in something a little easier than werewolves?"

"No."

Heather glanced over at Lisa. That was no help. Lisa had the mutinous expression on her face Heather knew all too well from their childhood. Lisa was fiercely loyal to Robin, had been since the day she'd been born. The closeness in their ages had provided a bridge for understanding that she, being ten years older, had to struggle to achieve. In reality, she never had. She'd always been the family oddball. Too purpose-driven to be spontaneous. And after their parents died just after she turned eighteen, too overwhelmed fighting too many battles to do anything but work, sleep, and worry.

She sighed. No, Lisa wasn't going to help. This was important to Robin so that made it vitally important to Lisa. Heather gave her oatmeal another stir, envy rising with frustration. She'd often thought it would be nice to have someone side with her with such unflinching loyalty.

She looked up. Donovan was watching her. The sympathy in his gaze made her feel like he could see right through her carefully composed expression to that moment of insecurity. She raised her brow back at him, expecting him to take advantage, to maybe say something cutting. Instead, all he said was, "You look tired."

She *was* tired. "I'm fine."

"I'm sure you are, but I'm also sure this discussion can wait, can't it, Lisa?"

Lisa opened her mouth to argue. Donovan caught her eye, and Lisa, indomitable, spit-in-the-Devil's-eye, take-orders-from-no-one Lisa, closed her mouth, clenched her hands, took a breath, and relaxed before letting it out on a sigh.

"It can probably wait until after she gets settled," she conceded.

Heather gave up pretending to eat and pushed her bowl away. This was just too unnerving. "Okay. Who are you and what have you done with my sisters?"

"Maybe we grew up," Robin offered softly, looking like the sister she remembered. The one who'd throw herself in front of a bus to stop an argument.

"No way."

Lisa shrugged. "It was bound to happen sometime."

"And all it took was a couple of werewolves to make it happen? Wow. Who'd have thought?"

As soon as the comment left her mouth, Heather wanted it back. Sarcasm was not going to help anything. Robin flinched. Lisa sighed. Damn.

"I'm sorry. I'm tired and . . ." What the hell could she say? In full capacity of her mind? She smoothed her hand over her braid. "I'm just tired."

Robin sighed. "And we hit you with the worst right off."

"If it'll make you like me better," Donovan said, "I voted for waiting to drop that bomb on you."

She looked at him askance. Was he serious or joking? "I'll keep it in mind."

"I didn't want to tell you at all," Kelon offered, the smile on his lips not matching the worry in his eyes as Robin stood.

Heather pushed her chair back. She needed a break. She couldn't muster a smile. "Then, right now, Kelon, I guess that makes you my favorite."

SHE was expecting the knock at her bedroom door. She wasn't expecting the person on the other side. Kelon. The shadows in the hall cast his face in a sinister light, emphasizing the bold angles, diminishing the softer planes. His eyes seemed to glitter with hypnotic magnetism. And against her will, she made the comparison. Like a wolf's.

"I noticed you didn't eat."

He was holding a tray in his hands, and on it was the most decadent-looking French toast she'd ever seen. She reached for the tray. "Is that white stuff on top arsenic?" She was only half-joking.

He didn't let go immediately and didn't smile.

"We've given you a lot to digest."

"Don't remind me—it'll ruin my appetite."

She supposed she could call that quirk of his lips a smile.

"The eggnog's for your sour stomach."

"Eggnog?" She loved eggnog. She loved French toast. She couldn't remember the last time anyone had even noticed that she hadn't eaten, let alone cooked her favorite foods for her. Even if the consideration came in the form of an apology, she was touched. "I'll have to thank them."

"Them?"

"My sisters."

"Ah." There was another infinitesimal pause. "They're concerned about you."

"I know."

"No one expects you to blindly accept what you can't believe."

"Robin does."

He shook his head and sighed. A thick swathe of his long black hair slid forward over his right shoulder. "No, she doesn't. She's just in a rush to have things work out."

She observed him carefully. "Because her kidney's failing."

A spasm of emotion flickered in his eyes. "You know?"

So much for the idea that that knowledge would send him running. "I get the bills from the insurance company."

Another "Ah." Then "If it will help you to know, when the time comes, she won't be alone."

It didn't help. Nothing helped with knowing her sister was dying, that nothing she did could fix it. "Thank you."

He took the tray back from her and carried it over to the small table beside the burgundy upholstered wingback chair. She had no choice. It was either follow or lose the best meal she'd seen in months. He motioned to the chair. "Sit."

"Bossy, aren't you?"

"So Robin tells me." With a nod of his head that made her think of the old days, he said, "Enjoy your meal."

If she had any sense, she'd let him leave before she got too upset to eat. She held out until he was halfway to the door.

"I don't mean to sound like such a bitch. It's just sometimes it feels like we live on different planets." Especially when her sisters declared they were married to werewolves. Her stomach churned. She took a sip of the eggnog. It was cool, smooth, and perfectly spiced. Her stomach didn't rebel. "There's ten years' difference in our ages, you know."

He turned back. "Those ten years enabled you to do what you had to for your family."

"Yes." And left her feeling like a dried-up old woman at the age of thirty-three.

Those dark eyes of his ran over her face, over her figure. There was nothing sexual in the look—there never was when men looked at her—but the feeling that he was assessing her was not at all comfortable.

"You should know the man who hit her, Buddy, and his friends are still a threat."

"You mean you big bad werewolves didn't take them out?"

"Not yet, but we did take care of the man that wanted to return her kidney to the original donor."

She didn't think she could take any more. "The donor's dead."

"He didn't see that as a problem."

She pressed her hand to her churning stomach. "Oh my God."

Kelon reached out. She jumped. All he did was tip the forgotten glass of eggnog to her lips. She shook her head and put it back down. "The police got him?"

This time his smile raised the hairs on the back of her neck. "He's been taken care of."

She wasn't touching that with a ten-foot pole. "Why are you telling me this?"

"Because we're leaving tomorrow for the compound, and you're coming with us."

Nothing luxurious and cozy ever carried the appellation "compound."

"I prefer to stay here."

That was a lie. She'd rather be back in the city in her hectic, too-busy-to-think life that she understood than stuck here in the woods isolated by so many trees she'd never see a stranger coming even if she was looking.

"Among my people, family is everything, and women are not left to stand alone."

"I'm not getting your point."

He smiled, the first genuine one she'd seen from him. "You're family now."

Now why did that sound so ominous?

Two

DONOVAN and Kelon had arrived. And not alone. Wyatt straightened carefully, favoring his broken ribs. They'd brought Robin and Lisa and some other woman that Wyatt didn't recognize. She was taller than Lisa or Robin, and more restrained. Her figure was more refined, her face more delicate, but there was definitely a family resemblance. Her movements as she got out of the big SUV were efficient and controlled. She reminded him of a finely strung doe, all nerves and tension.

Just what he needed. A time bomb waiting to explode in the middle of a keg of dynamite. He sighed and wiped the blood from his cheek with the towel. Through the window he could see Carl watching the house. His next challenge. Normally, Carl wouldn't be much of a fight, but stoved up as he was and without time to heal, it just might be a fair match.

"Are they still waiting?"

He hated to look at his father, a wasted shadow of the burly man he remembered. "Yes."

"If you'd just kill them, it would put an end to this."

And his father could get on with the dying that would reunite him with his mate.

"I'm not killing men I grew up with."

"They're trying to kill you."

Fresh blood trickled down his cheek. He pressed the towel to it. The constant challenges were taking a toll, which he suspected was part of Cam's strategy. The man was a master strategist. Wyatt was tiring, not healing as fast as he would normally. Eventually, he wouldn't be able to win the challenge thrown at him. No doubt the Alpha he lost to at that point would be Cam. "Yeah. I got that impression."

Movement in the compound drew his eye out the window. The arrivals were attracting a whole lot of attention. Especially among the males. Visitors were rare. Usually males from other packs either on business or looking for mates. Females were unheard of, and yet the pack Protectors had brought three. He sighed. Maybe the distraction would keep the males off his ass for a bit.

"Donovan and Kelon have arrived."

"Good." His father reached for the water beside the bed. "They're good men. As good as their father was." He shot Wyatt a glance. "Keep them near."

For a moment, Wyatt thought he saw concern in his father's eyes. A blink and the moment was gone. He must be more tired than he thought. If there was one thing Big Al saw in black and white it was pack law. Any variation was weakness. And he definitely saw Wyatt's not killing the men who challenged him as a weakness. If Wyatt died as a result of the challenges for power, his father would mourn but there'd be no call for blood justice. His father would see it as his own fault.

"Never breed outside a true mating, son. It weakens the line."

Or blame it on his mother. Wyatt sighed mentally. He'd been paying his whole life for the perceived weakness bred into him by his father's failure to wait for a true mate and mating with a compatible instead. "I'll keep that in mind."

His father grunted. It could have been a laugh. It was hard to tell with his skill at disguising his thoughts behind a blank expression. "No, you won't. You'll do just as you damn well please."

Wyatt smiled, glancing out the window. "And here I thought you didn't know me at all."

"I know you."

He probably did. And beyond Wyatt's skill at fighting, didn't approve of a goddamn thing he saw. Wyatt wasn't surprised to see the unknown woman had now, apparently, taken charge of emptying the SUV. She looked the type to try and take charge of everyone and everything. Still, there was something appealing about her—an excessive amount of energy in need of release. He bet she'd be hell on wheels in bed for the man who could tap that endless well. "Donovan and Kelon brought women."

His father lay back against the pillow, his breath shuddering out as if he'd run twenty miles just from the small effort of getting a glass of water. Hell, he couldn't get used to seeing him like this. Frail and vulnerable, clinging to life not because he wanted it, but because he feared for the pack to which he'd devoted his life. Feared what his son would do to them. It galled Waytt deep inside.

"Good," his father growled, his hand shaking as he replaced the glass on the nightstand. "The pack needs them."

The pack needed a lot of things, including being brought into the twenty-first century.

A tall were female with black hair and a way of walking that said "get the hell out of my way" crossed the compound, heading in the direction of the arrivals. Vera Campbell. In the last fifty years, Vera's single-minded pursuit of Donovan had developed into an expectation of mating. The mating had been speculated to death until it had received pack sanction based on the potential strength of the offspring alone. Donovan's wishes, apparently, weren't relevant. All because Vera came from a line of Protectors. Though her mother had produced only two females, no one could see Donovan throwing daughters, and it became universally expected he would eventually ask the beautiful were to mate. If anyone had ever bothered to ask Wyatt, he could have told them it would never happen. Settling wasn't in Donovan's nature.

"What are you looking at?"

"Vera."

Al laughed. "She is determined, isn't she?"

"She does have the look of a woman staking her claim."

Which wasn't going to go over well when she found out Donovan was mated. With the exception of her pursuit of Donovan, Wyatt wouldn't exactly call the woman predictable.

"Donovan ought to just mate with her and get the next line of Protectors started."

"It'll never happen."

"She's perfect for him."

"She's not a true mate. Aren't you afraid it will weaken the line?"

"The pack needs Protectors. Humans are squeezing us out."

"Which only means we should learn to blend with them."

"Blending will mean destruction of the pack."

Through weakening of bloodlines. Wyatt got that, he just didn't agree with it. "Inbreeding is already doing that."

"It's better than the alternative."

Wyatt opened his mouth and then closed it. His father would never accept the reality.

Vera was bearing down on the group. From this angle, he could see the frown on her face. "Shit."

"Trouble?" his father asked.

"It looks like Donovan brought back a mate."

His father smiled, a spark of anticipation in his eyes. "Vera isn't going to like that." He pushed up on his elbows, straining to see around Wyatt. Wyatt didn't move and didn't offer to help his father to a better position. "Does it look like she's a good fighter?"

"She's small." And she was a hell of a fighter, but no match for a werewolf. Wyatt didn't add the last.

"Vera will make her life hell."

"Yes." And likely kill her unless Donovan stepped in, which would result in the rest of the pack making Lisa's life hell. Donovan shouldn't have brought her here, wouldn't have brought her here if there had been any other choice. Damn.

"I think it might be time to practice my diplomacy skills."

Vera was closing in on the small group fast. Other wolves, noticing the direction of her anger, fell in step behind. Wyatt couldn't really blame them. Things had been pretty boring around here, and Vera did put on a good show. He just couldn't let her put one on today.

"Won't do you any good if Vera is spoiling for a fight." Al smacked his pillow into shape. "No Campbell ever listened to reason when they were spoiling for a fight."

That was the truth. Wyatt let the curtain fall back over the window. "Then I'll have to lay down the law as her future Alpha."

Al settled back against the pillow, with a weary sigh. "Now, that I'd like to see."

Wyatt grabbed his hat off the hook and yanked open the door, knowing Big Al wouldn't hesitate to knock down a woman who questioned his authority, to beat her if she refused to acquiesce. It was the old way, the old law—dominance through brawn—the only method of rule to which his father subscribed. "I know you would."

Three

HEATHER didn't know what she expected, but for a den of were-wolves the compound looked ridiculously normal. She looked over at Robin and Lisa. "Is this what you expected?"

Lisa pursed her lips and leaned back against the hood of the SUV. "Honestly? I was sort of hoping there'd be a bit more of a woo-woo factor."

Donovan looked over from where he was taking suitcases from the back of the car. "I thought you couldn't handle any more woo-woo?"

Heather couldn't help but smile at Lisa's shrug as she watched a good-looking man approach. "From you, but I'm open to other experiences."

Donovan growled as he followed the trajectory of her glance. It was a surprisingly realistic sound.

"Like hell you are."

He grabbed her arm and spun her around, aggression settling over him in a dark cloud. Heather looked around for a weapon. Lisa laughed and relaxed against Donovan's chest.

"You are so easy."

His grip lessened, became caressing. "And you like to play with fire too much."

She arched her brows at him, clearly taunting him. "You could always bring me into line."

His hard mouth quirked in a grin Heather didn't understand. "I'm not that easy."

There was a yelp behind her. She turned to find Robin rubbing her rear and Kelon standing arms folded across his chest with a very masculine smile on his lips.

"I am."

Heather blinked. They were talking about spanking, and apparently while Lisa wanted it and wasn't getting it, Robin was and enjoyed it.

"Ew."

"What?"

She wasn't going to admit she was both appalled at the thought of her sisters playing sex games with their boyfriends yet at the same time titillated by the thought of the games themselves. She brushed at her jacket sleeve. "Road slime."

"You worry too much about appearances," Robin offered, looking supremely content, now tucked into Kelon's side.

Heather had noticed the McGowans were big on touching and always kept her sisters close. The behavior was at once protective and romantic. A loving relationship with a man who cherished her was something every woman dreamed of, something Heather knew Robin had despaired of ever knowing. Now that she had found it, Heather should be happy for her. She knew that. Instead, what she was experiencing felt an awful lot like jealousy.

She couldn't remember the last time she'd had a boyfriend, let alone felt carefree enough to let go and relax. And the last time "carefree" had happened in a man's arms was never. She'd never been able to let go with a man. There had always been too many responsibilities, too many variables, too many what-ifs of which her mind couldn't let go.

"It's a habit," she answered as Robin stared at her. Left over from the days when Social Services watched her like a hawk, waiting for her to mess up so they could take her sisters away.

"Maybe one that you should let go."

The voice came from behind her, a deep, smooth rumble of sound that slid over her skin like rich velvet. A voice like that hadn't been heard since Elvis died.

She turned. "I don't think so."

Especially when faced with a man that defined sin with his aggressively masculine features, near amber eyes, and pure sexual way of looking at a woman. She had to ask. "Do you believe yourself a werewolf, too?"

"That depends." His gaze left hers, moving down her face, lingering so long at her mouth she wondered if the chocolate she'd eaten on the way here had left a smudge.

"On what?"

"On which answer you'd prefer."

With the same lazy perusal, that gaze came back to hers.

Good grief! He was flirting with her.

Heather quelled the instinctive urge that said to smooth back her hair and straighten her skirt. She wasn't the type to primp, but when, out of the corner of her eye, she saw a tall, stunningly beautiful woman with black hair and a very angry expression coming toward them, she wished she was. "Then I guess my answer would depend on what you, wolf or human, did to tick that woman off."

The man's gaze never left her face. "Oh, she's not here for me. She's here for Donovan."

"What?" Lisa pushed away from Donovan. "Some old business you forget to tell me about?"

Heather heard Donovan's response, but the words didn't impinge upon her consciousness. Not when the stranger was still looking at her, still showing signs that he liked what he saw. Not when she was suddenly picturing them in bed together, rolling around in the sheets, exchanging kisses, touches. She took a breath. It'd been a long time since she'd indulged her carnal side.

The man held out his hand. "Wyatt Carmichael."

Electric sparks shot up her arm as she took it. "Heather Delaney."

"Ah, the older sister."

Suddenly she felt as desirable as stale bread. With a sigh, she released his hand. "Yes, the older sister."

His eyes narrowed, focused. The air around her seemed heavier, more intense. Beneath the thickness of her coat, her breasts responded to the surge in energy, swelling and lifting, the nipples peaking.

"That wasn't an insult, Heather. Your sisters have had nothing but good things to say about you. You're very responsible."

Older. Responsible. Oh yeah, those were exactly the things a woman wanted to hear when confronted by a sexy hunk she had just been considering inviting to share her bed tonight. She forced a smile. "Thank you."

The woman, apparently tired of waiting to be noticed, pushed through the crowd and stood before Donovan. She was nearly his height. She flipped her hair over her shoulder with a toss of her head. The impatience in the gesture was emphasized by the hands she settled on her slender hips.

"Donovan, who is this?"

There couldn't have been more disdain in the word *this*.

Lisa reacted predictably. Her shoulders squared. The light of battle entered her eyes as she came up on her toes. "A better question might be who are you?"

Donovan caught her arm and tugged her behind him. "I'll handle this."

"I can take care of myself."

The men might have a screw loose, but Heather was relieved to see that at least they had common sense. Attitude could only carry a woman so far against brawn, and if Lisa went up against this giant, she'd get her butt kicked. She grabbed Lisa's hand. "No, you can't."

The were female sniffed, wrinkled her nose as if she smelled something foul, and took a step back. "You brought humans here?"

"Who I bring to my compound is not your concern."

"Humans are not welcome here."

Wyatt took a step forward as a murmur rippled through the crowd. Heather wondered if it was coincidence or design that placed his big body between her and the others. "It's not your call, Vera, as to who's welcome here."

Even when reprimanding someone, Wyatt's voice was sexy. Vera spun around and gasped. "You cannot approve!"

Wyatt folded his arms across his chest. "But I do."

"But everyone knows—"

Wyatt cut her off. "If Donovan wants to bring his mate to his home, he has my permission. That's all anyone needs to know."

A flush streaked Vera's cheekbones. The glare she cut Donovan was vicious, but not nearly as mean as the one with which she fixed Lisa. "You mated *her*?"

Donovan kept a tight grip on Lisa's arm. Kelon had Robin pinned against the car. Their behavior confirmed her instinctive response. This was a dangerous situation.

"Can she fight?" Vera asked with a jerk of her chin toward Lisa.

"No."

"Yes," Lisa snapped.

Donovan turned and shook Lisa's arm. "No, you cannot."

"How do you know?"

"Because you're not wolf. You don't have a chance."

"Do you realize how insulting that is?"

"No."

"It's not your place to interfere in a challenge," Vera snapped with a certain smugness.

"But as Alpha rising, it *is* mine," Wyatt interrupted. "There will be no challenge. I forbid it."

Vera opened her mouth. All it took was a glance from Wyatt to shut it.

"Leave. Now." Wyatt didn't raise his voice, but the order hit the woman like a punch. The starch left her stance and she lowered her gaze.

Heather might have thought her totally cowed except for the tight set to her mouth and the evil glare she cut Lisa as she turned on her heel and left with the same aristocratic bearing with which she'd approached. If looks could kill, Lisa was a walking corpse.

"That's all it took to make her go? An order?"

The last had Wyatt looking at her. Heather was used to looking up to men, just not like this. Not to the point that she felt like she was going to get a crick in her neck. The man had muscle to go with that height, too. Not to mention a nice set of shoulders, a square chin, and a handsome face set off by brown eyes so light they were almost golden. The bruises on his face didn't detract one bit from his looks. They actually added to them in a rugged, macho, I-can-take-on-the-world kind of way.

"Would you prefer that I hit her?"

Away from the car the wind gusted freely, biting through her coat, almost pushing her toward him. "No! Why would you even think that?"

Wyatt froze, his nostrils flaring, and stared at her as if she'd morphed into something he didn't recognize. She took a step back. He made a rumbling sound in his throat and reached out. His eyes looked strange. Almost eerie.

We're werewolves.

The preposterous popped into her mind. She crossed her arms over her chest and rubbed her hands up and down her upper arms. Inside, there was another flutter of interest.

Kelon intercepted Wyatt's movement by simply reaching across and taking his hand. "Good to see you, Wyatt."

Wyatt blinked and with a small shake of his head seemed to gathered his senses. "Good to see you, too."

The wave of his hand included Robin, Lisa, and herself. "I take it you weren't able to clear up that problem back home."

"We cleaned up one of them," Donovan said, ignoring the press of strangers staring at Heather and her sisters with too much interest for her peace of mind. "The others are still outstanding."

"There was more than one?"

Kelon's "Yes" was more a growl than speech. It was surprising how Heather was getting used to the strange habit, and how it didn't effect her the same way it did when Wyatt did it. Wyatt's growl was sexy.

"I handled it."

Donovan grabbed her suitcase out of the car and glanced at Wyatt as he set it beside the fender. "Damn, you look like hell."

The man did look worse for wear. His face was all bruised up and he was standing awkwardly. Heather had worked enough ER shifts to recognize the probable signs of broken ribs.

"The wannabes keeping you busy?" Kelon asked.

"They're helping me stay in shape."

"An interesting way to keep yourself fit," Heather said.

Despite the fact it had to hurt his bruised face, Wyatt didn't flinch as he raised his eyebrow the way Kelon and Donovan often did. Obviously, it was a family trait. "You don't approve?"

"When the results look like you're getting the stuffing knocked out of you?" She reached for her suitcase. "It seems counterproductive."

"I'll admit I'm not making the headway I was predicting."

Her hand closed over the handle the same time his did. She didn't miss his flinch as he bent.

"I've got this."

He rumbled in that unique way he had. Her body responded in the completely feminine way it had before. "With those ribs, I don't think so."

His fingers curled around hers, prying them gently but resolutely from the handle. "This is one thing you don't have to think about. When it comes to the heavy lifting, you use me."

Four

THIS is one thing you don't have to think about.

Following Wyatt as he led her to the place where she'd be staying, Heather couldn't help but wonder: Was that a lucky guess or did Wyatt really know that she had trouble shutting her mind down?

"Here we are." He stopped in front of a ranch-style home with large windows and a wraparound porch.

"Where is *here*?"

"The best accommodations in the compound."

She glanced at the next cabin over where Lisa and Heather were passing through the door. "Why can't I stay with my sisters?"

"There are only two bedrooms."

"I have no problem staying on the couch."

"Yeah, but I have the feeling you'd have a problem listening to your sisters and their husbands all night."

She wasn't a prude, but when it came to her sisters she seemed to have a conservative side because she blushed every time their sex lives was mentioned. A fact that seemed to amuse Wyatt if the creases by his mouth were anything to go by.

"I appreciate your consideration."

The dryness of her gratitude just deepened those lines until they formed a grin. "True matings are passionate affairs."

She rolled her eyes. "Why do you have to use that language?"

He took her arm, helping her up the last stair with old-world courtesy. "What language?"

"*Mate.*"

"Because that's what werewolves do. We mate."

He just had to go steal the charm from the gesture by belaboring that point. She turned. Standing a step above him, she was about even to him in height. "You know I don't believe in werewolves, don't you?"

"I imagine you don't believe in a lot of things, right now." His finger brushed her cheek. "But I have every faith you'll work it out."

Anyone else she would have smacked for touching her so. With Wyatt, it just felt right. Instead of remaining cool and uninterested, her skin warmed under his caress. He pushed the door open and motioned her in. As Heather stepped past him, his scent wrapped around her with the same welcoming warmth as the the interior of the home. She turned and looked at him, a new question rising inside right along with a feeling of desperation.

Could she handle an affair with a man like this?

She blamed her sisters entirely for the moment of insecurity. If they didn't appear so content, if their men didn't look so head over heels in love with her pretty sisters, her mind wouldn't have gone down the forbidden path of maybe just maybe thinking there was a Prince Charming for her, which inevitably led to the mental jolt that such things didn't happen to practical, logical women like her. "I don't believe in fairy tales."

"No one's asking you to. However, as long as you're here you might want to keep your mind open to the possibilities in front of you."

Meaning him? "Why?"

"Because you don't know all you think you do." He closed the door. "That being the case, you also might want to pick up some smelling salts."

"Am I supposed to deduce from that that I'm going to be shocked frequently?"

"If you believe I'm human, yes."

"Well, so far, I haven't been able to get anybody to prove to me otherwise." She blew her bangs off her forehead. "Lisa won't let Donovan change because it'll be 'too much for her to absorb,' and Robin forbids Kelon to change because she wants me to believe her without proof. So"—she shrugged—"I'm living dangerously."

He motioned her to a leather recliner. "She's testing you."

Why not? Lack of sleep and food had left her tired. "Apparently. I just wish I knew why."

"Probably because she's running out of time."

The chair all but swallowed her in softness as she sat in it. "You know she's dying?"

Wyatt leaned over and grabbed a cushion off the couch before tossing it to her. She caught it.

"I didn't until just now."

"Don't tell her you know."

"I wouldn't dream of it. What's the problem?"

Heather hugged the pillow against her chest, squeezing against the pain of the reality she had a hard time forgetting. "She's had two kidney transplants. This one isn't doing any better than the first."

"Shit."

"That about sums it up."

"They can't give her another kidney?"

"She's a tough match to begin with, and after two rejections she's not a good candidate for a third."

"I'm sorry."

There wasn't anything to say to that except a stupid, paltry "Thank you."

"Can I get you a drink?"

"Are we talking with or without alcohol?"

"Whatever's your preference."

It was a perfectly innocent statement, and maybe it was just her hormones making more of it than it was, but she had a feeling he was offering her more than a drink. That was promising if she wanted to move ahead with an invitation to her bed. "I'll take a glass of wine if you have some."

"Coming right up."

Watching him walk across the room was a study in the grace of motion. There was a glide to each step, a placement to his feet that made her think of an animal stalking its prey.

We're werewolves.

The idea didn't seem so far-fetched anymore. Glass clinked against glass.

"Are you staying long?" he asked over his shoulder.

"Here or in Haven?"

"Let's start with here."

Another clink of glass on glass, followed quickly by the sounds of ice plopping into liquid.

"I don't like ice in my wine."

She felt like a complete idiot when he turned. He had a wineglass—a big wineglass—in one hand and a highball in the other. The highball contained something stronger, maybe whiskey from the amber color.

"I'll keep that in mind."

"I'm sorry. I can speak without thinking sometimes."

He handed her the wineglass. She had a thing about men's hands. His were strong, big boned, and well-balanced. Sensual. She bet those hands gave women a lot of pleasure.

She took the glass. He didn't immediately move away. Just stood there, staring at her until she couldn't stand it anymore. She ran her hand over her hair. She didn't feel anything out of place. "Is something wrong?"

He took a couple steps back. "No. Nothing at all."

That rumbly sound was back in his voice. She couldn't suppress her shiver. With a voice like that, he could probably talk a woman to orgasm.

Maybe you'd like to give me a try.

His head snapped up and his eyes narrowed.

The flush started in her toes and just kept climbing, consuming her face with heat that she hadn't experienced in years. "Please don't tell me I said that out loud."

"I could, but that would be a lie."

At least she had wine to get her through this moment. She took a long drink, polishing off the contents in several large swallows, telling herself she was entitled. It had been a rough two days, culminating with her humiliating herself in front of the sexiest man she'd ever seen. God! She hadn't blurted things out like that since she was thirteen! She settled the glass on her thigh. "Then can you spare us both and just pretend you didn't hear it?"

Out of the corner of her eye, she saw his approach in the increasing light reflecting off the amber liquid in his drink. His fingers curled under her chin, pressing on the outside, bringing her face around to his. The scent of scotch blended with the more earthy fragrance of his skin. Of the two, his scent packed the hardest punch to her senses, but nothing hit her harder than the look in his eyes. All the promise any woman could ever want burned there.

"Now, why would I want to do that?"

She wasn't much of a drinker, but she could use another about now. "To spare us both a lot of frustration."

"I'm not following you."

No, she supposed he wasn't. He probably had his choice of women. They probably threw themselves at him. And when they got in his bed, they probably didn't lie there wondering what the fuss was about, wondering if this time would be different, and eventually, end up wondering what was wrong with them that they lacked sizzlocity between the sheets. She held up her glass. "Can I have some more wine?"

"Absolutely."

She sat back in the chair, welcoming the haze from the wine. With things a little foggy, she was even less distracted from the beauty of his movement as he crossed the room. The man defined *poetry in motion*—if *poetry* was a purely masculine tendency to prowl. She frowned. With a broken rib the beauty of his walk should have had a few hitches. He refilled his glass while he was over there, bending with no problem to get more ice out of the small refrigerator below the bar.

"You're not hurting anymore?"

"Werewolves heal fast."

The reference to being werewolf wasn't the turnoff it should have been. The one thing Lisa and Robin definitely looked was sexually satisfied. If werewolves could do that for all their lovers, she was signing up. Wyatt handed her back her glass. She took it, sliding her fingers over his. Electric shocks skittered up her arm. She tried not to get her hopes up. A few times in the past things had looked promising at the start only to fizzle out.

"Do me a favor: drop the reference to werewolves."

"Why?"

"It's ruining my mood."

His eyebrow crooked up in that way she was fast finding sexy. "What mood is that?

It only took four swallows to drain the glass. She debated asking for a refill but considering she hadn't really eaten since yesterday, two glasses were probably enough to take the edge off. "I'm considering asking you to kiss me."

"Only considering?"

She smiled. "Well, you *are* off your rocker."

He stretched. His T-shirt clung to the hollow of his stomach, clearly defining his six-pack abs and the impressive pectorals above. "Because I'm a werewolf?"

She licked her lips. "I'm beginning to consider that a minor inconvenience."

"I'm glad you're flexible."

She might have misjudged her tolerance level for alcohol. The end of her nose was already tingling. "Do you have some pretzels or chips to go with the wine?"

"Are you hungry?"

"Some food would be good about now. A peanut butter sandwich, anything like that."

He took a sip of his whiskey, studying her face over the rim. The impression that he was seeing everything she wanted hidden made her very aware of him. And of herself.

"I'm no Kelon, but I probably can manage a peanut butter sandwich."

She couldn't feel the end of her nose anymore. "A sandwich is fine." She put her glass on the end table. "If you point me in the direction of the kitchen, I can make it myself."

A simple hand gesture from Wyatt kept her in her place. Well, that and the fact that the room was swaying.

"A sandwich is the least I can do."

He headed toward the kitchen, leaving her with the burning question: *The least he could do for what?*

Five

By the time Wyatt got back to the living room, Heather was leaning back in the chair, her eyes closed, obviously feeling relaxed from the effects of the expensive wine she'd chugged like water. Not that that was a bad thing. The woman packed way too much tension. He much preferred seeing her face relaxed than tight with tension.

She had a nice face, too, not beautiful, but compelling. Her features were strong, bold, expressive, matching her personality, reflecting the way she carried herself: with the confidence of someone who'd had to fight to get where they were and knew what they were worth. The woman had trouble written all over, from her tightly braided hair to the don't-mess-with-me boots hugging her shapely calves. She had the look of a woman who could strip a man to his soul with a glance. She also had the look of a woman who could wrench a man's heart from his chest with the next.

And she was his.

Heather opened her eyes—grey eyes, not blue like her sisters', with darker flecks at the edges. Her smile was as fuzzy as her focus—she was well on her way to being drunk. Wyatt just wasn't sure why she'd felt the need. He placed the sandwich on the table beside her. "One sandwich as ordered."

Her gaze locked on his cheek where the cut had been. She frowned. "Your cut's gone."

"I told you. I heal fast."

"It's not possible."

"For a human."

She sighed and reached for the sandwich. "You just have to keep going there."

"Does this mean you're not thinking of kissing me anymore?"

She frowned, debated, and then shrugged. "Oh, that."

"Yes, *that*." *That* was very important to him. He was very interested in *that*.

Bringing the sandwich to her lips, she opened her mouth, sighed, and put it back on the plate without even a nibble. "It probably wouldn't have amounted to anything anyway."

"You sound pretty sure of that."

She shrugged. "I have lots of experience."

Not many of his dates were this honest. He played with the end of her braid where it hung over her breast, not touching her skin, just teasing himself with the possibility.

"Do tell."

She cracked an eyelid. "You're not one of those weirdos who gets off listening to his partner's latest exploits, are you?"

"No. I like to be the action, not hear about it."

"Well, that makes up for a bit."

"Makes up for what?"

"The fact that you're off your rocker."

"I'm not off my rocker, sweetheart."

She waved her right hand in the air before letting it plop to the arm of the chair. "For what I've got planned it doesn't matter even if you are."

"You've got plans?"

She nodded. "Big ones. Life-altering ones." Her voice dropped to a whisper. "Scary ones."

She was getting off topic. "*Scary* as in you're thinking of kissing a werewolf?"

"Much scarier."

He couldn't imagine anything scarier than that. "What?"

From the slowness with which she gathered her thoughts to answer, his little mate was soused. On twelve ounces of wine. He ran his gaze over her again, taking in her too-drawn features, too-thin body, and stressed-out energy. He guessed it wasn't surprising. From appearances, Heather had been running on nerves a long time.

He repeated his question.

"I'm quitting."

"Quitting what?"

"My job. I'm a nurse."

She sighed. Her next breath was deeper, slower. If he wanted answers before she put that wall back up, he'd have to press. And he definitely wanted answers. Especially about anything that scared her.

"Do you like being a nurse?"

She rolled her head back and forth on the couch cushion, seeming to get distracted by the sensation. Or maybe she was stalling as she battled with a truth she didn't want to admit. He didn't know.

"Heather? Do like being a nurse?"

"Good grief, no. I hate the sight of blood. I hate seeing people sick and sad."

"Then it's good you're going to quit."

She cracked both eyes open that time. "No, it's not. Lisa and Robin depend on me for the money. Especially now that they have the inn. But I just can't do it anymore. I just . . . can't."

Her constant tension was beginning to make sense now. He

knew that Heather had taken over for her parents when they had died. Lisa often alluded to how strong her sister was, bragging about how Heather even won when the state wanted to take them away. But now, looking at the woman before him, knowing how young she must have been, seeing the heavy toll the effort had taken on her, he realized she gave a whole new definition to the word *determined.*

Hell, no wonder she was running on nerves. No one knew better than him how doing the right thing could tear the heart out of a person, destroy their hope, weaken their convictions.

"Maybe this isn't the best time to be thinking about scary things."

That popped her eyes all the way open. "I really wanted a kiss."

"Kisses aren't scary, Heather."

"Easy for you to say. You probably snap, crackle, and pop with the best of them."

She lost him there. "Not always."

He slid his hand up her braid, expanding his fingers as it thickened toward the base. He bet if he unraveled that fat braid, her hair would be smooth as silk against his skin.

She wrinkled her nose. "Oh, puh-lease."

Her neck barely filled the width of his palm. Her personality was so strong it was hard to reconcile the fragility of her build with the force of her drive. Harder still to see her doing an emotionally draining job that she didn't enjoy for twelve years. "Please what? Kiss you?"

She raised her hands and let them drop listlessly. "Why not?"

Because she was drunk. Because she was scared. Because she was vulnerable. Those were all excellent reasons why he shouldn't kiss her right now. They didn't amount to a hill of beans against the one reason why he should. She was his mate, and she was hurting.

"Come here, sweetheart."

It was easy to bring his mouth to hers. All it took was a little flex of muscle in his fingers and her mouth was within easy reach of his. Her full lips parted. A hint of wine scented her breath, enhancing but not overshadowing her natural sweetness. He didn't immediately take what was his.

This was their first kiss, the first step in the mating game. If he did this, he was accepting whatever fate handed him. There'd be no going back. He'd either have to convince the pack to change their ways—something the daily challenges were convincing him wasn't going to happen—or he'd have to walk away from the people he loved and the life he'd always seen as his. Walking away was not an option. He was the Carmichael Alpha rising.

"Wyatt?"

No one had ever said his name with such hunger, waited with such hope for the touch of his mouth on theirs. No one had ever made themselves so vulnerable to his whims. Cradling her cheek, he made his decision. The pack was just going to have to move into the twenty-first century. "Right here."

The bite of her fingernails on his shoulder was sublime. The first request of a female to her mate. "Did you change your mind about kissing me?"

There was nothing vulnerable in the tone of the question. It was matter-of-fact. If a man discounted that she'd asked the question.

Sliding his fingers through her hair, Wyatt cradled Heather's skull in his palm, savoring the way it seemed to fit his hand perfectly. "Just enjoying the anticipation."

Her "Yes" was a sigh. "The anticipation is always good, isn't it?"

Implying the reality often wasn't. He was beginning to get the gist of her concern.

"The reality is going to blow your socks off."

"That would be nice."

Another sigh. This one deeper, longer, trailing off. If he wanted to get this kiss he'd better hurry. She was almost asleep.

With his thumb against her chin, Wyatt tipped her face a little bit more to the right, and closed the gap between them. His "Very nice" whispered against the cushion of her mouth.

Heather didn't move, just froze in the chair, her mouth going tense under his. He did want to know how many failed attempts at sizzle it took to put that much nervousness into a woman. Fitting the edges of his mouth to hers, taking her breath as his, absorbing her tension, letting it play out, not rushing, he waited. Her eyes opened. He smiled down at her as if they had all the time in the world, as if his wolf wasn't howling for him to do exactly what she expected—to thrust in and claim that moist heat that tempted him.

When he was sure that it was him she saw and not the failures from the past he said, "Hi, sweetheart."

She frowned at him.

"Are you ready for our kiss?"

Each word was spoken against her lips. Each movement brushed against the sensitive nerve endings at the edges of hers.

"We're already kissing."

"Nah, that was just a get-acquainted moment. This is our kiss."

All it took was a tilt of his head to mate his mouth to hers. All it took was the tease of his tongue and her lips parted. On the sigh of her breath he tasted wine, hope, and the faintest hesitation. She wanted this. She feared this. And with what he was beginning to recognize as her method of handling fear, she took charge of the kiss.

He held her carefully. She was so vulnerable in her aggression. So easily hurt in her charge to make sure this went perfectly. Her tongue met his with undoubted skill. Each move calculated to give him pleasure. And it did. She did.

Her taste flowed through his mouth, sating his need for discovery. He closed his eyes, letting it sink deep, memorizing it, letting it blend with her scent in his soul. His. She was his. He wanted so much more for her. He wanted to give her sizzle.

Gradually, so as not to spook her, he took control away from her, becoming the one initiating, the one choreographing the erotic duel, smiling as she fell into his lead, deepening the kiss when she surrendered her weight into his hands.

"Yes," he groaned into her mouth, "I've got what you need. Just relax and let me give it to you."

Relaxing didn't come easily to her. She was a woman who used control as a defense, who didn't let herself be vulnerable. But she was vulnerable to him, would always be vulnerable to him.

Satisfaction surged at the thought. He caught her lower lip between his teeth, biting down, feeding the ache in his canines with the parody of what he really wanted to do. He wanted to nibble on her neck, her breasts, her sweetly flowering pussy. He wanted to bathe in her intimate scent as he marked her thighs, her clit.

Her fingers came up, fluttered by his cheek before dropping back. Another betraying hesitation.

Ah, damn. He wanted her like hell on fire and he had to go slow. Very slow. The wrong move and she'd spook, and nothing, not the aphrodisiac in his saliva or mating passion, would halt her retreat. He'd have no one to blame but himself if he scared her back into her shell.

Catching her hand, he brought it to his cheek.

"I want your touch, sweetheart. I want your fingers on my skin."

"How?"

"However you want." He scooped her up. Her breath caught as he lifted her easily. He catalogued the little tell, adding liking to be carried to his growing pile of information about her.

As he sat back down, the scent of her arousal grew richer. She definitely appreciated a man's strength. Settling her on his lap, cuddling that pert little ass over his throbbing cock, he leaned back against the chair. Her head naturally fell into the hollow of his shoulder. He met her gaze without flinching. "You're the hottest thing I've seen in a long time, and pretty much I'm one big ache when it comes to the thought of your touch."

"Really?" She said that as if it were a marvel.

"Oh, yeah."

Her smile came slowly, but when it came it was his turn to be breathless. The gradual stretch of her lips showed even white teeth and transformed her face from gamine to earthy. She opened her fingers against his cheek. "You really are good at this."

"I've been waiting a long time."

"For a drunken woman to fall into your lap?"

She had a sense of humor, too. Better and better. Bringing her fingers to his lips, he gave her the truth. "For you."

"You need better dreams."

"No, I don't. I just need you."

"How about another kiss instead?"

That was a mistake on her part. He only needed an opportunity, but by the time she figured that out, he'd be well and truly under her skin. "I'll take it."

She tilted her head back and that smile didn't falter. "Good."

Stroking his thumb over her lips, he agreed. "Yes. It is."

Intensely feminine, naturally sensual, she responded to him like no other woman ever had, following his lead as if she'd been born to it, enthusiastically improvising when she could, tempting him with the arch of her spine, the press of her nails, the softest of moans. He needed her closer. "Damn, come here."

She twisted against him, her nipples prodding him through the knit of her turtleneck and the cotton of his shirt, pulling herself closer, offering herself to him, offering him everything.

His hand closed over her breast, accepting the taut peak burrowing into his palm. He'd never had a woman offer him everything so hard, so fast. No wonder she had her defenses so high. Once a man got past them, there was just her, ready and waiting, trusting her lover to take care of her, to put her first.

He broke the kiss, dropping his forehead to hers. Son of a bitch, he had to put her first.

He stood. She linked her hands behind his neck, gazing at him with half-drugged wonder and unconscious trust. “Where are we going?”

“To bed.”

Six

HEATHER woke up alone. It wasn't the first time, and likely wouldn't be the last, but this was the most devastating. Exhaustion and alcohol were apparently not a good combination for her. Or maybe it was her sisters' fault. Seeing them with their boyfriends, seeing the carefree way they were with them had opened up that old longing that just wouldn't die. But the reality was she wasn't a cuddly type of woman. She was practical, logical, and efficient, and while doctors trusted her to carry out their orders and patients trusted her to take care of their needs, no one ever saw her in need of being taken care of.

Lisa and Robin were the type of women men fussed over. She'd worked hard to make sure they had softness in them, to make sure they never had to grow up too fast, and she didn't begrudge the sacrifices she'd made. She just missed feeling . . . feminine sometimes.

She stretched her arm across the bed, pressing her palm into the far side, seeking proof of life. No lingering body heat warmed the sheets. She grabbed the pillow, rolled on her back, and held it to her nose. There was no lingering essence of Wyatt's scent. Clutching the pillow to her, closing her eyes, she accepted the reality. He hadn't stayed afterward. He'd taken what she'd offered, and left. Like any sane, rational person would.

"Damn, you're awake."

She didn't need to open her eyes to know Wyatt was by the door watching her. She could feel it.

"I can pretend to be asleep if you want me to." That would be preferable to being caught clutching his pillow to her face, searching for his scent like a lovesick cow.

"Nope." There was the sound of something thudding to the floor. "That won't be necessary. I can improvise."

There was another thud, closer. Pulling down the pillow far enough to see what he was up to, she was just in time to catch a glimpse of his chest as he shrugged out of his shirt. It was quite a chest. She'd seen bodybuilders that would have killed to have that much muscle. But at the same time, his muscles didn't have that artificial look that came from pumping iron. There was a leanness to the length, a flexibility to his moves that implied those muscles came from everyday work. She couldn't imagine what kind of work he did that would produce such muscle, but she was grateful. He caught her gaze and smiled.

"Like what you see?"

"Oh, definitely." She pulled the pillow the rest of the way down, holding it against her chest. His hands went to the fly of his jeans. She licked her lips.

"Do you mind telling me what you're doing?"

"Well, the original plan was to take care of business and be back here before you awoke."

"But?"

He left his jeans on. The fly, however, was unfastened, creating a little vee like an arrow that provided a glimpse of that intriguing line of hair that started beneath his navel and disappeared at the base of the zipper.

"Business took longer than I expected."

He crossed to the bed, the look of a predator stronger this morning for some reason. Maybe it was the way he was studying her. Like she was his first morning cup of coffee and he couldn't wait to get started. She licked her lips, eyes drawn to the impressive bulge beneath his jeans. She rubbed her thighs together, testing for lingering sensitivity. There wasn't any.

He put one knee on the bed. The mattress dipped as he came over her with that smile on his face. He was devastating when he smiled. Heck, who was she kidding? He was devastating no matter what. His hand slid over hers under the covers.

"Checking for memories?"

Good God! Had she been that obvious? She could feel the flush rising, her chin rising right along with it. One thing she'd learned over the years was that any embarrassment could be handled by bluffing. "Yes. And I find myself distinctly lacking any."

He laughed, undeterred by her accusation. Threading his fingers through her hair at her temple, he said, "Then I guess it's up to me to do something about it."

She clutched the sheet to her chest. It was one thing to consider taking on this man when she was half-drunk. It was a whole other thing to consider it when she was sober and aware of just how a different they were. There was a world of experience in his eyes that she couldn't match. A world of experience she couldn't bluff her way into.

"Before coffee?"

He tipped her head back. "Uh-huh."

His mouth was just a lift of her head away. "You know, I'm not much of a morning person."

His breath caressed her lips.

"Then I guess you'll just have to lie back and let me do everything."

God, he made that sound so good.

"Does that little shiver mean you're interested?"

What the hell? Taking a werewolf lover worked for her sisters, and when was she ever going to meet a man like this that was interested in her again?

"Is there coffee in it afterward for me?"

Another chuckle ghosted her flesh in a whisper of what might be. Heck, even his morning breath was good. He kissed the end of her nose. "Already got it brewing."

She threw her hands back over her head and pressed them into the mattress. "Then do with me as you will."

His thumb tested her temple, grazed her cheekbone, settled beneath her jaw. "A blank check. Awfully bold for the first time."

"First time?" You mean . . . ?"

"Sweetheart, I like a woman conscious when I make love to her."

"Thank goodness. I was feeling shortchanged."

This time he kissed her eyelashes. It tickled. She flinched. He laughed and caught her earlobe between his teeth. She held her breath. He made her wait—one second, two, three. Then he bit, the sharp sensation shooting straight to her core, softening her muscles.

She moaned. "Do that again."

He did, holding the pressure, sustaining the delight. "Are you going to be a talker?"

"Are you going to mind?"

"Hell no."

"Then yes."

"Good."

He didn't head for her lips like she expected, but moseyed his way down her neck. She hunched her shoulder. He laughed and persisted.

"Stop."

"Why?"

"That tickles."

"So?"

Opening her palms against his chest, she tested his strength. "I don't think laughter is what we're shooting for."

"Sweetheart, there's nothing better than laughter in bed."

"Not even an orgasm?"

She couldn't believe how bold she was with him, but there was something about Wyatt that encouraged it, invited it, made it feel natural. "Why do I feel like I've known you forever?"

"Because you were born for me."

He said it the same way Donovan and Kelon declared their devotion to her sisters. He said it with the same calm certainty with which he declared he was a werewolf. He said it so easily she couldn't believe him. Tears stung her eyes.

She arched her neck, facilitating the next caress, forcing back the sadness, reaching for the laughter. "That's sweet."

His lips left the cord of her neck. The air felt cooler where they had been. Her flesh hotter. She didn't think to resist when he caught her chin between his thumb and forefinger and turned her face to his.

"If it's so sweet, why the tears?"

Oh shoot, why hadn't she resisted? She turned her head and kissed the inside of his wrist. "I don't need fairy tales, Wyatt."

Those amber eyes of his studied her face. Nothing in his expression betrayed his thoughts. "What do you need?"

"Honesty."

"I haven't lied to you."

"Your . . . beliefs are a little fantastic."

"But not impossible."

He might as well be asking her to believe the moon was made of cheese. "I don't want to argue."

"Neither do I."

"I want to make love."

"So do I."

"Then I guess we don't have a problem."

Except this was never going anywhere. She debated it a minute and then made a decision. It'd been so long since she'd been held. So long since a man had fired her hormones. She was a grown woman. She didn't need forever. She could handle a one-night stand. Arching her back so her nipples took the heat of his skin, she faked a pout. "Just the fact that the fire's gone out."

The sheet dipped as he hollowed his fingers between her hands. "Hmm, that is a problem."

He was back to teasing her lips with the pulse of his breath that came in the rhythm of his speech. Heather leaned her head back, parting her lips in a blatant invitation. "Not if you do something about it."

He gave the sheet a tug. It didn't move.

"Why do I have to do something about it?"

"Because you promised me I could just lie here and do nothing."

"So I did." Another tug, and then a sexy smile that reached his eyes. "But in order for me to take over, you're going to have to give up a little."

"Give up what?"

"Your grip on the sheet."

Oh good grief, she was back to clutching it to her chest like a frightened virgin. She let go. "I'm sorry. It's just that you're a little overwhelming."

"Hmm." Taking her right hand in his, he positioned it above her head. He did the same with the left, crossing her wrists. "Keep them like that."

"Why?"

He hitched himself up, notching that thick cock into the vee of her thighs. Her imagination kicked into overdrive, leaving her with the impression of a throb that echoed her pulse.

"Because it turns me on."

That was good enough for her. "Okay."

No one had ever restrained her in bed before, literally or figuratively.

The right corner of his lip quirked up. "So obliging."

"I'm experimenting with being adventurous."

"Lucky me."

She dug her heels into the mattress and pressed her hips up into his. The divine pressure of his cock against her straining clitoris sighed through her in a blissful prelude. It felt good. Beyond good. "I'm hoping it's going to be lucky me."

Wyatt cupped Heather's hip in his palm, sinking his fingers into the soft flesh behind. He'd noticed her ass right off. Tight, cute, with just enough padding to cushion a man. "Count on it."

The moue of disappointment Heather made as he pushed her hips back to the bed jostled another smile loose. She was a bossy little thing, and her hands above her head did little to inhibit her need for control. He wondered how long it was going to take her to realize he wasn't going to leave her any.

Another tug and the sheet was tossed to the side.

"You're beautiful, sweetheart."

"I'm too thin."

Yes, she was, but she was also beautiful, all long, lean lines that encouraged the sweep of a man's hand complemented by curves that enticed him to linger. Cupping her breast in his hand, he met her eyes. "You don't feel thin to me."

Her grey eyes searched his for a lie. He rested his thumb very lightly on her nipple.

"And these I definitely like."

"They're so big."

"Yes." He loved big nipples on a woman and she had the prettiest ones he'd ever seen. As big as the tip of his finger. Big enough to easily capture in his mouth. Big enough to feast on all day. "Perfect."

"You think?"

He recognized a prompt when he heard one. Rubbing his thumb across the swollen tip, he smiled as she shuddered. "Want me to prove it?"

Her teeth sank into her lower lip as she watched his thumb with a hunger that dragged a growl from his chest. "Yes."

Another brush of his thumb, another jerk of her body.

"Your breasts are very sensitive."

She was still watching his thumb. "Yes."

"Has anyone made you come from sucking these pretty nipples?"

Her eyes flashed to his and then a shake of her head. "No. They're usually in a hurry for other things."

It wasn't hard to imagine what *other things* were. With a mouth like that there wouldn't be a man alive that wouldn't want it wrapped around his cock as soon as possible. With her willingness to please and her take-charge attitude, all it would take was a hint and she'd be back in control, making sure her partner was pleasured, doing it all right while leaving out the most important ingredient—giving herself time to enjoy the encounter, too.

"I bet."

He rolled onto his back, taking her with him. Her hair tumbled around him, sliding down the sides of his chest. It was his turn to shudder. The narrowing of her eyes let him know she hadn't missed the betraying movement. "Kneel up."

Slipping his hands between them he freed his cock, arranging it to his satisfaction. He stopped her before she could settle back down. "No. Wait."

"For what?"

She was so innocent in some ways. "For me to enjoy the view."

And it was a pretty view. Her delicate torso in front, her breasts suspended like ripe fruit above, his cock, hard and aching between his legs, lifting toward the liquid heat of her pussy. Reaching down, he grabbed his shaft and tipped it up. The fat head nudged into the pink folds, pressing them apart, holding them separated until he eased it back to dip into the well and be swallowed into hot bliss.

"Shit."

A calculating look came into her eyes. "You like that."

Yes, he did, but they weren't going there. "Yes, I do, and later you can show me how grateful you are."

She pressed down. "For what?

His counter was instinctive. Muscles as delicate as the rest of her began to part as he pushed up. Wrapping his hand around her neck, he drew her face to his, taking her mouth with the surge of desire, thrusting with his tongue, giving her enough play that she could rub against him but not enough that she could achieve entry. When he couldn't go without another breath, when she was taut above him, her natural passion enhanced by the aphrodisiac flowing through her system, he broke off the kiss and caught her nipple between his fingers. Holding her gaze, her squeezed gently, steadily. "For giving you your first breast orgasm."

She made a sexy little high-pitched sound in her throat.

"I'll take the squeak as agreement, so bring those pretty little breasts up here."

He liked that he didn't have to tell her twice. He liked the way she threw herself into the experience. He liked the way she didn't let her insecurities stop her from having what she wanted. She wanted this orgasm.

Almost as much as he wanted to give it to her. Wyatt loved pleasuring women, loved watching them come, loved that moment when they trusted him to keep them safe when their control slipped away, but there was more to that with Heather.

Everything he did to her was much more intimate with Heather. Deeper, more connected. Every sigh she made, every twitch of her muscles found an echo within him, edged between his desire and his control, fanned the flames of his passion. She made him burn.

"Is that a deal?"

Her breast dangled above his mouth, that full nipple pouting at him, pink and engorged, but not as hard as it could be. Would be. With a flip of her head she shook her hair back. Like her, it had a mind of its own, tumbling back over her shoulder, falling around his face, sheltering them in a cocoon of need.

He couldn't want any longer. "Come here."

With his hand in the middle of her back, he didn't give her a choice. The way Heather watched his lips close over her nipple was a caress in itself. The turgid bud swelled as he sucked it slow and easy, gradually increasing the suction until he heard the breathless gasp that said, "Right there."

He suckled, nibbled, and licked. She moaned, twisted, and pressed, whipping his lust to a frenzy with the lash of her hair, the earthy scent of her passion, the willingness with which she gave herself. It was almost too much to switch breasts, the brief separation wrenching another growl from his chest, his head pounding with one thought. His. His. His.

She answered with a growl of her own. The small, feral sound dug into the boundaries of his control and ripped off another layer. He yanked her down, holding her breast to his mouth, pushing up with his hips as she ground herself down on his cock, her hand holding his mouth to her breasts, desperate little cries of "please" exploding from her in throaty pleas.

Shit, he couldn't stand it. Wasn't going to last, but he had to last with her. He'd promised her. Heather's hips worked on his, sliding her pussy along the ridge of his cock, bathing him in her essence, flooding the room with the rich scent of impending orgasm.

His canines lengthened and ached. Marking hormones swelled the glands under his tongue. *Now!* The thought tore through him. *Now!*

He caught her nipples between his canines, arching his back off the bed, driving the length of his cock along her clit. He bit down, piercing her just enough. She screamed his name. Her torso snapped back into the palm of his hand as her pussy grasped at his cock with desperate fervor.

She tried to wrench away. He didn't let her. Instead, he transferred his attention to her other breast, repeating the procedure, sending her into a new frenzy of marking ecstasy before lifting her hips and lowering her tight little pussy onto his cock, pushing past the resistance, snarling when she tired to pull back, holding her nipple, holding her pleasure in his hand as her channel clenched like a fist around him and her cry rang in his ears.

"Wyatt!"

Slow down. He needed to slow down, but he couldn't. She was too small, too tight. He needed her, all of her. Releasing her breasts, he stopped her next cry with his mouth, breathing it deep as his cock sank to the hilt. She shuddered against him. He bucked up, suspending her on the plateau of his hips, keeping her impaled on his cock for two heartbeats, not letting her rest, not letting her come down, kissing her hard and deep as he transferred his grip to her hips.

"Hold on, sweetheart."

Any other time he would have been concerned about the dazed look in her eyes, but, right now, all he could think of was marking her, with his mouth, his seed. He lifted her up, and then brought her down hard, setting the rhythm, ordering her to keep it, slapping her ass lightly when she did, spanking her harder when she jerked and cried out, driving her higher with every thrust, every spank until she screamed and fell forward. He finally let go himself, pumping into her as the explosion reigned, catching her to him with his last conscious thought, holding her to him as her hair settled over them both, exhaling softly as satisfaction flowed through him. "Mine."

Seven

HE deserved to have his ass kicked. Wyatt circled with Carl within the challenge ring, looking for an opening. The man held his right arm down too far, turned his shoulder out a little too far. When the time came, it would cost him.

"Human lover," the wolf sneered. It wasn't the most original of insults. Then again, Carl wasn't the most original of men. He was a solid beta, loyal to the old ways, but more loyal to his cousin, Cam.

"It's early in the morning, Carl. If you're going to talk when you challenge, make it interesting."

Carl spat to the side. "You don't give me orders."

"For that I'm grateful."

"Fuck you."

"No thanks."

Carl feinted in.

Wyatt easily blocked the attack, sending the wolf backward with a punch to the gut. The other man's expression revealed his surprise.

Wyatt smiled, feeling the adrenaline rise. "What's the matter Carl? Did you think it was going to be easy?"

Carl had had every right to expect an easy time of it. The challenges of the last week had been designed to systematically weaken him. Cam just hadn't planned on Wyatt's mate showing up, hadn't planned on Wyatt claiming her. Hadn't counted on that claiming restoring his energy.

There were murmurs from the male werewolves forming a circle around them. Weres who would stand witness to the results. Friends with whom he'd grown up. Friends he was expected to kill if they stepped forward with a challenge.

Carl snarled and lunged, lashing out with his claws. Wyatt sucked in his gut and jumped back. Teeth snapped inches from his face. Damn, he'd better keep his mind on what he was doing. Falling back, Wyatt catapulted the other man over his head, coming up on his feet behind him. In the split second before Carl turned, he had his opening. Head bent, Carl unwittingly presented his vulnerable nape. All Wyatt had to do was strike at the base of his skull, severing the spinal cord, and it would be all over. He drew back his arm, letting the heat of battle take him past his reluctance. This had to end. Only death would accomplish that.

A small gasp drew his attention. Out of the corner of his eye, he saw Carl's mate, Fiona, standing on the fringes, arms folded, expression impassive. A good were female doing her mate proud, facing his death with her chin high and agony in her eyes. His gaze dropped to her obviously pregnant belly. Battle heat took a backseat to knowledge. Damn it.

Wyatt took the shot, delaying a split second long enough for Carl to twist out from beneath, his claws slicing a nonlethal blow along his shoulder. Pretending to trip, he took them both down, growling in Carl's ear. "Don't make me kill you."

Carl's head snapped around, fury and confusion in the depths of his gaze. Driving back with his elbow, Carl threw Wyatt off. Pain exploded through Wyatt's midriff. He stumbled back under the force of the blow. Hands caught his shoulder.

"What the hell are you doing, Wyatt? Finish him off," Donovan snapped, shoving him back into the ring.

Wyatt shook off the nausea. "I'm working on it."

"Work faster. You can't afford the energy loss dancing with him is costing you."

He knew that, just like he knew if he killed Carl a woman who'd sat with him the night after his mother's death, just holding his hand as the grief had battled for dominance, offering her sympathy to an Alpha who wasn't supposed to need it, would be without her mate and her child without his father. All because tradition held the best leader wasn't the smartest, the most compassionate, or even the most suited, but the one with the most blood dripping off his claws. A tradition that demanded he kill Carl or die. A tradition the hard stares of the males around him said they expected to be supported by him.

He glanced at Fiona again, saw the break in her control that came in the form of a single tear. Saw the acceptance of the choice he no longer had. Either he killed Carl or the pack would kill him. Yet, still he hesitated.

Out of the corner of his eyes, he saw Carl attack. Coming in low, moving faster than Wyatt anticipated. Too late, he jumped back. The only thing that kept him from being disembowled was the last minute contraction of his abdominal muscles. It wasn't enough to save him. Agony rose in a hot tide, temporarily blacking out his vision. He heard a woman scream, Kelon shout, and suddenly everyone seemed to be in motion, disguising the one sound he needed to locate. And then it came from behind, too late for him to defend against, the sound of a killing blow whistling through the air.

So, how was he?"

Heather shifted position on the hard kitchen chair, discreetly trying to relieve the pressure on the deliciously raw flesh between her legs and duck Robin's question at the same time. From the look Lisa gave her she wasn't being particularly successful. "How was who?"

Robin rolled her eyes. "Wyatt."

Lisa handed Heather a cup of coffee and pulled out a chair at the small square table in the middle of the comfortable kitchen. "Personally, I always thought Wyatt would be hell on wheels in bed. Besides being sexy as all get-out, he's got that bad-boy, happy-to-show-you-a-good-time aura about him."

Anger caught Heather by surprise. She took a sip of her coffee, grateful for the sting as the hot liquid hit her tongue. It gave her the distraction she needed to keep her voice even. "You've speculated about sleeping with Wyatt?"

Robin laughed. "I don't think there's a woman who's met him that hasn't."

"You, too?"

"Hey, I'm not dead yet."

That had Heather looking at Robin again, not just because she wasn't used to talking to her sisters like this, but because Robin was looking far from death's door this morning. There was color in her cheeks and an energy about her she hadn't seen in ages. "So I can see. How have you been feeling lately?"

"Good, and no changing the subject." Robin plunked herself in the chair across the table. "How was he?"

"Yeah. Spill."

Wild. Uninhibited. Perfect. "He was okay."

"You can't sit comfortably, and you want us to believe he was just *okay*?"

There was no stemming the tide of heat rising up her cheeks. "Yes."

Lisa snorted. "Bull."

"Too bad he was challenged this morning, otherwise you could have experienced the benefits of being soothed."

"Soothed?"

"Oh man." Lisa practically melted in her chair. "I like being soothed."

Heather had a feeling she'd been cheated out of something important. "What's *soothed*?"

Robin got the same dreamy look in her eye. "It's when your man makes up for the hard use of the night before."

She just stared blankly at them.

"Along with an aphrodisiac in their saliva, wolves also have a healing agent," Lisa explained.

"Which they apply"—Robin waggled her eyebrows—"with their tongues."

Heather didn't think it was possible, but her cheeks burned hotter.

"They're very dedicated about it," Robin said, a cheeky grin on her face.

"Yeah. In case you haven't noticed, wolves are devoted to their mates."

"Mates? Whose talking about mates?" She left the statement about wolves untouched. "I had a one-nighter with a sexy man. Nothing deeper than that."

Lisa frowned, her hand going to her shoulder. "You're not telling me after making you scream like that, Wyatt didn't mark you?"

"You heard me scream?"

"Honey," Robin said on a sigh, "the whole compound heard you scream." She smiled and hid her face in her cup. "Which definitely inspired Kelon."

As soon as she found one, Heather was crawling into a hole and never coming out.

Lisa was still frowning. "Donovan was sure he'd marked you."

She said that as if Donovan had the last say on everything. "I hate to crack your rose-colored glasses, sis, but Donovan is not all-knowing."

"You're not cracking anything, but there's no way Wyatt would have made his claim of you so public by putting you in his house if his intentions weren't serious. Not only that, Donovan wouldn't have allowed it. Weres are old-fashioned when it comes to women."

"Maybe the fact that I'm human had something to do with the break in protocol."

She didn't like to think that Wyatt saw her as something less than respectable because she didn't share his delusion, but then again, she didn't like that he saw himself as wolf.

"And what is *marked* anyway?" Though she didn't want it, it irked her that whatever it was, Wyatt hadn't felt she was worthy of it.

"When a were finds his mate, he bites her in a certain way. It leaves a mark and binds them together."

This was getting more preposterous. She couldn't keep the dryness from her tone. "And you've both been 'marked.' "

Robin looked at Lisa. Lisa at Robin. In silent agreement they bared their shoulders. On each woman, just to the right of the spot where their neck met their shoulder there was a faint shadowy discoloration under the whiteness of their skin, barely visible, seeming to shift with the light.

"It's just a bruise."

Like no bruise she'd ever seen and identically placed on both her sisters. A shiver whispered down her spine. This was getting too eerie.

"A bruise that heats when you're mate's near, that can send you into orgasm if he pays enough attention to it?" Lisa shook her head. "I don't think so."

"Are you sure Wyatt didn't mark you?" Robin asked.

Heather pulled aside the collar of her bright pink shirt. Both

Robin's and Lisa's faces fell. Robin's "Oh" conveyed the disappointment for both of them.

Lisa frowned. "Donovan is not going to be happy."

"What does it matter to Donovan?"

"You're my sister; he feels responsible for you."

"Another part of that archaic mind-set he seems to favor?"

Lisa shrugged. "It grows on you over time."

"So much so you won't let him change in front of you?"

Lisa grinned. "Are you kidding? I let the man strip as often as he wants."

"That's not what I meant."

Lisa sighed. "I know. I'm just not ready for that."

The strain in her face tugged at Heather's conscience. For most of her life she'd been taking care of her sisters. The instinct to make everything right for them wasn't one easily turned off. She put her hand over Lisa's. "Because you don't want to have to accept the truth?"

"Because I just couldn't accept it before."

"But you're ready to now?"

"Yes. He's bound his life to mine. It seems silly to prevaricate after that."

Robin gasped.

Heather cut her a quick glance. Robin didn't notice. She was staring at Lisa.

"What exactly does that mean?" Heather asked, not taking her eyes off Robin.

"It means if I die, he's committed to follow immediately."

Robin turned a ghastly white. Her "How?" overrode Heather's snort of disbelief.

"What?"

"How did he do it?"

"He cut his hand and put it over my mark and said, "My soul to yours, this life—"

"And the next. We are bound," Robin finished for her, a sick note in her voice.

"Oh God," Lisa gasped. "Kelon . . . ? But he *knows* you're dying."

"How could he?" Robin looked at both Heather and Lisa, disbelief and horror in her eyes. "How could he do that to me?"

Lisa shook her head, disbelief and compassion etching lines into her face. "He loves you."

Robin trembled and pushed her coffee away. The cup tumbled off the table and fell to the floor. No one moved to pick it up. "He needs to love me better than that. He needs to live."

When your sister's time comes, she will not be alone.

Kelon's solemn promise to Heather took on a whole new meaning.

"Maybe it's not true." The weakness of Heather's conviction wobbled in her voice.

Robin pinned her with her gaze. "I've seen him change, Heather. The night he saved my life, he was in wolf form. I saw him change back. We're married to werewolves. Not the kind from horror movies, but the real kind. It's permanent, and all the logic in the world isn't going to change it."

"You were drugged. Are you sure . . .?"

"She's sure," Lisa snapped.

Heather bit her tongue on a retort, not only because it wasn't the time to argue, but because the boundaries between belief and disbelief were blurring for her, too. She wanted to believe a man was capable of that much devotion, wanted to believe she could be loved like that.

"Maybe it can be undone. Nothing's ever that extreme."

It was all she had to offer.

"That's true," Lisa chimed in. "In all the best fairy tales, there's always an out clause. We'll just find him and make him use it."

"What if he doesn't want to?"

Heather cut her sister a glance, taking in the huge tears hovering. Robin wasn't a pretty crier, but she was an effective one. "Then you look at him just like that and ask him again."

Eight

It wasn't hard to find the men. They were with everyone else, forming a ring around a spectacle taking place in the center of the compound. Heather assumed it was a fight, but the lack of cheering was eerie. Robin ran toward that wall of broad, muscular backs calling Kelon's name. He burst out of the crowd, gun drawn, hair blowing behind him, looking deadlier than any image Hollywood had ever created. Robin didn't slow, just launched herself at him. He caught her, holding her close, tipping her head back with his hand in her hair as he frowned down at her.

Heather followed at a slower pace. She knew what Robin was asking, but while she couldn't hear Kelon's response, the way Robin started beating on his chest made his answer clear.

Beside her, Lisa whispered, "Damn."

Even though she told herself she didn't believe in everything happening here, Heather felt the sting of tears. The one thing Robin never wanted to be was a burden and yet the thing she always saw herself being was a burden. "Doesn't look like there's an out clause."

A few men looked over their shoulders at the spectacle Robin was creating, but whatever was happening inside that tight circle had more pull.

"Let's get her out of here. I don't think spectacles are looked upon favorably around here."

"What makes you think that?"

Heather jerked her chin in the direction of a big were with a streak of grey in his hair. "The disapproving frown that man just shot Kelon."

"He can just suck it up."

The response was so typically Lisa, Heather couldn't help but smile. "I can see being married to a werewolf hasn't totally mellowed you out."

"Donovan has hopes."

"I guess he'll have to suck it up, too."

"Yeah." Her smile was faint. "I guess he will."

She was watching Kelon and Robin. "He really loves her, you know."

This close it was hard to miss. Love was evident in the protective way the big man held her sister, the way his fingers stroked over the tear-wet surfaces of her cheeks. It was especially evident when he bent his head to hers, his hair falling around her face, shielding her from view, and whispered, "The decision's made. There's no reason to cry."

Robin's hand stretched up around his shoulders. "I made a wish for you to live."

Kelon kissed the top of her head. "And I made a wish to live only with you. Looks like we're both getting what we want."

"This isn't the way I wanted it."

He dropped his forehead to hers. "But it is the way I wanted. Never doubt it."

I think I'm going to cry."

Lisa glanced over at her, tears on her cheeks. "You never cry."

Heather wiped at her cheeks. "Well then, I'm overdue."

Kelon looked up, saw the tears, and shook his head. With a last kiss to Robin's cheeks, he pushed her toward them. "You need to take her back inside. It's not safe out here, and I can't protect you right now."

"Protect us from what?" Lisa asked.

"Challenge."

"Is that Vera woman still holding on to hope?"

"It would be better for you if she did."

"Why?"

There was a murmur from the crowd. "I don't have time to explain. I need to get back to Wyatt."

"This"—Heather waved to the crowd forming a human barricade—"is about Wyatt?"

"He's been challenged again. They seem determined to stomp his ass back to the beginning of time."

Challenged. She remembered his face from last night, the blood, the damage. Even if he was a werewolf, there had to be a point of no return with injuries. "Is it dangerous?"

"Challenges are to the death."

To the death? Wyatt was in the middle of these barbarians fighting to the death and she was out goo-gooing over the way Kelon touched Robin?

Heather pushed through the men, ignoring Kelon's shout, poking and jabbing as needed to get the big oafs to notice her efforts to get through. Closer in, she ran into a few women. They were harder to move than the men, but when Vera got in her way, Heather lost patience. She stomped as hard as she could on her toe. As the were female hopped about, Heather ducked around her and burst through the crowd, her stomach churning with nausea and dread because now she knew what those strange thumping noises were. Fists meeting flesh. Maybe Wyatt's flesh. Because they kept challenging him. To the death. Who the hell did that?

Wyatt was in the circle with another man. It was probably

wrong to be relieved, but Wyatt wasn't bleeding. The other man was. Blood soaked his shirt and sleeve. It didn't seem to be slowing him down. A woman on the sidelines sobbed, the sound more wrenching for the solitariness of the protest. She was pregnant. Very pregnant. And her eyes never left the man circling with Wyatt. Wyatt looked at the other woman, too, hesitated, and within that split second of inattention the man attacked, charging in, swiping with—oh my God—huge claws on his hands.

Heather's warning scream caught in her throat. Blood sprayed. Wyatt staggered to his knees, his eyes dazed. The other man snarled a horrible sound. Three realizations came in the next heartbeat—Wyatt was critically injured, no one was going to help him, and the other man was going in for the kill.

Rage freed the scream from her throat. She ripped the rifle from the hands of the man standing beside her. Holding it like a club, she swung, catching the stranger in the face. The force of the blow reverberated up her arm. Wyatt's opponent grabbed at the rifle with a snarl that sent chills down her spine and inspired another scream, this one of terror. There was an explosion and then a burning pain in her hip. Someone pulled her off; she spun, clawing at his face.

She was shaken twice, hard enough to rattle her teeth. The rifle fell to the ground.

"Settle down, Heather." Holding her dangling off to the side, Donovan looked around. "The challenge is called."

"Challenge is to the death," a square-jawed man at the edge of the crowd called.

"If you want it to be your death," Donovan shot back, setting her down but not letting her go, "challenge the call of a Protector again.

"Do you accept my decision, Carl?"

"No, he does not. He defeated the Alpha. The title is his."

"Shut up, Cam."

Carl looked around, his back straight, a hunted expression in his eyes. The pregnant woman covered her mouth with her hands, and shook her head. "Oh no. No."

Carl looked between Cam, Donovan, and Wyatt, who'd staggered to his feet. Blood gushed from his wound. Heather gouged at Donovan's arms. She needed to get to Wyatt. "Put me down."

"Stand your ground," Cam snarled at Carl.

Carl shook his head and took a step back.

"Yield," Donovan murmured.

Carl took another step back. Wyatt wavered unsteadily. Heather didn't know how he stood at all. She slipped her hands free of her coat, dropping to the ground while Donovan swore, holding the empty garment. As soon as she got close enough, Wyatt snatched her to his side, snarling at the men around, bracing his feet.

She slapped at his hands. "Stop fussing and let me see your wound."

"Get back to the house."

"Only if you come with me."

"I can't until this is settled."

Good God, he honestly thought he was going to fight some more? The rifle lay two feet away. She snatched it up, gasping at the burn in her hip, eluding Wyatt's grab—something she could never have done had he not been wounded—and pointed it at Carl. "It's settled, isn't it, Carl?"

With a snap of his teeth, the other man whirled. His form seemed to shimmer, blur. There was a strange crackling sound as he dropped to all fours, and then he was no longer a man but a wolf. Complete with fur and fangs.

She dropped the rifle.

Nine

I'M a werewolf.

Heather shook her head, blinking. Men came up beside her. She lashed out.

"Easy."

Donovan. That was Donovan. Relief collapsed under reality. He claimed to be a werewolf, too. She pushed him and took a step back only to bump into Kelon. Another werewolf. She was surrounded. And in front of her, Wyatt was bleeding to death.

"Oh God."

"Now is not the time to fall apart," Donovan snapped.

"Take this." Kelon growled, shoving the rifle back into her hand. He slung Wyatt's arm over his shoulder. "If anyone tries to follow us, shoot them."

In her current mood, that wouldn't be a problem. "Gladly."

Donovan cocked a brow at her as he grabbed Wyatt's other arm, suspending Wyatt between him and his brother. "Feeling hostile?"

All Heather could see was the blood soaking the remnants of

Wyatt's shirt before dripping in bright red splotches to the dirty snow. "Absolutely."

"Then you might want to turn off the safety," Kelon suggested.

She checked the side of the rifle. "This thing?"

"That would be it."

She heard footsteps behind her. She threw the safety, and spun around, firing blindly.

"Son of a bitch." Cam grabbed his shoulder.

Blood seeped between his fingers. She brought the gun back up, aiming for his chest.

"Get the hell away from here."

He didn't move. "Put the gun down."

"Do the words *no way* and *hell* mean anything to you?"

"They mean you're in need of discipline."

She tightened her grip on the trigger. "Or maybe they just mean I need to be a better shot."

From behind her there was a chuckle. Wyatt. Instead of moving he was standing there appreciating her sarcasm. When this was over, they *so* needed to talk.

"If you don't want to be breathing through your belly button, Cam, I'd suggest you do as my mate said."

She'd really appreciate it if Wyatt would just do as he was told. The rifle was getting heavy and her nerves were fraying.

Cam sneered. "She's human. What can she do?"

A hell of lot, as he'd find out if he didn't be quiet.

She was getting sick of this "who's more macho" crap.

Glancing over her shoulder at Wyatt, she snapped, "You need to save the taunts for later and let Kelon and Donovan get you inside. And you"—she recentered her aim on Cam—"need to shut the hell up."

"Can't take the truth?" Cam asked, that irritating sneer still in his voice.

"No, but my arms are getting tired. And before I let this gun drop, I'm going to blow a hole in you, something you might want to consider when you talk to me."

"You think you can take on a wolf?"

Her finger tightened on the trigger. "I think I can do whatever the hell I have to, and if this bullet doesn't kill you, I know for sure it will slow you down long enough for one of them"—with a jerk of her chin she indicated her sisters' lovers—"to finish the job."

"She's got a point," Wyatt interjected in a deliberate goad. Her last nerve snapped.

"Shut up Wyatt and get back to the house."

Wyatt paid her no mind, just kept on goading the other man as if the rifle wasn't getting heavier by the second.

"And if you don't want to be totally humiliated in front of your pack mates, I suggest you back down before she proves she can take you out."

"She's just a woman."

"She my woman, and there's nothing 'just' about her."

"You're weak."

"But getting stronger by the second."

"I'm not," Heather said, just in case anyone was interested.

Cam lifted his lip in a snarl that made her feel very human, very fragile. Very threatened.

Wyatt snarled back. "Come here, Heather."

"No."

"Do as I say."

"I'm taking orders from Donovan right now." And Donovan had told her to stay where she was and hold her ground.

"A wolf woman only takes orders from her mate."

"Sucks for you I'm human, then, doesn't it?"

Her forearms burned. The rifle wobbled.

"Damn it, Wyatt," Kelon growled. "Come on."

"Not without Heather."

"Now."

There was an ugly snarl, the sound of bodies hitting the dirt, and then an arm came around her waist, yanking her backward. Her finger jerked on the trigger. The rifle went off. Cam ducked, crouched, and looked like he was going to leap. The crowd that had gathered scattered to the sides. She fired again as she was carried along. The bullet hit the ground beside the big were. He rolled to the side. The stunned look on his face did her ego good.

"Take that, you chauvinistic son of a bitch!"

The thrill of danger had to be getting to her, because for no reason she could discern her nipples swelled and ached almost to the point of pain as Wyatt dragged her along.

"Drop the gun."

That was Wyatt growling in her ear.

"No."

Kelon jerked the rifle from her hand. Donovan took up a position in front of her. Kelon fell into step beside him. The width of their shoulders and ease with which they held the defensive position made her feel better. The wetness soaking her coat and the back of her jeans did not. Wyatt's blood.

"Put me down."

"In a minute."

"Now."

"You don't give me orders, sweetheart."

"Someone with sense has to be in charge."

"That would be me."

She eyed the trail of blood behind them. "Says the man bleeding all over the place."

"Says your Alpha." Her breasts pressed on his forearm with every step. The ache built to the point that if she could have she would have rubbed them to ease the discomfort.

"Saying it doesn't make it so."

"I'm aware of that."

"I don't like your tone."

Wood thudded under his boots. They were at the house. Wyatt

leapt onto the porch, groaned, and then growled. "You'll probably like the rest even less."

Donovan was right behind him. Kelon brought up the rear. She wasn't any happier with them, using their bodies like shields. Lisa and Robin would never forgive her if anything happened to them. As if thinking of them conjured them, Robin and Lisa came out of the house. Their husbands shoved them right back in.

"Get inside."

Robin and Lisa went without protest, a miracle in itself. Heather met Kelon's gaze. "Where were you when they were growing up?"

Kelon scanned the compound. "Searching for them."

She supposed if she was going to believe they were werewolves she could believe in their mating practices. "Oh."

The muscles in Wyatt's arms began to relax, letting her slide down his hard body, stretching her breasts just a little. The erotic ache built to an almost unbearable pressure. She licked her lips and groaned. Immediately, she was lowered to her feet and three pairs of male eyes fastened on her. Just what she needed.

"You're hurt."

They weren't looking at her breasts, but at her hip.

Not all the blood was Wyatt's. "Oh."

The ache in her nipples was far worse than the burn in her hip. She crossed her arms over her chest, at a loss to understand the reaction.

Wyatt dropped to his knees, swaying. She reached for him. He held her back with one arm. His claw sliced her jeans.

"Wyatt!"

She grabbed for the pants. Neither Donovan nor Kelon turned their backs. "Perverts."

"Someone needs to catch him when he falls."

She stopped Wyatt before he could strip her bare. "I'm fine. You're the one in trouble."

She needed to get in the house before she caved to temptation and grabbed her breasts and polished off the impression she was currently leaving with her butt cheek flapping in the breeze.

"I'll be the judge of that." For all his talk, Wyatt's face was a ghastly white.

"That's it. I have officially had it." She snapped her fingers at Donovan. "You and Kelon pick him up and get him into the house."

"He won't go until he's sure you're fine, and the struggle could be too much for his body to take."

She held Wyatt to her, bracing him. God, he needed help, and she needed relief.

"Then knock his ass out."

The brothers glanced at each other.

"I'd be willing to do that," Donovan volunteered with a bit too much enthusiasm.

"Like hell, if anyone gets to knock out Wyatt it'll be me," Kelon countered.

"Age before beauty."

This had the sound of a long-running argument. Why didn't they get that this was serious? "Oh for goodness' sake. Lisa, get me another gun."

"Coming up."

Donovan smiled. "That won't be necessary."

He took Wyatt's shoulder. "She won't go inside until you do. You need to let me help you while Kelon helps her."

Wyatt's gaze was alarmingly unfocused. "Kelon has her?"

Heather practically leapt into Kelon's arms, almost losing her pants in the process. "Yes."

"Okay."

Wyatt staggered to his feet. Donovan put his arm around his waist and dragged him into the house before carrying him to the bed.

Kelon followed. She pushed against his chest. "You can put me down now."

Kelon shook his head. "Not yet."

"Are you having an inappropriate macho moment?"

He didn't even glance at her as he asked, "Will you stop struggling if I agree?"

"Yes."

"Then yes."

"Good grief." There was nothing to do then but wait it out. One thing she'd learned was that it was easier to humor these men when they got like this than to fight them, and since Kelon was following Donovan, she could afford to. At least the ache in her breast was subsiding.

As soon as Kelon put her on her feet, she raced to Wyatt's side. He'd lost so much blood. She motioned to Donovan. "Do that claw thing and cut off his clothes."

"That claw thing?"

She didn't have time to play word games with him. "Now."

"What can we do?" Robin asked.

Kelon's "Cook up some steak" overrode her "Call a doctor."

"What good will that do?

"He'll need it to replenish after he heals."

"Rare," Wyatt ordered in a weak voice.

Robin rolled her eyes. "Of course."

Heather looked from the horrible gaping wound. "Steak will help him heal?"

"It will help him to recover."

"I'll get some towels to clean him up."

"Thanks, Lisa."

Wyatt needed more than cleaning up. He needed a doctor. "I'd feel better if he saw a doctor."

"We don't have doctors."

"Then I'll take whatever you have."

"We're already here."

Heather ran her hand through her hair. She was a nurse. She knew how bad this was. She could see his intestines for God's sake.

"I'll keep watch," Kelon said heading to the front.

"What are we watching for?"

"The way the fight ended left some loose ends."

Bad loose ends from the way Kelon unslung his rifle.

In the kitchen, she could hear Robin cooking. Lisa came back with a bowl of soapy water and several towels. Heather debated putting something under Wyatt, but decided against it. Better the mattress suffer than Wyatt.

Donovan took the bowl and placed it on the nightstand.

"Thank you." She picked up the towel, dipped it in the water, and started wiping the trail of blood from his skin. "Wyatt?"

"What?"

"If you die, I'll never forgive you."

His hand caught hers, pressing it against the hard muscle of his stomach, and that fast the ache in her nipples was reborn.

"I won't leave you."

"It's not like you have a choice."

"Look at the wound, sweetheart. It's already closing."

She did, and it was.

That's not possible. She didn't voice the thought for the simple reason it apparently was.

"Is infection a risk?"

"No. Werewolves have strong antibodies," Donovan explained, handing her a clean towel and taking the blood-soaked one.

"I liken them to rotweillers on steroids," Lisa interjected. "The suckers can't wait to go on the attack to make things right."

"You've seen them in action?"

"Yup. Donovan got a belly wound, too, when Buddy's friends tried to run me off the mountain."

"What!"

"I thought we agreed not to tell her about that for awhile," Robin called from the kitchen.

"Sorry."

Heather didn't care. She just needed to know Wyatt was going to get better, that when this wound healed, the spectre of infection wasn't going to lurk over them. "Why is he unconscious?"

"He's not." Donovan glanced out the window again. "He can hear you, but his body is using every bit of energy to heal the wound. If he had to, he could wake up."

"Oh."

She followed his glance out the window. The compound residents—werewolves—were mingling in groups. A lot of discussion was going on. From the body language and hand motions, none of it was positive.

"Is he going to have to?"

"Not right now."

"But later?"

He frowned, glanced at Wyatt, and then smiled. "It'll all work out."

She wiped at the blood on Wyatt's hip bone. "You're not very good at the reassuring smile thing are you?"

"Apparently not." He glanced out the window again.

"You need to go."

"It's okay."

She licked her lips, and rubbed the sides of her breasts with her arms, trying to ease the ache. "I'm a big girl, Donovan. If all he requires is watching, we can handle it."

She glanced over at Lisa, who was gathering up the bloody clothes Donovan had thrown aside.

Lisa nodded. "Go Donovan, we'll be fine."

He studied them a second, weighed his decision, and then nodded his head. He crooked his finger at Lisa. She smiled and crooked her finger back. Shaking his head he cleared the bed, caught her chin in his hand, and kissed her. It wasn't a gentle kiss, or a polite kiss, but a strip-naked-and-climb-on-board kiss. When it was over, Lisa was weaving on her feet, her expression dazed. Donovan was as controlled as always, though he was breathing heavier and a sizable erection strained the front of his pants. He tapped Lisa's butt. She moaned.

"Don't leave the house."

Lisa's response was a vague nod.

As soon as Donovan left the room, Heather snapped her fingers, bringing Lisa back to reality. "Whatever he packs in that kiss, I'm going to bottle it."

Lisa blushed, her hand going to her shoulder. "If we could, we'd make a fortune."

"Are you hurt?"

"No, it always takes a bit for the sensation to go away."

Heather shook her head, stroking Wyatt's stomach. Even lying in the bed with a wound the size of Florida in his stomach, he still managed to look powerful. She blinked. As big as the wound was, it was still half its original size as evidenced by the red scarring indicating newly knitted flesh.

This was going to take some getting used to. She glanced back to Lisa. "Sensation?"

"From the mark. It burns and aches like Hades whenever Donovan is near."

Heather glanced down at Wyatt, felt the erotic burn in her nipples.

She was going to kill him.

Ten

WYATT didn't like the way Heather was looking at him. Four hours after he'd had that near-fatal loss of attention during the fight, three since he'd healed, an hour after her sisters left, and she was still glaring at him as if she were contemplating removing his balls with a rusty knife. He finished the last of the steak.

"Do you want more?" The words were solicitous; the tone was not.

"Nah, six should do it." Truth was, five would have done it. Asking for the sixth had been a distraction. He'd hoped by the time he'd finished she would have lost her anger, but—he glanced over at her again—she hadn't. He didn't want to fight with Heather tonight. There'd be enough fighting tomorrow when the repercussions from today exploded out of control. Whatever way the decision went, it was going to tear the pack apart. There was no way to avoid it. Not with a battle that had been brewing for seventy-two years.

Heather reached for the plate. He caught her hand and pulled her to the side of the bed. The sound she made was as close to a growl as he'd ever heard a human make. Holding her there, he placed the plate on the floor.

"Care to tell me what's eating you?"

"Not particularly."

"Why not?"

"Because there's been enough bloodshed today."

"Meaning you want to kill me."

"Yes."

Threading his fingers between hers, he tugged her down. She refused to bend her knees. He refused to give up. She fell across him in an awkward heap. Immediately, she groaned. Too late, he remembered. Her hip.

"Damn it."

He switched their positions with a quick move, lifting the hem of her skirt in quick jerks as she lay blinking up at him, startled by the suddenness of the maneuver. A shallow groove carved a line across the side of her hip just beneath the band of her sexy little high-cut thong. The thong he appreciated. The wound he didn't. "This should have been healed."

"Will it get infected?" she moaned and shuddered as he turned her on her side.

"No, my antibodies will protect you."

"What if they don't like me?"

"Can't happen. They don't have a preference when it comes to marked tissue."

"Then ignore it. That's not my problem."

He looked up along the trim line of her torso, pausing at her breasts. His gaze lingered on the way they belled slightly with the pull of gravity. A perfect curve to fit his palm. The nipple, hard and eager, poked against her T-shirt. Perfect for his mouth. "What is?"

The swat she delivered to his head rattled his teeth. "You are, you bastard. You marked my nipples!"

"What?"

He vaguely remembered the need to mark her, the lust, the drive, loving her gorgeous nipples. But marked them? "Hell."

He hitched up over her, rolling her to her back, straddling her slender hips. He grazed his fingers down the side of her breasts, knowing if it were true, she'd feel it in her engorged nipples. Just thinking about her breasts responding to him like that was as erotic as hell. "Marks are very sensitive things."

Her head thrashed. Her hands came up, fisted, and fell back. "Which you knew."

"Yes." He inched his hands up. He just hadn't been fully aware when he'd marked her.

Her spine arched, in a display, a plea. "I've been in agony all day."

"I'm sorry."

"Make it go away,"

"Marks are permanent."

"No, damn you."

He leaned forward, catching his weight on his right elbow. The mattress dipped. She rolled with it, her nipple skimming his cheek, bumping the corner of his mouth.

On a "But the effects don't have to be" he took her nipple into his mouth through her shirt.

"Oh God!"

"You're not wearing a bra."

"I'm too sensitive."

Rubbing his chin across the hard tip, he smiled. "I'm not complaining."

"Well, I am!"

"Pull up your shirt."

"What?"

He couldn't resist her mouth. It'd been hours since he kissed it. Such a deliciously full, hot mouth. "Pull up your shirt and show me how hungry those pretty little breasts are," he whispered against her lips.

"Perv."

The insult lacked heat.

"But you like it."

"Maybe." She kissed him lightly, her sharp little teeth sinking into his lower lip. "What's in it for me?"

"You, my sexy kitten, get to come."

Arching against him, she rubbed her breasts against his chest. "Just once? Hardly seems worth the effort."

"I might be persuaded to put forth a little more effort than that."

"You'd better."

He laughed, fitted his mouth to hers, taking in her scent and her breath, holding both deep. "Has no one ever taught you to respect your Alpha?"

Completely unconcerned with the dangerous path she was walking, she shrugged. "I guess not."

"We'll have to work on that."

"You do that."

He shook his head at her daring. "You don't want to tempt the wolf, Heather."

"Why? Are you going to go all dominant on me?"

There was a slight catch in her voice as she asked the question. The way her gaze skirted his betrayed the secret she thought hidden. Catching her chin between his fingers, he leaned in, pinning her with his weight, kissing her hard and deep, not letting her control the kiss, keeping her where he wanted, inhaling the scent of her arousal, swallowing her little moan. He could be as dominant a lover as she needed. "Lift up your shirt."

She did, first one side and then the other, drawing the material in taunting little teases, baring her midriff, the undersides of her breasts, stopping just short of what he wanted to see most.

A glance down confirmed it was on purpose. "Challenging me, seelie?"

"Just giving you something to think about."

Taking her hands in his, he placed them above her head. The almost imperceptible shiver indicated her delight. He didn't bother to hide his. Dominating a woman in bed was one of his favorite pleasures. "I think you *are* challenging me."

She raised her eyebrows. "And?"

"And that comes with consequences."

"Hrrmph."

Her shirt offered no resistance to the brush of his palm, slipping up and over the pert mounds, tumbling willfully to her upper chest, revealing everything he wanted to see, and maybe a few things she didn't want him to. Beneath the red of her succulent nipples, beneath the red brown of her areolae he could see the shadow of his mark. A permanent, erotic brand. He hadn't meant to mark her breasts, but now that he had, he was glad.

He touched his finger to one tip, her immediate cry pleasing to hear. "For the rest of your life, whenever I'm near, these will ache for my touch, my mouth, my cock . . ."

"Bastard."

"No, just a very appreciative mate." He flicked the hungry peak. Her body jackknifed into his. Her small scream whistled past his ear. She reached down. He caught her hands and gently slammed them back into the pillows, adding a bit more pressure, absorbing her shudder of delight with his much bigger body.

"No. Keep your hands here."

"Now you're going all macho?"

"Losing fights have that effect on me."

She frowned. "You didn't lose. There was no reason to kill him."

"That's not how the pack will see it."

"Screw the pack."

There was no reason for her to understand what the pack meant to a wolf. How it was the half of his soul not owned by a mate. "I'd rather screw you."

"What's stopping you?"

Dropping his gaze to her breasts and their nipples—so swollen he swore he could see her pulse in them—he smiled.

"Not a damn thing." Tucking his palm in the small of her back, he pulled her up, increasing the pressure until her torso arced in invitation. "Come here, kitten."

He took a hard peak in his mouth, sucking lightly, letting her thrash under the whip of sensation, letting her come to terms with the powerful need on her own, before taking her higher with a steady suction, bringing her up hard and fast, catching her nipple between his teeth as she twisted, biting down gently, watching her eyes fly wide as the nip of pain blended with the pleasure. He pulled gently, firmly, held her as the orgasm broke over her in a harsh cry, watched the pleasure take her, transform her, cradling her as she screamed, holding he safe as she came floating down into reality, sheltered in his arms.

Wyatt nuzzled her cheek, teased the corner of her mouth with his tongue, lingering there because it sent goose bumps chasing over goose bumps, wanting to give her pleasure. "Damn, you're beautiful."

She still had it in her to argue. "No, I'm not."

He kissed his way down her neck, nipped the tempting curve where her shoulder blended with her neck before moving lower, his destination clear. "Another challenge?" he whispered against the upper curve of her right breast.

"No." She reached for him, hesitated at his look, and resettled against the pillow. With a shake of her head she thought to deny him. "It's too soon."

"I disagree." It would never be too soon to see her eyes get that unfocused look again, to surround himself in the scent of her satisfaction, to feel her convulse with the ecstasy he'd given her. "I love to watch you come."

The flush on her cheeks deepened, but she didn't hide. "You do?"

"Yup."

Turning his head to the side, he blew a stream of air across her right nipple. "I want you to come for me again."

"I need a break."

He shook his head. For such an up-front woman, she didn't know herself that well. "You'll come harder this time."

"Says who?"

It only took a slight bend to capture her other nipple in his mouth and to start the process all over again. His cock throbbed and fought for freedom, wanting the heat and moisture just a scant width of material away. "Says your Alpha."

She rolled her eyes, the gesture ending on a gasp as he bit down, this time piercing her a tiny bit. She screamed and thrashed, throwing her hips against his, searching, seeking—until she found the position she needed. A tiny droplet of blood spread across his tongue as he milked her breast with his hand and his mouth, feeding the mating hunger, nourishing his mark while she rubbed that swollen pussy along the ridge of his cock, giving him the gift of her trust as she struggled to find the pinnacle that eluded her. He slid his hand down from the small of her back to her buttocks, sinking his fingers into the taut curves, tilting her hips up, angling his down until her clit rode the rough seam of his zipper. She flinched at the new sensation, and then her thighs fell open and she thrust against him, once, twice, three times.

Her hands came down. He growled a warning. She snarled one right back, working her fingers between their bodies, unbuttoning his fly, unzipping his zipper, pulling him out into the cool air, before, with the delicacy of a butterfly, she lifted that pussy against him, sliding him along her slick crease, caressing his length with her engorged clit, wrapping him in the flow of her desire. She took his hand and brought it against her nipple. The hard rubbery tip throbbed in the center of his palm.

"Make me yours, Wyatt. Make me yours as you fill me with your cock."

She wanted the bond.

"No." He wouldn't abuse her that way. Commit her life only to take it tomorrow when the council ruled.

"Yes. Fill me with your cock, make me come, and when the world's shattering away and I feel like I don't know where I am, bind me to you so I can never get lost again."

"Ah damn."

Heat, hunger, need, they careened out of control as she lifted her hips, drawing his cock down with the help of gravity until it nestled in the well of her vagina.

"Bind me, Wyatt."

Yes. He pressed, temptation taking over for duty, sinking into the fiery heat of her pussy, closing his eyes as the feminine channel rippled along his length, the muscles milking him hard, tempting him deeper, demanding he thrust and give her what she wanted—him and her together. For eternity.

He buried himself to the hilt, capturing her blissful cry in his mouth, holding himself deep, absorbing the moment, the beauty, His palms ached; his wolf howled. *Yes!*

No. He wrenched himself free. He was a selfish bastard, but he wasn't that selfish. Heather's moan of disappointment lashed at him. His palms throbbed with a hunger that went deeper than passion, deeper than lust. The need to bind her to him forever in this life and the next flowed along the rush of his blood, gathered with his climax, growing in power.

He gritted his teeth against the agony. Her gaze flinched from his, taking the rejection hard, curling on her side facing away from him.

"Heather."

She flinched from his touch. "It's okay, Wyatt. I just got carried away."

She thought he didn't want her that way.

He stroked his hand over her shoulder blades, down over her back, pausing in the small of her back before cresting the swell of her buttocks.

"I can't give you that, Heather. Not now, but I can give you something almost as good." His hand dipped between her cheeks, probing lightly at the tightly puckered rosebud hidden between. He was willing to bet no one had ever had her ass.

"Not until you tell me why."

He shook his head. She still fought for control. He coated his fingers with her juices below and returned, swirling his fingers in a circle as tight as her clench. She gasped and arched.

"Yesterday's fight can only be settled one way."

"What way?"

"By council decision."

Which would likely be a call for his death.

He pressed. There was the slightest give. She squeaked, but then she pushed back, instinct overriding fear. "Did you like that, Heather? Did that hot little stroke feel good?"

A blush ran up her torso, spread over her face, but she didn't pull away. "Yes."

It only took a little more pressure and she took his finger to the second knuckle. She cried out as she struggled with the foreign sensation. Brushing her hair off her cheek, he kissed the corner of her mouth. "Easy. Just relax into it and be easy."

"I can't."

"Yes, you can. You wanted to give yourself to me. This is what I want."

"This isn't forever."

"This is what we have." Reaching into the drawer, he pulled out some lube. He gently fucked her with his finger, getting her used to the idea as he unscrewed the cap. It rolled off the bed, plopping to the floor. He withdrew his finger and replaced it with the nozzle of the lube. She shivered as the cool gel worked inside. Tossing the tube to the foot of the bed, he pressed her to her stomach, pulling her back until her legs draped over the end of the bed, tugging on her hips until she supported her weight on her toes. With a nudge of his foot, he widened her stance, leaving her perfectly displayed, the full heart of her ass flowing into the long lines of her thighs, open to his pleasure. His cock bobbed between them, throbbing.

He lifted the heavy shaft and stepped in, aligning it precisely before letting go. The fat head dropped onto the crease in an erotic little spank.

"Oh my God." Heather bucked back, fucking him along the crease.

It wasn't enough.

Wyatt worked one hand between her hips and the bed. Bracing his weight on his forearm, he found her clit. Rubbing it gently, he slipped in one finger, then two, stretching her, readying her. He whispered in her ear, "Come for me."

She shook her head. "Not like this."

Wyatt plucked at her clitoris, playing her desire in staccato pulses. Her breath drew shorter; her hips bucked harder. "Are you sure?"

She nodded, her hair falling forward, revealing the vulnerability of her nape.

"You," she gasped. "I want you."

She wanted to come on his cock. Shit. She was hell on his sense of right.

"It'll be easier for you this way."

"I don't want easy."

She didn't know what she was asking for. He kissed her nape.

"You'll like this."

She threw her head back along with her hips, forcing his fingers deeper, crying out when they bottomed out. When she caught her breath she asked, "Why did you even bother asking me what I want if you didn't intend to give it?"

He was dying to give it. "It might hurt."

"I don't care."

He aligned the tip of his cock with the impossibly tiny opening. "I won't stop."

"Wait until you're asked."

He shook his head. She was like a pit bull when she got hold of an idea. He leaned in, watching the small hole flatten, the creases around it smooth out as the muscle stretched to his demand. "It may be more than you're expecting."

"There's no way it can be more than I'm expecting because I'm expecting a lot. I want you to brand my ass with your cock. Mark me with you seed, fill me with your come. I don't care if it hurts. I don't care if I tear. When it's over, I just want to know I'm yours."

He understood then. She was coming at him from a different angle, seducing him with this submission so he'd take the other. "You want all that?"

She tossed her hair over her shoulder, looking at him from the corner of her eye, rocking back against him. Challenging him. "Can you give it to me?"

"Baby, I can fuck this sweet ass until you're raw, until you feel me filling you even when I'm not around."

"Uh-huh." She waggled her rear at him like a red flag in front of a bull, apparently under the delusion that he was reluctant. As if there was anything she wanted that he wouldn't give her. "Talk is cheap."

But she wasn't. She was precious, and even though she thought she needed hard to remember, he knew differently. There were many ways for a man to imprint himself on a woman's soul. Some of them hurt. The best ones didn't.

He kissed the soft white skin of her nape and leaned in, gradually giving her more of his weight as he milked her clitoris, timing the possession with the rise of her passion, holding back while his balls swelled and filled, eager for the dark heat beyond, more eager for her cries of pleasure. It was an unequal battle from the beginning, her natural resistance no match for his insistence. She opened that first bit, her ass spreading over the head of his cock in an intimate kiss. The muscles in her back tightened, her fingers laced through his, holding tight as the stretching continued.

"That's it. Just like that."

"Easy for you to say," she gasped, full of sass even now.

"Not so easy," he growled, battling with his nature that commanded he take, claim, mark, knowing she needed time, wanting to give it to her.

Another inch and he'd be in. One small, vitally important inch. The hardest one.

He set his teeth to her shoulder, biting down, holding her pinned as he thrust in tiny increments in time with his stroking of her clit, feeling her tension rising, scenting the approach of her climax in the air around them. Rich, feminine, perfect.

She threw back her head, screaming his name. "Wyatt!"

"Let go, Heather," he growled against her shoulder. He thrust forward with his hips, tunneling past the last of her resistance. "Let go and come for me."

The shock of his entry sent her tumbling into the mattress. She screamed again as her orgasm overtook her, clamping down on his cock. He followed her down, pumping into her ass, taking his rhythm from the rippling spasms of her climax, holding her clit, her pleasure in his hand, as he gave her his seed, his soul, his heart, holding her until the last sighing pulse faded away. Holding her as she gasped his name, kissing her shoulder, her ear, her cheek as the words rose up from within. He couldn't give her forever, but he could give her this.

"I love you."

Eleven

THEY don't have a preference.

The knowledge burst into Heather's mind, snapping her out of a sound sleep. She blinked, staring up at the ceiling, listening to the echoes, trying to attach importance to her subconscious's shout for attention.

They don't have a preference when it comes to marked tissue. Kelon had marked Robin.

They meaning the antibodies. Of course, the antibodies! The antibodies didn't have a preference! She threw back the covers and jumped out of bed "Wyatt! Wake up."

He didn't just wake up, he sprang out of bed, claws extended, a warning snarl on his lips. She halted one step short of leaping into his arms.

"What is it?"

Spinning around she searched the floor for her clothes, muscles not used to the workout Wyatt had given her pinging in protest. "Robin."

Pulling on his pants with far more efficient movements than

she was able to coordinate, he asked, "Did she take a turn for the worse?"

"No. Oh no. I just have to see her."

He glanced at the clock. "It's four in the morning."

"No one's going to care."

"I care."

She yanked on her shirt and headed for the front door, buttoning as she went. "I don't."

"So much for my lessons in discipline," he muttered under his breath.

She rubbed her butt, feeling the lingering heat of his spank. The delicious stretch of his cock. "Trust me, I'm thoroughly chastised."

"Want to do it again?"

"In a day or two?" It seemed to take him forever to get into his boots. "Absolutely."

"I'll look forward to it."

He grabbed their coats off the hook and held hers out. "You forgot something."

"I wasn't going to bother."

He had that I-can-outlast-you smile on his face. "Humor me."

"Will it get you to move faster?"

"Yes."

She stuck out her arms. As soon as her wrist cleared the shoulder holes, she made a grab for the door handle. Wyatt was there before her, rifle slung over his shoulder, revolver in the holster at his hip. "Wait."

She didn't want to wait. Her news couldn't wait. "Is this really necessary?"

"Yes."

"Well, hurry up."

It took another three minutes for him to decide the path was safe. She was so excited she ran across the yard, reaching the house where Lisa and Robin were staying one step ahead of Wyatt. She pounded on the door. There was a thump of feet on wood. A male curse and the distinct sound of a gun being cocked. Maybe she'd better identify herself. "Robin, Lisa, it's Heather."

The door swung open. Kelon frowned at her.

"Do you know what time it is?"

"Four A.M." She pushed past him and rushed to Robin, catching her by the shoulders, studying her face. The hint of rose beneath her skin was still there. Her eyes were bright and clear. And she was moving very well, especially for four in the morning. "What's wrong?"

"Nothing." Heather hugged Robin tight and spun them both around, laughing when Robin tripped and Wyatt had to catch them. For once, she could give the answer she'd always wanted to when Robin asked her that question. "Nothing at all."

Because she couldn't help her it, she hugged her again, before holding her at arms' length. "How are you feeling?"

"Fine, but I think the question should be how are *you* feeling?"

Lisa came into the living room, drawing on her robe, grumpy as always when woken out of a sound sleep. "I think the answer to that is obvious. She's finally lost her mind."

"No, I haven't." She let Robin go and stepped back into Wyatt's arms, looking around. "I just think I have really, really good news." They were missing someone. "Where's Donovan?"

"He was called up to the council a couple hours ago."

Behind her, Wyatt stiffened. Heather tilted her face back and checked his expression. He was composed as always, the tension not immediately evident around his eyes. "Do you need to go?"

"No. They won't need me until the council meeting at nine."

"So what's the news?" Kelon asked, a frown on his handsome face.

"You're about as pleasant to wake up as Lisa," Heather groused. She didn't want any wet blankets on her announcement.

"That's not news," Robin interjected with a small smile.

"Well, this is."

"Everyone might get a lot happier if you would just spill the beans," Wyatt offered, his hand on her hip, the feel of his chest against her back transferring in a frission of delight to her nipples. She quickly stepped away and crossed her arms over her chest.

"Robin isn't dying."

Four "what"s echoed in the wake of her declaration.

"Kelon's bite cured her."

Kelon pulled himself to his full height and glared at her, while at his side, Robin looked at her with the same hope and faith in her eyes as she had when she was five and wanted to know if the tooth fairy would really come.

"That's not possible."

"Actually, it's not only possible but probable."

"A bite can't cure disease."

Heather pushed her hair out of her face. "If you'd stop being a killjoy, Kelon, you'd see what I'm talking about." She ignored his growl. "While Robin lost her kidneys to disease, she's losing this one because her antibodies see it as a foreign object and are attacking it."

"But were antibodies—" Wyatt began behind her.

"Have no preference for tissue, Wyatt says." Heather finished for him.

"Oh my God!" Lisa gasped, covering her mouth with her hands, tears sparkling in her eyes. "You're not going to die."

Robin shook her head, reaching out, grabbing Kelon's hand, wrapping his arm around her abdomen, eyes shining with the wonder of a new beginning. "No wonder I felt better when I stopped taking my medicines."

Kelon spun her around. "You did what?"

She shrugged. "They were making me too sick to enjoy our time together."

"You should have told me before making that decision."

She shrugged. "And you should have told me you were binding your life to mine. I guess that makes us even."

"No, it doesn't."

"But if what I suspect is true," Heather interjected before they could get into an argument, "you will have a long time to balance the scales."

Kelon pulled Robin up into his arms, buried his face in her neck and sniffed loudly. "I've been so busy I didn't notice, but your scent isn't off anymore."

Robin pushed him away. "Excuse me. Are you saying I stank?"

He let her slide down his body, his expression one of a man who'd been on the rack and had just earned a reprieve.

"You always smell perfectly sweet and feminine, but before there was an underlying something that didn't fit. It's gone."

Joy, fear, love, disbelief, they all warred for dominance in his expression, but in the end, only one emotion thrived. Love. For her sister.

Heather glanced up at Wyatt. "I think I'm going to cry."

"Get me a tissue and I'll join you."

He wouldn't, but it was nice of him to lie for her.

"Heck," Lisa sobbed. "I'll join you and you don't even have to bribe me with a tissue."

"Deal."

Robin reached behind Kelon. Her arm jerked and something came flying at them. Wyatt caught it. It was a box of tissues. She wrapped her arms back around Kelon, holding tight to her man, her dream.

"So we don't have to stop the lovefest to mop up the floor."

Twelve

In the end, it was Donovan's return that broke up the joy. Wyatt, watching him stride up the path through the window, noting the squared set of his shoulders and the angry length of his stride, knew he wasn't bringing good news. He excused himself from the table, leaving the women arguing over what culinary great of the time Kelon was better than. Slipping out the front door, he headed Donovan off before he reached his cabin.

"Were you looking for me?"

He nodded and adjusted his rifle on his shoulder. "Yeah."

Wyatt glanced at the house. They were out of sight from the kitchen windows.

"Why so glum? You knew it wasn't going to be good news."

"I didn't think it was going to be this bad. They want to kill you."

Wyatt nodded. "I figured that."

"They're afraid of you. If they weren't they'd settle it differently."

"But using this to get rid of me makes it all nice and tidy."

"I'll back you when they announce the decision. So will others. The pack will not tolerate such blatant abuse of the law."

It had finally come to this. Wyatt shook his head. Civil war. "Thanks."

Donovan jerked his Stetson down, anger seething in his scent. "The Alpha wants to see you."

"I imagine he does." Wyatt looked around the quiet compound he'd called home for all of his life. On every rock, beneath every tree there were images from his youth, memories from his past, good ones, bad ones, normal ones, all of them different, all of them shaping him into the man he was today. And through them all ran one constant influence, the security of being pack.

Wyatt faced Donovan, seeing the same torn loyalty in his eyes that raged in himself. No, civil war was not the answer.

He held out his hand. Donovan took it, his handshake as familiar as the knowledge that he had Wyatt's back. Donovan would kill pack if it came down to a choice between life and death. The same way Wyatt would if it came down to a choice between family and pack, but if it came down to that, if it came to brother on brother, family on family neither of them would ever be the same. Nothing would ever be the same.

Wyatt forced a smile on his lips and slapped Donovan on the shoulder. "Go on up to the house. There's good news waiting for you there."

Donovan's eyes narrowed. "What are you going to do?"

"Go talk to my father."

HIS father was waiting for him, frailer than ever, looking as if sheer stubbornness was the only thing keeping him in this world. Which it probably was. Big Al had the aura of a man waiting. Wyatt just wished he knew for what.

"I hear you've pissed off the council."

"I'm good at that."

"Maybe too good this time." He reached for the water glass by the bed. "They're calling for your blood."

Wyatt shrugged. "Nothing new in that."

"This time they mean it."

"And they didn't before?"

The glass shattered against the far wall, "Damn it, Wyatt. Ask me for my help."

"Why? So you can tell me how I have to kill good men I've grown up with? Make widows of the women I knew as a child? Take fathers from children who deserve to know them? All so I can try to drag a pack that doesn't want to go out of the dark ages into the future so they have a prayer of survival?"

"We've been doing fine the way we are for a thousand years!"

The hold on his temper snapped. "But your way won't take you another thousand!"

"Damn, you're stubborn just like your mother!"

"And you hate me for it."

"No, but I sure as shit don't want to lose you because of it."

Wyatt froze, the unfamiliar response to a habitual refrain pulling his argument up short.

Al sighed and ran his hand over his face, looking every inch his age. "Bring me that box over there."

Against the wall was a small wooden chest. Wyatt fetched it and placed it on the bed. Al placed his hand on it. There was a reverence in the gesture that surprised Wyatt.

"I've heard you've also taken a mate."

"Yes."

"And like Donovan's and Kelon's mates, she's human?"

"Yes."

"Hrrmph, wouldn't know it from looking at her."

"What do you mean?"

He motioned to the window. "She sure set Cam on his ass yesterday."

"She was a little annoyed."

"Uh-huh." His father grinned, revealing his canines and a hint of the man he used to be. "Well, after seeing her temper in action, I'd suggest you take care not to annoy her."

"That thought had crossed my mind."

"I bet."

Al looked at the box, rubbing the surface. "All these years, I'd always thought you'd come round with time to my way of thinking."

"I know."

"It didn't mean I didn't love you, just that I hoped that, through you, I could go on."

Wyatt thought he'd become immune to the knowledge that he was a disappointment to his father, but apparently that kind of pain a man didn't outgrow.

"Watching the challenge yesterday, watching your reluctance to kill Carl, watching your mate handle Cam, I realized things have changed."

"Excuse me?" His father admitting things were different was the equivalent of his admitting pink was a masculine color. It was just something no one ever expected to happen.

"In my day, it was kill or be killed, and a woman knew her place and didn't get involved. But watching yesterday I saw what Helen had been trying to tell me for years. There are all kinds of strengths and all kinds of people." He pushed the box across the bed. It snagged on the sheets. Wyatt tugged it the last few inches.

"Open it."

He did, seeing it was filled with envelopes. "You aren't the first man to mate outside pack, and we're not the only pack to forbid such unions."

Wyatt opened a letter dated two years ago. It was from a woman whose human mate had died, asking to come home. Her loneliness and longing for pack came clearly through her letter. He looked up, knowing the answer before he asked the question. "You didn't let her."

"Couldn't. It was against tradition."

"She has children. Were children in characteristics according to her letter."

"She's a desperate woman wanting to come home. Her assessment couldn't be trusted and if her children ever exhibited any human traits, they would have been picked on and eventually killed. You know that."

And killing children always upset pack balance. "So you told her no."

Al waved to the box. "I told them all no."

There had to be a hundred letters in the box. He opened a few more. They all sang the same lonely song. Disenfranchised weres looking for a home. He touched the "please" at the bottom of the first woman's letter, tracing the tearstain that smudged the period. "I wouldn't have."

"I know. That's why I drew this up. I'll be declaring it at council today." He handed Wyatt a paper. The parchment was thick, old-fashioned. Official. "You can keep that copy."

Wyatt read, his eyebrows raising as each word of the shakily written declaration revealed his father's intent. "You're giving me my own pack?"

It wasn't done. New packs meant competition. Often war. It'd been two hundred years since the last had been created.

"You're a good leader, Wyatt." Al motioned to the box. "And there are a whole lot of weres who've been been waiting a whole lot of years for someone like you to step up to the plate."

"Someone weak." He knew how his father saw compassion.

Al sighed and shook his head. "Someone strong enough to carry compassion alongside strength. Someone not afraid of change. Someone brave enough to kick tradition in the teeth."

Wyatt looked at the paper again. A pack of his own, formed by his own law, uncrippled by tradition. The paper rustled as his grip tightened. He wanted this. "The council won't go for it."

"The council can't do shit as long as I'm alive."

That wasn't going to be much longer. Al easily read his mind.

"I can hold on long enough to give you time to get a pack together, time enough to train who needs training. Donovan and Kelon will go with you. So will Carl and others. That will give you a start."

He didn't know what to say. "I always thought you hated me."

"Lying here longing for Helen has given me time to realize a lot of things, one of them being the only things I've hated are the times I haven't had the courage to do what my heart said was right when faced with the expectation of tradition." His smile was rueful. "It's not as easy as it looks."

"No. It isn't." Wyatt picked up the box and stood by the bed. "Thank you."

A traditional "thank you" seemed so inadequate for this moment.

"You're welcome."

Al held out his hand. Wyatt took it, feeling the outer frailty housing that will of iron. Halfway through the handshake, he gave it up. "To hell with tradition."

He dropped the box on the bed and hugged his father.

Epilogue

Dear Sarah Anne:

I apologize for the delay in response to your letter. My name is Wyatt Carmichael of the sanctioned Pack Haven. Your letter was passed on to me by Al Carmichael of the sanctioned Pack Carmichael.

I am aware of your situation and would like to offer pack status to you and your children. You should be aware we are a new pack located in the high mountains of Montana. Our Protectors are Donovan and Kelon McGowan. I'm sure you've heard of them. Their reputation is legendary as is their devotion to the pack they serve.

I mention them because I know your first fear will be for your children. While we follow pack law, Pack Haven is a progressive pack. We do not discriminate. You will find the McGowan seal affixed to the bottom of this letter. Consider it their promise, along with mine, that your children will always be safe.

You can contact me at the address or phone number on the

head of this letter should you wish to accept our invitation. Upon word from you, an escort will be immediately dispatched to bring you home.

Sincerely,
Wyatt Carmichael
Alpha, Sanctioned Pack Haven

HEATHER read the letter over Wyatt's shoulder, sliding her arms around his neck as she read. "Very nice."

"It's too formal." He reached for it, no doubt planning on crumpling it up and tossing it with the others littering the floor around his chair. She stopped him, placing her hand on his.

"There's only one word in that letter Sarah Anne is going to care about."

"*Pack?*"

She shook her head and leaned in, moving her finger to the right so it underlined the last word. "*Home.*" She kissed his cheek. "You've promised her a home, acceptance, and safety for her children. There's nothing any woman wants more."

Tension flowed through Wyatt's muscles. Hope. He hoped so much, fought so hard, this man of hers.

"Then I'd better get to work on that house we bought in town so it'll be ready when they get here."

"Which one?" The men had been buying up a lot of houses, offering a fair price. Residents chained to a dying town through poverty had been accepting, relieved to have the cash that would enable them to start over elsewhere. The only thing that would have made it perfect would have been if Buddy had been one of them.

"The cape. It's got a nice yard."

He was thinking of the children. Her breasts ached, but not as much as her heart. Heather kissed Wyatt's neck. He was such a good man, and a heck of a leader doing everything right even by pack he hadn't yet met. If Sarah Anne didn't accept his invitation, she'd drive down to Missouri and drag the woman back herself. "Have I mentioned how much I love you lately?"

"Not in the last two hours."

He lifted his arm, allowing her to slide around to sit on his lap, arms still linked around his neck. "I seem to have been remiss."

"Yes. You have." And it was time to fix this one last thing between them.

His right eyebrow kicked up in that way she found both sexy and endearing. "We've got an hour before Kelon's going to have the celebration dinner on the table if you want to make it up to me."

"For what?"

She took his hand and brought it to her breast. The immediate sear of fire stole her breath. Centering her nipple in his palm, she smiled up into his handsome face, toying with the buttons on her shirt. "If I remember correctly, you owe me a bonding."

His eyes lit from within, his joy pouring over her like sunshine, sinking into her along with the heat of his touch. She bared her breast. He slit his palm with his thumbnail. His gaze held hers as the growl rumbled from within, wrapping around her with the promise of forever he held only for her.

"So I do."